"Sometimes a love story ends in tragedy and a tragedy leads to a love story. And sometimes a hero turns a bit villainous and a villain turns a bit heroic. In this unique story within a story, Deese delivers all of the above with the finesse of a clever storyteller. *The Words We Lost* is thought-provoking and tender, capturing the transformative beauty of surviving."

—T. I. Lowe, bestselling author of *Under the Magnolias*

"A poignant, masterful exploration of the enduring power of friendship and love, and the links that sustain and nurture us through all of life's complications and losses. Deese once again takes readers on an emotional journey filled with heart and hope."

—Irene Hannon, author of the bestselling HOPE HARBOR series

"Poignant and intriguing, Nicole Deese's latest takes readers on a heartfelt journey, one that will stay with them long after they've reached The End. From its deeper themes of grief, trauma, and healing, to its bubbling romance and moments of lightness, *The Words We Lost* is a beautiful story!"

—Melissa Tagg, *USA Today* bestselling, Christy Award-winning author

"Few things in life can be depended upon as reliably as the magic of a Nicole Deese book. No one breaks my heart and pieces it back together, better than before, quite like Nicole. *The Words We Lost* more than lives up to the standard of beauty and brilliance we've come to expect."

—Bethany Turner, author of *Plot Twist* and *The Do-Over*

"*The Words We Lost* is a poignant tale of grief, healing, and all that falls in between. Deese is a master at getting to the heart of emotion and letting the reader experience it as well. This novel is a testament to the power of fiction and a must-read."

—Toni Shiloh, author of *In Search of a Prince*

"*The Words We Lost* is as deep, beautiful, powerful, and restorative as its ocean setting."

—Angela Ruth Strong, author of *Husband Auditions*

"*The Words We Lost* is a poignant masterpiece. Intertwined with grief and hope, friendship and family . . . and a God who gathers us up with tender strength and begins to heal. This story strikes a chord that will resonate long and deep in the very best, most beautiful ways."

—Amanda Dykes, author of *All the Lost Places*

"Interwoven with an intoxicating second-chance romance, *The Words We Lost* delves into murky secrets that can shipwreck even the most precious of friendships and brilliantly carries readers through waves of heartbreak to the satisfying shores of healing and wholeness."

—Connilyn Cossette, Christy Award-winning author

"Deeply romantic and wonderfully emotional, Nicole Deese's effortlessly exquisite voice sings in another book that evokes All the Feels. "

—Rachel McMillan, author of the THREE QUARTER TIME series
and *The Mozart Code*

"A picturesque small town, a past to unravel, and hope for the future. Nicole Deese handles the complexities of life with grace and finesse. A truly standout novel."

—Rachel Fordham, author of *Where the Road Bends*

A FOG HARBOR
······ ROMANCE ······

The Words We Lost

NICOLE DEESE

BETHANYHOUSE
a division of Baker Publishing Group
Minneapolis, Minnesota

© 2023 by Nicole Deese

Published by Bethany House Publishers
Minneapolis, Minnesota
www.bethanyhouse.com

Bethany House Publishers is a division of
Baker Publishing Group, Grand Rapids, Michigan

Printed in the United States of America

Library of Congress Cataloging-in-Publication Data
Names: Deese, Nicole, author.
Title: The words we lost / Nicole Deese.
Description: Minneapolis, Minnesota : Bethany House Publishers, a division of Baker Publishing Group, 2023. | Series: A fog harbor romance
Identifiers: LCCN 2022044046 | ISBN 9780764241185 (paperback) | ISBN 9780764241406 (casebound) | ISBN 9781493440719 (ebook)
Subjects: LCGFT: Novels.
Classification: LCC PS3604.E299 W67 2023 | DDC 813/.6—dc23/eng/20221208
LC record available at https://lccn.loc.gov/2022044046

Cover design by Susan Zucker

23   24   25   26   27   28   29   7   6   5   4   3   2   1

823 3522

To my baby sister, Aimee Brooke.

July 26, 1987—November 25, 2013
Missing you always.

"The sincere friends of this world are as ship lights in the stormiest of nights."

–Giotto di Bondone

1

Every *tap, tap, tap* of my editorial director's blood-red fingernail against her ceramic coffee mug feels like another second closer to the death of my career. And unfortunately, my only chance at an exoneration is currently limping his busted bicycle through the soggy streets of San Francisco on this uncharacteristically wet day in July. Below the conference room table, I twist the black sea glass ring on my right index finger, wishing it held the power to summon an ETA text from my assistant. Preferably one that starts with: *Just arrived! Be right up!* But instead, when a notification brightens my silenced phone, it reads: *Can you stall for ten more?*

"You're up next to pitch, Ingrid," SaBrina Hartley says, managing to draw my two-syllable name into three. It's a practice she's perfected since her transfer and subsequent promotion to our division nine months ago, along with her many lectures on the importance of signing *established authors* with *established platforms*. "You ready?"

This, of course, is a rhetorical question. Nobody ever tells SaBrina they're anything but ready.

"Uh, yes. Sure." I surrender my phone face-up on the conference room table, as if Siri might sense my panic and offer me a preemptive bailout plan. Sadly, no such thing happens. Heat prickles at the base of my neck when I open the cover of my iPad and stare down at the proposal for a dual-time novel I know far too little about to discuss intelligently.

Of the two critical meetings scheduled during the summer publishing season, this is the one I'd allocated to Chip, the young, enthusiastic editorial assistant I'd trained straight out of college. He's also quite possibly the only reason I still have a corner office and the title of Senior Acquisitions Editor. While I'd been overloaded with deadlines for our national sales conference at the end of the month, he'd completed all the prep work for today's meeting. Not only was Chip the one who'd reviewed the manuscript and researched every comparable title for the proposal we'd planned to pitch together—with Chip shouldering the majority of our shared talking points—he was also the one best-equipped to answer SaBrina's cross-examination questions about the book and author. Truth is, I'd only managed to read the first couple chapters before I handed it over to Chip, and not even the most accomplished editor in the world could successfully pitch a manuscript for publication after reading so little of the story.

Another truth: there's no mystery on how long it's been since I last acquired a new book contract.

More than nine months and twenty-six days ago.

I hook the lock of dark hair obstructing my vision behind my right ear and lift my gaze to the exposed brick walls of our rectangular conference room. The space is bookended on either side by shelves filled with plaques and awards and the internationally recognized bestselling fantasy novels most of those accolades belong to. Their astonishing success single-handedly launched our midsize printing press into an entirely new stratosphere roughly five years ago. Consequently, they are the same best-selling titles that shoot a flaming harpoon through my ribcage whenever my gaze lingers too long in their direction.

I divert my attention to the half dozen unsmiling faces of our acquisitions team: four editors and two assistants who rarely lift their eyes from their laptops. It's strange to think that once upon a time—back before SaBrina Hartley arrived from our New York imprint

8

and before my brain short-circuited to a pace slower than dial-up internet—that *this* was once my favorite meeting of the month.

Under past leadership, this space was a welcome reprieve from the endless cycle and demands of publishing—a safe launching pad where fresh ideas and premise hooks sailed back and forth like a crowd-pleasing game of hot potato. We'd laugh over the scrambled coffee orders we'd have delivered and swap them with ease the way we once swapped inside jokes and stories from around the Golden City. The only stories we share now are the ones we pitch in an atmosphere as hospitable as Alcatraz.

I tap my iPad screen and stare down at the proposal Chip emailed on my behalf to each editor in this room while I'd been cramming for a sales conference I might be uninvited to after today. I clear my throat and twist the underside of my ring with the tip of my thumb, turning the band around until the oblong piece of frosted black glass is tucked safely against my palm.

"*Moonlight on Sutter's Mill,*" I begin in my most professional-sounding voice, "is a dual-time narrative that's unique for several reasons, the first being that the setting is the iconic sawmill in the foothills of the Sierra Nevadas where gold was first discovered in 1848." I swallow and try to remember any other snippets of interest Chip might have shared with me while I continue to panic-skim the digital proposal. I glean whatever I can from the summary, throwing key terminology out like a magician practiced in sleight of hand: generational family feud, unsolved mysteries, debauchery and scandal, and a secret Romeo and Juliet love affair. "'But perhaps,'" I read directly from the fourth paragraph, "'the most interesting fact is that the author herself, Mary B. Jespersen, is a direct, albeit distant, descendant to the Sutter family.'"

My vision warbles in an obnoxiously familiar warning. I blink twice in vain, though I know from experience that the only remedy for the coming onslaught of brain fatigue is time.

Unfortunately, time is the one thing I never have enough of.

"And is this the reason you've listed no previous works in her bio—because she has a connection to a distant, dead relative?" Sa-Brina interjects before I can locate the notes Chip wrote about the author's platform. But in the same way I can predict the ending of nearly every work of fiction I've ever read, I can also predict Sa-Brina's next words. "As I've stated before, Ingrid, I have no interest in taking on a debut author in our current market—far too much risk for far too little reward. Fog Harbor Books is interested in authors with established platforms only." She sighs in that dramatic way Chip loves to emulate, second only to his perfected pronunciation of the capital B in our boss's name. Rumor has it, SaBrina only became S-a-B-r-i-n-a upon her transfer here, as if adding a second capital letter to her first name would give her more professional clout. "Established authors mean established readerships, which in turn equals higher pre-order sales, visibility, and marketable placement on best-selling lists." Her gaze finds me again. "Great story hooks don't sell books. Platforms do."

I clamp my teeth together as a rebuttal builds behind my closed lips. It wasn't too long ago that Fog Harbor Books said yes to a no-name author after she was submitted to an editorial director via a no-name editorial intern who was so passionate about the power of story that she was willing to sacrifice her career track to see it published. But I don't say this. Not only because the legendary tale of how I snuck Cecelia Campbell's manuscript onto Barry Brinkman's desk is as well-known as the five-book deal she struck because of it, but because it still hurts too badly to speak about my best friend in past tense.

With everything in me, I fight to recall the reason why Chip was so convinced he could get Ms. Jespersen's novel sold despite all the contracted authors SaBrina hasn't renewed for lack of sales this last year. But try as I might, I can't remember, so instead, I go with what I can remember about the two chapters I managed to read. "Mary Jespersen writes with a rare blend of old-soul and a twist of modern snark. She also has a pitch-perfect sense of time and place. The tension and conflict is evident from the first few sentences in each storyline, which isn't often the case with dual-timelines. I was impressed with the current-day plot and the focus on the great-granddaughter, who is the historical protagonist, and the inheritance she means to—"

"Again, Ingrid, you offering a recap of the story won't fix the fact that Jespersen remains unproven." SaBrina's perfectly groomed eyebrows arch in exasperation. Due to her high-end fashion and expensive cosmetics, her age is nearly impossible to pinpoint, but given her career track my guess is she's hovering close to forty.

Early on in her invasion, when employee morale was still as much of a priority as analyzing the concerning downward trend in book sales, I chose to believe Barry must have seen something special in her, the same way he'd seen something special in Cece's writing all those years ago. The same way he'd once seen something in me, too.

But now I'm convinced that whatever Barry saw in SaBrina when he and the board selected her as our new director was exactly what SaBrina had *wanted* them all to see. After all, she is nothing if not strategic.

SaBrina pushes her chair away from the conference table and stands with covetable grace in her dark pencil skirt and heels. When she sashays toward the bestseller shelf, my pulse trips over itself, ratcheting higher with every step.

She stops in front of a framed picture I know almost as well as the books standing guard on either side of it. The woman staring out from behind the glass is holding up an award for *Editor of the Year* on a stage bigger than any she'd stepped foot on before that evening. Her ruby lips are a perfect color match to the glamorous, floor-length gown that hugs her curves as if it was designed with her figure in mind. The hazy aura cast from the spotlights on her long, shiny black-brown hair illuminates the amber flecks in her dark eyes and her bare, naturally tan shoulders. Due to the sweeping success of her best friend's series, the outcome of that award ceremony hadn't come as a huge shock to the editor smiling in that photo, or to the publishing house she represented.

But three years and two major plot twists later, I can hardly believe the woman in the framed photo is the same one I saw reflected in my bathroom mirror this morning.

When SaBrina turns her gaze on me it's clear she, too, is playing the spot-the-differences game between the Editor of the Year Ingrid in that picture and the one who's struggled to pitch a single manuscript since that dark day last September. It's not that I haven't tried to keep up the professional appearance SaBrina requires. I still follow the business casual dress code at the office; I still style my shoulder-length hair in headbands and clips; I still dab my cheeks with blush and swipe my lashes with mascara and blot my lips with the same sheer gloss I've worn for a decade. But it seems no matter how I try to conceal it, grief's shadow is permanent.

The ball of nerves at the base of my belly squeezes tight as SaBrina reaches for the familiar spines of the Nocturnal Heart series beside her. She taps the special edition titles of all four of the epic fantasy novels one after the other: *The Pulse of Gold, The Keeper of Wishes, The Art of Thieves, The Twist of Wills.* She stops there, her fingernail sliding up the spine of book four, the wildly infamous cliffhanger that sparked nearly as much commentary as news of the author's sudden and tragic death.

Unbidden, the text from Cece's dedication page inside her fourth and final published work scrolls through my mind.

Joel—there are a billion sappy quotes for siblings and next to none for cousins, so it's a good thing that you and I have never been much for sap. However, I would like to point out the fact that I'm the one dedicating a book to you. May this also serve as a collection notice that you still owe me a blackberry lemonade slush for beating you to the lighthouse.

We had a witness. Pay up.

And then, just like that, I'm there with the two of them all over again—seventeen and filled with the kind of blissful, adolescent recklessness adults fear most. The sea breeze whips through our hair and tugs on our shirts as we race to the base of the hill before the start of the climb to the top of the rocky bluff. Cece and Joel are neck-and-neck on their flashy trail bikes, standing on their pedals as they pump their legs hard to reach the top first, when Joel suddenly squeezes his handbrakes and plants his feet. In an instant, Cece shoots out of sight, leaving the two of us behind on a deserted bath pike. With little more than the sly wink he tosses me over his shoulder, Joel rolls backward down the hill while I pedal the rust out of my secondhand ten-speed. His chest is still heaving from the exertion of his climb as I pull even with him, yet it's his hypnotizing smile that suspends my breath—that calming presence he carries with him everywhere as if he's never known true fear. As if he doesn't even believe it exists. As soon as he's able, he takes hold of my handlebars and eases me so close our front tires kiss. The simmering heat of his arm when it settles against mine feels like the warmth of the afternoon sun when it finally breaks free from the clouds. When his fingers clasp around mine he says, *"Cece can gloat about her win all she wants, but a few minutes alone with you is the real prize I'm after."*

My skin prickles in remembrance as SaBrina's voice snaps me back to the present. Back to this meeting in which I'm failing to pitch a book I've never read. Back to this life I built from scratch after the one I wanted was washed out to sea.

"This"—SaBrina holds up Cece's last novel—"this is the kind of golden goose we're after, folks. Stop searching for a trendsetter and start targeting the genres and readerships that are eager for a comeback. Cecelia Campbell's fans have been champing at the bit since her last book left them hungrier than ever." Her statement slices through me. "Your job is to find an established author who can fill the shoes Cecelia Campbell left behind."

"That's not possible," I fire back with the confidence of an editor who never could have imagined consulting a grief therapist about her declining comprehension of the written word. "Cece was a prodigy

13

of the pen." The same quote forever memorialized on her headstone. "Her instinct for story and mastery of prose isn't replaceable—not by any author, in any genre."

A reverent hush descends over the room, and my right hand curls tighter around the ring still cupped into my palm. For the first time since SaBrina's takeover after our beloved Barry Brinkman took his position on the board, SaBrina actually appears chagrined. Her gaze shifts uncomfortably around the room. But unlike whatever cutthroat work environment she's tried to shape us into, we aren't some heartless crew of ladder-climbing monkeys. The authors we sign at Fog Harbor Books San Francisco have always been more than names on contracts. And Cecelia Campbell was certainly so much more than an author to us all.

"Well, of course not. I'm not suggesting she can be replaced," SaBrina backtracks. "But Cecelia's colossal fanbase, loyal as they've been to her series—albeit an incomplete series—are still ravenous for comparable content. They want angst and danger, intrigue and adventure, and most of all, they're craving an original high-stakes romance promising to entertain multiple generations in the same household. That's what her books offered the world." She holds out *The Twist of Wills* like Rafiki holds baby Simba in *The Lion King*. "It's *our* job to give them the fiction they want. It's *our job* to stir the coals Cecelia's imagination ignited with her record-breaking saga." She studies the group of us, then locks eyes with me once again. "And short of locating her missing final manuscript, it's our job to carry her legacy forward by bringing the world more of what her voice gave us—addictive storytelling."

There are a few murmurs of agreement, but I can't bring myself to join in. SaBrina may be a pro when it comes to persuasive speeches, but she can't possibly have any real understanding of the legacy Cece left behind for the few who knew her best. In the lull that follows, I remind myself that today can't be about Cece's contribution to the publishing industry or even about the plummeting bottom line Fog Harbor Books is desperate to recover from in light of the incomplete Nocturnal Heart series. Today has to be about proving to SaBrina that I'm still an editor who can pitch a book worthy of a contract and—

The conference door bumps open, and Chip, my ever-faithful assistant, drips his way across the threshold. Even with his half-drowned appearance, his prep-boy grin and teddy bear brown eyes steal the room's attention. He fists several paper towels as he makes his way toward the empty chair to my left. He dabs his face and hair, all while his loafers slog a path across the gray carpet squares. Astoundingly, the cross-body messenger bag at his waist appears unscathed from whatever drama he's encountered on his commute to work.

Chip bows his head low before issuing his regrets with the impeccable manners of a kid whose given name is Chadwick Knightly Stanton the Third. "Please forgive my tardiness, Miss Hartley." The corners of his eyes crinkle at SaBrina before he scans the rest of the group. "My back tire went flat about ten blocks east, which caused me to miss the BART by a whopping six seconds. And you may not believe it by looking at me now, but I was actually successful at dodging the worst of the rain with my bike until a delivery truck found a puddle as deep as the bay and decided to give me a test swim." He gestures at the splattering of mud displayed on his tan pants from hip to ankle and takes full advantage of the comedic interruption he's causing. I've only known two people in my life who can shift the mood of a room in less than thirty seconds: Chip and Cece.

He glances over at my lit iPad. "I hope I didn't miss too much discussion about this dual-time proposal. I happen to be a huge fan." He gives me an affirming gaze. "When Ingrid told me it had the grit and intrigue of *Yellowstone* and the tension and romance of *Outlander*, I couldn't wait to read it for myself. The deep-seated family connections and betrayals throughout the historical thread adds a palpable, page-turning punch, as does the twist in the great-granddaughter's story. When she took that DNA test in order to receive her inheritance only to find out she's actually related to her great-grandfather's rival . . . *whew*." He shakes his head, laughs. "I might have let a few choice words slip. And that was all before I realized how networked this author is—I'm sure Ingrid told you about the documentary being made of Jespersen's own great-aunt and uncle? She'll be a featured narrator." His grin is huge as he unveils what I'd failed to remember. "Couldn't ask for a better marketing plan than a simultaneous documentary and book release."

For the millionth time since Chip was assigned to our department, I'm floored by his ability to command a room and deliver exactly what that room needs to hear most. He may only be four years my junior, but his exuberance for life often makes me feel thrice his age.

SaBrina's lips twist into something resembling amusement and, at least for a moment, the conference room curse seems to be broken as several editors begin to comment on aspects they enjoyed about my—*Chip's*—proposal as well as the sample chapters he provided them. With his timely jog of my memory, I'm able to add what I hope is valuable feedback to the discussion. If only my reading speed and comprehension could be jogged as easily.

Clearly satisfied with his performance, Chip drops his chin onto his fists and smiles in a way that only serves to highlight his innocent and enviable perspective of the world.

After our pitch earns the covetous stamp of approval to be pushed through to the publication board, I will my body to release the nerves it's been harboring since last month's uncomfortable meeting. Only SaBrina's gaze continues to linger.

For the next hour and a half, she continues to eye me with unnerving interest, and it's a struggle to track the storylines my colleagues pitch to the group. Chip comes to my aid multiple times, seamlessly pulling me into conversations as if the two of us have discussed each editor's proposal at length prior to this meeting.

At the wrap-up, relief comes in the form of a full breath as I gather up my belongings to make a quick exit on a quest to find Chip and fill him in on what he missed before he granted me yet another career-saving stay of execution. I'm guessing he's in the hallway sorting out his lunch offers for the day. If Fog Harbor had a yearbook, Chip would be voted *Most Popular Lunch Companion*. Ironically, the only person he's interested in lunching with is the elusive, pink-haired barista in the lobby coffeeshop he's been pining after for months.

I'm halfway across the carpet squares toward the exit doors when SaBrina says, "I think there are a few things you and I need to discuss, Ingrid. I'll plan to stop in for a chat when I return from my lunch meeting."

My blood cools to a thick sludge inside my veins, and I rotate in her direction. "After lunch as in . . . today?"

"Were you planning on going out?" There's no challenge to her question as she knows the answer already. I eat lunch at my desk. I don't have time not to.

"No." I work a polite smile onto my lips, reminding myself that I've earned my place here. Despite the devastation of the last year, I'm still a good editor. "But if there's something more on the dual-time you're wanting, I'm happy to send it off to you as soon as I'm back in my office. I can get you the market analysis you requested and more on the family's documentary—"

"There's absolutely nothing I need from your pitch today or any other day that I can't get from Chip." Her words hit their intended target with the accuracy of a marksman whose patience has finally paid off. "Keep your schedule open this afternoon." She zips her laptop into its case, slips the satchel strap over her shoulder, and smiles a grin that fills in the blanks of my overtaxed brain.

My execution hasn't been pardoned after all.

2

The second I'm clear of SaBrina, Chip pops out from around the corner like an over-friendly puppy who matches me stride for stride down the long hallway. "On a scale of one to cataclysmic, how bad was it?"

"You mean before you arrived in need of a bath towel?"

"Yes, sorry about that by the way." He laughs easily. "But on the bright side, your stalling skills have greatly improved!"

"I wouldn't be so sure about that." Anxiety churns low in my gut.

"Why not?" he asks, obviously noting the change in my tone. But before I can elaborate further, his mud-spattered slacks steal my focus. He tracks my gaze and winces. "I know. Of all days for Eugenia to blow a tire. If she wasn't made of hollow aluminum and rubber, I'd swear this was some kind of jealous prank." His sigh is smothered in mock annoyance. "Correct me if I'm wrong, but this look doesn't exactly scream you-won't-regret-saying-yes-to-a-date-with-me, right?"

"Ah, Chip." Suddenly, I understand the reason behind the extra polish to his attire choices and the hint of cologne I detected from him in the conference room. "Today was the day you were going to ask her, wasn't it?" I offer him a sympathetic shake of my head. "Do you have a change of clothes?"

"Not unless you count Trevin offering me a pair of unwashed gym shorts."

I scrunch up my nose. "I definitely do not count that." Trevin from the IT department might be a great guy and all, but borrowed gym shorts aren't the way to impress a girl bent on playing hard to get. "I vote you wait for a clean pair of pants."

"It's unanimous then. Tomorrow it is." He nods decidedly before he reroutes our conversation. "How about you catch me up on everything I missed at the meeting over lunch? My treat."

His lunch offer triggers my pace to quicken as I imagine SaBrina finishing up her Greek salad sometime in the next hour and coming to knock on my door. "Sorry, but I really can't today. I need to prepare for a meeting."

"What meeting? I cleared the majority of your schedule for conference prep this week."

Only six more doors until I reach my office. I do my best to mask the fear in my tone and punch the words out in rapid succession. "SaBrina requested a meeting with me this afternoon."

"What? Why? If there's more on that Sutter's Mill proposal she wants then I'll—"

"It's not about the proposal."

His cadence slows to a crawl. "Then what's it about?"

From experience, I know how impossible it will be to divert Chip's attention away from something he wants, so when he tips his head toward the alcove sandwiched between the women's bathroom and the break room, I don't decline the invitation. One way or another, this conversation is happening.

Once we're hidden from view, I move my hand to my chest to feel for the fabric that rests directly under my clavicle. Absently, I rub at the spot, finding little comfort as I speak the truth I've been afraid to say for months. "I think she's figured out you've been covering for me."

He lifts his shoulders in a slight shrug as if completely undaunted by my admission. "I'm an editorial assistant; assisting editors is literally what I'm paid to do here. My work on that proposal shouldn't be a big deal."

I exhale and try my best to look like an authority figure, though at the moment I feel about as powerful as a cocooned butterfly. "You and I both know you've given me far more help than any editor should request of their assistant—which is why it can't continue. Today was the last time you can help me like that."

His voice collapses into a hush. "You didn't request anything of me, I *offered*. Just like you offered to take me on as a college intern two years ago when not a single editor here was willing to give me a chance. I wouldn't have a job if not for you." The permanent glint in his eyes turns mischievous. "You do realize it's not possible to load every manuscript into that robotic reading app you've been using, right? If you turn the listening speed up any higher on that thing, you'll put yourself at risk for a stroke." He shakes his head as if this is all a simple misunderstanding and not an elaborate scheme we've been playing at for months. "I'm a freakishly fast reader and you're . . ." *Broken*, I think, as he pauses to select his word choice before finishing with, "Experiencing a temporary setback. Your therapist said your brain fog would normalize in time, right?"

That's not exactly how Dr. Rogers had put it, but this alcove isn't conducive to such a personal conversation. What my therapist had actually said was that if I was willing to do the work, willing to walk backward in time and navigate the loss that stifled my ability to comprehend the written word, I might improve. *Might*. But he also made certain to tell me that trauma responses like the one I've been experiencing for the better part of a year come with no certainties or guarantees.

A life lesson I know all too well.

I stop scanning the dozen or so empty cubicles in the center of our third-floor office building and return my gaze to Chip, willing the courage to come. "I think it's time I tell her the truth about what's really going on with me."

I knew I couldn't keep such a limiting handicap a secret for long in an industry built on books. Chip's superpowers in speed-reading manuscripts may have bought me borrowed time, but now that time is up, and I can't allow his career to sink with mine. I know too much about life at sea to let Chip jump in after me when I'm the one flailing and sputtering for breath.

"You can't." All pretense of calm washes from his face. "SaBrina isn't like Barry." He eyes me as if I've somehow missed the last nine months under the command of an editorial dictator. "If you tell her you can't keep up with the reading requirements of this job, she won't suddenly respect you for your honesty, she'll fire you for incompetence. She's fired staff for a lot less—just think about how many receptionists we've gone through."

I know he isn't wrong, but I don't see another option. Sometime within the next hour SaBrina is going to march into my office and accuse me of using my grief as some kind of unethical hall pass to shirk my work responsibilities onto my assistant, and I have no real defense. Because in some twisted version, it's true. Once again, grief has stolen something irreplaceable from me.

Needing to move, I make a break from the alcove and into the fresh air of the hallway. Chip follows at a clipped pace.

"Okay, I say we grab a couple of subs from Luigi's and talk through a new game plan because unlike you, I'm not used to biking twenty miles each morning on my Peloton. And even though I'm not sure how many miles I biked in the rain with a flat, I do know my brain cells will combust from lack of sustenance if I don't eat something soon. I also know your hangry eyes are starting to show."

"You're not hearing me, Chip. There are no more game plans for the two of us to make together. This is *my* problem to fix. I made this mess, not you."

"But—"

"No." I shake my head, cutting him off. "I appreciate everything you've done for me, but from this point on, it's best you're not involved. I can handle SaBrina on my own."

He eyes me unconvincingly, but Chip doesn't know how many

times SaBrina has badgered me on the whereabouts of *The Fate of Kings*, or how many times she's insisted I turn Cece's laptop over to our IT department so they can scour the hard drive more closely, or how many times she's managed to work in questions about my current relationship status with the Campbell family into professional conversations—particularly why I was named one of the two trustee holders of Cece's intellectual property. Given that the estate details have never been public record, I still haven't a clue how SaBrina gleaned that tidbit of information. Somehow, the woman has eyes and ears everywhere.

"Go save your brain cells from combustion," I encourage Chip, now standing outside of my closed office door and testing out what is likely a sad and pathetic version of a smile. "If you hurry, maybe you can catch a sidewalk sale on a pair of pants so you can ask Chelsea out before the end of the day." I'm not sure I've ever used her actual name with him before, but I need Chip to leave because I can't think when he's looking at me as if I've already been given the ax.

"Fine," he says resolutely. "I'll go, but I still say that telling SaBrina about your brain fog is a huge mistake. There has to be another way."

He walks away without looking back, and I watch until he reaches the elevator lobby. Maybe he's right. Maybe if I could just think for a minute there might be a way to keep my job while also keeping Chip out of trouble. I skim my teeth over my bottom lip and reach for my office door, thinking of the lone protein bar at the bottom of my desk drawer. Maybe Chip's right about my hangry eyes showing. First, I'll eat; then I'll strategize.

I push into my office and immediately startle back.

A heart-stopping, electric current stuns all five of my senses at once at the sight of the broad-shouldered man staring out my office window. For the briefest of seconds, every shattered thing in my world pushes to the periphery to make way for a hope that hurts nearly as badly as the heartache it's desperate to replace. On sheer instinct, my body moves towards him, desiring a reunion I've never allowed, a restoration I've never believed possible. But as soon as he faces me, it all comes rushing back into focus again. The place and time I yearn for in my restless dreams no longer exists. And yet somehow, the past I fled is standing right in front of me, hundreds of miles off course and a handful of years too late.

For an immeasurable amount of time, neither of us speaks, allowing my brain the space it needs to thrust my last in-person memory of Joel Campbell to the surface. Joel: sitting in the front row of Lighthouse Community Fellowship at Cece's funeral next to a leggy redhead who fiddles with the yellow marigold pinned to his lapel. Me: sitting two rows behind them in the not-quite-family-but-more-than-friend section. Perhaps the most honest definition of the in-between I straddled as Captain Hal's daughter and Joel Campbell's . . . whatever we once were to each other.

Though his stance is as unwavering as it's always been, I can't help but note the weariness anchored to his shoulders and the faint brush-strokes of silver interspersed through his thick, cinnamon-brown waves. It's the same dignified shade of silver his father embraced sometime in his early thirties. And likely what Joel himself will embrace in only a few years' time. His solid frame is a far cry from the lanky, athletic build of his youth, as if his once-familiar dress code of blue jeans and a logoed work polo is no longer acceptable. This Joel wears slacks and a button-up shirt. Yet it's the hauntingly empathetic way his gaze fuses with mine that renders me motionless.

"I'm sorry, Ingrid" is all Joel gets out before I'm reaching for something solid. A door, a wall, anything that will keep me upright as my reconstructed world begins to collapse in on itself.

"Is it Wendy? Has something happened to—"

"No, no." He shakes his head emphatically, as if realizing only then that he chose the same words to start this conversation as he did on the two darkest days of my life. "Aunt Wendy is . . . she's fine. Everyone back home is fine." He pauses again, and I wonder if his definition of fine is as fluid as my own has become. A word used only in relativity. "What I meant to say is that I'm sorry to show up unannounced like this, but I didn't come to report bad news."

As my adrenaline recedes, my mind races to catch up on what I've missed. I eye my open office door, confused at how he—

"I told the receptionist I was here to see you."

"And she just let you in here?" I'm in too much shock to feel violated by such a careless oversight at the hand of our newest receptionist and too well-versed in the paralyzing appeal of one Joel Campbell to feel indignant.

"I refrained from correcting her when she assumed we had a lunch date." His pause is only as long as a breath, and yet I'm still holding mine when he adds, "But even if she hadn't offered to let me wait for you inside your office, I came prepared to wait for however long it took to see you today."

It takes great effort for me to cut the invisible tether between our gazes, but I'm not sure how much longer my knees will hold me if I continue trying to stand. Before I start toward the sanctuary of my desk, I make the cognizant decision to keep my office door ajar. Sharing such a confined space with Joel is an intimacy I can't allow myself, not even at the cost of privacy. In true Campbell fashion, he waits for me to take my seat before he claims the chair across from my desk.

"It seems a phone call would have been more efficient than catching a flight," I say with a candor that seems to surprise us both. "For the record, I do check my voicemail daily."

"This deserves more than a voicemail." He shifts in his seat and tugs out a small, slightly crumpled manila envelope from a satchel on the floor, only he doesn't hand it off to me right away. Instead, he holds it hostage near his chest in a protective manner that hastens my pulse. "Do you remember Marshall Evans? He graduated a couple of years ahead of me, and he's the attorney who took over Cece's estate dealings after his grandfather's stroke last fall."

"Lloyd Evans." The name of the Campbell's former family attorney sails off my tongue easily. A kind man in his late seventies with a broom mustache and a small-town demeanor. Lloyd had phoned me regarding Cece's initial wishes soon after her service, but it was

Marshall who followed up with me a couple months later, after Lloyd's stroke left him nonverbal. For his own records, I'd repeated the same conclusion I'd come to with his grandfather, and we hadn't had a reason to speak since.

"Marshall's spent the better part of this year transitioning Lloyd's clients and accounts to his own practice, which took some effort, seeing as his grandfather's organizational system was mostly kept up here." Joel points to his temple. "Marshall had every reason to believe Lloyd kept all his notes regarding Cece's estate in the same filing location." He pauses. "But he called me in to his office yesterday after he found something odd tucked away in an old cabinet. Something that was supposed to be delivered to us three months after Cece passed." He holds out the envelope so it hovers in the gap between us. "This."

My voice is as thin as my breath. "What is that?"

But the instant I reach for it, I see the red confidential logo stamped on the back and pull my hand away. Despite Cece's wishes for Joel and me to hold the rights to her intellectual property together, I declined the title of trustee. I'm not a Campbell. I will never be a Campbell. Whatever business decisions are required, Joel is more than capable of handling them on his own.

"I've already told Marshall that I don't wish to review any documents or reports regarding her estate or—"

"Open it."

I eye him warily. "I'm sorry you wasted a flight out here for this, but like I said—"

"Just open it, Indy. *Please.*"

The use of my nickname kicks through a deadbolt inside my chest, and despite my resolve, I take the envelope from him and turn it over in my hands. I lift the gold brad at the back, which reveals a second envelope tucked inside. *Yellow.* This envelope doesn't have the attorney's confidential logo stamped across the back. Instead, there's a note paperclipped to the front, written in a script I'd know as well as my own: *In the event of my death, please follow my previously stated instructions and deliver this letter to Joel Campbell and Ingrid Erikson.*

Panic sloshes up my esophagus as I contemplate the cruelty of such a terrible, terrible prank. "Tell me what this is, Joel. Stop playing games with me and just tell me what this is all about."

"I don't know what it's about," he says in a see-for-yourself kind of way. "The letter is still sealed. I wasn't about to open something from Cece that was addressed to us both without you present." Which explains why he caught a flight south, knowing it would take nothing short of an act of God to get me on a plane headed north.

I run my fingers along the crisp edges of the envelope several times, as if doing so might provide a clue for the content inside.

When I glance up at him, he nods for me to go ahead.

With my pulse pounding hard in my throat, I press my lips together and carefully peel back what was likely one of the last documents my childhood best friend touched before she died alone on an operating room table.

The opening process is slow as I tug the thin yellow stationery from its matching envelope. When I unfold it, my lungs refuse to refill. I stare down at the familiar writing, at the way Cece's g's and y's double loop, and at the whimsical dashes above her i's that look like the curve of a smile. The way each letter slants just a bit too far to the right, as if poised and ready to waltz right out of the margins, revealing the old soul she was, even at the age of twenty-six.

"Would you mind reading it out loud?"

"Sorry." I clear my throat. "I wasn't actually reading it, I was just . . ." I shake my head, reminding myself that I don't owe him an explanation. I don't owe Joel anything anymore. After another thorough glance at Cece's beautifully unique penmanship, I slide the letter across my desk toward him. "You should be the one to read it. You're her family."

Unblinking, he takes it back, dragging his gaze from me to the fragile piece of paper in his hands. And then, he begins to read it aloud:

"Joel and Indy,

If you're reading this letter, then we've all had a pretty big shock. Although mine ends with streets of gold and treasures far more valuable than any my beloved pirate friends ever managed to discover. I'm sorry I can't send you any pictures. On that note, I'm sorry I couldn't stick around a little longer. I wanted to.

I'm sure you're wondering what this letter is all about and why I had Lloyd wait to deliver it until a few months after my heavenly housewarming, and I promise, I'll get to that. But there are a few things I need to say first.

Losing someone dear to me has always been at the top of my fear list. Perhaps my only real-life experience with grief is wrapped up in an absentee father who didn't deserve the tears I shed for him as a young girl. But when I close my eyes today and force myself to try and replay the best moments of my life without either one of you in them . . . the pain that brands itself onto my chest is nearly unbearable. And yet I know you are both well-acquainted with this kind of loss, the same kind I've never been brave enough to face outside the pages of my fiction. And for that, I'm the most sorry.

During these last few years, I never lost hope that the two of you would find your way back to each other again—or that the three of us would be reunited as if we'd never been apart. After my surgeon told me the risks involved in the surgery to remove my brain tumor, my priorities became clearer while my options grew fewer. There are things I promised myself I'd be brave enough to do long before now. And yet now is all I have left.

I've read that it's not advised for those who are grieving to make any big decisions within the first year, but I couldn't make you wait a year for something I wish I could have given to you sooner. I asked Lloyd to hand-deliver this letter to you three months after my death in hopes that you'd be open to receiving something I've set aside for you both. Something outside the parameters of my estate. Something far more substantial than my words in this letter.

I'm asking you to put your differences aside and retrieve a package

*I've left in the care of my trusted attorney. Lloyd will give you my in-
structions from there. I love you.*

*Yours always,
Cece"*

There's a slight tremor to Joel's hands when he lowers the letter to
his lap. And once again, when our eyes meet, neither of us utters a
word. I don't even know how to begin to process what I just heard.
But I do know I absolutely cannot process it alone with Joel.

On restless legs, I ease away from my desk and pace the length
of my window that overlooks the back alley of a sandwich shop and
two bakeries. My office isn't large by any stretch, but it's big enough
to house a floor-to-ceiling bookshelf, an L-shaped desk, and the
Peloton bike I couldn't fit into my tiny studio apartment after Dr.
Rogers prescribed cycling as a part of my therapy. I study it now,
wishing it wasn't mounted to a go-nowhere stand. Wishing even
more that it could take me far, far away from here.

"Seven months," I murmur, trying to wrap my brain around it.
"That letter has been sitting in a dusty file cabinet for seven months?"

To his credit, Joel doesn't look any less stunned than I feel. "Apparently so."

"This is crazy." I continue to pace. "People don't just leave random
packages for their friends to retrieve after they've . . ." I don't finish.

"People? No. But it's not as if Cece's ever been the conventional
type," Joel amends. "The longer I sit with it, the more on-brand it
feels for her."

I hate how accurate his statement is, but Joel knew his only cousin
as well as I knew her, which also happens to be as well as we knew
each other once upon a time.

"This coming Saturday would have been . . ." Joel trails off, swallows, tries again. "Her twenty-seventh birthday." A date I've done
my best to pretend doesn't exist, because Saturday will also mark

28

ten months to the day Joel called to tell me her surgery wasn't successful. "My parents are hosting a dinner in her honor that night."

It doesn't take much imagination to visualize the kind of tribute the Campbells might be hosting in honor of their late niece. The parties they've held at their hotel have always been memorable, meaningful occasions. Grand end-of-summer soirees, formal dinner affairs at the pier, outdoor family seafood nights sprawled across dozens of picnic tables overlooking the Sound.

"It's invite-only. Just friends and family." Joel stands and tucks his hands into his pockets as he watches me pace. "They'd welcome you, Indy. We all would." Without taking his eyes off me, he adds, "I know Cece intended for us to read this months ago, but the timing of this has to be more than coincidence. She always did prefer giving gifts on her birthday over receiving them."

It takes work to stop the barrage of memories his words have provoked, to realize that Joel assumes my decision to return to Port Townsend for a package neither of us knew existed until today has already been made. It's as if he thinks Cece's request—which was obviously made out of a guilty conscience, seeing as no one knew the true odds of her procedure—is enough to cause me to forget everything else Port Townsend represents. But there is more than one tragic death hovering in the fissure between us, and while Joel had nothing to do with the outcome of his cousin's surgery, he will forever be the last person to see my father alive. He will forever be the last person to speak to him mere moments before he boarded the Campbells' charter boat and died alone at sea. And he will forever be the one person I trusted enough to care for the only family I had left before it was too late.

A truth that's haunted me almost as much as the hurt I buried after walking away from Joel on his family's dock five years ago.

"Unfortunately," I say with as much conviction as I can summon without looking at him, "I won't be able to make it up this weekend. It's a busy season here in publishing, and I need to stay close to the office." I try not to think about Cece's mother, Wendy, as I add, "Please give my regrets to your family."

"Cece asked us to collect the package together, Ingrid."

"I know what she asked, but I don't see any reason why we'd both need to be present. I trust Marshall can oversee the process and contact me about the contents." I cross to my desk again and reach for a pen and the memo pad that says: *Edit or Regret It.* "I'd be happy to sign something so you can collect it without me—some kind of permission slip." With a slight tremble to my fingers, I scrawl out the words: *I, Ingrid Erikson, give permission for Joel Campbell to receive the package from Cecelia Campbell addressed to us both.* I date the memo and sign my name near the bottom before tearing it from the pad. "Please tell Marshall he's welcome to contact me if he needs anything more." I hold it out to Joel, but he makes no effort to retrieve it.

"That's not what she wanted."

I tamp down the desire to blurt, *"Look around! None of us got what we wanted, Joel!"* and instead I say, "As I said, it's terrible timing for me. I can't get away right now."

His jaw flexes twice. "You're telling me you can't take *two days* over a *weekend* to honor your best friend's last request and attend a birthday dinner? Maybe I'm missing something here, but that really doesn't seem like too much to ask of a woman my cousin called her best friend for over a decade."

His accusation lashes through the tender scar tissue of an old wound, exposing a hurt I've worked to shield for years. I narrow my eyes as heat flares in my chest. "And I really don't think you're in any position to judge me on what it means to honor a friend's request—last or otherwise."

The acute flicker of pain in his expression forces me to bite the insides of my cheeks so I won't take the words back. But even still, my insult doesn't stop whatever pre-programmed autopilot our bodies were set to long before this unplanned visit. There seems to be no off switch as the space between us thins enough for my spine to tingle with a sensation I swore I banished half a decade ago. When his focus downshifts from my eyes to my mouth and then finally to the fabric of my blouse concealing a tattoo that rests just below the ridge of my left collarbone, I actively remind myself to keep breathing.

"Aren't there enough regrets stacked between us, Indy? Please don't let this be another one." His emotion-laced question curls around my ribcage and squeezes with the strength of a python. "Come home."

My throat begins to burn right as the familiar tap of a nail on my office door breaks us apart.

"I hope I'm not interrupting something important." SaBrina's eyes skirt to Joel, and she extends her manicured hand as if she expects him to kiss a signet ring. "SaBrina Hartley. I'm the Editorial Director here at Fog Harbor Books."

"Joel Campbell." Though he's the picture of well-mannered professionalism, I fail to miss the way his eyes narrow at her ever so slightly. "I'm an old friend of Ingrid's."

And like a collision one can see coming from miles away, I watch the exact moment SaBrina connects the dots and registers Joel's full name.

"It's a privilege to finally meet you in person, Mr. Campbell." SaBrina shoots a brief but pointed glance my way before steering her attention back to him with rapt interest. "Does the rest of your family happen to be joining you in the city? I would love the opportunity to host a VIP luncheon for—"

"I'm afraid it's only me." His smile is unnaturally tense. "I had some family business to discuss with Ingrid."

In the lull that follows his explanation, there's an awkward dance of gazes, as if each one of us is trying to figure out the next steps. Only there are no next steps to be choreographed between the three of us. Joel has never been a part of Cece's publishing life, just like SaBrina has never been a part of Cece's personal life. And I see no reason for the two to intermix now.

I twist the ring on my finger and rotate to face Joel, panic slipping into my voice. "Thank you again for taking the time to stop by today. I don't want to keep you from your flight. Traffic in the city is never predictable."

"Not much in life is." And then, as if the two of us were still on casual touching terms, Joel reaches out to still my nervous hand with his, the same way he did a thousand times in the life we shared a thousand years ago. Every rational thought in my brain vacates in a single blink as his voice lowers. "For the record, I'm not the only person who'll take note of your absence if you're not with us on Saturday. You were her family, too."

He dips his head to SaBrina and then to me as he lifts his hand from mine and slips out of my office almost as suddenly as I slipped out of his life five years ago.

3

My legs feel as boneless as if I've just ridden an extra ten miles on my virtual circuit. Every nerve ending in my body screams for a reprieve, only there's no time for one because I'm now at the mercy of a woman who has only ever seen me at my worst—and by the way she's eyeing me now, it doesn't seem likely that will change any time soon.

"It seems a visit from one of Cecelia's family members would be something you'd think to mention to your editorial director, Ingrid." SaBrina's voice holds an unnerving amount of calm, though her meaning is razor sharp.

"I wasn't aware he was coming."

She tilts her head to the side as if weighing my statement. "This family business matter Mr. Campbell mentioned—it wouldn't have anything to do with a missing manuscript, would it?"

"No," I rush to get out. "He only came to invite me to a birthday gathering on Saturday—one I won't be attending." Of the two invitations Joel extended involving Port Townsend this weekend, this is the only one safe enough to mention to SaBrina. She never needs to know about Cece's letter or the mysterious package Cece left behind for reasons I still can't comprehend. Only once had I overshared the details of a private conversation held between Cece and myself regarding the deadline of *The Fate of Kings*, and SaBrina hadn't let me forget it.

"In Port Townsend?" she asks.

At my obvious confusion, she tries again, this time at an irritatingly slow pace. "Is the birthday event you declined taking place in Port Townsend with the Campbell family?"

I nod. "Yes."

Her face remains contemplative, her silence dragging from one minute into the next. It lasts so long that I begin to think it's a test—a waiting game to see if I'll step up and take the lead. Perhaps this is the moment I should come clean about my reading issues and beg her for a pardon. Only, instead of a polished speech I had zero time to prepare, what comes out of my mouth is a simple: "I can do better."

Her gaze flashes with renewed interest as she continues her study of me for a few seconds more.

"I still remember what I was doing the day I heard about Barry Brinkman signing a twenty-one-year-old debut author in the San Francisco office for a five-book fantasy series." She takes a turn around my office, her eyes skimming my sparsely decorated walls. "The rumors spread like wildfire. Some people thought Barry had lost his pulse on the market, while others began to question his moral integrity, especially after the story broke on how he'd secured that first manuscript—or perhaps I should say, *who* he'd secured that first manuscript from."

My stomach sours at the careless way she speaks about the character of a man who quite literally scraped me off my office floor and put me in a cab home the day Joel called to tell me the outcome of Cece's surgery.

"As a senior editor working in New York at the time, it was easier for me to believe the rumors than the hype about some small-town writer from nowhere Washington with an affinity for pirates." She chuckles to herself. "But I'm not too proud to admit I was wrong—about that series, about Cecelia Campbell's talent, and even about you." A soft wrinkle forms between her eyebrows. "Ingrid Erikson, the legendary college intern who took this office by storm, seemed to be the whole package—beauty, brains, ambition, and story instinct."

It's the first compliment SaBrina's ever paid to me, and yet I know it won't be without a catch.

"Which is the reason I've put off this conversation for as long as I have. But I can't put it off any longer. You may have struck literary gold for Fog Harbor Books when you discovered Cecelia Campbell, but your sales numbers have taken a nosedive since her last release. Barry cautioned me about your bleeding heart when it comes to debut authors looking for their big break, and if that was your only issue, I might have been willing to overlook it. But we both know your performance this year has been abysmal. Your lack of sales, your lack of professional discretion—not to mention your gross overuse of your editorial assistant—has made you a liability to Fog Harbor Books."

The finality in her tone causes my throat to burn as I try to imagine what it will feel like to walk out my office door for a final time, or to email a professional farewell to the coworkers I've collaborated with since I was an intern, or to take the elevator down to the lobby and buy one last Americano from Chip's pink-haired crush, or to say good-bye to an assistant who became an unexpected friend when I'd had so little to give in return.

And then the scariest feeling of all begins to quake through me: *What will become of me?*

Working in editorial is the last piece of myself that still resembles who I was before so much of my world went black. In the short span of five years, I've lost my father, my closest friend, my ability to escape into fiction . . . and the man who promised me a future secured by trust and love.

With the bone-chilling clarity that only comes after one's life has been upended, I know I will not survive losing one more thing.

"*Please*, SaBrina," I say, throwing whatever pride I have left at her feet. "I know I've fallen short of Fog Harbor's standards—of my own standards for that matter. But a life in publishing is where I belong, it's what I know best." *And it's the only thing I have left.* "I can do better. Please, give me another chance to prove that to you and I will. I swear I will."

"I believe you." She glides toward my office door and then promptly closes us inside. When she faces me again, her smile is as bold as it is telling. "You can start by accepting Joel Campbell's invitation to Port Townsend this weekend."

Nearly three hours later, I'm trudging down Sutter Street in Lower Nob Hill, my anxiety as impossible to contain as it was when SaBrina laid out her ultimatum. I mute her voice from my thoughts as I trudge up the steps into my apartment building, swipe my access key card, and nod at Mr. Winslow, who sits behind the security desk. He offers me his standard two-finger salute and I reciprocate in kind, thankful he doesn't strike up a conversation that would require anything more than muscle memory tonight.

When my phone buzzes in my pocket, I silence it the same way I've done the previous three times. There is still too much unsettled business in my head to answer Chip's questions—the majority of which will likely center around an encounter I can't seem to stop reliving, no matter how many times I've tried.

I see and hear it all again as if viewing the scene on playback: the captive way Joel watched me pace across my office floor, the precision of his fingers as he refolded each crease of the yellow stationery, the earnest reprimand in his voice when he said, 'You were her family, too.'

I take the stairs to the seventh floor, hoping the extra steps will slow my overactive brain cells. Within a minute of stepping into my four-hundred-square-foot studio, I'm out of my work clothes and into my vintage *Twilight* tee and coziest pair of drawstring shorts.

A minute more and I head to my spot.

Technically, the rooftop isn't one of the highlighted amenities listed on my apartment lease. And it's also technically not open to tenants since it's been "under construction" for as long as I've lived here. But for whatever reason, Mr. Winslow has never outed me to management, even though I know he's seen me on his security camera at least a hundred times. Maybe it's the children's books I've gifted him at Christmas for his grandkids, or maybe he's just a nice guy who doesn't peg me as a threat to myself or others. Whatever the case, I'm grateful for the far northeast corner of this concrete island where I can pretend there's still privacy to be found in one of the most populated cities on the Pacific coast.

I settle on the wide, bricked ledge where a whirling exhaust fan nearly drowns out the slamming of car doors, trolley bells, and drunken shouts ping-ponging in the alleyways below. Along with the soundtrack of the city, the unique odor of sulfur and urine is also dulled from up here, though I don't make this trek for the change in air quality. I make it for the tiny sliver of bay I can see on a clear evening like this before sunset.

The water is miles away, but the reflection of the dipping sun within its mirrored surface has a profound and provocative effect on me nonetheless, both a beckoning and a rebuke. And a silent reminder that all is not lost inside me.

I hug my legs, rest my chin on my knees, and slip my phone out from my pocket. I tap into my photos and scroll to the last selfie I took with Cece, just six months before she died.

Due to our busy work deadlines, we hadn't seen each other in person for several months, so when she'd called to say she was desperate for some story help and an old-fashioned slumber party, we agreed to meet somewhere between my bustling city and the suffocating seaside town I refused to return to. She booked us a mountain cabin in Sisters, Oregon, for the following weekend. "*The town name was too perfect for me to pass up,*" she'd said, hauling a duffle bag nearly as big as she was from our rental car through the log cabin door. "*I think this place was made for us, Indy.*"

In the selfie, our cheeks are smashed together in a way that contrasts the dark and light shades of our hair and eyes as well as the difference in our skin tones—the golden hue of mine, the pinkish pale of hers. Unlike so many pictures we share together, it's not Cece's signature blond curls that steal the limelight, but the extra-bright smile that consumes her face. Yet another distinction between us. Cece's smile was always halfway to a guffaw—a wide, open-mouth grin that showed all her teeth as well as her vivacious spirit. My facial expressions have always been far more controlled, my smile little more than a closed-lipped curve prepared to shift with the ever-changing winds of life. Only an hour after this photo was taken, the winds shifted again when Cece told me the truth about her perplexing bad headaches. They weren't the barometric pressure migraines she'd diagnosed herself with. Cece had a brain tumor. Benign. Operable. Low-risk.

"*I wanted to tell you in person, Ingrid, so you could see that I'm okay. See?*" She'd crossed her eyes and stuck out her tongue. "*This is me giving you permission to save your tears for the tragedy that is the last season of* Gilmore Girls. *On that note, can you also save your time off? I'm hoping you'll agree to be my official recovery plan when I'm declared tumor-free.*" Her voice was confident and assuring. "*You'll come stay with me at the cottage afterward, won't you?*"

Without a second's hesitation I'd said, "*Of course. I'll come sooner if you need help to prepare—*"

She cut me off with a hard shake of her head. "*Believe me, between the smothering of my mom and my aunt, I'm having a hard enough time finding pockets of quiet to finish drafting* The Fate of Kings. *I'm nearly there, though—don't worry.*" Though she didn't mention Joel in her family inventory, there wasn't a doubt in my mind he'd be there with her, too, along with his father, Stephen. The Campbells stuck together that way. It used to be the thing I admired most about them. "*My goal is to turn it in to you before the surgery. Just in case.*"

"*No.*" It was my turn to be adamant. "*You are officially off deadline as far as I'm concerned. I don't want it until you're ready to trade it in for a giant bowl of cheddar-caramel popcorn and an episode of* Gilmore Girls."

Her smile brightened. *"Deal."*

A single tear splashes onto my knee as my phone rings in my hand, blocking the image with a contact name that startles me out of the memory and back to the present—one lived in a world without Cece. I wipe at my face, clear my throat, and swipe to accept the call.

"Hey, Chip. Sorry about the delay."

"Is there a politically correct way to ask your superior if she's still employed? It's not in the employee handbook—I've already checked."

"I'm not sure."

"About what part? Being politically correct or still being employed?"

"Both, actually." I huff out a tired sigh.

This is usually when I'd power myself on to work mode and fill the void with talk of our never-ending deadlines and to-do lists. But tonight feels different. Tonight I don't need an assistant as much as I need a friend.

"You still there?" he asks.

"I'm here." Only, I'm not exactly sure where *here* even is anymore. Sometime in the last few hours I've been sucked through a cosmic portal and dropped into a past life. One I've already lived once and never planned on repeating. But Cece's letter, the words she'd penned, and the mysterious package waiting in an office a thousand miles away have me cornered in a mental dead end I can't U-turn my way out of.

Or perhaps SaBrina's ultimatum is what has me cornered: submit the missing manuscript within the probation period she's outlined for me—AKA the ten days of paid vacation time I'd stored up for Cece's recovery—or lose my job.

As I watch the fog crawl across the bay, I force the inevitable aside to prioritize the answers I know Chip wants first. "I didn't tell SaBrina about my reading issues."

His relief is audible. "Thank God, that was what I was most—"

"But even if I had, I'm not sure it would have made a difference."

The words are more difficult to say than I thought they'd be. "She was planning on firing me this afternoon."

"What?" he all but shouts. "On what grounds?"

"Your lawyer side is showing again." Given that seventy-five percent of Chip's family works in the legal system, this is a common occurrence. "You already know on what grounds. There's no need to rehash every area I've fallen short this last year. It's a long list."

"You've been grieving. Is she really so heartless? So you haven't hit your sales quota for the year; what about all the novice authors you've responded to? Does she even realize you're the only one of her editors who personally responds to queries the way you do? And what about the virtual story workshops you've taught online? Or the—"

"Chip, I appreciate what you're trying to do, but that's not the stuff she cares about. And truthfully, she's not paid to care about it. She made it clear that if not for my past successes, I would have been gone months ago."

"So why aren't you, then? What did you say to convince her to keep you on?"

I close my eyes, replaying the events of the day all over again as I muster up the courage to tell him more personal information in this one conversation than I have in the past two years combined.

"Listen," he says tentatively. "I get that this is probably a lot weirder for you than it is for me—being my supervisor and all—but let me remind you that you know pretty much everything there is to know about me in case you ever require blackmail material." And then he begins to list off facts as if reading them from the headline on a supermarket gossip magazine. "My parent's *very* public divorce. My boarding school years in Monterey. The custody arrangement that kept me apart from my sister for so long we're little more than strangers now. My repulsion to the sight of seaweed. Every one of my failed pick-up attempts with Chelsea to date. Losing my grandpa to a stroke last Christmas Eve." He releases a sobering exhale. "For whatever it's worth and for however unprofessional it is to say this, when everything happened with Cece last fall I started to think of you like the big sister I never had growing up. If that makes you uncomfortable, then you can hang up now and we can just go back to—"

"Joel Campbell came to see me today at work." It might not be the ease-in approach I was prepping for, but Chip knows a decent amount about my history with the Campbell family. Working so closely with Cece over the last couple years, there were simply too many unavoidable questions. Even more so after her death when Chip was the one fielding my phone calls and scheduling my calendar.

After a brief exhale, I extend a conversational 4-1-1 to him and walk him through the drama-filled events of the day, taking great care to summarize Cece's letter to the best of my ability and ending with the probation plan SaBrina placed me on with orders to find a missing manuscript I've already searched for extensively on Cece's hard drive.

There's a long silence at the end of my monologue, and then I hear a muffled curse. "That was not at all what I was expecting."

I laugh at his candor. "That makes two of us."

This time his quiet is of the contemplative variety, and I wonder if he's experiencing the same nagging thought that has been buzzing around my head like a gnat ever since I stepped off the Bart. But like an author who hasn't given herself adequate space and time between her first draft and her developmental edits, I can't trust my own discernment. I need an outside perspective.

"This might be totally off base, but do you think there's any possibility the package Cece has for you might contain *The Fate of Kings*?" The reverent, almost cautious way he asks prickles the skin on my neck.

"I don't know," I all but whisper, too afraid to hope it could be that easy. That simple. "Maybe?"

Again, he falls silent. "If it is, then why would she give it to an attorney to hold on to when she knew it was under contract with Fog Harbor?"

Perhaps for the same reason she'd name her cousin and me trustees. Because Cece never stopped hoping that the two of us could overcome the past for a future that was never meant to be ours. Once a matchmaker, always a matchmaker. "Maybe because she wanted to give me time to read it with fresh eyes and not with . . . grief eyes." Ironic, considering my current situation.

"Okay, sure. But what does her cousin have to do with *The Fate of Kings*? It's not like the two of you can shop it around to other publishers looking for a better deal. The deal was already made—she signed it."

That answer, I realize, is far more complex than I'm willing to hammer out on the phone, but I know with glaring certainty that her reasoning for including Joel would have nothing to do with seeking better deal points or bigger royalties from a different house. Cece was as loyal to Fog Harbor as I am. So instead, I take the simplest approach to this one. "There's an added level of accountability when two people you trust have to sign off on a project together—especially one as big as the end of a book series." And wouldn't Cece have relished in the idea of Joel and I having to stay connected throughout the duration of a publication process—having to agree on every little decision until release day.

Cece's real-life plots were often as intricate as her fictional ones.

"You realize how insane a discovery like this would be, right?" Chip's volume begins to escalate. "The ripple effect would be huge. Can you even imagine what her fans would do? The media would lose their minds. Not to mention all it would mean for Fog Harbor Books, and for you, the heroic editor who brought the most coveted manuscript in the world back from the . . ."

"Dead," I finish after he bails.

"Sorry. I didn't mean—"

"I know what you meant. And you're not wrong. Finding that manuscript and turning it in after all this time would be an ending better than fiction." My eyes sting at the thought of offering a conclusion to Cece's millions of diehard fans, all those readers left on the edge of a cliffhanger who deserve to see justice done. Could this nightmare really come to an end in the span of a single weekend? Could one quick trip back to Port Townsend really be the answer? The magnitude of such a question begins to unfurl inside me. My future at the publishing house would be secure, Chip's promotion to editor inevitable, and the world would finally have what's remained elusive to me for five years.

Closure.

"What are you going to do, Ingrid?"

This time, I don't stop my wandering thoughts from traveling in a direction I haven't allowed in over half a decade. Because this time, there's no room for second guessing.

"I'm going to find *The Fate of Kings*."

4

idway through the ferry ride across the Puget Sound, I zip up my windbreaker and cut a path through the congested passenger area for the viewing deck on the stern. Though I'd escaped the frenzied pace of the San Francisco airport and the bumper-to-bumper traffic of downtown Seattle, the nerve-wracking anticipation that vibrates from every happy tourist aboard this hollow sea vessel pushes me toward the open air.

As soon as I step alone onto the viewing deck, it's a battle to stay upright against the bluster of the wind. There's a reason most passengers have chosen to remain inside where it's warm and stable. I grope along the railing until I find a secure place to anchor myself until we're docked in Bremerton. After that I'll drive for an additional hour to reach the northeastern tip of the Olympic Peninsula in a rental car that's only available through Sunday. But if my growing suspicions about the secret package from Cece are true, then I won't need to stay any longer than the weekend, anyway. No matter how trying the events of the next thirty-six hours might be—or the estranged company I'll be sharing the majority of those hours with—every minute will feel worth it if it ends with the retrieval of *The Fate of Kings*.

Not surprisingly, the time it took to book my plane ticket, ferry passage, and rental car was only half as long as the time it took me to summon the will to text Joel. Due to the height of tourist season in this part of Washington State, the closest vacancy for a hotel room was more than a thirty-minute drive out of town. And even if I'd wanted to stay at the Campbell Hotel, I already knew their summer reservations booked out by mid-March. I also knew that if I asked Wendy for a room she wouldn't turn me down, the same way she hadn't during Cece's funeral, but I have no right burdening a grieving mother with a houseguest during the weekend of her daughter's birthday.

So instead, I'd sucked up my pride—after deleting the first six messages I'd attempted—and texted Joel about an alternative housing option only he could grant. Cece had willed her cottage to him, or rather, to the property management company he helps oversee in addition to the family's hotel. Wendy's financial needs had been more than taken care of through a separate trust Cece had set up for her mother, but her cottage was a different type of investment: a prime piece of real estate in a seaside town that lacked for vacation rentals.

It's also a place I deeply regret never visiting while the owner was still alive to receive guests.

Ingrid

I'll be coming into town this Friday. Can you arrange a meeting with Marshall on Saturday morning? I'll plan to attend the birthday party that evening.

Also, would it be possible for me to rent Cece's cottage from you for the weekend?

His reply came less than an hour later.

Joel

We're set to meet with Marshall at ten on Saturday morning. As for the cottage, it will be ready for you by Friday afternoon. I'll text you the gate code along with any other relevant information.

Thank you for choosing to come, Indy. You being here this weekend will mean a lot to my family.

I've reread the text thread a dozen times, and yet the surrealness of the exchange hasn't lessened. I replay his word choice over again in my mind, pausing like always at the recall of his last line. *You being here this weekend will mean a lot to my family.*

I wish I could build a box around that final sentence and toss it out to sea, casting with it the sickening guilt I haven't been able to shake regarding the Campbell family. Cece had been my only real link to them in the years following my move to California. She was eager to supply me with every necessary and unnecessary update of the hotel, the town, the people. She was even willing to fly her mom down to see me for a mini reunion and a tour of the Bay Area, though that trip had been far less about Wendy wanting to see Ghirardelli Square and far more about her checking up on me. Shamefully, I'd failed to do the same with her, with any of them. I hadn't picked up the phone once since the funeral. I just . . . I couldn't.

Perhaps that's the real reason behind why Joel had written that last line about his family, a dig to remind me of my many short-comings in relationships. Joel would have picked up the phone. I have no doubt that if the situation between us now was reversed, the ever-reliable, ever-responsible Joel Campbell wouldn't have waited a week—much less a disgraceful ten months—before making an inquiry to my family if I'd been the one to die on a cold operating table.

Then again, our situation can't ever be reversed seeing as I have no family left for him or anyone else to inquire after.

Despite the windblown state I'm sure to arrive in, I lean farther over the railing and stare into the inky sea below, allowing my thoughts to surf the rhythmic waves in seclusion, where it's safest. It's one thing to talk about my past with Dr. Rogers through a video screen, but something else entirely to be returning to it. The rumble of the vessel's engine vibrates the soles of my feet, and I can't help but wonder just how many days, months, years of my life could be measured standing next to a railing near open water? How many times had I watched my father at the helm of a ship, interpreting his wordless orders to me with a ready smile and an eager will to please him?

I twist the only possession he ever gave me around my finger and scan the vast horizon in search of answers I know will never come.

"Hello, I'm Emma." A small, tinny voice at my side startles me out of my reverie. "Is that a black agate?" She points to my finger while steadying herself on the railing. "We studied rocks at my school last year."

Two velvety brown eyes blink up at me from a girl who can't be much older than nine, ten at most. On instinct, my gaze darts around the deck in search of the child's guardian. I locate her immediately. On the opposite side of the glass, a woman holds a sleeping toddler to her chest and raises a hand to me with a smile, a gesture that confirms both her authority and awareness. I nod my acknowledgement and return the gesture before I bend to answer the girl, whose arms are now looped around the railing as she arches her back. Her gaze is still locked on my ring.

"This is actually black sea glass," I confirm.

She scrunches up her face. "I didn't know glass comes from the ocean."

"This kind does." I smile as she asks if she can touch it.

I release my grip on the railing and squat to give her a better look. Emma pokes at the ring. "But how does the ocean make this?"

The sunlight glints off my ring as the child twists the oblong piece of glass left to right. "It takes a very, very long time for the ocean to make a piece of sea glass," I explain. "Often it starts as a piece of a broken bottle that's pulled out to sea by the tide where it's tossed around in the surf, beaten against the sand, rocks, and shells for dozens of years until one day, something like this rolls onto the shore."

Her wide eyes blink in awe. "Will I be able to find one with my mom and my baby brother?" She looks back at her mother and waves with an enthusiasm that makes my heart swell.

"You just might. Sea glass comes in all different colors and shapes. This one was found on a beach in Port Townsend." I slip the ring off and hold it up to the sun for her to inspect it. "It's rare because it appears to be solid black until . . ."

47

"I can see the light through it!" she exclaims. "See? It *is* like an agate! I knew it!"

The wind whips my dark hair into my face, and it takes effort to tame it behind my ear. "I suppose you're right. You have a good eye."

A moment later Emma is called back inside for a snack, leaving me alone to recall some of my own beachcombing memories. Mesh bags swinging from tanned arms, worn sandals piled on driftwood, sand dollar collections, and sea kelp wars fought by teenagers in the tide.

As familiar as I was with a life at sea by my youth, I rarely spent my free time at the beach. If Dad and I were docked—either after the end of a chartering job or waiting on our next clients—then I was usually hunting for books, not seashells. But whenever Cece and her mother invited me to join them on their beachcombing adventures, I rarely turned them down. There was no first mate expertise required to walk on wet sand in search of treasures dancing in the tide. I could simply be an ordinary teenage girl doing ordinary teenage girl things.

One cool morning, under a narrow bluff on the northeastern side of the peninsula, where the tide crept in and out without warning, the two of us had stumbled upon a sight more coveted than any treasure Cece's pirates tracked across the dark waters of her fictional Cardithia: a glittering, multi-colored shoreline of sea glass. It was more than I'd ever seen in one place.

Inspired by the sight, I fisted a handful of sand and plucked out the colored pieces of pebble-like glass one by one. *"My dad says this is what happens when sadness and saltwater meet. It creates 'ocean tears.' He's called them that since I was young."* I dropped a nickel-sized piece of garnet-colored glass into Cece's open bag. *"He says the ocean is the only place big enough to hold all the sorrow in our world."*

I'd expected Cece to smile at the nickname and then continue on around the bend, but instead, her brilliant blue eyes misted, her voice cracking as she spoke over the soundtrack of rolling waves.

"My mom always says God sees every tear we cry—that He collects

them in a bottle. And I guess, when I think about it, it makes sense that God would use the ocean as His bottles." She faced the water then and waved her hand over it like a magician setting up their final act. *"What if all our tears are out there somewhere, tumbling around in the surf, just waiting for their chance to become something beautiful?"*

I hadn't answered her then, but I never stopped hoping she might be right.

When the ferry makes her final push for the Bremerton terminal, I trade the last remnants of this memory for a reality that's becoming as clear as the journey ahead of me. When an automated voice crackles an announcement over the speakers for drivers to gather their belongings and return to their vehicles to await further instruction on exiting the ferry ramp upon our embarkment, I allow myself a parting glance at the Pacific. And then, with determination in my step, I head to the bottom of the ship to locate my rented Prius and make the drive back to my past.

5

Just over an hour later, as the sun is beginning to make its descent, I roll up to the fence bordering Cece's daffodil-yellow, A-frame cottage and idle in front of a security gate I didn't even know existed until Joel texted me the entrance code. For as often as Cece had Facetimed me with her latest furniture finds and renovation updates, she'd never mentioned this addition to her property. Of course, I can understand why extra security measures might have been encouraged. After all, she was a single woman living alone, one whose private life had been catapulted into the public eye the moment her debut novel appeared on every bestsellers list.

I punch in the four-digit code and wait for the electric gate to slide open before I pull through and drive past the detached single-car garage to park at the bluff's edge. It overlooks a secluded, nameless beach, one we'd combed dozens of times together in summers past. I exit the car and take in the surroundings for the first time.

The early evening sun sits bright in a near cloudless sky and my breath catches at the one-hundred-and-eighty-degree view of the Strait of Juan De Fuca and the pocket-sized islands to the southeast. I squint at a cruise ship headed in from Victoria, British Columbia, and marvel at just how different this all looks in person than on a tiny, handheld screen.

Much like with my hair, the sea breeze tangles my emotions into a twist as I'm absorbed by memories of the day Cece FaceTimed me her good news.

"Guess what just happened?" Her blond curls had bounced in the frame of my phone screen as she waved a piece of paper in her fist. *"I just made a down payment on the cottage—the one on our bluff! And if things go as well as you and Barry project with these first two books, I should have enough to start renovating it by spring. Mom's already making me a vision board."* She rolled her eyes and laughed. *"She thinks we can save the floors. As long as we can dry them out, they should have this gorgeous driftwood-like finish."* She released a giddy shriek. *"Can you believe it, Indy? I just bought my dream house, and it's all because you forced Barry to read my first draft! Maybe instead of a book, I should just dedicate this entire cottage to you instead!"*

I twist now to scan the quaint cottage to my left, the one Cece had called her "dream house." Once an abandoned shack ravaged by storms and neglect and entrapped by thorns and thistles, Cece had seen something in this property that nobody else had. It was a gift she'd come by honestly, and one that didn't stop at foreclosed properties.

As I cross the pavement to the cottage, I startle at the sight of a Campbell Hotel club car parked under the shade of a maple tree in the side yard. How long has that been parked here? And where is the driver? Or perhaps a better question is—*who* is the driver? I run my fingers through my windblown hair and straighten my top. It wasn't that I hadn't expected to see Joel; I just hadn't expected to see him until tomorrow.

Random cleaning supplies and grocery bags peek out from the flatbed at the rear of the miniature vehicle. I slide my gaze from the open driver's door to a side entrance of the cottage, which has been propped open with a sturdy box of Grape-Nuts.

I lean into the kitchen and call out, "Hello?"

But the only reply I hear is in the form of a Taylor Swift song with a distinctly female vibrato. I recognize the lyrics about a lost first love immediately.

"Hello?" I try again, creeping into the entryway.

Cautiously, I trail through the narrow, galley-style kitchen I've glimpsed dozens of times while Cece made her morning coffee or popped her favorite brand of popcorn in the evenings. The walls are painted a soft, buttercream yellow, with cupboards refinished in crisp white to match the beadboard ceiling overhead. I touch the matte black hardware she went back and forth on for weeks until I finally convinced her to flip a coin. I wish I could tell her it was the perfect choice.

I wish I could tell her a lot of things.

A vase of wildflowers sits on the butcher-block countertop, and when I skim the petals with my fingertips, a sense of wrongness settles between my ribs. Cece would have reveled in the role of tour guide. I push away the thought before it gains any real traction.

As the mystery singer belts a new Taylor Swift song throughout the cottage from an undisclosed location, I step into the quaint living area, noticing the hardwoods for the first time. I smile at their driftwood-like charm she described. Looks like Wendy had been right about drying them out.

Just as I reach the far living room wall made up entirely of windows, a scream splits the air. I jump and scream back, throwing my hands above my head, ready to drop into a full duck and cover when—

"Oh my gosh! It's you! You're here!" A girl not much over the age of twenty squeals at the top of her lungs as she rips out her earbuds and hops up and down as if she's just stepped on something sharp. "You're Ingrid, and you're here!"

Before I can even attempt to lower my heart rate, she's velcroed herself to me with the kind of hug one might extend if they held proof of a matched blood relation. Which is more than implausible, considering her blond-brown hair and aqua eyes. Not to mention the fact that she's roughly as tall as Chip, who claims to be one pair of basketball high tops over six feet. As quickly as she appeared, she pulls back, the momentum swooshing her ponytail to the opposite shoulder.

"Um, hello?" I respond, unsure which kind of salutation should follow such an exuberant greeting. "Sorry I startled you, I did call out a few times but . . ." I shake my head. "But yes, I'm Ingrid."

"And I'm Allie." When she places her palm flat to her chest, it's clear she assumes this isn't our first introduction. "Allie Spencer."

Allie Spencer. There's a faint ping of remembrance when I hear her full name, but I have no clue as to why.

"I job shadowed under you and Cece at the hotel for a few weeks the summer I turned fourteen while my older sister was off at ballet camp—or maybe it was fashion camp." She smiles, shrugs. "It was one of those. My folks arranged for me to get some work experience with the Campbells while we were in town that summer, because heaven forbid I actually get to relax during a vacation or anything." Allie rolls her eyes good-naturedly while I work to sort through my memories of those last couple of summers at the hotel.

Allie must interpret my struggle to place her face and she's quick to come to my aid. "I was about a foot shorter then and had braces and a pretty janky haircut up to my ears because I did it myself," she amends with a grimace. "Zero stars. Do not recommend."

I nod as the image she's painted comes to life in my mind. "I do remember you, yes. You were the best linen napkin folder we ever had." I chuckle at a memory I hadn't thought of in years—a night of origami napkin folding in the basement with a teenage helper who was far more creative than either Cece or myself when it came to folds. "It's good to see you again."

"It's good to see you again, too." She beams. "And I'm definitely not the only one that feels that way. It's actually why I was delayed in getting here on time tonight." She leans in conspiratorially. "Let's just say, I was given a lot of instructions about how to make your stay here as comfortable as possible—most of which came from Joel's daily task lists for me, but still. To quote my mother, 'People's opinions are the heaviest kind of traveling companion.'" She laughs and once again rolls her eyes. "Pretty sure I could have pushed a wheelbarrow up that hill faster than it took to collect everybody's requests."

Everybody's requests? Joel's task lists? "I—I apologize for any hassle my stay might have caused. I certainly don't require much of anything."

"Oh, it's no hassle at all. I was joking—*mostly*," she says with another thousand-watt smile. "The cottage needed some basic essentials replenished, and the pantry and fridge needed to be stocked. But then of course when Patti and Stephen heard the news you were coming, they wanted to make sure I ordered you a fresh pastry plate from the bakery along with a deli plate of meat and cheeses. Then there were all sorts of discussions revolving around what linens I should bring over from the hotel since the family did a pretty thorough clean-out of the closets here a few months back. Oh, and then just as I was headed out, Joel had me wait while he asked his aunt to arrange a vase of flowers for you—"

"Wendy arranged those flowers on the counter?" Just speaking her name out loud constricts my next breath.

"Oh yes." Allie nods. "I hadn't seen her smile so big in months when Joel told her you were coming to the birthday dinner tomorrow."

Shame pummels me as an image of Cece's mother crystallizes in my mind; a mosaic of a thousand tiny snapshots pieced together during the most formative years of my life—each one of them underscored by Wendy's life motto: door open, arms open, heart open.

The only thing I deserve from Wendy is a slammed door.

When Allie stops to take a breath, I feel as if I need to take one, too. It's rare to be in the presence of someone who can out-talk Chip. "Is your luggage still in your car?" She peers around me in search of a suitcase I don't have. I brought a single carry-on with me from California, with exactly three changes of clothes, a wrinkle-free party dress, and a pair of pjs. "I'm happy to put it away for you. Joel said as far as he was concerned, you're my number-one priority. So if there's anything you need—*anything at all*—I'm your gal. Well, except for baking. In that case, my mom can be your gal. She's the head baker at the hotel now and she claims my technique with filo dough is criminal, but honestly, what does she expect? I played varsity volleyball for three years. I'm not the dainty dancer Spencer. That'd be my sister."

I blink multiple times. Perhaps the repetition might rewind my brain back to the part where she'd mentioned her work assignment from Joel. "You said you work for Joel?"

"Technically, I work for the family, but it's pretty much all the same. Work for one Campbell, work for them all," she says in a sing-song tone. "He would have been here himself if not for the flooding issue in the hotel laundry room. He told me to say he'll meet you tomorrow as planned though—at Marshall's. But again, if you need anything until then, I'm happy to be of service."

Allie laughs at whatever mystified expression she must find on my face. "In case I wasn't clear before, I'm one of the Campbells' property hosts for their vacation rentals in town. It's an upgrade from napkin folder for sure, and it's easy to step back into whenever I'm on break from Wentworth."

I nod, though I have an embarrassingly low comprehension for this entire exchange. "Sure, that makes sense."

Only I'm not so sure it does. Allie nods as if everything has been straightened out and like she didn't just tell me that Joel took her off her usual duties to act as my . . . as my what? Personal butler? Lady's maid? What is the proper, modern terminology for a female house manager? And it's that thought that strikes the match on a new one.

I rub at the dull ache starting in my right temple as she practically prances toward the kitchen.

"Wait, Allie, can I ask you something?"

"Absolutely!" She spins on her heels. "Anything." Her expression is as eager as the one Chip wears when I ask him to review my critique notes on an author's manuscript.

"Was this house rented for the weekend? I mean, before I confirmed I was coming. Was there a cancelled reservation?" Or perhaps a reservation that had been cancelled on my behalf, is what I don't ask.

Her grin sobers as she shakes her head. "No, ma'am. It wasn't rented."

"You're sure?" I press.

Her nod is resolute. "Only three people have keys to this cottage. Wendy, Joel, and myself. It's never been rented, not even for a night. You'll be the first guest to sleep here since . . . well, since, you know." For the first time, Allie's peppy demeanor diminishes. "Cece was an incredible person and my all-time favorite author. I couldn't believe it when my mom called me that day." She rubs her lips together and then stares me straight in the face. "It felt so wrong, it still feels so wrong. I know how close you two were, we all knew." She meets my eyes then and says, "I'm sorry she died."

Her words reverberate in my skull as I take special note to catalogue what she didn't say, not "I'm sorry for your loss" or "I'm sorry God needed her in heaven more than He needed her on earth" or the very worst of condolence offenses: "At least she lived a good life."

Something about the raw, refreshing truth of Allie's sentiment makes me hope this won't be the last time our paths cross this weekend. "I'm sorry, too."

She clears her throat and motions to the kitchen door. "I better grab the rest of those groceries and supplies. I'll be around for a few more minutes if you need anything else."

"Thanks."

After she's gone, I tour the rest of the cottage, braced for a sneaker wave of grief that never comes, not even when I open Cece's master bedroom and inhale the faint scent of the peachy-vanilla body spray she's worn since her eighteenth birthday. It had been on one of those BOGO sales at our favorite candle, lotion, and perfume store in the mall we visited twice a year.

"This can be my signature scent, Indy. Every lady who has ever made history has a signature scent. Did you know that? It's true. I read that J.K. Rowling wears a spicy, woodsy blend that reminds her of the trees she grew up around."

A Cece fact if ever there was one.

The final space in the cottage to be explored is the upstairs office in the converted attic. But as I stand on the bottom step of the narrow staircase, a searing pain begins to radiate from underneath my ribcage.

"You in the bedroom, Ingrid? I'm heading out." Allie's voice trails through the hallway, and I step down to level ground once again. I'll tackle Cece's office later.

"I'm right here."

Allie halts as she rounds the corner and holds out a key. "I wanted to give you this before I take off. I'm not sure I'll make it back over tomorrow—my mom needs about ten extra hands during special events, and this one is obviously more special than most. I wrote the garage code down for you as well. It's on a sticky note on the fridge."

"I appreciate that, thanks." I try my best to smile, but by the way she eyes me, I can tell it doesn't quite hit the mark. "Would you remind me what time the dinner starts tomorrow?"

"Six. Although I'm sure there will be plenty going on before and after. You know how these kinds of things go."

Maybe at one point I did, but I wasn't sure of much that went on here anymore.

"Oh"—she holds up a finger—"I also left my number on the counter for you. Please don't hesitate to call. You're only a seven-minute club car ride away from me."

"But only when it's not loaded down with other people's opinions," I remind her, and she laughs at that.

"True."

"But, really," I say, "thanks for treating this place with such special care."

"It's been my privilege. Cece was so kind to me after we moved here. One time, she even invited me over on one of my breaks to make milkshakes with her, which neither of us knew how to make." Her lips quirk as if she's reliving the memory. "We ended up with a sad sort of cold soup by the end of it. But she was super cool to let me ask her a million questions about her characters and series and even about the book she was working on at the time."

My thoughts sharpen at the mention of the timeline. "When was this milkshake meeting?"

"Um, let's see." She thinks for several seconds. "I guess it would have been when I was home last spring break? Middle of April last year."

"She was working on *The Fate of Kings* then," I say, more to myself then to Allie.

She nods. "I actually analyzed her entire series for my literature and pop culture class last semester. I'm an English major. Same as you were, right?" Her smile brightens again when I nod. "I was thrilled when she told me that Ember and Merrick would finally get their happy ending, but I guess that was never meant to be. . . ." Her sentence slides away, but I'm not quite ready to move off this topic.

"Did you actually see her working on it here at the cottage?" My heartbeat ticks a bit harder in my throat because I know this is the biggest clue I've been given in a year. A firsthand account of somebody who saw the manuscript in progress.

Her nod is more vigorous this time. "Yes, she had all her notebooks spread out on the dining room table, along with her laptop and all the maps and timelines. She showed me her plotting system, and we talked through her outline. I honestly felt bad for interrupting her that day when I knocked on her door, but she ushered me in and told me she was due for a mental break and a milkshake."

I smile. "That sounds like her."

"Oh!" She gasps and reaches for her phone. "I have some videos from that day, if you want to see them." In only a few swipes and taps, Allie pulls up the videos, and for a moment I'm not sure if I can do it, if I can see Cece's face or listen to her voice. But Allie's expectant smile causes me to push down my instinct. The video she plays reveals a countertop slick with milk and littered with ice cream cartons. Allie is talking into the screen, laughing at the mess they've made, when suddenly Cece's face pops into view and my breath all but leaves my body at once. Her smile is as vibrant and lively as my memory recalls, as are her corkscrew blond curls, which spill out from a messy bun atop her head. By the looks of it, it was not a wash day. Whenever she was super-focused on a writing deadline, she'd go up to a week without washing her curls. "This right here," Cece says, pointing to the sloppy blender on the countertop before slinging an arm over Allie's shoulders, "is procrastinating like a pro!"

The video ends, and Allie looks over at me. "She gave me permission to post it to my social media, and when I did, my writing club went crazy. Everyone wanted to meet her, so Cece invited us all to come to the hotel for a private luncheon after she was finished with her draft and her recovery from surgery, but . . ."

But Cece didn't live long enough to fulfill her invitation.

Allie goes quiet then, and I know it's because there's no easy way to transition out of this conversation. So I do it for her.

"You know, I just thought of something you might be able to help me with," I say, swallowing back the tears lodged in my throat as I conjure up a request.

"Sure, ask away."

"I'm thinking I might need to upgrade the dress I brought to wear to the birthday dinner tomorrow night. Are there any stores in town you'd recommend? Preferably a place that doesn't feature a colorful sarong or a Port Townsend windbreaker in the storefront window?"

Allie belts out a laugh, and I'm grateful for the reprieve. "You're in luck. My sister owns a clothing boutique next to the hardware shop called Madison's Wardrobe. It's where all the bougie tourists shop, but she really does have some beautiful formal wear. I'm sure she'd give you a discount, too."

"Sounds perfect. Thanks."

Once Allie takes off for the hotel, I tuck the cottage key into the pocket of my shorts and pull out my phone. Allie only represents one person in this town, and yet the information I confirmed in twenty minutes about Cece's final months is more than I've discovered all year. If I had any doubts that Cece hadn't been working during her sickness, that worry has now been put to rest. Maybe SaBrina was right to suggest that somebody in this town held the answer to where Cece's manuscript's been hiding out all this time.

And the most obvious choice by far is Marshall Evans. It makes sense to me now. Why wouldn't Cece entrust her last manuscript to a man who was legally bound to keep it safe?

What if for once in my life I don't have to suffer to find the answers I'm in search of? What if, for once, those answers might simply be handed to me in a package on the morning of my best friend's birthday?

6

I wake disoriented. It's as if the lack of police sirens and sidewalk musicians busking to make their next rent payment has
muddled my memory. That is, until I register today's date on
my phone's home screen. Like the swift bang of a gong, my brain
clears in full: the ferry, the cottage, the run-in with Allie, the vase
of wild flowers arranged by Wendy at Joel's request. And then the
loudest clang of them all, Cece's twenty-seventh birthday. It's this
last reality that pushes me from the comfort of the bed and into
the shower. I'm dressed and ready with an hour to spare before my
scheduled meeting at the law office, but I have no desire to sit in an
empty house. Not today.

Unlike yesterday's harried drive from the ferry terminal to Cece's
cottage, my pace through town is tourist-slow. If all goes as I hope,
there's a better than decent chance I'll be booking an Uber from the
San Francisco airport by this time tomorrow morning. Funny how
differently time is prioritized when it's in short supply.

Sunlight glistens off the storefront windows and highlights the
litter-free alleys and sidewalks as I roll through the freshly paved
streets of downtown Port Townsend. Dozens of fishing vessels and
wooden sailboats line the harbor to my right, each one biding their
time for their next day at sea. A handful of nautical-themed tav-
erns, coffee shops, and best-view-in-town restaurants have come

into focus now, too. And before I can look away, I'm searching for the most obvious of landmarks along Water Street: the renovated, Victorian-era hotel owned by a family I once loved as if they were my own.

My speed is barely above a crawl as I recall the first time I roamed these streets with my father as a wide-eyed adolescent. The cotton-candy-colored Victorian architecture had awed me back then, encouraging my belief in the magical fables I collected from used bookstores at ports up and down the West Coast. But unlike most children who outgrow fairy tales, it wasn't age that had squashed the magic of this seaport town for me; it was the inescapable reality of unmet promises.

With just over twenty minutes to spare, I swing a left just past the docks and head up the hill toward Marshall Evans's office. A white, steepled church comes into view and kicks my pulse into an erratic beat. For all my controlled reminiscing since debarking the ferry, I'm not prepared for the collision of snapshots and soundbites that thrash against me like a battered piece of sea kelp at the memory of Cece's funeral. The somber gray skies. The eulogy delivered by Joel. The security detail instructed to keep onlookers out of the private service.

Ten months suddenly feels no longer than a blink; five years no longer than a breath.

Two stop signs away from the law office, my gaze pulls to the right, where a familiar purple-and-yellow-striped food truck idles with a banner advertising *The Peninsula's Best Blackberry Lemonade Slush.*

And just like that, I veer into the beach parking lot with Cece's voice resounding in my ears. *"Come on, Indy. You can't miss birthday slushies on the beach. It's tradition!"*

How many summer days had the three of us shared right here, year after year, laughing and listening to Cece regale us with imaginary tales about pirates on the high seas that felt as real as our friendships?

"Ma'am? Can I help you?" A woman with bohemian braids smiles at me through my driver's window. She tips her head to the small sign directly in front of my bumper, reading Drive-up Orders Only, and lifts her ordering device. It's then I realize how I want to spend the next twenty minutes.

Despite the early hour and brisk morning, I order a medium slush with a slice of lime and a splash of orange juice—Cece's standard order—and leave the rental car behind so I can meander the nearby shoreline, a path I could walk in my sleep.

Transfixed by the spellbinding swells and tantalizing rhythm of the tides, I face the Sound and inhale the briny air in one greedy pull. Just like I did as a young girl, I count all the buoys I can see— six—and watch as seagulls dip to play with the catches in their beaks. With an unsteady hand, I raise my slush a few inches toward the horizon and whisper the words my heart aches to shout to the best friend I'll ever have, "Happy birthday, Cece."

When I finally twist away from the water and head to the bench where so many book plots and secret hopes were shared, my steps falter. On the far right side of the old wooden bench where three sets of initials are carved sits a man who slowly raises his own blackberry lemonade slush in my direction.

If this were anybody else, any other two people reuniting in such a serendipitous way, I could easily imagine the fumbling of words that would follow such an encounter: the cheap quips about great minds thinking alike, the uncomfortable chuckles and insecure small talk, the shock over the happenstance of such a random meeting. But this moment isn't random for Joel and me. It's the result of a synchronous connection neither of us seems to know how to sever even after the world broke us apart five years ago.

He gestures to the empty spot at the opposite end of the bench—*my spot*. I don't hesitate to take it, though I'm careful to leave adequate space in the middle. For Cece. And perhaps for everything else that will never be named between her cousin and me.

Like the ceasefire in war on Christmas Eve, there are no words exchanged during this brief reprieve where we pretend to be nothing more than two grieving strangers who cared for the same remarkable human being in our own unique ways. And for a moment, this shared silence feels like a gift.

When Joel clears his throat a few moments later, my back muscles tense. "It's time, Indy. You ready?"

As I stand and face him, something inside me begins to crack, but I refuse to let it crumble. So I hold it back, lift my chin, and lie. "I'm ready."

Joel holds the door for me as I enter Marshall Evans's office. Though it's my first time inside, the place is exactly what I imagine any small-town law office in America would look like, with its dark-stained bookshelves and executive-type furniture, complete with inspirational wall hangings and metal sconces. I can't help but wonder how much of his grandfather's practice still resides in this space.

"Ingrid, Joel. It's good to see you both." He shakes our hands. "I'd first like to offer another apology regarding the inexcusable delay in getting Cecelia's letter to you. After our discovery, I hired an additional assistant to help me comb through every nook and cranny of my grandfather's old files and lockboxes." He offers us a kind smile. "Good news is, I don't anticipate any more surprises will be surfacing from this point on."

Joel nods in response, his manners reflective of the respectable upbringing I witnessed firsthand. "Please tell your parents my family's been praying for Lloyd's recovery, Marshall."

"I will. They'll appreciate that." Marshall nods and gestures to the oblong table on the far side of the room. "Please, feel free to take a seat anywhere you like."

"Thank you," I say, wishing that I hadn't left the remainder of my slush in the rental car. My tongue feels like a sea sponge on the sand.

Joel waits for me to select a seat before he claims the chair beside mine, despite the fact that there are six others at this table. Strangely, our proximity in this office feels infinitely closer than on the bench we occupied together only minutes ago. I pick up a hint of sea salt and spruce from the fabric of his shirt and make a point to detect the other scents around the room to drown it out. Coffee. Leather. A fresh linen fragrance wafting from the wall plug-in near Marshall's bookshelves.

Marshall himself is a generic kind of familiar to me. One of the many faces of the kids who grew up dining at the hotel restaurant where I waitressed and whose parents rented out banquet rooms for game nights and birthday parties. He's matured since I last saw him—stockier build, slightly thinner hair, and a wedding band encircling his left ring finger. If there's an inventory to be taken of me, I imagine it would be over in a single glance.

My straight, obsidian hair—once worn long—has since been chopped to my shoulders, and the early wink of fine lines around the corners of my amber-brown eyes have already begun to make their appearance. The years acting as my father's skipper under an unassuming sky didn't do my future skin many favors. My natural tan, inherited from my mother's Chinook heritage, deterred the rosy burns that often plagued my father's milky Norwegian complexion, but the sun doesn't play favorites. I'm sure in time it will prove just as unforgiving to my skin as it was to my father's.

Marshall sits at the head of the table and places a thick padded envelope in front of him. Instantly my spine straightens, my eyes scanning the dimensions of its rectangular shape while he delivers a series of disclaimers and legal jargon my ears won't absorb. My fingertips tingle with the urge to reach out for this precious parcel my friend saw fit to keep locked away for reasons I might not ever understand. And I'll simply have to be okay with that, because what might have felt like a farfetched hypothesis only days ago now feels like the only outcome possible. That package contains Cece's last written words. I can *feel* it, the same way I can feel the quickening thump inside my ribcage.

"... of course, if either of you has any other questions about the trust itself or the protection it offers to Cecelia's written works, you're welcome to call me anytime." Marshall's hand rests atop the package as my mind wanders down a new path.

In only a few moments' time, I'll be holding the conclusion to my best friend's fantasy series—the closure her readers have been waiting for. The closure that will mend the fissure dividing her massive fanbase over the cliffhanger she left us with in *The Twist of Wills*. And just maybe it could be responsible for fixing something else, too.

What if these are the very words that can stitch the broken pieces in my brain back together again?

Marshall pushes the package toward us. "Then I suppose there's only one thing left to do."

Joel nods at me with a resolve that feels as certain as the one that's anchored inside me. I wouldn't be surprised if he's guessed the contents of this package by shape alone. He knows Wendy gave me Cece's laptop after the funeral, the same way he knows my searches for *The Fate of Kings* have been fruitless ... until now.

"Go ahead," he says. "You can do the honors."

"Thank you," I reply, gently pressing my fingertips to the dusty surface. "And thank you again for meeting us on a Saturday, Marshall. I have a feeling this discovery will mean a great deal to a great many people."

I break the seal at the top of the padded envelope and reach inside to grip a ream of paper. The sturdy feel of it in my grasp is confirmation enough, but my eyes still burn to see it. I slide the bulk out in one single motion of bittersweet relief. The overall volume isn't quite as hefty as I remember her last manuscript being, but when my gaze falls on the emboldened "PROLOGUE" header midway down the first page, I exhale a year's worth of unmet hope and fight to keep my emotions reined in.

I scroll my pointer finger under the first words, and then along the first sentence, and then down the entire first paragraph.

And then I'm frozen.

My hand. My head. My heart. All of it a brick of unthawable ice.

"Is it what you were hoping for?" Marshall inquires hesitantly.

I'm unable to answer him. I'm not able to do anything but stare at the blurring ink on the paper in front of me.

"Ingrid?" Joel asks as he slips the manuscript out from under the dead weight of my arm to read it for himself.

His mouth opens and shuts. Twice. And though his eyes never lift from the page, his voice is as piercingly intimate as if he were holding my face between his palms and speaking directly into my soul.

"This isn't fiction." When his eyes find mine, they brim with an audacity that throws me back to the night I spoke my final good-bye to him on a dock not too far away from where we sit now.

Blood swishes in my ears at such a high velocity that I shake my head in an attempt to mute the sound. But it only increases, beating out a chorus of *this is wrong, this is wrong, this is wrong . . .*

Joel slides his finger along the paragraph a second time as if the words printed there might have changed in the last sixty seconds. But even as he reads them aloud, they are the same.

"'I suppose their friendship began the way all good stories begin—with a promising hope delivered at just the right time and place. But as in all good stories, theirs shouldn't be judged midway through or even by one poorly executed chapter. Their story should only be judged upon its completion . . . which is still writing itself.'" He continues to scan the page in silence. When he finally speaks again, my ears strain on the rough timbre of his voice. "This is about the three of us."

I'm actively drowning in a sea of confusion when I reach for the pages again and riffle through them as though somewhere hidden beneath this odd prologue is the *real* manuscript. The one she spent years of her life crafting. The one *we all* spent years of our lives crafting—*together*. But as I flip through the pages and find each chapter ascending in order, my hope of discovering a stowaway manuscript expires. *It's not here.* My eyes blur as the only lead I had morphs into a riddle I'm not sure I'm strong enough to solve.

Joel's lifting the envelope and reaching inside for something more, but I . . . I can't seem to remember how to breathe.

I tug at my shirt collar, at the fabric trapped against my clammy skin, and push out my chair.

"I'm sorry, Marshall." The rasp breaks halfway up my throat. "I need a minute."

The crumbling is happening inside me again, boulders falling and crashing, a landslide of dangerous debris threatening to flatten me if I don't leave now. If I don't find air *now*.

Joel is speaking words I can't decipher, his voice like a steady pulse to restore the order I've disrupted. But unlike Joel Campbell, I wasn't born into polite society. I was born a salty sea captain's daughter, and I have nothing to prove and no reputation to save.

On unstable legs, I stand and break for the exit.

The instant I'm out the office door, my walk quickens to a jog, and soon I'm at the end of a dead-end street in my canvas dress flats, staring down at the steep, rocky shoreline below. The air pressure is different on this side of the point, the wind gustier and mistier than at surrounding beaches, which makes this beach both unappealing to tourists and ideal for me.

The panic that fuels me down boulders and over seaweed-slick driftwood numbs my inhibitions, and in only a moment my exposed skin prickles with a chill that does little to tamp the pain splitting my chest wide open. Scattered shells and pebbles cut into the bottoms of my thin soles, but I'm as unbothered by my footwear as I am by the tide creeping inward. All I know is that I must keep moving forward.

"Ingrid, stop! *Wait!*"

From somewhere behind me Joel's voice distorts on a gust of wind that manages to untuck my shirt. The gauzy fabric has become like flightless wings at my sides, flapping in place without purpose. Without direction. Without one last remaining hope.

He catches me around the elbow and pulls me to a stop, but whatever he sees reflected in my gaze causes the jump in his jaw to slow, to soften, and then to disappear altogether. "You can't just . . ."

He scrubs his opposite hand down his face and starts again. "This shoreline isn't safe to walk when the tide is out, much less now. "

"Did you know?" I ask him, my lips trembling against my will. "Did you know she was writing something about us?"

"No." He speaks the word like a swift punch. "I don't have a clue what that is back there. As soon as Marshall brought the package to the table, I figured it had to be the manuscript your publisher's been after all year."

I cut my gaze to the overcast horizon, swallow. "That's what I thought, too."

A beat passes before he says, "She left something else for us inside that envelope." He reaches into his back pocket for a familiar yellow piece of stationery, only I'm still trying to process the prologue I struggled to read in Marshall's office. "If you'd rather read it on your own first, then I'll give you space to—"

I shake my head. "I just want to understand what's going on."

He nods. "So do I."

And then, much the way he held Cece's letter in my office, he holds this one out, too. In a voice that projects over the wind and waves, Joel reads his cousin's words to us both.

> *"Joel and Indy—*
> *There are so many things I want to say to you, but I know if I could come back, even for a moment, the first thing I'd say is that I miss you. I've often wondered if missing people from heaven is even possible, given the whole 'no more sadness' assurance . . . but missing someone doesn't always have to be sad, does it? If not, then I'll miss you happy. And I'll miss you laughing. And I'll miss you with every ounce of joy I possess until I'm with you again.*
> *By now, Lloyd has given you the memoir I've been working on for some time. Years, actually. When I started it, I had every intention to finish and hand it over soon after Indy moved to California, but a story is so much harder to write when it's true.*
> *I'm under no illusion that these last few months have been easy,*

which makes asking something more of you even more difficult. <u>But I</u>
<u>need you to read this memoir</u>. Not on your own, but together. And not
only for me but for everything the three of us meant to each other for so
many years. This is more than a last wish—it's an imperative truth that
deserves to live even if I do not.

Once you've finished, I pray you'll find the rest of the answers you
seek and know how to move forward.

I made you the trustees of my intellectual property because I trust
you'll guard my words and work well. But I made you my closest friends
because I trust you'll also guard my love and intentions for you well, too.

I love you both. Forever.

Missing you happy,
Cece"

The sky has morphed into a marbled gray mass overhead, beckoning emotion long buried in me to rise to the surface—which is
exactly why I cannot possibly agree to what she's asked. Honoring
my best friend's legacy by protecting her life's work is one thing, but
reading an entire book of memories *with* the man I hold responsible
for the questions that plague me most about my father's death? The
very idea of it feels like a betrayal. How could she possibly ask this
of me?

I'm shaking my head, shaking all over, and yet I can't utter any
one of the hundred thoughts Joel seems to perfectly interpret from
my gaze.

"I know this isn't what you wanted or what you were expecting—
it's not what I was expecting, either. But this is it." He holds up the
letter and the wind immediately molds it to his fist. "This is all we
have left of her. We may not understand why she did it, but she
wrote that memoir to us. *For us.* The least we can do is honor her
request by reading it."

"Cece was my closest friend," I petition, willing my stance to
hold firm in the shifting sand, "and when she was here, there was

nothing I wouldn't do for her. But she's not here now, Joel. Only we are." I thump a hand to my chest as if to scare the shake from my voice. It doesn't work. "Think about this for a minute, about what she's actually asking of us. What can a memoir written about our pasts possibly tell either of us that we don't already know? That we haven't already lived and experienced?" *That one of us barely survived.* I shake my head and stare into his unblinking gaze as the ceasefire we reached earlier this morning rapidly disappears. "Do you have any idea how—"

"How what? How hard it is for you to be here with me? Believe me, you've made that quite clear." He thrusts the envelope into his back pocket and twists to stare at the horizon. "You're not the only one whose life changed that night, Ingrid."

"Don't." It's a warning, and yet it's so much more than that. A locked door on a portal I refuse to open, even for Cece.

When he turns back, he stays me with a look of such crippling desperation I struggle for my next intake of air. "Until this week, I've asked you for nothing. I've gone to every estate meeting and reviewed every account and document with Marshall. I've read the trustee reports and secured the properties and overseen Aunt Wendy's trust and monthly budget. And I've done every bit of it for her, for Cece. But this is not something I can simply add to my calendar reminders. This is bigger than that." His mossy eyes bore into mine. "Out of everyone in the world, she entrusted her last written words to the two of us. That *means* something to me, and it should mean something to you, too." At his gentle chastisement, a fresh wave of guilt crashes over me. "I'm not asking you to forgive me or even to forget the past we've shared—I'm asking you to help me honor the life of someone we both loved deeply." He steps in close, the plea in his voice sucking me into a past dimension I can't revisit. "I'm asking you to give yourself permission to stay here a little longer—for her."

Somewhere inside me lives the remnant of a desire to push back, to protect the last undamaged piece of myself at all costs. But my mind is as wrung out as my heart, and the vulnerability in his expression roots me to this rocky shoreline until he's all I can focus on. Not the polarizing wind or the swelling tide or the turbulent clouds overhead.

Just him. Just Joel.

For several heartbeats, I'm lost in the eyes of the man who once showed me the kind of love I'd only read about in pages of fiction. The man who once cradled my dreams and cherished my secrets and fought my demons when I wasn't brave enough to face them on my own.

But I'm brave enough now, even if the battle I have to fight is against him.

I'm still working to formulate an adequate response when water rushes for my heels. In one swift move, Joel launches me out of danger and onto the dry shore. Only this present danger, the one where his hands grip my arms and his eyes memorize my face in a way that makes bumps scatter over every inch of my exposed skin, is far more dire than a pair of wet flats and a narrowing beach.

Dazed, I work to reorient myself on the sand as his fingers trail a faint path down the backs of my arms. Before I can fully register the touch, he drops his hands to his sides and clears his throat.

"A few more days, Ingrid," he reiterates. "Will you agree to that?"

I close my eyes in an attempt to capture my fleeting thoughts, but the gathering storm has blown them too far out to sea to be caught. When I open my eyes again, he's still there, still watching me, still waiting for an answer.

"I need some time to think," I say in a voice so feeble I'm not sure he'll be able to make it out over the weather. But he must because he nods and says, "I think that's fair. Today has been . . . a lot. We can talk later tonight."

At first, I'm lost at his reference of time, unable to connect with anything outside the here and now. But then slowly, surely, it all comes back and I remember. Today is Cece's twenty-seventh birthday. Just one of the many reasons why *fair* won't ever be a part of my vocabulary again.

7

I lost track of the afternoon while in the driver's seat of my rented Prius. The marbled sky had finally cracked open to weep into the sea for the better part of an hour while I pretended to take in the blurry coastline ahead. But at the first wink of sunshine, I was ready for a change of scenery. I was also ready for some much-needed retail therapy. Shopping for an upgraded party dress wouldn't require me to provide answers I wasn't prepared to give.

Allie hadn't steered me wrong by recommending her sister's boutique. It wasn't fancy by any means and the dressing room was nothing but a curtain strung across a narrow closet in the back, but the stylish employee in her mid-forties may as well have been Mary Poppins and the narrow shop her magical carpetbag. Dress after dress appeared in my changing room until a perfect match in both the style and color I'd requested could be made. I left the shop with a floor-length, golden chiffon A-line that boasted a halter neckline and a side slit that roamed to my mid-thigh. Quite remarkable for a last-minute purchase in a sleepy beach town.

Using the reflection of my passenger side window, I double-check the bobby pins securing my loose updo in place and then lift my gaze to the four-story Victorian building situated a block past the marina I know as well as my studio apartment in San Francisco.

The siren's call of live music drifts from the hotel's private deck and bounces off the water like an amplifier to the streets of downtown.

My pace slows in time with the bluesy jazz, and my therapist's coaching techniques *to deal with hard feelings as they come* confronts me head on. I stand at the mouth of the busy marina, where skilled sportsmen come from all over the nation to try their luck in the Sound, spending thousands on chartering excursions with seasoned captains. I scan the moored inventory, noting the empty slips of boaters enjoying the pleasant summer evening and then the dry-docked vessels, waiting to be repaired by skilled hands. For a moment, I'm sixteen years old again in search of my father's red cap and Norwegian beard. I can almost hear him call my name, hollering for me to climb aboard quickly because we have a big day planned with paying customers who don't much care to wait on a teenage girl. But as quickly as it comes, the memory is gone.

I arrive at the hotel twenty minutes prior to the start of dinner as planned, opting for an early arrival and exit time. I also opt to use the patio entrance off the narrow sidewalk that borders the hotel instead of walking through the lobby, but I'm as surprised by the security detail stationed there as I am by the No Trespassing and Private, Guests Only signs distributed around the Campbell's property. The security guard verifies my name and then opens the gate for me without further comment.

I pause for a moment in a shaded corner of the grand deck to observe the well-oiled machine that is the Campbell Hotel staff and work up the courage I need to get through this night. My eyes sweep the perimeter of the grounds in search of a familiar face, but the only employees I find buzzing around the expansive waterfront space in tidy black aprons embroidered with updated logos are strangers to me. Some balance trays of appetizers and champagne flutes for nearby food and drink stations, while others are tasked with setting out flatware and buffet plates—two jobs I've done hundreds of times. Tall tables meant for mingling have been placed throughout the deck, interspersed with unlit heaters in case the evening turns too breezy after the sun goes down. The Campbells' favorite jazz band continues their sound check on a stage closest to the access point of the stairs that lead to the long floating dock. Much like at the marina, I take inventory of the small gathering of close friends and family who have likely been here most of the day and are now milling about with plates of shrimp kabobs and fresh crab cakes.

My breath stalls as I see Joel's mom trailing after her husband with a tier of yellow frosted cupcakes. I've never been to a Campbell function where Stephen and Patti weren't working twice as hard as their employees. Tonight, it seems, is no different. There's no question as to why their hotel has been named the Best Accommodations in the Olympic Peninsula for the past decade. My search continues for the face I most want to find this evening, when a sweet, feminine voice catches my ear.

"I'm always envious of a woman who can pull off such a striking shade of yellow—marigold is a stunning color on you. I knew Rhonda wouldn't steer you wrong."

My gaze lands on a beautiful young woman with delicate features and flowing strawberry blond hair that spills down her back in cascading waves. Her dazzling, sleeveless olive romper is cut in such a way it reveals a splattering of sun-kissed freckles on perfectly toned shoulders and arms. And despite the fact that she's wearing strappy, flat sandals to my four-inch heels, we're practically eye-to-eye. Yet there's something about the familiar way she addressed me that gives me a déjà-vu-like sensation.

She switches the near-empty champagne flute from her right hand to her left, and then with soft, pastel pink fingernails, she touches my elbow. "Please tell me she remembered to offer you the twenty percent friends and family discount? If not, I'll be happy to adjust your receipt tomorrow."

"I'm sorry," I finally say, shaking my head. "Do we know each other?"

"Oh gosh." Her laugh is bright and melodic. When she flattens her palm to her chest, the gesture harkens back to an earlier introduction that took place yesterday afternoon. In Cece's living room. "Forgive me, I'm Madison Spencer. I'm—"

"Allie's sister," I conclude at the same time she says, "Allison's big sister."

"Yes," she practically sings, and I'm struck by the family resemblance. Madison is a tad shorter than her baby sister and definitely built more like a willowy ballerina than a varsity volleyball star, but they are equally matched in spirit. They are both the kind of home-grown gorgeous that stems from a confidence imparted early on in life. "Allie said you'd settled in at the cottage but were a bit short on party attire. I wish I could have assisted you at the shop myself, but I've been here seeing to odds and ends for the family most of the day," she explains. "Anyway, I've heard so much about you, Ingrid, and I've been looking forward to meeting you in person this time around. I nearly introduced myself to you last year, but the timing never seemed quite right considering the occasion."

Immediately, her cheeks bloom the shade of her nails. "I promise that sounded far less insensitive in my head. What I'm failing to communicate is that it's good to meet you, and that I'm truly sorry for your loss. Cece was one of a kind." Her expression hints at the bewildered kind of innocence I envy most. "May I salvage this horrible first impression by offering to get you a drink? I think I could use a pre-party refill." She downs the last of her champagne and lifts her empty flute into the air. "What can I get for you? Champagne? Pinot Grigio? A huckleberry martini?"

"Actually, I don't drink."

Madison's eyes widen as if she's tallying up another point against herself. "Wow, it seems I'm on quite a roll tonight."

"You're fine," I offer with a smile. "Really."

"Then can I get you a sparkling water, lemonade, punch?"

"Actually, I'm wondering if you might know where I could find Wendy?"

She offers me a slow nod. "Last I knew, she was downstairs working on flower arrangements."

"Great, thank you. It was nice to meet you, Madison."

And it's only then, when she turns toward the golden horizon and wades into an arriving circle of guests, that I realize Madison doesn't only resemble her younger sister. She resembles another woman, too. The one I observed from a distance throughout the entire duration of Cece's funeral.

Madison from Madison's Wardrobe is the leggy redhead whose identity I've speculated about for the last ten months.

I'm still chewing this over when I step away from the shadows and start for the cement staircase at the side of the building. I zigzag my way around several clusters of people, offering polite but minimal small talk so as not to get caught in an unwanted conversational web. Even still, if I had a dollar for every time I heard, *"You and Cece were like sisters, you must miss her so much,"* I'd have enough to pay off this dress, even without the friends and family discount.

I've just broken free from the last circle of sparkling water drinkers when a sensation that causes chill bumps to rise on my arms beckons me to look back. Sure enough, Joel is making his way toward me, determination in his confident gait. But I'm not ready for him or for the questions I read in his gaze.

He's roughly an arm's length away when a horrendous crash erupts from the opposite end of the deck. And for a fraction of a second, everything freezes—the music, the conversations, the heartbeat inside my chest as Joel's eyes lock with mine—and then in a snap, the spell is broken and everyone is rushing to clear the stack of broken plates from the deck floor. With a regretful expression I don't have time to interpret, Joel tears his gaze from me and locates the young employee who's apologizing profusely for bumping his service cart into the buffet table. I watch with fascination as Joel's hero radar is activated.

In a blink, he's striding toward the disaster, toward the new hire who's reaching for shards of glass with his bare hands, and my mind can't help but compare a similar instance on this deck during my first summer as a Campbell employee. Only instead of a stack of broken dinner plates, it was an entire porcelain tea service. And instead of a teenage boy, it was a teenage girl who couldn't afford to lose her first job and was terrified she would be fired for such a careless misstep. And instead of a throng of people jumping in to help, it was Joel alone who'd come to her aid while a dozen finely dressed ladies gawked at the commotion she'd caused when she knelt to pick up each delicate shard of china while blood trickled from her fingertips. The ladies had gawked all the more when Joel knelt beside her with a broom and dustpan. *"Hey, don't even worry about this, okay? It happens to everyone. You're fine."* His assurance left little room for doubt. *"Go in and wash up in the kitchen. I've got it from here."* She'd started to protest, but he merely set the dustpan down to pluck the fine china from her trembling hands. *"I said, I've got you, Indy."*

Four words she was certain she'd never heard quite like that before. Four words she hoped she'd hear again from this boy she hadn't been able to shake from her thoughts since the day she met him. Four words she hoped would remain true.

I blink the haze of the past away as Joel works to secure the area around the food table and delegate tasks to each of his employees, including the shaken teen boy whose cheeks are now a flaming shade of crimson. It's not until Joel pats his shoulder that I turn away to focus once again on the reason I'm here.

By the time I step onto the cracked cement stairs that lead to the hotel's basement kitchens and wine cellars, I'm rolling my shoulders to ease the tension in my lower back and wishing I'd worn more practical shoes. Heels are always better on display in a storefront window than on actual human feet. But all thoughts of practical fashion vanish the instant I catch a glimpse of Wendy Campbell's silk floral kimono. A spark of grief catches fire under my ribcage.

She's bent over a floral arrangement of yellow dahlias when I slip under the arched doorway. I'm no closer than twenty feet when she straightens and twists in my direction. And then in no time at all, those twenty feet morph into an embrace that rocks me off-center.

There are no thoughts in my head as I sink my face into Wendy's blanket of graying curls and feel the way her hold on me seems to soften all my hard edges in seconds. I breathe in her familiar honeysuckle and lavender soap scent, wishing I could keep it with me always. Wishing I could keep so many things about her with me always.

We don't speak, only it's not because there aren't words to be spoken. It's because the words Wendy cares about most are not the ones filtered by the tongue, but those that pulse through the heart. When her arms loosen, I pull back just enough to see her sorrow-rimmed eyes and the dark half-moon circles imprinted underneath them. But those aren't the only differences to be found in this woman who loved me like a daughter even when I was little more than a stranger.

Wendy's once radiant mid-fifties glow has dimmed considerably since I saw her last. Her skin isn't plump or dewy but rather etched in the familiar markings of stress and loss. My focus snags on the way her kimono slips off her too-sharp shoulders, exposing collarbones that look as if they might snap in two if she exhales too quickly. But when her eyes flood with tears for what is obviously not the first time today, I shove my own pain deep into a pocket I vow to keep closed out of respect for her.

The hierarchy of grief will always belong to a childless mother.

"I knew you'd come," she whispers as she touches my cheek with cool fingertips. "And you wore her favorite color."

"Of course," I say, my voice a choked betrayal of itself, because the only thing I want to express is *I'm so sorry I didn't come sooner.* She deserves so much more than a simple apology from me, and yet I know I'd fail at trying to explain the more complicated reasons for my absence. Postponing grief may not be the healthy approach my therapist encourages in our sessions, but sometimes it feels like the only approach a person can handle. Being back here on what should have been Cece's twenty-seventh birthday has made it real.

Being back here makes it *all* real.

Wendy doesn't bother to wipe the tear streaks from her cheeks as she gestures to the array of flowers strewn along the butcher block table where she's arranged thousands of floral centerpieces over the years as the hotel's hospitality manager. "As you can see, I'm running a bit behind schedule tonight. I just wanted to make sure Cece's favorites were included in these arrangements."

"I'm happy to help." Words I should have spoken months and months ago. "Where can I start?"

As if I were eighteen again, I reach for a pair of floral scissors as Wendy points to the three bouquets of greenery at the end of the butcher block. "Those still need to be trimmed."

"On it," I say, securing the wholesale bouquets to prep for the two oversized vases, all too aware of the fact that I've never known Wendy to purchase flowers for any gathering. "Were these flowers donated for the dinner tonight?" It's the only possible conclusion I can come up with for such an extreme departure from her usual routine.

She looks at me from across the butcher block and shakes her head in a way that communicates so much more than her words. "We've been ordering them from a floral supply warehouse in Seattle for a while now."

I nod, though my lungs seize at her simple explanation. What's become of her luscious gardens? Of the greenhouses Joel and his father assembled for her on their property the summer we turned seventeen? Of the rows of flowers and flora and herbs she meticulously labeled and tended to year-round for every special occasion at the Campbell Hotel?

"And your gardens? How are they?"

"I haven't done much gardening lately," she says with a tentative smile, as if trying to reassure me. But Wendy without an active garden is like Cece without writing, and me without reading—*impossible*. "I've actually been working on a—"

"Wendy? Are you ready for me to carry those arrangements up to the deck? Our guests are arriving."

I recognize the deep timbre of his voice long before I see the face of Joel's father round the corner into the basement. Just three steps in, Stephen Campbell stops as he registers me.

"Ingrid, hello. Goodness, it's great to see you here again. You look beautiful tonight."

Though we haven't had any relationship to speak of in more than five years, Stephen's fatherly presence doesn't fail to take me back a decade. He'd given me my first real job. Truthfully, he'd given me so much more than that.

"Thank you, Mr. Campbell, and thank you for the platters and blankets you and Patti sent to the cottage for my stay. That was thoughtful."

"You'll always be a welcome guest." His stride is as evenly paced as his personality. "I hope it goes without saying, but Patti and I hope your visit here is a good one. If there's anything you need, please don't hesitate to ask." He glances at Wendy, and I can't help but note the concern that touches his brow. "I see Wendy's already put you to work."

"Ingrid's always paid such close attention to detail." Wendy's smile is tender as she slides the fragile vase toward him. "It's part of what makes her such a brilliant editor."

Stephen winks at me as if I'm still part of the exclusive network of faithful employees who make this family business tick. "Is this one ready to go, sis?"

Wendy confirms with a nod. "And the second should be ready in a few minutes. Ingrid's just trimming the last of the greenery for me."

He lifts the vase with ease and carries it out of the cold room and up the concrete steps.

I snip the stems at an angle and open my mouth to speak to Wendy in these last private moments, only to close it again. Because the questions knocking around in my head are not suitable for a birthday dinner, even if they are the questions that keep me awake at night.

"How long will you be here, Ingrid? I'd love to spend some time with you while you're in town."

The question churns my insides, harkening back to Joel's plea on the beach and then even further back to SaBrina's ultimatum in my office at Fog Harbor Books. "I haven't set a date quite yet, but I would love to see you, too. I can work around whatever hours you're keeping at the hotel."

Her eyes water again. "You're my priority. Whenever is good for you will be good for me. I'd actually like to get your professional opinion on something when you come over." As Wendy plucks a tiger lily from the arrangement, my mind is still stuck on *professional opinion*. What would she possibly need an editor's opinion on? Curiosity worms its way into my subconscious and I store my brewing questions away for later.

She lifts a single bloom in her hand, and I know immediately what she's thinking. I bend my head toward her and she slides the stem of the tiger lily under my hair pin. "It's a perfect match." She swipes her thumb across my cheek in a maternal gesture that causes me to blink away tears. "You've always been stunning, but especially so tonight."

By the time Stephen returns to grab the last arrangement of Cece's favorite lilies, Wendy and I are cleaning up the remainder of the floral scraps and sweeping them into a large trash can. I trail behind her as we climb the concrete stairs, and I'm as vigilant of every step she takes as I am about the frailty of her thin frame. By the time we reach the top stair, Wendy has been swept away by a sea of well-meaning guests, yet my anxiety over her fragile state doesn't dissipate.

The party is fueled by moody jazz, seafood skewers, and heartfelt birthday tributes given by the same family and friends I saw ten months ago at Lighthouse Community Fellowship. Surprisingly, Joel isn't among them. I haven't seen him since the broken plates.

By the time the sun starts to set, I've been pulled into all sorts of conversations, asked dozens of questions about the future of Cece's books, and deflected giving my opinion on the memorial landmarks scheduled to be voted on at city council next month due to the large donation Cece gifted her beloved community. Opinions belong to residents, not to sporadic weekenders like myself.

As soon as the cupcakes are served, I begin to contemplate making the trek to my car when I feel the familiar tug of an invisible tether. My attention sweeps the deck until I find a man dressed in a sky-blue shirt whose expression suggests our last interaction has left him as unsettled as it has me. Perhaps he's reconsidered his emotion-packed request for me this morning. Perhaps he's realized, as I have, that we're both better off leaving the past in the past.

Joel makes no effort to break his concentrated stare, not even when Madison taps his bicep and blinks up at him with those innocent doe eyes of hers and the kind of smile that doesn't need practice to maintain. Waitstaff and mingling guests cut a path between us, allowing me a reprieve, but I'm unnervingly aware of Joel's exact location from that point on.

As Stephen and Patti conclude the evening with their standard benediction blessing and excuse themselves to escort Wendy home, my high-heel-hating back begs me to follow their lead and do the same. But instead, I slip off my shoes and take a path I've walked hundreds of times on cool summer nights just like this one.

I'm halfway down the floating dock, following the blue sheen of an almost full moon out to sea, when I hear him behind me.

I expected he would follow. But this is record time, even for someone as studiously observant as Joel.

As soon as he settles beside me, my voice falters to a whisper. "You should have told me about Wendy."

"You haven't exactly made yourself available to us."

I rotate just enough to see a silvery reflection of moonlight dance across Joel's strong jawline. "I would have come back for her."

The shift in his stance is unmistakable, and it's not difficult to deduce how he's interpreted my comment: *I would have come back for her, but not for you.*

His next words are so quiet I strain to hear them above the waves that roll beneath us. "What did you decide about the memoir, Ingrid? Are you staying or are you leaving?"

A question I've asked myself at least two dozen times since the beach this morning and yet still don't have a final answer for. If I stay and read the memoir with him, it will offer me the time I need to search for *The Fate of Kings*. But the risks to that option are high and uncertain. Yet if I go back to California emptyhanded, there is no doubt about the certainties I'll face there. In a matter of days, I'll be without a job, and soon thereafter without an apartment or any of the life I've built there from the ashes.

So instead of answering, I deflect back to him. "Where were you tonight? You missed more than half the party."

"I didn't realize you were monitoring my whereabouts so closely."

"Everyone else in your family gave a speech in Cece's honor. Your absence was obvious."

"I was dealing with a guest dispute inside the hotel."

So none of them would have to is what I know he doesn't say.

A suffocating silence descends over us then and I refuse to be trapped in it for another second. "I know you expect an answer from me, but I don't have one yet."

"Why not? I don't understand what more there is to think about. Either you're willing to stay and honor Cece's request or you're not."

"It's not that simple, and you know it. I need to be sure I can process this memoir in a healthy, logical way. I can't afford to let emotion drive this decision."

"Wow." He whistles low. "And to think, I actually thought I saw a glimpse of the Ingrid I knew all those years ago out on that beach today."

"She's the last person I want to be again."

"You're right." The bite in his tone has crested the edge of his impatience. "Because this guarded and cynical version of you is far superior."

"Not superior, just necessary."

And then, more gently than I expect, he speaks again. "I'm sorry . . . that was careless of me."

I shrug my bare shoulder, the movement causing the silky fabric of my gown to swish against my legs. "It doesn't matter."

"It absolutely does matter." The dock creaks as he moves in close. "Everything between us would look different now if it didn't."

I shake my head as if to block out his words. "You want to know why I can't make a decision? It's because of this right here. If I agree to stay and read Cece's memoir with you, then this kind of talk between us absolutely cannot happen."

"And what kind of talk is that, Indy?"

I fight the effect his honeyed baritone has on every nerve ending in my body. "Anything pertaining to the way things used to be, to the us that died on this dock five years ago. I have no intention of going back there—not to that night, and not to each other." My throat is dry, and the words feel as rough on my tongue as they do on my heart. "If we do this for Cece, then it has to be about her. Not anything else."

The moon has arced above our heads. Its light exposes my face to him while it casts a shadow on Joel's, but even still, I can sense his expression so strongly that if I were to brush my hand over his features, I know exactly what I'd find. I'd start by smoothing the pad of my thumb along the tension furrowed in his forehead before sliding the rest of my fingertips down the stress crease that sits between his eyebrows, and then lower still to where his narrowed eyelids fan an impossibly dark curtain of thick lashes. I'd glide my pointer finger down the masculine slope of his nose, careful not to skip the ridges of his brooding mouth. And there I'd rest, just beneath the swell of his bottom lip, in the faint, crescent scar one can only detect under a sky much like this one.

I blink, breathe, and hear him swallow.

"I can do that," he says.

My reply is little more than a strained whisper. "Okay."

"I'll be over after church tomorrow with the memoir."

I hold my breath for what will undoubtedly come next, an invitation like so many he's extended me in the past: to join his family at the second service and to interact with the community they love.

Only Joel doesn't offer me an invitation. He simply takes a step back and bids me good night.

8

"The Girl Who Came from the Sea"

It all started on a particularly warm day in early June. It was the kind of overly stuffy day that required Cecelia to prop open the third-floor window of the hotel suite she shared with her mother for fear she'd die of heatstroke. Unlike the desert-dry Nevada heat she'd grown up in, there were few buildings in Port Townsend ducted for air-conditioning. At least, that's what her Uncle Stephen explained, and he seemed to know everything about this prehistoric sea town where nothing of significance ever happened. Sure, the Victorian buildings looked like they were straight out of the novels she borrowed from the library when her mom wasn't with her—the ones with shirtless men embracing fancy ladies in low-cut gowns with titles that boasted words like Duke or Duchess, Rogue or Rake.

Cecelia liked the historical romance genre well enough, but not nearly as much as the sweeping adventures she collected about life on the high seas. She'd always had a thing for pirates, which was precisely how her mom had lured her to the tippy top of western Washington in the first place. Only so far, every deckhand, fisherman, and sailor she'd met could either be classified as geriatric or reeked worse than the fish guts the hotel cook flung into the compost pot her mom insisted be saved for the gardens.

Cecelia took one final glance at the carefully scripted good-bye letter she'd penned to her mother and placed it underneath the jewelry box her dad had given her on their final Christmas as a whole family. Zipping up her backpack, she took one last glance at the movie poster she'd hung above her bed before closing the door to room 312.

Contrary to what the diehard fans of *Pirates of the Caribbean* may believe, not every history-centered seaport town held the mysteries and inspiration needed to write an epic fantasy. After thorough investigation, Cecelia had concluded that Port Townsend could win a contest for the most boring, predictable place ever to be established on planet Earth. Furthermore, there were exactly zero persons in this town who resembled a young Orlando Bloom.

Which was why she was headed back to the desert. Today.

There, at least, was a true mystery waiting to be solved. No matter what her mom told her, Cecelia knew better than to believe her father didn't want to be found. After all, wasn't the best fiction just a couple lies south of the truth?

She'd researched her plan of escape for weeks, stockpiling her backpack with essentials while her mom organized ego-stroking events for folks who only came to this town to eat crab cakes and drink too much wine in one sitting, all while rambling on about how exquisite the sunsets were over the Sound. Although *this* weekend, everybody would be chatting about the same thing: the annual Summer Dayz Festival, sponsored by none other than her own extended family.

It was both the alibi and distraction she needed. When she didn't show up for her shift to wait tables in the dining room later this evening, everybody would assume she got caught up downtown, enjoying the street musicians and socializing with the masses. But in reality, Cecelia would already be halfway across the water, bound for the airplane she planned to catch in Seattle. By the time her mother found her note, it would be too late. The festival traffic would make getting to the airport by car nearly impossible, and the nighttime ferries were too infrequent to get anywhere quickly. Her mom would never make it to her in time to stop her plans. Cecelia had, however, left her mom the number of her new prepaid phone. Yet another part of her carefully researched plan.

Oddly enough, though, it wasn't her mother's wrath she feared most when this elaborate scheme came to light. It was her cousin's. Sure, her sweet mother would be disappointed in her, maybe even angry. But Joel would be . . . she shook her head. She didn't have to wonder what he would be. Sometime after Aunt Patti decided to give up the fertility battle for more children after suffering through many, many losses, Joel had become unbearably protective of everything and everyone around him, reminding Cecelia all too often of the whopping thirteen months he had on her. But as sad as she felt for Aunt Patti, Cecelia had never been interested in filling the role of Joel's younger sister. Nor was she in need of a big brother. She was an independent woman of sixteen, full of ideas and dreams, and old enough to make up her own mind, *thank you very much!*

But the minute she stepped onto the hotel patio where VIP parties were held and where old couples shuffled to music that should only be played in elevators, something tugged at her conscience, enough to cause her feet to slow. Was she really going to leave without telling her cousin good-bye? She bit her bottom lip and then quickly swung her backpack around to her front, rummaging through it for a notebook and pen. She had plenty of time to jot something down and hide it for him somewhere on the property. She began scribbling out a message. She'd send him a text in a couple of hours and tell him where to look—

Cecelia stopped mid-note as her gaze snagged on a blur of thick black hair attached to a girl reading at the far end of the Campbell's private dock. A girl who looked to be around her age. One she was certain she'd never seen in this town before. She glanced at her watch. Her bus to the ferry was leaving in thirty-two minutes, plenty of time for an introduction to a stranger for the sake of character research.

She dropped her backpack on the patio and started for the dock. The closer she got, the more curious she grew about the book that had so enraptured this stranger's attention that not even the sound of Cecelia's approaching footsteps turned her head. It had been a long while since she'd been so engrossed in a fictional world that she was able to escape her real one.

"Whatcha reading over there?" Cecelia asked as water lapped against the dock underfoot.

Like in a poorly written comedy, the girl on the edge of the dock startled, causing the book to leap from her hands like a hooked fish arching toward the water.

A collective cry rang out as Cecelia dove for the paperback mid-air, arms outstretched, as her body thrummed with an adrenaline that had her straining for the novel with muscles she was certain she'd never before engaged. Miraculously, she caught it, the trophy now safely cupped between her palms as if it were the Holy Grail itself. Both girls stared at it wordlessly before moving their focus from the novel to each other.

It was Cecelia who spoke first. After all, it was Cecelia who almost sent the book swimming in the Sound.

"Guess that proves I have at least one athletic bone in my body, right? You're my witness." An opener that earned a smile from the dark-haired, tanned-skin girl. "Few things in life are worth the risk of getting soaked—and books are at the top of that list." She handed the tattered—*but dry!*—copy of *Island of the Blue Dolphins* back to the gawking stranger. "I'm Cecelia, by the way. But you should know I'm in the process of changing it to Cece."

The girl's dark eyebrows rose an inch as she tilted her head in a way that suggested she didn't quite know what to make of the curly-haired maniac who was still splayed on the dock like a dying starfish. Or perhaps the tilt was because she didn't understand her? Maybe she didn't speak English?

Cecelia's cheeks grew hot at the possibility. There wasn't exactly a ton of diversity to speak of up north, not that her hometown in Nevada was much different. But still . . . there was something almost otherworldly about this girl with her rich skin and sharp, dark features. Her eyes were the color of warm honey, yet her waist-length hair was an indistinguishable black-brown. She glanced down at the cover of the girl's book once again, her eyes noting the similarities anew.

"You're changing your name?" the enigma asked with crystal-clear English.

Cecelia sighed internally and crisscrossed her legs beneath her, ever-aware that her getaway backpack was still waiting for her up on the hotel patio. "Not legally or anything. It's not that I hate the name Cecelia, it's just that I think it sounds like a stuffy aristocrat who wears a girdle, ya know? Cece is more my speed." The girl smiled. "Unfortunately, though, the only person who ever calls me Cece is my cousin. And seeing as he's been calling me that since I could fit into the hotel's laundry chute when I'd visit on family vacations, I don't have a lot of hope the others will join him anytime soon. But like my uncle always says, 'Success is a slow, long process of repetition.'" She rolled her eyes, realizing only then that her "nickname process" would stop once she boarded her ferry.

In twenty-six minutes.

The girl nodded like she could relate, though she probably had some rare gem of a name like Saraiya or Arianna or Catalina— "I'm Ingrid."

Cecelia blinked. "Ingrid?"

She nodded again.

Of all the names she could have guessed, *Ingrid* would not have made the top thousand. All the *Ingrids* Cecelia had ever read about were fair-skinned Scandinavian women with hair the color of a ripe apricot. Also, they were usually being held captive by a Viking king.

"It was my dad's mother's name," Ingrid supplied. "She grew up in Norway before she moved to the States when my dad was a kid. I never met her."

"It's a strong name," Cecelia added politely, realizing now that her private thoughts must have leaked onto her public face. Joel always said she should never play cards. She made sure to smile extra big just to spite him. "We both have the namesake thing in common. That's where I got my name from, too—a great-aunt on my mom's side who died before I was born."

Ingrid's decidedly pensive gaze wandered from Cecelia back to the cover of the book in her hands.

"What's that about?" Cecelia asked. "Sure looks like you've read it lots."

The spark in Ingrid's gaze was unmistakable. "I have. It was my mother's favorite—a survival story about a young girl named Karana who was aban-doned on an island for years after her people went in search of new land." She tapped on the picture of a girl who shared many of Ingrid's characteristics.

"All she had for a friend was a wild dog. She creates an entire world for the two of them, never giving up hope that one day she'll be rescued."

"And does she? Get rescued?"

Ingrid studied her, her eyes practically aglow under the sun's rays. "You should read it for yourself. It won some pretty big awards in the sixties and seventies. It's also a movie, though I've never seen it."

"Then I can't believe our library doesn't own a copy of it."

"It does." Ingrid's voice boldened. "I saw it there in a display of classics the last time we came to port, but since I can't get a card, I have a list of others I read through while we're in town."

"Oh, wait." Cecelia shook her head and upped her volume to be heard over an obnoxious seagull. "I wasn't talking about the community library. I meant the library at the hotel—my uncle's a huge book nerd. My mom says it must be where I get it from because she can hardly get through a novel. Give her a book on art or gardening and she'll read for hours, but give her an adventure story and she'll be asleep within five minutes."

Ingrid's smile was soft as she asked, "So Mr. Campbell is your uncle?"

Whenever Cecelia was asked this question, she wanted to throw out a bunch of caveats to include with her answer, share that even though her uncle owned the most affluent hotel in town, he wasn't the stereotypical rich jerk who barked orders at his family and staff. Truth was, he was everything opposite that.

But this time, all she said in reply was, "Yeah, he is."

"He's at the marina with my dad—he's a captain, looking for charter work for the summer." Ingrid pointed across the water at the marina, which was only a short swim away. Cecelia squinted her eyes to see if she might spot the men between sails and boat lifts. But there was already triple the usual number of people to scan through. Looked like today's festivities were already underway. "Since the library's closed, your uncle said I could read anywhere on his property if I didn't want to sit at the marina all day. I already spend too much time on boats as it is, so this sounded like a better way to spend the afternoon."

Cecelia's ears perked up at this, and she readjusted her position. "Do you always go on the boat with your dad while he works or something?"

Ingrid scrunched her lips together for a moment before answering, "Usually, yes, but we've lived on a boat since I was six."

Cecelia nearly gasped as she switched positions once again, this time propping herself up on her knees to face Ingrid fully. "You *live* on a boat?" She slapped a palm to her chest. "How absolutely magical!" She closed her eyes, wishing there was an ocean breeze that would sweep her hair back at this very moment to confirm her deepest of desires. "If I lived on a boat, I'd have all the inspiration I'd ever need to write my series."

"Your . . . series?"

Cecelia nodded vigorously. "I'm an author—or I will be one day. But for now, I'm still working out the kinks in my plot and waiting for the right muse to come along. That's a big part of being an author, you know—finding your muse. Most non-writers don't know that." Ingrid shook her head slowly as if to say she hadn't known, either. "It's going to be a pirate fantasy set in the brutal Kingdom of Cardithia." Her hands worked in animated gestures. "There's hidden treasure, capsizing ships, secret stowaways, magical spells, kingdoms conquered by evil rulers, and many epic battles to the death. Oh, and of course, there will be a forbidden romance between a ruggedly handsome pirate and an orphaned princess."

Ingrid's previously reserved demeanor blossomed to life before her eyes. "I would read that series in a heartbeat."

Cecelia beamed at her new friend. "Then perhaps you should help me plot it? I need someone I can get inside information from—someone who knows life on the high seas."

Ingrid's expression withdrew. "I'm not sure I'd be any good at that. I just like to read."

"Are you kidding? You'd be perfect! You've traveled from port to port, town to town, living the kind of adventurous life I've always dreamed of living." Cecelia flung out her arms for extra emphasis, scaring a duck skimming the waters below into flight.

"You've always dreamed of living on a boat when your family owns *that?*" Ingrid's voice pitched as she pointed to the old Victorian hotel behind them. "I'd give anything to live on land for longer than a week. It's why we're here actually. My dad promised he'd try to settle us in a town for as long as he can find work."

Cecelia's mental gears began to crank. "It's really too bad we don't look more alike because I'd totally suggest we pull a *Parent Trap* swap on our two families."

Ingrid stared blankly.

"What? You've never seen *The Parent Trap*?"

"I haven't seen many movies. I mostly just read anything I can get my hands on . . . which hasn't been much lately."

Cecelia thought for a moment. "Have you read *The Prince and the Pauper*?"

Ingrid nodded. "A few years ago. It was on my homeschool list."

"Well, it's pretty much the same story line."

Ingrid looked as if she was about to comment on that when one of the festival bands started their sound check for the evening. The electric guitar strum reverberated across the water. Cecelia scrambled to her feet. She needed to get going. The shuttle bus would be unloading festivalgoers in no time now—the same bus that would start her journey to find her dad. She'd saved up enough tip money to stay in a motel for a month before she'd have to secure work as a hostess somewhere . . . but she'd locate her dad before that. She knew she would. Grown men didn't go missing; they simply got distracted and lost their way. She'd be the one to help him find it again.

"I have to go," Cecelia said with a level of regret that surprised her. "But I definitely think we should exchange numbers. I think you're the perfect person to help me with my stories."

Ingrid rose to her feet, and her height soared several inches above Cecelia, which wasn't difficult to achieve given she'd barely reached five-foot-one by her sixteenth birthday. Puberty had been a real letdown.

"Oh . . . I don't have a phone."

No phone? How did a teenager have no phone? But then a worse question struck her. What if this was the last time they'd ever see each other—this girl who'd come from the sea and mysteriously docked herself at her family's hotel? Cecelia couldn't fathom the possibility of walking away with nothing to show for their meeting. With nothing tying them together if their paths should cross again.

It was only then she recalled what Ingrid had said earlier, about her visits to the local library. About not having a card of her own. Likely because she didn't have a permanent address. Librarians were sticklers about that kind of thing, especially Mrs. Camden.

Cecelia glanced at the hotel and then back at her watch. If she skipped her plans to grab a blackberry lemonade slush on the way to the shuttle, she'd have just enough time to show Ingrid to the library reserved for hotel guests. Once inside, she'd encourage Ingrid to pick out a book or two, and then Cecelia would put her own name down as the borrower. She'd be states away before anybody found out.

"Come on, I want to show you the hotel library."

"Oh, I don't know if I should. I'm not really dressed for"—Ingrid tugged at her tattered T-shirt and cutoff shorts—"for anything that nice."

"You're dressed fine. Now, come on." Cecelia hooked her arm through Ingrid's, lengthening her strides to the point of an almost-run. They dashed over the grassy knoll and up the steep steps to the back patio. Only a minute had passed when the two made it into the back door of the hotel lobby. But given she only had eleven minutes to spare, she felt every second of it.

Cecelia pointed to the hall on the lobby floor and tried not to rush her new friend as she oohed and ahhed over the echo of their footsteps across the ivory marble and again at the twinkling chandelier above them. From the corner of her eye, Cecelia watched Ingrid tug at her cutoffs. But she didn't have time to reassure Ingrid that the only guests they'd see were those checking in their luggage.

With half the flair as usual, Cecilia opened one of the two glass doors leading into the library. And something about the way Ingrid staggered backward at the sight of it stabbed her in the gut. It had been a long time since she looked at anything with that kind of wonder and amazement.

"I've never seen anything so beautiful in my life."

Cecelia swallowed. "My uncle has been collecting books for a long time. There's even a lending system so it feels like a real library when our guests come to stay. You can use my card, though. Go ahead, pick anything out. Pick out two or three if you want . . . just . . . it kind of needs to be quick."

Ingrid didn't seem to hear her as she stepped toward the bookshelves with a reverence Cecelia had only ever witnessed inside a church. As Ingrid

95

neared the tall mahogany shelves, she didn't lift her hands to the books the way most people did. Instead, she only skimmed the spines with her eyes, as if too afraid to touch them.

An ear-piercing clatter resounded somewhere in the direction of the lobby, and Cecelia told Ingrid she'd be right back.

"Oh, Cecelia, thank goodness," her frazzled, petite Aunt Patti said as she rounded the hallway into the lobby. "Could you give me a hand with these serving platters? They're heavier than they look. I don't know how Joel managed to carry such a large load," Aunt Patti called out, nearly toppling under the strain of at least eight stainless steel platters.

"Sure, I've got you." But then Cecelia really needed to get out of there, especially with Joel lurking somewhere inside the hotel. She knew the minute they spoke, he'd be able to tell something was up. Just one of the many annoying things about her only cousin.

Seconds after Cecelia set the platters on the cook's immaculate kitchen counters, she raced back to the library to tell Ingrid good-bye before she collected her backpack and dashed off to the shuttle stop down the street.

But as soon as she reached the open library doors, her heart stuttered to a stop, and she quickly slid into the shadowed alcove to the left of the room, where she gawked at the nightmare playing out in real time.

Joel was inside! And worse, he had Cecelia's backpack slung over his shoulders. Why was he always the one to ruin her best plans?

Yet her frustration quickly gave way to curiosity as she studied the rare look of amusement on his face. She followed his line of sight to where Ingrid stood, both hands raised in the air as if Joel was about to quote the Miranda rights to her. But from the looks of it, the only thing he was doing was leaning against the doorjamb with his own hands casually stuffed in his pockets.

"I—I swear, I wasn't stealing anything," Ingrid uttered.

"That paperback in your back pocket might suggest otherwise," Joel said with a suave-sounding voice that made Cecelia roll her eyes to the ceiling.

Ingrid pawed for the tattered novel sticking out of the back pocket of her denim cutoffs. "Oh no, this isn't . . . this one is mine."

"You carry books on your person often then?"

"Yes."

Joel raised his eyebrows at this, then smiled in full.

"I swear, Cece was right here with me a minute ago. She can tell you." She rose on her tiptoes and appeared to be searching the space. "I'm just not sure where she went."

"Cece, huh?" He laughed as he spoke the nickname. "I'm not sure I've ever heard anyone else refer to her as that before. Maybe if there's two of us, her campaign to change her name might actually stick. Still"—he lowered his voice a smidge—"you should probably know that Cece has a bad habit of wandering off at inopportune moments."

If Cecelia wasn't actively trying to hide from her cousin, she'd tackle him. How long was he going to hold that particular grudge? It wasn't as if she'd planned to walk away with their only flashlight that night. Sure, Joel had been waist-deep in dark waters at the time, and sure, he had asked her to light his way back to shore after he retrieved the runaway crab pot, but she would have lost the rare Moon Snail shell to the tide if she'd waited even a few more seconds. But the way Joel told the story, she all but planted that fish hook on the sand for him to step on.

Joel pushed off the doorjamb and held out his hand for Ingrid's book. "Mind if I take a look at that?"

Seconds passed before Ingrid handed her book over to him, and Cecelia wondered if her new friend was even breathing while Joel examined it. "I read this one in fifth grade," he finally said. "I enjoyed it. Especially the protagonist's relationship with the dog. Probably because I've never had a dog of my own."

And much like the way Ingrid's eyes lit up on the dock, they did once again, turning a shade of melted gold.

"I never have, either," Ingrid said. "But I love Rontu. I'm trying to get my dad to name our next boat after him, but he said dog names don't make good boat names and that if I want to use it, I'll need to either buy my own boat or save it for a dog."

Joel turned the book over with care before handing it back to her. "Which confirms you are indeed Ingrid Erikson."

Ingrid took a step back. "How do you know that?"

"My dad just called me from the marina—said I should keep an eye out for you seeing as he just hired your father to be the hotel's charter boat captain this summer. I'm Joel." He smiled, and Cecelia noticed it wasn't his usual smile. While it had taken her some time to get used to the baritone of her cousin's post-puberty voice—and to the way he'd practically bulked up overnight—she'd rarely seen him interact with peers their age. And certainly not with exotic, sea-bound, book-loving newcomers who'd just been granted a reason to stick around town for an entire summer. Cecelia bit her bottom lip and studied the second hand of the clock in the grand hallway across from the lobby. *Two minutes.* She had two minutes to make a decision she might regret forever. "I'd planned to introduce you to my cousin," Joel continued. "But it sounds like she got to you before I could."

"That's right, Joel. I did." Cecelia practically leaped out of her hiding place. "Which means as of right now, you are officially the third wheel."

He shook his head and laughed while Ingrid looked between the cousins curiously.

Joel slid the backpack strap from his shoulder, allowing it to dangle in the space between them. "I found this on the patio. Seems to be packed pretty full for a casual day at the beach." Suspicion gleamed in his eyes. "Care to explain?"

Cecelia's cheeks flamed in their silent standoff. "How about if I *don't* explain and instead we take our new friend for a blackberry lemonade slush and show her around town before our shift starts tonight?"

He narrowed his eyes and Cecelia held her breath. "You buying?"

She grinned and nodded. The tradeoff was very much in her favor. She swiped her backpack off his shoulder with a hard yank. "I just need to run upstairs and grab something really quick." Like the good-bye letter she left for her mom. Perhaps she'd store it away for another time, when things in this town returned to their typical, mind-numbingly boring existence.

But something told her that if she left on that ferryboat today, she might just miss the most epic adventure to ever happen to this town . . . and to her.

9

As Joel concludes reading Cece's first chapter aloud and lowers the stack of printed pages to his lap, I'm thinking how strange it is to have known a person so well and still be a stranger to their inner thoughts. While her written narrative brought an instant recall to the dramatic inflection of her voice and to her unique way of stretching every detail to the fullest, it wasn't without surprise. Although, Joel seems to be focused on something else entirely: a cautionary tale I've heard a hundred times.

"She really did make a horrible lookout," he reports with feigned indignation. "I still have that scar on my foot from when she abandoned me on the beach without our one and only flashlight." He shakes his head. "If that fish hook had been—"

"Even a centimeter off you would have needed surgery, which would have resulted in more than the five stitches you needed," I conclude for him.

"It was six." Joel's smile comes easily as he reaches for his mug on the coffee table, although the wooden serving platter filled with an array of brunch items remains untouched by us both. It appears I wasn't the only one with an anxious stomach prior to our first reading session.

"I forget," he adds lightly. "You've heard that one a few times before."

"Just a few." It's an effort not to crack a smile of my own as I remember the two cousins going head to head over who was more at fault the evening of Joel's accident: Joel for not taking the time to pull on his rubber boots before wading into the dark waters, or Cece for not staying on task. I refused to choose a victor because secretly, I'd reveled in their over-the-top rivalries. Their banter had filled a sibling-size hole that was otherwise empty.

After Joel had arrived wearing his Sunday best and carrying a platter of delectable-looking foods, we'd sat on opposite sides of Cece's living room. With the curtains pulled back on either side of the oversize windows, the view offered a neutral focal point, highlighting a powder-blue sky and sailboats in the distant waters. Given their high speeds, the wind has picked up considerably since my morning jaunt across the sandy beach.

"Did you know she was planning to run away that day?" I ask, picking at the *Ahoy, Matey!* pillow on my lap.

"No." Joel selects a tangerine from the tray and tosses it from hand to hand, his face contemplative. "But I don't think she would have gone through with leaving. Even if she would have boarded that ferry and made it all the way to the Seattle airport, I think her common sense would have caught up to her well before Nevada."

Spoken like a man who has never been without two loving, supportive parents. "Her plan sounded pretty solid to me. I mean, she even wrote a good-bye letter to Wendy. It certainly doesn't seem like one of her more impulsive exploits." Joel purses his lips, appearing to mull my opinion over as I continue. "I think she was determined to see her search through, at least until the money ran out. Her dad may not have played a lead role in her life, but she carried his absence with her everywhere she went."

Joel's eyes slide to mine, and I take a quick detour from this too-close-for-comfort subject. "I never realized how close the timing was, though."

"The timing of what?"

"Never meeting each other." Though I intend for the reference to be about Cece, it's impossible to pretend that the three of us weren't intertwined into a single meet-cute that day, separated only by minutes. "Do you think that could be the point of this whole thing?" I gesture to the bulk of pages left to be read on his lap. "Some kind of life lesson about fate and friendship?"

"I'm not sure what point she's trying to make. Not yet anyway." He bends forward on a sigh, elbows to knees, and rolls the tangerine between his palms. "I'll admit, I don't think I heard a word of Pastor Gray's sermon this morning. I spent most the time speculating over what we'd read in that first chapter." The slight flush of his cheeks triggers warmth to simmer in the base of my belly. "I'm relieved, I think. It wasn't as if I thought she was going to out some big family secret or something, but it's unnerving to know we're the main characters of this story." He shrugs as if he's finished, but I can tell he's not.

"What else?" I prod.

"It was good to hear her voice again." He stares down at his hands and offers a nervous laugh. "Which is probably a weird thing to say, considering it was my own voice I was hearing as I read."

"It's not weird," I say, as I release my tight grip on the pillow. "I felt the same. Her narrative held true to her nostalgic, jovial point of view, though her tone and phrasing were slightly less dramatic than in her fiction. Still, she drew me in with her distinct perspective and her willingness to explore something so personal. Despite the differences in technique and style, her voice remained authentically her own."

"Spoken like a true editor." The admiration he speaks with now holds none of the edge I heard in his voice last night. "I doubt there's another person in the world who knows her writing like you do. She always admired the way you told her the truth, even when it was hard to hear."

I glance out the window to mark where the blue horizon kisses the sea. For the first time since the discovery of this memoir, I don't want to push Cece's words away out of fear, I want to draw them in close. I want to cherish them like the gift Joel deemed they'd be if only I'd give them a chance.

"The real truth," I say, "is that Cece was one of a kind in every way."

Joel lifts his coffee mug from the antique chest doubling as a coffee table and stretches across the divide toward me. "I'd offer cheers to that. You?"

This time, I allow a small curve of my lips as I lift my mug of tepid caffeine in his direction.

After we toast to Cece, he stands to prepare his brunch plate in earnest. Patti's famous cinnamon rolls are among the mix, next to a pile of crisp maple bacon, crustless quiche, smoked salmon, and fresh baguettes. "I'm going to warm some of this up in the microwave. Should I add yours too?"

I spot the two fruit and yogurt parfaits, which is my usual go-to for breakfast, and nearly tell him I won't be needing anything more, but the intense growl of my stomach gives me away.

The amused gleam in his eyes causes me to crack another half smile.

"Yes, thank you."

I make quick work of adding various specialties to my plate before handing it off to be heated and wonder if Joel realizes the milestone we've passed this morning: fifty whole minutes together without a single argument or sharply spoken word between us. It seems he took my request to keep our interactions focused on Cece to heart last night. Well, good. If Joel is willing to shelve our history for the sake of this cause, then I certainly can, too.

When I stand from the sofa, I remember the clothing I'd donned this morning—the last of my clean options, a pair of navy bike shorts and an oversized, white zip-up hoodie. They were perfect for an early morning beach walk, but not for much else around town. Before I return my rental car at the drop-off location in Oak Harbor this afternoon, I'll need to run to the superstore and stock up on a few personal necessities like shampoo and conditioner bottles larger than my thumb, for starts.

The sweet aroma of cinnamon and sugar wafts through the cottage, and my stomach clenches in want. "I doubt there's a person on this planet who can resist your mother's cinnamon rolls."

"My mom actually retired from kitchen work last fall." Joel strolls into the open dining area and sets our warmed plates on the table. I would have happily eaten in the living room, but Joel has always been one for eating at tables. The result of a family-born habit the two of us don't share.

"Allie made a comment yesterday about her mom being the head baker," I remark, "but I didn't realize that was because Patti had retired." I move toward the whitewashed wooden table and work to adjust my sweatshirt from where it's slipped off my shoulder, briefly exposing my thin tank top straps and the inked skin I do my best to keep hidden. Joel freezes at the sight, and I quickly tug the zipper north. Heat prickles at the base of my throat as I move to sit in the chair he's pulled out for me.

"Thank you," I say, hoping we can move past the awkward moment and continue down the path of keeping things light—as light as two people who once promised their futures to each other can keep them anyway.

I pick up a piece of candied bacon and bring it to my lips just as Joel bows his head and blesses our food with a prayer. I murmur an *amen*, though it feels as foreign on my tongue as this high-brow meal to my low-class belly.

I appreciate when he steers our conversation back to the breezy topic of hotel staff changes. "My mom enjoys the flexibility of retired life and spending as much time as she can with Wendy. Thankfully, the guests seem pleased with Barbara Spencer. She's made a good impression."

And so has at least one of her daughters, I think to myself. An image of Madison Spencer's graceful fingers wrapped around Joel's forearm at the party last night materializes in my mind. Her affection for him is obvious, and why wouldn't it be? It's easy to visualize the things she'd find most appealing about the man sitting beside me. Confidence, intelligence, leadership qualities, loyalty to his family and career, and a face that's only grown more attractive with time . . .

I squint and imagine the two of them together, like the cover couple on a summer beach-read romance. I fork a bite of cinnamon roll into my mouth, hoping the sweetness will drown the acidity lining my belly.

"Is there a reason you're squinting at me?" he asks, narrowing his own eyelids to match mine. "Is this the way people look at each other over brunch in San Francisco?"

"Sorry, no." The tips of my ears burn hot. "I was just thinking."

"About how many dishes our new summer waitstaff has dropped since June? Or something else?"

And because I can't say, *Actually, I was just thinking about how you and Madison must be the golden couple of Port Townsend*, I lead with the first layer of a plan I've been working on since I woke up to a text from SaBrina at dawn. As if I'd forgotten my purpose for being here, she'd reiterated my mission to retrieve Cece's missing manuscript as well as the consequences of what would happen if I didn't. And seeing as I have no new leads to follow, I need the gatekeeper of the Campbell family as my ally, not my enemy. "Allie mentioned seeing Cece working on *The Fate of Kings* here at the cottage a few months before her surgery."

Joel's fork hovers above his quiche. "Makes sense."

I pick around at the food on my plate. "I was thinking I might poke around a bit while I'm here, see if it might turn up somewhere."

"I thought you searched Cece's laptop. Aunt Wendy told me you took it with you after the service."

"I did, but there was no trace of it on her hard drive, and honestly, I wasn't in the best frame of mind to think outside of the box. Maybe there's a second laptop nobody knew about? Or an iPad she was using instead? Or maybe it's as simple as her saving it to an external hard drive that could be in a junk drawer in the kitchen." I pop a grape in my mouth, hoping my quest will be that simple. "I'm thinking of mentioning it to Wendy when I visit her tomorrow, see what she might know about it."

"She doesn't have it," he says a bit too flatly to be nonchalant. "Believe me, if she did, she would have turned it over a long time ago. I'm pretty sure she'd be fine never hearing about that missing book again."

My shoulders tense. "It's not like I was planning to accuse her of holding it hostage. I just thought she might know something about—"

"She doesn't. And you're hardly the first person to ask." He sets his fork down. "If you want to search the cottage, do it. Have at the garage and the storage unit, as well. But please leave Aunt Wendy out of it."

The finality of his request rubs me all sorts of wrong ways, but I clamp my jaw closed to keep from saying anything I'll regret. Instead, I nod once and lift my coffee mug to my lips. It's empty. I set it down and circle back to Wendy. My mind can't seem to let thoughts of her go. "Did you know she's been ordering her flower arrangements from a wholesale vendor in Seattle?"

Why I expect him to show the same level of surprise I experienced last night when Joel is only a half-step away from inheriting the hotel is beyond me. Of course he knows.

"I'm aware, yes," he says, slowly. "But it's not a subject we discuss with her much."

I feel the tentacles of frustration beginning to weave their way into my subconscious. "Is there a list of all the acceptable conversations and activities I'm allowed to have and do with Wendy? I didn't know there was a special protocol I should be following."

An exasperated sigh escapes him. "There isn't a protocol."

"Are you sure?" I push. "Because I certainly wouldn't want to skip over any necessary permissions in order for me to assist her with a gardening project tomorrow."

To my annoyance, he doesn't come back at me with sarcasm. "I assumed, by the workload you mentioned last week, that you'd be spending much of your time here working remotely."

"There's some work I can do from here, yes, but I have an incredibly reliable assistant at my office." At the mention of Chip, I cringe inwardly. There are currently five unanswered text messages waiting on my phone from him.

"Gardening projects are fairly involved."

I eye him pointedly. "As in water, soil, sun? Yeah, I'm pretty sure I can handle that."

"And time," he challenges. "Projects like that take time."

"Two weeks may not be long enough to see an entire garden bloom, but it's certainly long enough to help prepare her beds for the months ahead," I blurt without thought.

The air shifts between us as I watch the information take root for the first time. "You're here for two weeks?" The stunned, almost hopeful way he asks spears through me. I don't want Joel to find reason to hope where I'm concerned. And I certainly can't afford to find any hope where he's concerned, either.

"I talked to my boss." My palms grow damp as I dig for a half truth. "She insisted I use up my PTO days so I don't lose them. I figured staying a little longer made the most sense—takes the pressure off us having to finish reading the memoir in only a couple days." I swallow, thinking also of the time staying will afford me during my search for *The Fate of Kings*. "Unless, of course, you have other plans for the cottage?"

His eyes are firmly fixed on me now. "It's yours for however long you want it."

"Thank you." With anxious fingers, I reach for my phone and tap the screen to check the time. *1:21 p.m.*

He clears his throat. "Should we start the next chapter? I can refill our coffees if you want to take the lead on the next one and—"

"Actually, I can't do another one today. I need to return my rental to the drop-off site in Oak Harbor by three." The hour-and-fifteen-minute drive wouldn't leave much time for running errands, but it might be enough time to clear my head. Alone. Something I'd likely have to do in between all the future chapters we read together. "I need to run a few personal errands, too."

"Anything Allie can bring over for you from the hotel?"

"Not unless she has a secret stash of women's clothing hanging around in my size."

"Allie wouldn't, but her sister, Madison, might. She owns a women's clothing boutique here in town. Obviously I haven't shopped there myself, but from what our guests report it's become a popular tourist destination on the peninsula." His description conjures an image of the golden gown I purchased and wore last night from said shop. "Madison's brain for marketing is remarkable," he goes on. "She actually pitched a winter campaign idea for the hotel to my dad a couple weeks back. He was so impressed he asked if he could hire her on the spot."

The favorable way he speaks about her fills in the holes of what I couldn't conclude last night at the party through a simple observation: Madison's admiration for Joel isn't one-sided.

He cares for her, too.

He slips his phone from his pocket. "I'll put a call in to her."

"Oh, no. That's okay." My wind-chapped lips stretch to the point of pain as I reach deep for a smile I don't feel. "Upscale boutiques don't generally carry the kind of clothing options conducive for gardening."

"Believe me," he chuckles. "Madison has more closets stuffed with clothing in her house and storage facilities than we have rooms in the hotel. She'd be insulted if I didn't at least ask what she has available."

He knows her closets? Yet I have exactly no time to process this as he scrolls through his recent call list and taps on her name.

"Joel, please don't—"

An instant later he drops the phone from his ear. "Straight to voicemail."

I'm so relieved I nearly thank God for intervening on my behalf, as if that's actually something He's been known to do for me.

Suddenly itching for a reason to get up from this table, I swipe my empty coffee mug and make for the kitchen to buy time to collect myself when I hear the familiar buzz of my own phone. Which I left next to my plate.

"Your phone's ringing. Need it?"

Unlike Joel's lengthy list of recent callers, my own such list is limited at best. And by limited, I pretty much mean Chip. Based on the texts he's sent, I know he's calling about the email SaBrina sent, the one letting him know I wouldn't be returning to the office until after my PTO was used in full. She basically told him he'd be tackling the bulk of my work responsibilities, effective immediately. Though he knew there was a chance of this outcome, I hadn't yet told him about what had occurred at Marshall's office yesterday. I'm simply not ready to talk about the memoir yet. Not even to Chip.

"It's a . . . Chip Stanton," Joel announces, with a decidedly different tone of voice than the one he was using before.

I set my steaming mug on the counter and hold up my hands. "I actually should take that—can you toss it to me?"

Joel's eyes widen as I catch the phone mid-arc and swipe the green arrow to accept the call.

"Hey, Chip. I'm sorry I haven't texted you back yet. Things are . . . busy," I say, turning my back on the dining room and the man seated there.

"It's a good thing you answered because my next step was to call the local police there and ask for a wellness check like I used to do for my grandpa. Only since I don't have your address, I would have had to say, 'Can you please go door to door until you find my missing boss? She's about five-six, likes fantasy fiction, has dark hair and speaks fluent sarcasm—'"

"Thank you, but that won't be necessary. I'm fine, really." I release a soft chuckle, though the worry I hear in his voice makes my eyes prick with tears. Or perhaps it's the truth that lives just beneath it: Chip, my work colleague, is likely the only person in my life who'd even think to question my absence in the case of an emergency. I swallow to find my voice again. "I need to stay a bit longer."

"So that means the package wasn't—"

"Unfortunately, no. It wasn't."

"So you're just going to stay there, in hopes you find it?" *In hopes*

108

that you have a career to come back to? is what he doesn't ask. But I can tell he's more concerned than he's letting on.

I glance over my shoulder at Joel, suddenly hyperaware of the mounting sense of injustice between our two lives. While I've fought to survive these past five years as an orphan in a strange city, Joel's life—which he's lived in the only place I've ever called home—has continued on, continued to thrive, the same way it always has: through faith, family, job security, and a future of promising relationships.

He still has the whole package, while I'm at risk of losing the only thing I have left.

"Hello? Ingrid? Is this a blink-twice situation?" Chip cuts in. "Is there a safe word you forgot to tell me ahead of time? Because my offer to call the cops is still—"

"No, no, I'm good." I breathe out. "Why don't I call you back a little later when I'm in the car. Does that work for you?"

"As long as you won't be alarmed when I ask you a list of identifying questions first."

"I won't," I amend softly. "I'll talk to you later."

After tapping the red icon at the bottom of my screen, I slip the phone into the front pocket of my hoodie. I refuse to meet Joel's concentrated gaze while I move to collect the dishes from the dining table.

"How were you planning to get back to the cottage after dropping off the rental today?" he asks, though by the sound of it, it's not even close to all he wants to ask me right now.

"I can manage a ride." Which, at this moment, I'd accept from any source other than Joel. For future note, the time stamp on our civility ends promptly at the one-hour mark.

He carries the wooden platter of food into the kitchen and sets it on the counter with more restraint than I would have given him credit for, seeing as his jaw is keeping time with the second hand on the clock above Cece's oven.

"Just leave all that," I say, putting away the coffee creamer. "I'll clean it up later."

Joel pauses for a beat. "Allie's planning to stop by in the morning; she can bring the platter back to the hotel then."

"Actually, I'll drop it off there myself." Indignation simmers in my stomach as I twist toward him. "I appreciate you letting me stay here, but I don't need a house manager. I'm perfectly capable of running my own errands, folding my own laundry, washing my own dishes, and sorting out my own transportation needs while I'm here. You don't need to treat me like a broken little bird. I can manage just fine on my own."

He rotates slowly from his place near the sink, and it's only when my rump collides with an ill-placed oven handle that I realize I have nowhere to go in this too-narrow kitchen.

His gaze drags along the edges of my face until the mossy green of his eyes paralyzes my ability to look away. "I don't think you're broken—but I do think you're still punishing yourself for what you had no control over. It's okay not to have it all together all the time and to receive help." In a different life, I would feign ignorance to what he's referring to, but Joel knows my past as well as he knows his own. "It's okay to let yourself talk about him. He was your father—you're allowed to grieve him, to miss him."

"*No.*" Ice crystalizes in my veins until the words burst from my encapsulated heart. "I didn't ask for your permission, Joel, and I don't want it. *You* are the last person who gets to talk to me about my father or about my feelings. You lost that right five years ago when you left him alone to die!"

I ball my shaking hands into fists at my sides as the silence between us contracts and expands like the rising panic in my chest. I'm braced for a fight I've been too scared to have, only Joel doesn't take me up on it. Instead, when he speaks again, his voice is a bruised kind of tender, a raw form of undone. "You're absolutely right. I did lose that right. It won't happen again."

I trail my tongue along the dry roof of my mouth, desperate to avoid the telltale swallow that's sure to reverberate like thunder in this tight space, when he retreats to the opposite side of the kitchen.

"If your plan is to catch an Uber from Oak Harbor, your choice of drivers will be slim. Most aren't willing to commute this far due to the construction on the bridge—the delays are long." He pauses. "Allie will be on standby with the hotel car if you need her. I won't insult you further by offering you a ride myself."

He moves into the living room to gather his things while I work to thaw my senses long enough to form a coherent reply.

"Joel, wait. I'm—"

But my plea is cut short by the click of the front door.

10

After replaying the tense moments with Joel in the kitchen a dozen times throughout the night, I wake with a heaviness I haven't been able to mask with caffeine or even a sunrise beach walk. Upon my return to the quiet cottage, I distract myself by searching every drawer in Cece's kitchen, bathroom, and spare room for an external hard drive or secondary device I'm not even sure exists. And still, the weight of our last interaction presses against my conscience

As if on autopilot, I reach for my backpack in search of the only thing that's brought me any kind of relief this year. I slip Cece's laptop from the padded pocket like the comfort item it's become and tuck it securely under my arm. This morning I'll perform my weekly routine in a new location, one that's been calling to me since the day I arrived.

When I stand at the bottom of the narrow staircase leading to Cece's office, it doesn't take me long to bolster up the courage I need to climb. Some part of me wants to believe that the simple act of returning Cece's laptop to its rightful place of origin—an atmospheric attic brimming with concentrated doses of Cece's imagination—might make her feel a little less far away.

Clearly, I'm no lightweight when it comes to fantasy plot lines.

I flip the light switch and inhale as the room glows a warm amber from the twinkle lights strung at the top of the walls. I tiptoe across the floorboards and set her laptop on the desk before pulling out the fuzzy, sherbet-orange desk chair. Slowly, I rotate in a circle, taking in the funky lamps, the pile of boho floor pillows, and the miniature bookshelf where an intricate Lego pirate ship is displayed. She'd worked on it whenever we Facetimed late into the evenings.

I recline the chair into a nearly horizontal position and stare up at the expansive mural painted on her A-frame ceiling—something she and Wendy worked on diligently for the better part of a year after she moved in. The colorful, detailed map of the Kingdom of Cardithia and all its surrounding seas and ships is the most unique aspect of Cece's writing attic. She used to tell me that whenever she was lost, she only had to look up to find her way again.

How many times had I wished that was true in my own life?

I peer up at the detailed painting, my throat uncomfortably tight. "Where is it, Cece? Where is *The Fate of Kings*?"

But like every other time I've asked that question, no answer comes.

I grip the chair lever under my right thigh, and in an instant I pop back to a sitting position. My gaze falls once again to a laptop I've spent more time with than most people spend with their significant others. Even though I gave up searching for the digital file of *The Fate of Kings* on this hard drive months ago, there were other hidden gems I found during my explorations.

I twist the sea glass ring on my finger around twice before I open the lid and click into the bookmarked browser at the top right: Cecelia J. Campbell's Memorial Page.

This was once her most active profile page on social media, with a handful of trusted admins and virtual assistants to keep her fans both entertained and in the know about her latest book release news, exclusive giveaways, and any extra tidbits she wanted to offer. Now though, it is simply a place to remember.

Here there are always new posts, pictures, graphics, and favorite quotes to scroll through from at least a handful of her most loyal

2.3 million fans who have been contributing to it since her death. Despite having zero personal connection or regard for any social media outside of this one space, this ritual of mine has become a rare source of solace. That this group of strangers, these beloved readers of Cece's fictional creations, can share such a unique kinship with me has been reason enough for my visits to continue.

Only this time, as I place my finger on the touchpad and scroll through the most recent admin posts, a familiar name and face jumps out among the masses: Allison (Allie) Spencer. I click on the profile picture of the same girl who regaled me with stories of college dorm life as she drove me home last night from the car rental place in Oak Harbor. The same girl who's named a top contributor in this online group and one of only five administrators with the power to edit, delete, and generate announcements.

I willingly hop down the Allie Spencer rabbit hole—noting how many accounts she follows that have to do with Cecelia Campbell and the Nocturnal Heart series. She's definitely earned the title of *huge fan.*

Though I stumble through multiple profiles like an arthritic ninety-year-old navigating the abyss that is social media, I finally land on the milkshake video she showed me a few days ago. She wasn't kidding about the views or the feedback. I watch it five times over, zooming in to search the blurry background for any possible clues I could have missed the first time, but all I see is a stack of notebooks anchoring the four curled corners of Cece's favorite nautical charting maps on the dining table.

After closing the laptop, I stand and immediately smash my skull on the low, angled ceiling.

And it's then, as I press my palm to the throbbing ache, that Joel's face resurfaces amidst the distraction of pain. It's as if he's been there this whole time, perched on the edge of my subconscious. I sigh and slip my phone out of my new pink cotton shorts, scrolling past the empty text thread between us, pretending not to notice the unanswered question I'd asked late last night like an extended olive branch.

Ingrid

When would you like to schedule our next reading time?

There had been no reply.

I tap into my contacts and dial Wendy.

When she doesn't answer, I leave a message. Is it possible she's working at the hotel today?

With a palm still pressed to my head, I navigate the stairs on a quest for an ice pack when I spot the hotel's wooden serving tray from yesterday's brunch with Joel. I forget all about my injury. It feels like a sign, or at the least, an arrow pointing me in the next right direction. I can drop the platter off, connect with Wendy, and maybe even ask some questions about Cece's lost manuscript while reviving a dead garden.

There was still time to make this day count for something, especially when I only had thirteen of them left.

Turns out, four miles on foot while carrying a chunk of wood that might as well be a tree stump should be one of the exercises included in those tire-flipping, rope-whipping competitions. It's maybe seventy-five degrees out by the time I reach the front steps of the hotel, but given the burn in my biceps and the way my T-shirt clings to my back, I'm certain I look like I've just crossed a marathon finish line.

I give myself no more than a few seconds to take in the lobby before I push myself forward, with little more than an I'm-already-checked-in-but-thank-you-anyway smile at the welcoming front desk staff. My biceps shake as I return the serving platter outside the kitchen, then slip into the employee restroom and take a minute to blot my pinked cheeks and neck with a cool paper towel. It's not until I return to the admin hallway and read each header above the five doorways that I realize what comes next.

Anxiety flares as I pass Wendy's darkened office door near the end of the hall and peer into the rectangular glass window. There's nothing inside but a bare desk and empty bookshelves. I wonder when she was last here?

When I twist to stare at the door at the end of the hall, the pang in my chest registers before my brain has a chance to catch up. Sometime in the last five years, Joel Campbell was promoted to Hotel Manager. It's the only position that would make sense after all this time, and yet it's different to see something you speculated about for years materialize before your eyes.

From the time Joel could procure a work permit, he has held more than a dozen known job titles inside his family's business— a signature piece of Stephen's leadership philosophy for any employee willing to commit to the long haul. I'd bet there isn't a single executive-level employee who hasn't worked every entry-level position the Campbell Hotel offers. And much like his father, I've seen Joel pressure-wash decks after windstorms, load dirty dishes in the wee hours of the morning, fold fresh linens after scheduled housekeepers call in sick, and restore order to disastrous suites when party guests become too reckless.

I lift my fist and knock on his office door.

A strange yelping sound, followed by a round of short, encouraging commands, rocks me back a step.

"Come on in, we're ready," Joel's unmistakable voice calls out from somewhere behind the door.

I shift on my feet, wondering if Joel would be quite so welcoming if he knew I was the one waiting on the other side of his door.

"Come in," he says again a bit louder.

The instant I step inside his office, he's on his feet.

As is the most adorable puppy I've ever laid eyes on.

"Ingrid," Joel announces like a question. "I didn't know you were coming."

"Yes, I was just—" But before I can pretend to know how to

finish that sentence, I'm crouching to reach for the insane bundle of mottled brown-and-white fur circling my calves at high speed.

"Oh my gosh, who is this little guy?" I laugh as the pup places his paws on my thigh to bump noses with me. I hold his little face between my palms and forget my surroundings entirely. "Aren't you just the sweetest thing ever?" The puppy licks my cheek as if in agreement, and I laugh again.

"And there goes every last minute of office training I've been working on with him this month."

I glance up at Joel in time to see the twitch in his cheek. "So he's yours, then?"

"By default, yes."

I'm too busy drowning in puppy kisses to ask for clarification.

"It's good to hear you laugh again," Joel says, studying me in a way that flips my insides. My smile holds as I look from him to the puppy.

I stare into two yellow-brown irises. "What's his name?"

Joel's hesitation forces my attention away from the happy pup once again. Only this time, when our gazes collide, I feel every syllable he pronounces like an arrow through the chest. "Rontu."

"Rontu?" I repeat, breathless.

He tugs at his neck. "He's not quite as wild or scraggly as his namesake, but . . . it seemed a good fit regardless."

Rontu, the feral, untrusting dog from *Island of the Blue Dolphins* who sacrifices his life for Karana's. The same name I'd planned to give a dog of my own one day if ever I was able to own one.

"Rontu, sit." Joel waits for the puppy to respond to his command, and amazingly he obeys despite my distraction. "Good boy. Now, go to your bed." Rontu looks forlorn as he tilts his head intuitively and searches my eyes before obeying his alpha's command. Impressed, I smile at Joel. "Looks like he's retained more than you thought."

"A miracle." He offers me his hand and pulls me to my feet. Rontu whimpers at the edge of his circular pillow.

Joel lowers his voice. "Stay, boy. Stay."

"What's his breed?" It was easy to see the golden retriever in him, but there was something else mixed in I wasn't certain of.

"He's a beago. A beagle-retriever mix." Joel rolls his eyes. "I've never been one for designer dog breeds, but Madison and Cece were all googly-eyed over them the spring before . . . her surgery."

I try my best not to react in surprise at the pairing of names he's mentioned, but like usual, Joel sees right through me. "They became friends a couple months before Madison opened her shop here." His eyes stray from mine, and I wonder if he's uncomfortable discussing Madison in my presence. I hope not. Joel owes me nothing, and Madison certainly seems like a great catch. "Madison's a big dog lover, and she managed to convince Cece that having a dog at her cottage would be good for creativity and companionship. They found a reputable breeder on Whidbey Island, and then one thing led to another and they both ended up putting deposits down on the next available litter. The puppies were born three months after Cece passed away."

"And Wendy didn't want him?"

Joel's telling expression suggests that it wasn't a matter of want, but a matter of capability.

"So you chose Rontu and Madison chose . . ."

"Rita, the only female in a litter of six. Madison considered taking on both puppies, but with her shop hours, she barely has enough time for one dog, let alone two. We try to get them together at least once a week or so, to share some of the load."

"How perfect," I say quietly.

Sure, Joel has always wanted a dog of his own, but his lifestyle at the hotel—like mine at the publishing house—isn't exactly the most pet-friendly environment. And yet, here he is, sharing custody of a sibling set with a young woman who seems as genuine as she is gorgeous.

Joel looks to be puzzling something out when our eyes meet again, and I can only hope it doesn't have to do with Madison. Thankfully, it doesn't. "Did you *walk* here from the cottage?"

I nod.

"The entire way?" He asks this like the distance between the cottage and the hotel actually is the distance of a marathon, and for a moment, I consider telling him just how brutal hefting that extra bulk around really was. But instead I simply say, "It's only about four miles."

I lick my lips before glancing at Rontu, who has now plopped his body down on his bed, preparing for a nap. "I sent you a text last night."

"Yeah." His gaze cuts to his desk where paperwork is fanned out in all four corners. "It's been a morning around here."

A torturous few seconds tick by before I finally say what's been brewing inside me since the moment he walked out the cottage door.

"I shouldn't have snapped at you like that yesterday. I . . . I'm sorry for what I said to you."

"I'm not." He twists to stare at me head-on. "It has to come out somehow. That kind of pain will kill you if you keep it bottled up inside."

My eyes prick. "Still, I have better self-control than that. I should have—"

"Ingrid." His expression is so excruciatingly sympathetic that even Rontu's ears perk at the curious change in his master's tone. "I've never asked you to hold back with me. Not once." He pushes a hand through his hair. "I know things are different now, but that doesn't change the fact that I've waited five years for you to return home. The last thing I want is for you to be here in body but stay absent in the ways that matter most."

His words hit so unexpectedly that it takes a moment for me to regroup. In all the months I've been in therapy, I'm not sure I've been anywhere near that bold with Dr. Rogers.

Joel reaches as if to touch my arm, but pulls back before his fingers find purchase. "I was wrong to speak so freely about your grief yesterday, but I'm hoping we might get the chance to talk more about—"

"Knock, knock. You here, Joel?"

Madison's distinctive voice, even from behind the closed door, carries the air of a southern belle, only I know from Allie that the two sisters grew up in eastern Oregon. Even still, her charm is impossible to ignore. Rontu stands at attention and whines for Joel to allow him off his bed.

Joel's eyes are trained on my face as he moves toward the door, but I suddenly don't have it in me to guess at what's going on in his head.

"I'll go," I say. "Let me know when you're free to read again." I pat Rontu's head just as Madison sweeps inside the room carrying her own bundle of puppy sweetness. Surprisingly, I don't have to force a smile when I greet the duo. Despite my conflicting emotions, my fondness for the lithe strawberry blonde comes as naturally as Rontu's affection for his high-fashion sister. Madison sets the petite, female version of Rontu on the carpet. Their size is far from the only difference between the puppies, though, as Rita is dressed in what can only be described as a doggie tankini.

"She's . . . wow. She's adorable." Despite myself, I release a light chuckle as Rita prances around the room in her ruffled, pineapple-patterned bathing suit.

"Thanks, I think so, too, even if I've entered the category of obnoxious pet owners." But Madison's laugh holds just enough self-deprecation for me to cross her off that particular list.

"You work in fashion and you love dogs. Rita's the perfect combo."

"*Exactly.*" Her smile brightens as she makes eye contact with Joel. "See, Joel? Ingrid gets it. Why can't you?"

He crosses his arms and gives a slight shake of his head. "No, Ingrid's just too polite to tell you otherwise. But that"—he points to the white pup spinning in circles as Rontu sniffs her with interest —"is embarrassing. She's a dog, not a doll."

I open my mouth to refute him, when Madison pipes up, stepping in close as if to include me in an exclusive club I'm fairly certain I'd rather not join considering Joel is likely the only other member. I don't need a refresher course on "Boundaries With Your Ex" for me to know that getting involved with them as a couple is not a good idea for any of us.

"So get this: A few weeks ago Joel and my mom tried to stage an intervention over Rita's outfits, claiming I was—what was it, Joel? 'Displacing my maternal instincts on a fur baby'?" She rolls her eyes good-naturedly and swats playfully at Joel's arm again, which I take as my cue to exit. It's one thing to acknowledge their compatibility, it's another to stick around and watch it unfold.

"Well, it's been nice to see you again, Madison, but I should leave you both to—"

"Would you like to join us for lunch?" she asks as I retreat. "I usually take the kiddos here for a beach walk on Mondays since it's my day off. They're still leash training, but the pier has some great outdoor dining options." She looks from Joel to me again. "And it's such a gorgeous day for an outing."

"It is," I agree, careful to keep my voice upbeat and steady. "But I actually have a commitment to Wendy this afternoon. And I should probably head over there sooner than later." I train my gaze on Madison. "Thanks anyway."

"Come to the shop anytime. I'm always up for some girl talk, and there's a lovely coffee shop next door. They make a killer iced mocha."

"That's good to know." I'm two steps outside the threshold of Joel's office when I turn back and take a mental snapshot of the happy family of four that I'm sure will haunt my dreams tonight. "Hope you two have a great walk with the kiddos."

Halfway down the hall, a raw, unfurling sensation builds in the pit of my stomach despite my attempts to reason with it. Like a defiant teenager with something to prove, the feeling intensifies when I'm dumped into a sea of strangers waiting to be checked in at the front desk. And though I can nearly spot the exit doors through the lobby, I take a hard left toward the kitchen and wind myself down another short hallway, past the alcove where Cece hid the day the three of us met.

I stop outside a set of French doors I haven't laid eyes on in half a decade. But when I grip the vintage bronze doorknob on the right, it doesn't give. I try the one next to it, hoping the first was simply locked by mistake, but it, too, remains rigid.

I peer through the glass pane into a library that once fulfilled every childish longing of my soul and wish more than anything I could experience it all again for the first time: running my fingers along the spines of stories that shared their world with me.

"The library requires a staff keycard to open now. Too many break-in attempts after Cece went and got famous on us."

At the sound of Joel's voice at my back, I close my eyes. My lungs pause as he presses in close to reach for the little black box on the left side of the door. Upon his swipe, a light from within glows green, and the doors double click in response. But when I don't make a move for either knob, it flares back to red.

"I thought you were going to lunch with Madison." My breath fogs the glass in front of me.

"And I thought you were going to Aunt Wendy's." He finds my eyes in the door's reflection. "But I happen to like this idea of yours better." He lifts his arm to reveal Cece's manuscript clutched in his hand. "It's the perfect spot to read the next chapter."

This time when he swipes his card and unlocks the doors, I push them open.

The library's welcoming scent ushers me in like an old friend, though so much of this space appears new. The paint is fresh, and there are added rows of shelving backlit by fancy lighting at nearly every angle. I move toward the ornate, fully enclosed display case featuring all four books of the acclaimed Nocturnal Heart series—special editions, bound in leather with gold leaf lettering and gilded pages. Barry gifted me a set two Christmases ago.

I press in for a closer look. Cece's last professional headshot, the one we nicknamed her "sorority girl grin," is framed and propped next to several of her awards and plaques. I touch the protective glass, mindful of the fingerprints I'll leave behind as soon as my hand drops away. But part of me wishes I could leave a permanent mark, the way she left one on me.

"Fog Harbor donated that to our family in Cece's honor."

As I turn from the display case, I feel for the ring on my right index finger and twist it into my palm. "They did?"

"Yes, her first editor, the director there . . ." Joel pauses, and it's clear he can't remember Barry's name.

"Barry Brinkman."

"Yes, Barry. He came up with his wife, actually. They stayed at the hotel for a few nights and took our family to The Steel Pot for dinner. Said he wasn't big on attending funerals but that he was big on paying his respects. He told us some great stories that night—his favorite Cece moments. It did Aunt Wendy's heart good to laugh." He shoves his hands into his pockets. "Honestly, it did us all good."

There's a damp heat behind my eyes as I picture the scene. Barry leaning back in his chair, nursing his third glass of root beer while surrounded by more appetizers than he could eat in a week in order to share with those at his table. The same generous way he shared from his heart.

"When did he visit?"

"A day or two after the new year. We were still taking down the lobby Christmas trees when they arrived." Joel inclines his head to the display case. "This came in a few weeks later—addressed to the hotel with a card dedicating it to the Campbell Library. The signature said it was from Cece's other family at Fog Harbor Books."

I think through the timeline of Barry's retirement, struggling to recall a work environment prior to SaBrina's arrival. November stands out in my mind—a dark month in an obscenely dark year. Time is difficult to keep track of when there is little good being celebrated. But a mental door opens to reveal Barry saying good-bye to his staff *before* Thanksgiving. I remember now because he said he was finally going to give his wife the honeymoon she deserved after forty years of marriage: a month-long vacation in the Maldives over Christmas. He sent me a postcard or two. Maybe even a few more than that. Chip would know the number if I asked him. I was only functioning via the daily reminder alerts Dr. Rogers suggested I set on my phone after beginning therapy with him. Reminder alert questions like: Have I consumed *at least* two meals today? Have I eaten *at least* one fruit or vegetable? Have I drank *at least* three sixteen-ounce glasses of water? For a man who hated the words *at least* when it came to empty grief platitudes, he sure used them a lot with his clients.

I funnel my thoughts to Barry again. To the days at the office following the news of Cece's death.

There were dozens of email threads crossing paths from every department at Fog Harbor. All with similar subject lines to "RE: Cece's Memorial Flowers/Gift Fund." And that didn't include the outpouring from her fans. The onslaught of letters and packages and media coverage was so massive that Barry had to hire two temporary employees to sort it all. I can only imagine how overloaded Cece's P.O. Box in Port Townsend became and who had been in charge of managing it. My guess: I'm looking right at him.

"I remember Fog Harbor sending flower arrangements and cards. And I think there were a few framed pictures from her international book signings, but this . . ." I point to the specialty case and shake my head. "I'd bet my Peloton that this was all Barry's doing."

The corners of Joel's eyes crinkle. "Did you just bet your Peloton?"

Sure, in retrospect, betting a stationary bike sounds pretty lame, but in actuality, it's likely one of my most valuable assets. I don't own a car. I sublease my apartment. And the washer/dryer set I bought two years ago doesn't exactly scream bet-worthy either. But Joel's smile feels like a gift, and I accept it by giving him back one of my own.

"Don't knock it till you try it," I say. "It's a good workout."

"I'd rather do a hundred burpees in the sand than pretend to ride a bike for miles."

I laugh unwillingly, then try to regain the ground I lost. "It's not a pretend bike."

He hikes an eyebrow.

"Okay, it's not mobile," I amend. "But it's responsible for muscles I don't even know the names of."

The glint in his eyes certainly doesn't reflect the platonic expression of a man who shares part-time custody of his dog with another woman. I prop my elbow on the closest bookshelf of western classics—his father's favorite genre—near the front corner of the library, and contemplate asking him about Madison. But the opportunity passes as soon as Joel flips to the second chapter in Cece's memoir, clears his throat, and begins to read.

11

"A Pirate's Life for Me"

Cece, as she was now called by both family and friends, had been right to assume Ingrid's arrival eight months ago would add some mystery and intrigue to her life. But what she hadn't anticipated was the two-for-one package she'd be getting with the Erikson daddy-daughter duo, or the spark of inspiration they would bring.

Her spark of a novel had finally caught fire.

"You should be writing about the great Nordic Vikings, not wasting your time on common sea bandits." Captain Halvor—Hal, for short—stepped away from the helm of her uncle Stephen's docked forty-foot custom charter and squatted into a fight stance, flexing his massive biceps until the fabric of his long-sleeved shirt looked ready to surrender. "Vikings were the true warriors of the sea."

"As long as you don't count the ruthless murderers who raped and pillaged the innocent for their own personal gain," Ingrid spouted flatly without bothering to glance up from the book she was reading on this chilly afternoon in mid-January.

Captain Hal side-eyed his daughter, tugged off his red knit cap, and threw out his arm. "Ingrid, my helmet and my war horn, please."

"Nope," she said plainly, flipping to the next page of her novel.

"*Elskede*, my beloved. Pretend this is my last request. You can't deny a man his last request."

"I can absolutely deny it when it's the same request you ask for at least twice a week." Ingrid released an exasperated sigh. "It's embarrassing."

The corners of Captain Hal's illuminating grin dipped south until Ingrid slammed her book closed and dropped it to the bench. Cece tracked her friend's movements across the bow and up the ladder to the second-story cockpit tower. A moment later she hefted the lid open on a storage box to reveal a bronze Viking helmet and some kind of animal horn the size of her forearm. Without a word, Ingrid returned and tossed them to her father.

In what Cece suspected was a typical response from the gregarious sea captain to his daughter, he pulled her in and smacked a wet kiss to her cheek, followed by a lyrical-sounding string of words in Norwegian that seemed to soften Ingrid's annoyance by half.

Cece watched the fascinating display with wonder. She hadn't been around many father-daughter duos, and certainly none who lived the kind of life she'd been dreaming about since girlhood. Then again, she suspected there weren't too many fathers out there like Captain Halvor Erikson. He was anything but predictable.

Captain Hal fit the snug skull helmet over his head and then brought the horn to his lips.

"Dad, *please* don't—"

The powerful tenor vibrated Cece's eardrums while simultaneously muting every other sound in the marina. She glanced around at the repair men within earshot, each of them paralyzed by the alarming bellow coming from Ingrid's father. An eternity later, when the sound dimmed at the end of his long exhale and he pulled the horn from his mouth, he smiled the kind of conquering grin she'd only ever witnessed in action movies.

"Now, do you know what that sound meant to my ancestors, Curly?"

Cece shook her head, her curls bouncing around her face as she did, smiling at the nickname Ingrid's dad had given her when they'd first met during a hotel staff meeting last summer. With a huff, Ingrid plopped on the bench beside her and rolled her eyes.

"That war was coming," Hal said with an accent that seemed to thicken whenever he spoke of his homeland. "People lived and died by that sound."

"Or were slaughtered in cold blood . . ." Ingrid muttered under her breath.

He held the war horn above his head like a victor's trophy. "To hold this kind of power in the palm of your hands was among the greatest of honors. By a single note, boys became men and corrupt kings were conquered under new rule."

"Bravo! Bravo!" Cece couldn't help but clap at his enthusiasm, wishing she knew a few key phrases in Norwegian to express the depth of her appreciation for the time he'd offered her over these winter weeks when the charter boat was mostly out of commission. That was, other than the rare fishing excursion and the Santa cruises he chartered in mid-December, where Captain Hal hooked ornaments to his beard to match his flashing elf ears. His antics were *almost* enough to convince her to shift her affections from pirates to Vikings, but her loyalty simply ran too deep. More than that, she knew Ingrid would never approve of such a major plot change at this point. They were much too invested in this storyline to start over now.

Captain Hal winked one of his sea blue eyes at her praise and then held up a finger. "Wait here." He ducked inside the main cabin into the living room. Cece watched through the windows as he moved the sofa cushions to the floor and opened a storage container, pulling out a rustic wooden box roughly the length of his forearm.

When he emerged onto the bow again, Ingrid said, "Dad, Cece didn't come for a show-and-tell of your superstitions. She's here to write her own story, remember? The one about *pirates*. She has questions about the ships you've captained."

"Exactly why I will show her a real piece of treasure." The box itself looked to be ancient, with a rickety copper lock and faded nicks, symbols and carvings covering the outside, none of which she could decipher. But just to the right of the lock were a few initials she could easily make out.

HE + SE + IE = family

The initials of Ingrid's father, mother, and her.

He opened the treasure chest to reveal a small hatchet of sorts—one that looked like it should be showcased in a museum and not on a boat docked in harbor. "This is the authentic bearded ax my great-great-great-great-grandfather Ivar passed down through generations. I've never sailed a day at sea without it. It comes with me on every boat I captain, just like it went with my father. It's protected me, so I've protected it. And one day, it will be Ingrid's to protect." He winked as Cece touched the deep grooved marking on the ax handle. "Tell my girl to bring you by our place sometime, and I'll show you some old battle maps you can use for your *research.*" He said the word with an element of amusement that Cece didn't mind in the slightest.

She wanted to jump at the opportunity to see more of his family heir-looms, but over the last eight months, Ingrid had never invited her over to the houseboat she shared with her father, despite the many times Cece hinted at wanting to visit.

Cece noticed Ingrid staring at her father with big, unblinking eyes until Hal finally cleared his throat and said, "If you have a list of questions ready for me, then fire at will, Curly."

"I do have a list," she said tentatively. "But I also enjoy hearing about your life in Norway."

"He only lived there for ten years," Ingrid supplied. "As opposed to the almost forty he's lived in America."

Captain Hal diverted his attention to his only child. "History is as perma-nent as DNA, daughter. And the Viking blood that runs through my veins is the same blood that runs through yours." He pushed his shirt sleeve up his forearm to reveal the curious tattoo Cece had only ever caught glimpses of from afar.

"Is it a map?" she asked. Only her question wasn't answered immediately, at least not by the captain. He was obviously waiting for his daughter to take the lead on this one. After a reluctant moment, Ingrid obliged.

"It's the coordinates of his hometown in Norway. The small fishing village he grew up in with my grandma until they moved to the States."

"Wow . . ." The uttering was more of a breath, and if not for Ingrid's clear annoyance with how long they'd been hanging out with her dad today, Cece would have asked to take a closer look. The ink was jet black against his fair skin, the coordinates small and the words underneath scripted in a language other than English. But even still, she understood what the map represented to him. Not an outline of a random location he once lived, but a *home*.

Home was a concept she'd struggled to understand for some time now. Did she have a home? Was it the place she was born? The place she lived with her two parents before her father left? Or was it here, in the town she'd grown up treating like nothing more than an annual vacation spot to visit her only cousin at her aunt and uncle's grand hotel?

Perhaps home meant something else altogether, something she hadn't quite figured out yet.

The questions bobbed inside her head like buoys as she followed the captain around her uncle's giant boat, ticking off each one of her research questions so she could write her next scene accurately. That was, as long as rule-follower Joel agreed to it. But she imagined her cousin would have little reason for pushback once she told him who would be involved. Because if Ingrid was to be her muse for Ember . . . then she knew Joel would do whatever it took to become her muse for Merrick.

She had no doubt he'd be calling the second his shift was over at the front desk.

As Captain Hal answered the last question on her list today—the one having to do with storm protocols and procedures—she rubbed her lips and glanced at Ingrid, who was, once again, nose down in a fantasy novel.

"Um, Captain Hal?" Cece started, zipping her coat to her chin and tucking her notebook underneath her arm. "I actually have one last question for you, only it doesn't have much to do with my research."

He cocked an eyebrow, amusement lurking behind his robust expression.

"With your permission, I'd like to hold an on-location writing session tonight. Here, if possible."

"Here, on the cruiser?" he asked, and she nodded. "And what would this *session* involve?"

"Just your permission to come aboard after dark." She held up her palm as if she was ready to recite a pledge. "It will only be the three of us—and only for the purposes of writing."

He narrowed his eyes, stroked his auburn beard. "And who is *the three of us?*"

"Ingrid, Joel, and myself, sir."

His brilliant azure eyes flicked to where his daughter sat immersed in story. "Why not ask your uncle? It's his boat."

Apparently, her silence was easy enough to decode. Uncle Stephen may be generous, but he wasn't a man who often colored outside the lines. He was black and white. Straight and narrow. Rules, rules, rules. Much like his son.

But she'd be willing to bet that Captain Hal was a man who thrived in the gray.

He leaned in close to keep their conversation confidential, and Cece's nose prickled at the hint of something sweetly sour on his breath. "And this cousin of yours, he's a good boy?"

"Obnoxiously so, yes." No need to stretch the truth there. If not for Ingrid, Joel would be the first to boycott this entire plan. But the Joel of last June was not the Joel of this January.

Hal chuckled and bobbed his chin. "I'll expect you to treat this vessel with the same respect you treat your uncle's hotel."

"Yes, sir. Of course."

"And you'll lock everything up before you leave the dock."

"Absolutely."

His eyes softened to a look Cece had only ever seen him give his daughter. "You've been a good friend to my girl—getting her head out of those books and into the real world. Keep it up."

Cece beamed at his high praise. "You should know she's been an even better friend to me. Like the sister I've always wanted."

He considered her for another moment before adding, "No loud music. No drinking. No shenanigans of any kind. And not a soul outside the three of you. Got it?"

"Yes, sir. Thank you, sir!" She spun to join Ingrid and tell her the plan for tonight when Hal called after her once again.

"*Curly.*"

She twisted back and a rogue curl caught between her chapped lips. She blew it away. "Yes, sir?"

"You're positive you don't want to write about the great Nordic Vikings?"

Her cheeks stretched so wide they crinkled her eyes. "I'm afraid it will always be a pirate's life for me."

He waved her off with a teasing gleam in his eye, and for just a moment, it felt like the only approval she'd ever need.

"I've been thinking," Cece announced as she tossed a stack of pillows for Ingrid to shove into the rolling laundry cart that would aid them in their escape to the parking lot via the staff elevators. Cece could hardly wait to see Joel's face when she told him they were headed to the marina overnight. Though Cece hadn't specifically asked Captain Hal for permission to sleep aboard the boat, he also hadn't mentioned a time they'd need to disembark. A fact Cece had taken note of when he slipped her the key earlier that afternoon. "What if you and I played matchmaker? My mom and your dad."

"What?" Ingrid jerked to a sitting position, her elbow accidentally knocking a line of travel-sized toiletries to the cement floor. She shook her head and crawled to gather the scattered bottles. "No way. Your mom is way too sweet and trusting, and my dad is—"

"Literally the coolest guy I've ever met. Believe me, my mom could use some adventure in her life. Her idea of a good time is getting up before sunrise to walk the beach. Oh, and checking out art books from the library that she never does anything with." Cece rolled her eyes. "We could totally set them up on an awesome blind date in town." Cece flung her arms out wide. "Just think how incredible it would be if they hit it off! We could be sisters—the *real* kind."

Ingrid slumped back on her haunches, as if considering the rich payoff of such a brilliant plan: the two of them legally bound together for life as sisters! Cece was certain Ingrid wanted that as much as she did—they'd discussed their desire for a sibling multiple times during the nights Ingrid stayed over. In fact, they'd discussed many of their shared desires. Whatever Ingrid did or did not believe about God, Cece knew the two of them had been brought together for a purpose. And perhaps that purpose was to become a family.

"I think you've watched *The Parent Trap* too many times." Ingrid didn't glance up as she finished restocking the toiletries on the shelf. "Besides, my dad doesn't date."

"First of all, there's no such thing as too many times. That movie's a classic." Cece heaved the three queen-size comforters into the belly of the canvas opening one at a time. "And second of all, it's not like my mom's dated anyone since my dad left us, either. It only takes the right person to . . ."

She stopped speaking as soon as she saw the distressed expression on Ingrid's face, one she'd never been privy to before.

"Ingrid, you okay?" The instant she crouched beside her friend, understanding punched her through the heart. "Oh . . . gosh. It's your mom, isn't it?" Cece cringed at her own careless insensitivity. "I'm so sorry. I didn't mean to—I wasn't thinking. I know it must be different for you than it is for me. My dad chose to walk away from us, but your mom didn't have a choice. I know if she did, she would have stayed with you and your dad forever." Cece gripped Ingrid's hand and squeezed. "Let's forget I said anything about all that, okay? It's just that you're my best friend, and I never want that to change."

Ingrid's shaky smile strengthened when she squeezed back. "You're mine, too, the best friend I always hoped I'd find."

"So that would make me what, then? Just the dude who drives the get-away car for Cece's elaborate schemes?" Joel stood in the doorway, his hands anchored to his hips and his gaze anchored on Ingrid. He gave her a wink before swiping a hand through his shower-damp hair. Another new development when it came to Cece's cousin—no longer did he simply shed his nametag, tie, and staff vest to meet up with them in whatever rumpled state he was in. Nope, now he was into long showers and spritzes of cologne. And Cece rarely missed an opportunity to tease him about it, though she'd let it slide today.

"At least you're not in denial about your rightful place, Joel," Cece sassed, relieved to see a genuine smile return to Ingrid's face.

Her cousin assessed the clean pile of pillows and bedding in the cart at their backs. "And how exactly are my services required tonight?" He reached down to help Cece to her feet, and she observed as he did the same for Ingrid that their hands stayed connected three seconds longer than necessary. She also didn't miss the way her cousin stroked Ingrid's knuckles with his thumb just before he released his hold on her.

"Glad you asked." Cece beamed at the two of them, finally ready to reveal her plan for her next scene. "Because tonight, Ember and Merrick will learn to dance aboard a sleepy ship under the moon's magnanimous glow."

The jaws of her muses slacked open, which caused Cece's enthusiasm to skyrocket. "Which means we should probably head to the marina now because I have a lot to write before my breakfast shift starts tomorrow at six."

The three of them made quick work of loading Joel's trunk, arriving at the marina just after ten that evening. And just like Cece predicted, Joel's obvious displeasure regarding the unspecified terms surrounding their sleepover wasn't enough to keep him from rolling with Cece's plan. The two girls had told their parents they'd be staying together at the hotel, and Joel hadn't bothered to say much of anything to Uncle Stephen and Aunt Patti. He said it was because he was only a couple of weeks shy of eighteen, but Cece knew the real reason was because Joel had never given his folks reason to doubt he'd be anywhere other than where he was supposed to be.

Cece set her bag inside the cabin on the cozy chair next to the galley kitchen, complete with a sink, microwave, and stove. Her uncle hadn't shortchanged himself on this purchase whatsoever. She'd heard many a hotel guest say it was the nicest charter in Port Townsend.

She met Ingrid on the open deck at the stern, curious about something she'd meant to ask her earlier today. "Is this cruiser set up like your houseboat, Ingrid?" She'd wondered if Ingrid's bedroom was as private as the captain's bunk room downstairs.

"Not really." Ingrid's breath made tiny cloud-like puffs in the night air as she layered herself in warmth, tugging on an extra pair of socks and then a knit stocking cap like the one Cece had seen Captain Hal wear. Ingrid rubbed her bare hands together, cupping them to her mouth to heat them with her breath. The two girls had walked the length of the dock in search of Ingrid's lost gloves to no avail.

After Joel dropped the rest of their overnight supplies inside the cabin, his concerned eyes found Ingrid immediately. "Here, take mine." He ripped his gloves from his hands. "You'll need these more than I do if we're going to stay out here for as long as Cece intends."

"I'm sure mine will turn up somewhere."

"Well, until they do, you can wear these. I've already warmed them for you, see?" He slipped each one over Ingrid's frozen hands, and Cece quickly reached for the notebook tucked safely inside her tote bag. She couldn't afford to miss a single moment of character inspiration. Apparently, these two weren't waiting for the dance floor.

For the next several minutes, Cece set the scene on paper, opening a valve in her mind and dumping words onto a clean page, all while she observed her subjects—how they moved, touched, and spoke to each other in soft tones. Two pages in, Cece directed them to cinch in close, giving instructions on where they should place their hands and which way she needed them to sway and move even though there was no music to keep time. After a single rotation, Joel went inside for a spare blanket and curled it around Ingrid's shoulders like a cape, tucking the ends beneath the collar of her coat and whispering something in her ear Cece couldn't quite hear. She was too busy transcribing the soundtrack of lapping water against the boat and the rustle of lowered sails around the marina.

When Joel's hands settled securely around Ingrid's lower back, Cece made sure to note the way her heroine studied her hero—as if his eyes held the answer to a thousand unwished hopes.

Even sitting cross-legged underneath two hotel quilts, she was chilled, but not enough to break for the heated space inside quite yet. Cece scrawled her thoughts on paper as fast as her frozen fingers would move. She lost all sense of time, place, and reality. She was deep into the Kingdom of Cardithia. Deep into the minds and hearts of her characters.

She didn't know when Joel and Ingrid had stopped dancing, but when she finally glanced up, long after midnight, the two were snuggled together under quilts on the stern, so close their noses were practically touching. Ingrid must have been teasing Joel about something—as Joel only made that expression when he was the brunt of one of her jokes.

Ingrid tipped her head back with a muted laugh and then immediately startled when she found Cece observing them.

"Oh, sorry," she said apologetically, pulling the blanket higher. "We were trying not to interrupt your focus. Did you finish?"

"Not quite, but almost," Cece said, though in truth, she'd been struggling with how to wrap this chapter up for a while now, crossing out paragraph after paragraph, looking for the right emotional hook to close out the scene.

"Then would you mind if we all went inside?" Ingrid's teeth chattered as she spoke. "My toes went numb a while ago."

"Sure," Cece agreed, smiling. "Let's go get warm."

Together, they moved into the main cabin and Cece pointed to the chair. "I'll take that spot so I can finish up while you two get situated for the night."

Joel immediately began preparing beds for the three of them on the floor of the cruiser's main cabin, dragging the bunkbed mattresses up the short stairway into the living area and shoving them together. Next were a few layers of the hotel's down comforters.

Cece took her seat across from them, enjoying the thaw of her frozen body as she reopened her notebook and plugged in her headphones to listen to some theme music from *Pirates of the Caribbean*. She chuckled as Ingrid, who looked like a walking burrito, dropped to the makeshift bed in one swift collapse before snuggling her head into a king-size pillow. Joel laughed, too, and then mimicked her less-than-graceful landing. He propped his head on his elbow and stared unabashedly at Ingrid.

With stealth-like skills, Cece slipped out one of her wired earbuds, hiding the cord in the hood of her sweatshirt as she peered through the dim light at the two people she cared for most in the world outside of her mother.

"You warm enough?" Joel asked Ingrid, his voice a notch above a whisper. "I can grab another blanket from my car if not."

"Yes, I'm good now," Ingrid said. "Thank you."

"I might need proof of that. You were shivering pretty hard a minute ago."

"Is that why you're weirdly trying to pat my face right now?"

"It wouldn't be weird if you stopped squirming," he teased. "I'm trying to take the temperature of your nose. It's what my mom always did when she was trying to convince me I needed to wear a coat when I was younger."

"Sounds quite scientific."

"Oh, it is." The outline of Joel's arm was white-washed under the moon's glow; even still, Cece could clearly see him touch Ingrid's nose. "Still feels pink to me."

"Not sure my nose has ever been pink. I'm half Chinook, remember?"

"I could never forget, trust me."

Ingrid propped her head on the heel of her hand, mirroring Joel's position. Then he reached out to touch the black ring on her finger.

"I'm guessing this must have a story." Joel's voice was a curious kind of content. "I've never seen you without it."

"I don't take it off," Ingrid supplied easily. "My mom had one just like it before I was born; my dad found it for her on a beach not too far from here. It was the only ring she wore—she wasn't one for fancy jewelry. It's said to be one of the rarest types of sea glass. The center is almost transparent, with a purple hue you can only see when the light shines through it. Most are over a hundred years old when they get to this stage."

"Cece told me you call sea glass 'ocean tears.'"

Cece quickly lowered her eyes back to her notebook. It was dark and shadowy inside the cabin, but the moon shone bright through the windows, casting an almost magical illumination on her cousin and best friend.

"My dad started calling them that after my mom died."

"So this ring wasn't hers?"

"No, Mom lost hers when we were swimming, back before she got sick. I don't remember it, but my dad said she cried for a week. He searched every beach to find her another one, even tried to buy one to replace it, but never found one large enough to fit into a setting. Until my fifteenth birthday. Dad and I were here, actually. In Port Townsend on a short fishing run. And the second we stepped out of the marina, it was there on the shore, just sitting next to my dad's big foot. He told me it must be a kiss from my mom to me. He's not really into birthday presents or gifts at all, but that year he paid for me to get it set into this band. I've worn it ever since and have never seen another one like it."

"That's a better story than I would have guessed."

Joel tucked a strand of hair behind Ingrid's ear, his hushed voice unusually tender. "Will you tell me about her? How old were you when she passed?"

Cece set her pen down and strained to hear how Ingrid would answer this sensitive line of questioning. Joel seemed to elicit something different from her friend. And strangely, Cece didn't mind being on the outside looking in this time.

"She died two weeks after my sixth birthday, almost twelve years ago now. My mom was sick for a long time. It's hard for me to remember moments with her outside of her bed." She paused. "I used to imagine what she'd look like using a vacuum or making dinner at a stovetop or walking to the playground with me like the moms I saw in my children's books, but I don't have actual memories of her doing any of those things." She took a second before restarting. "She taught me to love books and taught me to read by the time I was four. I was reading at a fourth-grade level when she passed away. I read everything I could get my hands on."

"Smarty," Joel teased quietly, and Ingrid smiled.

"Hardly. I'm sure there's so much I've missed by schooling myself on the boat—in math, especially. But Dad always says life experience is more important than book smarts."

"But you want to go to college?"

"More than anything. I want to understand the classics, how to think and speak about them, maybe even how to teach my own literature class someday."

"I'm sure your mom would be proud." Joel wrapped a strand of her hair around his fingers.

Ingrid made a contemplative noise. "There is this one thing I remember about her clearly—something she did only for me."

Joel released her hair, giving her his undivided attention. "Tell me."

"Toward the end of her life, when speaking took too much of her strength, I would crawl into her bed beside her, and she would slip her hand over her heart like this"—Ingrid lowered the blankets to flatten her palm to her chest—"and then she'd pat it three times. Once for every word." Cece strained to hear the sound of each one of the three thumps. "It was how she told me she loved me. And then I would tell her back the same way. It was our own secret language, not even my dad knew about it."

Joel's voice sounded constricted when he spoke again. "She sounds really special. Like you. Your dad's a pretty lucky guy."

"Not sure he'd agree with the lucky part." Ingrid shifted in the blankets and propped her head on the pillow, tugging the blankets underneath her chin. "He's missed out on a lot because of me. A lot of opportunities and jobs he would have taken if he wasn't stuck raising a daughter on his own."

"And yet I've heard him boast about you to the entire hotel staff on more occasions than I can count. He thinks you're brilliant, Indy. And I happen to agree with him."

She yawned and lowered her head once again, her silky hair spilling like ink over the crisp white pillowcase. "You're too nice to me."

He stroked her hair. "Not possible."

"I'm afraid if you keep that up I'll miss my watch alarm to meet my dad in the morning. He has a fishing job I need to help him with."

"Then I'll stay awake for both of us. I don't work till the afternoon anyway. You should sleep."

"I'm just gonna rest my eyes for a minute."

"Good night, Indy," Joel said in a tone that caused goosebumps to rise on Cece's arms.

The sleepy sound Ingrid muffled in reply indicated she was already half-way to dreamland. But as Cece observed the tender strokes of Joel's hand over her best friend's hair, she realized with sudden clarity that there might be another way—a better way—for Ingrid to become a permanent fixture in her family. One that didn't involve blind dates or matchmaking schemes involving Captain Hal and her mother. Because maybe whatever Ingrid and Joel shared ran deeper than the romantic inspiration Cece needed for her two muses. Maybe it ran so deep that the only thing she needed to do now was sit back and watch fiction become reality.

12

As Joel reads the final line aloud, the air in the library thins, making me incredibly aware of the solid bookcase to my right. I sag against it, pressing my fingertips into the woodgrain of the shelf while I try not to picture my father in a Viking hat with a war horn pressed to his mouth or hear his boisterous belly laugh that never failed to elicit one of my own. I try not to think about the way things should have been.

Joel says my name, and his voice sounds too far away and far too close at the same time.

I start to shake my head to tell him I'm fine, but the fat, hot tears filling my eyes are a dead giveaway I'm lying to him. I'm always lying to him.

I swipe at my cheeks and stage a protest against my tears until they stand down.

Joel sets the manuscript on the glass table behind him, and though his hands are no longer occupied, he doesn't reach for me. He doesn't move at all. He simply takes me in as if I'm a lit firework. And why shouldn't he be cautious? I'm the one who took all conversations pertaining to my father off the table. And yet Cece had gone and made Captain Hal into a conversational centerpiece so large it obstructs the view of everything else.

I stare down at my walking shoes as one rebellious tear slips from my bottom lashes, drips off my chin, and splashes into the center of my crisscross laces. "I'd forgotten how fun he could be," I say. "How he was in the in-between times. I'd forgotten all about that stupid horn and ridiculous hat." My throat is impossibly thick and my swallow impossibly loud. "How could Cece remember so many details about one random winter day years ago when I can hardly remember . . ." *Anything good at all anymore.* I don't speak the words aloud. They're too condemning. Too heavy to hold in my mouth let alone in my heart. I hear Dr. Rogers's voice inside my head, imploring me to go there, instructing me to step into the black hole I fear and grant myself permission to access the pain of a lost little girl who never knew which version of her daddy she'd wake up to in the morning.

Joel slides his hand across the bookshelf until it sits only millimeters from my own. His decision to remain quiet appears calculated. Only by the way he's staring at me, it doesn't seem like a punishment at all. My mind jogs back to the conversation in Cece's kitchen twenty-four hours ago, first to my harsh outburst and then to Joel's insightful assessment after I'd accused him of treating me like a broken little bird.

When I find the courage to speak, my voice is paper-thin. "What you said yesterday, about me punishing myself." Reluctantly, I nod. "It's not the first time I've heard that. My therapist has said something similar."

Joel spurs me on with his patient gaze.

"There's no manual on grieving a man like my father. If there was, I would have read it by now." An airy laugh escapes me. "Well, I would if I could actually read it, that is."

At the frustration in my tone, the crease between Joel's brows deepens. "*If* you could actually read it?"

I can see him trying to work out the context of my comment. But I know he won't be able to get there on his own. It took the better part of a year in therapy for me to understand it myself. And while I've had the practice of explaining it to two people now, sharing it with Joel is a different kind of real. A different kind of loss. Neither my therapist nor my assistant ever knew Ingrid the Bookworm, the girl who carried a novel curled in her back pocket wherever she went just so she could stay close to a world far different from her own. But Joel had known that girl well. He had more than known her.

I glide my tongue along the backside of my bottom teeth and then rub my lips together. "I've lost my ability to . . . to get lost in a book. It started soon after Cece . . ." I let the ending of that sentence hang, but Joel nods for me to continue. "It's so much work to concentrate on even a single page of words. I can see them, I can read them, but sometimes it takes me four or five passes to comprehend what I've just read. I took so many online assessments, trying to understand what was wrong with me. Like maybe I developed some kind of late-onset dyslexia or another type of neurological condition. And I suppose it is that, in a way. Dr. Rogers says it's a trauma response. Not ideal for an editor." I try to laugh, but it comes out like a pitiful-sounding cough. "Between the app I found that converts the screen-shot pages of my manuscripts to audible narration and the help of my assistant, I've managed to make it work." *Barely.* I lift my gaze to his. "But the pictures my mind used to create while I read . . . those have all but disappeared, and I'm not sure if they'll return."

There's a part of me that wonders if he'll think I deserve this—my penance for choosing to cling to a life submersed in fiction rather than deal with a reality I didn't have the tools for. The missing pieces surrounding my father's drowning. The broken promises from the man who vowed to look after him while I was at school. The secrets he kept from me when my father needed more than Joel knew how to handle on his own.

In a subtle movement, Joel's hand covers mine. And when he speaks, the gentle affection of his tone holds the power to crush me into a thousand tiny pieces. "I'm so sorry, Indy."

And somehow, I know this *sorry* encompasses so much more than polite sympathy. This *sorry* is backdated to a night neither of us can change no matter how much we want to. I stare down at his hand on mine as if this is still the role he plays in my life: to protect me at all costs. Only that cost proved too much for us both.

"I am, too." With these words, something inside me starts to shift. The sensation is so odd it's almost peaceful, which makes no sense, given our history. Yet there's a stillness present that wasn't present before. And perhaps it's why I decide to color inside the lines for him a little more. "I'd all but convinced myself the package Marshall had for us was Cece's lost manuscript." I swallow. "I needed it to be, not only for her fans or even for my publisher. But for me, too." A truth I hadn't even admitted to Chip. "I hoped the discovery of *The Fate of Kings* would be the antidote I needed to fix whatever's wrong with me. That if I could somehow bring closure to her characters, to her entire series, that it might also bring closure to me." I shake my head and release a soft laugh, gently extricating my hand from his hold. "I sound like a fool."

"No, you sound like someone willing to do whatever it takes to be healed." His gaze lights a flame in my chest. "If I knew where to find it, I'd tell you."

I want to believe him, yearn to believe him even . . . yet he'd kept something from me before. Something far more vital than a missing manuscript.

"I just wish I could understand the reason she didn't tell me where to find it. It doesn't make sense."

An old Carole King song I assigned to a contact in my phone long ago blares from my pocket and jumpstarts my heart. *Wendy.* Joel tells me to go ahead.

"Wendy? Hi," I say in way of greeting.

"Ingrid, hello, I'm so sorry I missed your calls earlier. I was already out on the beach when I realized I'd left my phone at home. Are you still free this afternoon? I'm not planning on going out again today, I've taken on a bit of a project in my yard. But I'd enjoy your company if you'd like to join me."

"Of course, yes. I'd like that very much." I glance at my watch, wondering if we'd still have time to stop by the nursery before it closes this evening. By the sounds of it, she's already knee-deep in the garden beds lining her backyard. "I can be there in about thirty minutes or so if that's good? I'll be coming from the hotel, on foot."

As we finalize plans and as I ask what I might pick up from the corner market on my way to her place, Joel makes no attempt to avert his gaze. Instead, his interest in my conversation only seems to intensify the longer I stay on the phone with his aunt.

He digs into his pocket after I hang up and places something cold in my free hand.

"What is . . ." *Keys.*

"Take my car," he insists. "It's parked in the staff lot below."

I shake my head and try to give them back. I've seen Joel's fancy, made-to-look-vintage sports car, and I'm not about to be responsible for something that valuable. But he stuffs his hands into his pockets and rocks back a step. "That walk is almost entirely uphill. It will take you way longer than thirty minutes, especially if you're planning to stop by the market first." He seems to read all the excuses I'm compiling in my mind when he adds, "Let's not make this into a bigger deal than it needs to be. It's only a car. And you need it more than I do today."

My palm is still open, the keys still there as if I have some right to them or to their owner. Only I have no rights to either. "I haven't driven anything but an automatic in years, Joel."

"The clutch on my old Honda would take deep offense to that after all you two went through together," he says with a hint of amusement as we share a knowing look that throws me back in time to the night Joel tried to teach me how to drive a manual after working the late shift at the hotel. I stalled out so many times I worried I was doing irreparable damage to his transmission, but he refused to give up on me until I was comfortable shifting into every gear with confidence. "But even so, you're in luck. It's not a manual."

"It's not?" The revelation is so unexpected I feel my eyebrows revolt. "But you always said automatics were made for lazy, distracted drivers."

"Wouldn't be the first time I was wrong about what the future held."

I close my fist around the keys, press the cool teeth into my flesh. I have nothing to say to that. Thankfully, Joel doesn't wait for a response.

"I can get a ride over to Cece's place in the morning to pick it up. Maybe we could get in another chapter or two if you're up for it?"

I nod slowly. "As long as you're sure."

"Positive," he says, his gaze reflective with thoughts I wish I could still read.

I retreat a step and offer a wave as I backtrack to the library doors. "Well, thank you. I appreciate—"

"Ingrid." His tone is so arresting, it locks my knees in place. "There are a few things you should know about Aunt Wendy before you go."

Something like acid pools in my abdomen. "Okay?"

He pushes a hand through his hair and grips the back of his neck. "Up until about three months ago, things were pretty dark for her. There were times we weren't sure if . . ." He pauses, closes his mouth, then seems to redirect the avenue of his thoughts. "There was very little light to be found in Aunt Wendy's eyes, and I wasn't sure if it would ever return or even if it could return. And then one day, she found something that lit a spark. And every day that spark seems to grow a bit brighter." He stares at me. "I know she'll want to show you everything herself, but I think it's only right you know the tremendous progress she's made over these past few weeks and months. She's taken a lot of steps to get healthy. She's eating again, going on beach walks again, and my mom told me she went out for dinner last weekend with a couple of girlfriends from her grief group. They've been a good support to her."

And by the concern etched onto Joel's face, it's obvious they aren't the only ones. "You have, too."

In typical Joel style, he doesn't pause to credit himself. "I know it will be good for her to see you, to spend time with you. . . ." He stops, his unspoken words dangling just inside my reach.

"But you're worried about a setback."

His nod is painful. "She can't lose the light again."

The raw conviction in Joel's voice takes me back to that day on the beach with him, to those tense moments after we left the attorney's office when he'd described his involvement in Cece's estate, all the requirements he met for reports and documentation. *"And I've done every bit of it for her, for Cece."* For the first time, I'm beginning to understand the burden he's been carrying since her death. All the days, weeks, months of taking on extra work, extra responsibility, extra stress loads so that others in his family wouldn't have to. I know the weight of the loyalty he wears well. I know its strength and its depth and its overwhelming chokehold of control. Because it was Joel's loyalty to me that kept me from saving my father from himself.

When I can finally form an adequate reply, my throat is hoarse. "I promise I'll be careful with her."

"I believe you will."

13

It's rare a person has the opportunity to sit in the driver's seat of someone else's life. But that's exactly what I'm doing now: sitting in Joel's fancy driver's seat. Over the years, I've driven my fair share of rental cars for out-of-state meetings and writers' conferences, but most of those cars were economy selections leased on my publisher's dime. I've never sat in anything so pristine, much less anything with a touch-screen display on the dash. The black leather interior is polished and pristine, as is the dark woodgrain around the chrome control in the center console. It's immediately apparent that no "new car smell" air freshener hanging in a Quick Mart can duplicate the real thing.

Even still, despite the newness, my entire body prickles with nostalgia as I click in my seatbelt, start the engine, and pull out of the hotel parking lot. It's not only remembering the night Joel taught me how to drive from the passenger seat of his old Honda that has my mind drifting back to the past, but the trademark way he positioned his hands on the steering wheel and how he always kept the classic rock station set a notch below what could be deciphered by the human ear. Just like how it's set now.

My vision takes on a wide-lens approach to the scenery all around me as I pull onto Water Street. From behind the many Victorian-era houses edging the coast, the beach slips in and out of focus like an old filmstrip, and I feel my mind begin to drift again. How many summer days did the three of us navigate these roads together, with Cece's face continually popping in between our two front seats while she threatened mutiny if Joel didn't turn up the radio? There'd been so many late-night runs for salty fries and chocolate milkshakes. So many spontaneous day trips to Seattle when all our work schedules aligned. So many adventures lived out as fodder for Cece's characters. It's then I remember the last scene Joel read for us today—the one of us dancing to the soundtrack of nocturnal waves, of me huddled in close and speaking in teasing tones, of him running his fingers through my hair as I told him about my mother's final days on earth.

I wrap my hands around the lower rim of the steering wheel in an all too familiar grip and imagine, for just a moment, that Joel's hands are here, too. That the two of us are on our way to his aunt's house to pick up Cece for a blackberry lemonade slush or a trip to the lighthouse after dark. But I keep the pages turning quickly in my mind, unwilling to settle on any one thought for too long.

After a quick stop at the market, I take the first right onto the Campbells' property, where their gorgeously restored coral and teal Queen Anne mansion welcomes me with rows of apple blossom trees inside a white picket fence. I slow my speed to a crawl and veer off the main driveway to a short gravel alley that divides Stephen and Patti's property from Wendy's.

The way Wendy always told it, it wasn't until after Stephen and Patti gifted her the small lot behind their grand home that she seriously considered a permanent move to Port Townsend. She'd been heartbroken after her husband left, but it was Cece she'd worried about most when the divorce was finalized. And it was also Cece she was willing to uproot her life in Nevada for—to create a new definition of home for them both.

The property they moved to, complete with a carriage house that was likely built for the caretakers of the mansion in the late 1800s, needed some massive TLC, much like the main house had when the Campbells first moved to the peninsula a decade prior. It had taken Wendy over a year and every dime she'd saved to restore it, but she'd done it. With finishing touches like scalloped shingles, gabled ends, and a wraparound porch, the vintage charm of this place more than makes up for the lack of closet space. As does her view of the Sound from her back gardens.

I tap the responsive gearshift into park and stare up at the miniature, multi-colored gingerbread house in front of me and will myself to cycle my breathing the way Dr. Rogers coached me during our last video call. Inhale for two, hold for two, exhale for two, hold for two. Repeat.

Though I stayed here with Wendy and Patti during Cece's memorial weekend last September, it feels much, much longer than that. It's as if those seventy-two hours of trance-like living never even happened. Only, they did. And unlike me, Wendy has remained here. In the same town, in the same house, in the same grief-stricken existence I refused.

I blink the somber thoughts away and exit the car on steady legs. Even as I walk the cobblestone path with grocery bags dangling from my arms, my efforts here today feel too little, too late. Then again, there's nothing I'd ever be able to give Wendy that could equal what she's given to me over the years.

I knock on her whimsical plum-colored door. And then knock again. It's only after the fourth time, just when I'm about to reach for my phone and call her, that Wendy appears in the doorframe with a smile that looks far less wilted than it did Saturday night at the birthday dinner. She swipes a graying curl off her cheek and behind her ear. "Oh, Ingrid—sorry! I got caught up out back and only heard someone knocking when I came in for some water. I figured you'd use your key when you arrived." She pulls me into a hug, and I don't hesitate to hug her back, though my arms are still loaded with groceries. "I hope you haven't been standing out here too long in the sun."

I assure her I haven't.

She welcomes me inside, and I'm struck by how right Joel is about the spark of light in her eyes. Whatever's keeping Wendy so busy out back has brightened her entire countenance since last I saw her. My chest warms at the pinch of peach in her cheeks and the way her mass of curls is pulled back by a sheer blue scarf that wraps the crown of her head and ties at the nape of her neck. She's even donned an old smock I recognize from years past. A wave of anticipation flares at the prospect of assisting her in the revival of her garden.

"Here, let me take a couple of those bags from you. We can set them in the kitchen before I take you out back. But next time, just use your house key."

"I'm afraid I don't have it with me." Truth is, my privileges to that key should be revoked.

She frowns slightly. "I'll have Joel make a copy for you at the hardware store. I'll send him a text as soon as we get settled."

When she closes the door behind me, my throat's too tight to respond as all I can picture is the card she pushed through the vent of my staff locker a week after she and Cece moved out of room 312. Inside the card's fold was one of the hotel gift shop's most popular anchor keychains with a single gold key attached to it and a simple note that read:

Our home is your home, Ingrid. You're welcome to stay with us any time, for however long you need. No questions asked.

XoXo,
Wendy

At eighteen, I didn't understand everything involved in a house renovation, but I definitely understood the desire for something solid and permanent under my feet. For something that didn't leak during a heavy rain or howl in the night from the wind. For something that, no matter how many well-intentioned promises were made, would finally be more than a Plan B. What Wendy had extended to me out of love for her daughter that day was so much more than a house key. It was a home.

For a short stint of time, I got to experience potted plants sunbathing on window ledges, dinner leftovers stacked in plastic containers in a full fridge, and colorful shower curtains with matching bath mats and fuzzy hand towels. And a reserved shelf in the linen closet of blankets and pillows purchased just for me.

"I'll admit, you're only the third person I've shown my little project to. And I hope you'll be honest with me—the way you're honest with your authors."

Her words make me a bit nervous as I think back to what Joel said in the library, about doing everything in my power to keep the light on. If being honest with Wendy meant dimming her light in any way, then I'd have to find a way around the truth, using my professional let-her-down-gently approach while still encouraging her efforts.

"Of course," I say with a pop of optimism. "I hope you've saved some jobs for me to help with."

She smiles and tips her head to lead me through a home that's remained somewhat of a time capsule inside my mind. We head straight for the kitchen to deposit the groceries, but all the while my eyes travel over every surface at hyper speed, simultaneously taking note of the old and familiar as well as the new and different.

She stops to stare me straight in the eyes. "You can't know how good it does my heart to have you here."

"It does my heart good, too."

We approach her back patio doors and I squint as the sun pours over me at such an angle that it's impossible to see beyond the glare of the glass. But as soon as I step onto the shaded patio, my breath hitches, and I blink several times at the view in front of me.

There's not a single garden bed to be found in her entire yard.

In their place is an assortment of outdoor furniture grouped by chairs, tables, benches, and stools. And next to them all are buckets of glittering, beach-tumbled ocean tears.

The sight is so arresting it takes me a minute to find my bearings.

Where there was once soil, seeds, fertilizer, and tools to tend to Wendy's prized flowers, there are now paintbrushes, gloves, and large cans of epoxy. A compact Bluetooth speaker is propped onto a work bench where a soulful gospel song croons about joy.

I scan the inventory of furniture—ten, maybe twelve pieces or so—and work to solve a puzzle without being handed any of the edge or corner pieces. Is Wendy put in charge of collecting donations for some sort of outdoor hotel auction?

"Joel probably thinks I've lost my mind, asking him to help me collect used furniture from around the community. But every time he brings me a piece destined for the dump, I'm shocked by how much life is left in it. And how willing someone was to just throw it away."

I'm listening to Wendy as I cross the lawn to her workstation, drawn to a shimmering array of colors I can't quite make sense of from this far out. But once I'm close enough to understand what I'm seeing, my heart stutters at the beauty of it. On the surface of a large circular patio table, a mosaic of ocean tears mimics the feel of a stained glass window in an old church—equally captivating and inspiring.

I touch the smooth, epoxied surface, studying the illuminated scene of ocean, surf, and a sky at sunrise. It's absolutely breathtaking. "You made this?"

She's standing close now, her eyes set on mine, her hands cupped tightly in front of her as if she's nervous. "Yes. It's the largest one I've done so far. The size made it fairly challenging. . . ."

Her voice trails off, but I can't stop touching it, can't stop running my fingers along the foamy white surf she managed to recreate out of tiny pieces of cloudy sea glass and beach pebbles. I knew Wendy was crafty—I'd seen her transform pitiful, wilted flowers into heart-melting bouquets time and time again. I'd watched her cast fresh vision on stale window displays and tired lobby decor and select furnishings for events and parties far grander than anything she'd choose to attend herself.

But this . . . this is pure artistry.

"I've never seen anything like this. It's stunning. I'm not sure I even have words for how beautiful this is, Wendy. Or how special."

"Really?" When she clasps her hands over her mouth, tears climb my throat.

Wendy's relief releases another layer of vibrancy to her eyes, and I know right then that even if my part in this project only involves scraping chewed gum off patio chairs that have sat in the summer sun for weeks, I'll do it. I'll do anything to see her thrive.

"I'd love to hear the story behind how all this started," I say, looking for more of her finished work. I spot two in the shade by the fence line, though I can't make out their design from here, just the high-gloss sheen of epoxy: a dainty metal tabletop no bigger than a bar stool with a glass overlay, and a painted garden chair with an artsy seat thanks to Wendy's creativity.

She gestures to the house. "How about I grab us some lemonade first, and then we can prep my newest donation while we chat. As long as you don't mind? It needs a good scrubbing before I can map out the design and hunt for colors."

"I'd love to help. Which one is it?"

She points to a garden bench with chipping robin's-egg-blue paint and a plethora of other issues, the most obvious of which is a rusted arm.

As she goes inside for the glasses of lemonade, I move the bench to the prep station and then pull out my phone. I need to share this discovery with someone, and there is no one else who can possibly understand the significance of it like Joel.

Ingrid

Wendy's art is incredible.

Joel

Hope those green thumbs 👀 of yours aren't too disappointed. Though you do make a compelling case when it comes to the essentials of gardening. What were they again? Sun, water, and . . . ???

Despite myself, I bite the smile from my bottom lip.

Ingrid

What if I'd shown up at her door in overalls and gardening clogs?

Joel

You could have shown up wearing the clown costume from IT and my aunt still would have taken you in.

Ingrid

Thanks for reminding me of the one and only Stephen King movie I ever watched. Now I'll have to sleep with the lights on.

Joel

I wait a full minute, thinking of how best to reply and finally settling on:

Ingrid

I'm glad I didn't leave before I saw this.

Joel's reply comes quickly.

Joel

I'm just glad you didn't leave.

I reread his text several times, staring at the words and pondering the conflicting sensation low in my belly.

The sound of the sliding glass doors opening and closing forces my gaze upward as Wendy traverses the lawn carrying two glasses of icy lemonade. "I feel spoiled getting to have you all to myself tonight when I'm sure there are a million other things you could be doing."

I take her offering with a smile. "This is the only one that matters."

14

Turns out, prepping secondhand furniture for art can work up quite an appetite. By the time we finished washing and stripping the old bench in preparation for Wendy's next step, our stomachs were grumbling. But I'd appreciated having something purposeful to do with my hands while we talked. Somehow, it alleviated my stress over trying to do and say the right thing and instead allowed our casual discussion to flow naturally.

By the time we cleaned up our mess in the yard and began chopping vegetables in the kitchen for a curry salad, we'd already circled the moon in conversation. We'd orbited around the simplest topics first—work updates, town updates, friends old and new—and eventually wove our way toward the missing core in us both: Cece.

The first time Wendy mentioned her name while I poured curry dressing over a bowl of shredded chicken, my entire body went rigid. I was unsure of the next right steps, of how to give her what she needed. Unsure if I was even capable of giving Wendy what she needed. My own experience with grief had been so isolating. A heavily locked room ready to trap an unsuspecting victim inside it without offering a way out.

I didn't want that for Wendy.

But then she touched my tense shoulder. *"Talking about her is good for my heart, Ingrid. It keeps her with me. The same is true for hearing her spoken of by someone she dearly loved, and by someone who dearly loved her in return. I hope I never have to grieve her alone. I'm learning that much like love, grief is meant to be shared."*

I wasn't familiar with the concept of shared grief. I hadn't stayed near anyone who knew my father before he was reduced to little more than a tragic headline in our regional news. Most people I'd been around in those early months after my move to California barely knew me. And even when Cece flew out for visits or took me as her plus-one on book tours or red carpet events, I'd closed that part of my heart off, to her and to everyone else. And yet here was Wendy, inviting me to join her in the most sacred of places, the same way she'd always done for me.

"I have the table all set for us out here, Ingrid," Wendy calls from out back. "Would you like a refill on your drink?"

"Yes, thank you. I'm just about finished in here." I put the last of the ingredients away in the fridge, then carry the two plates of chicken salad to the outdoor table. My nose tingles at the all too familiar candle fragrance of Peaches & Cream wafting on the patio. Cece's signature scent.

"I lit a candle in our girl's honor. Thought it would be nice if we included her somehow—she wouldn't have wanted to miss out," Wendy says, her voice noticeably more wobbly as she speaks now than it was in the kitchen. "Is that okay with you?"

Throat tight, I manage a nod as I set our plates down. "Yes, of course."

Once we're sitting she takes my hand, and I curl my fingers around hers instinctively. But before she bows her head, she gently smooths her thumb over the sea glass on my right index finger. "A black ocean tear. To this day, it's the only one I've seen come from our beaches," she adds with a smile. "Your father gave you something special with this, Ingrid. A reminder that no heartache has ever gone unseen, and no darkness is ever too solid for light to overcome."

I pinch my lips closed, already too overwhelmed to speak.

And then she bows her head.

Unlike when Joel prayed over our Sunday brunch, Wendy's prayer feels altogether different. I want to curl up in her familiar phrasing and cover myself in the raw hope rolling off her tongue. I'd always admired the way Wendy spoke to God when I was a teenager, as if she'd saved Him a seat at the dinner table and He'd actually shown up, but I can't help but feel the impact of every syllable she speaks now. Because of all the times for her to give up on an invisible God . . . it should be now. Yet as she holds my hand and expresses her gratitude for a dozen blessings, including my visit, her strengthened faith is as obvious as the tears that streak her cheeks.

I wipe my eyes before she says *amen* and offer her a clean napkin for her to do the same.

"I've learned to keep a tissue supply with me wherever I go. Tears come easily these days. In our grief group, my girlfriends and I often refer to ourselves as professional criers. We've even created a rating system for each tissue brand based on their absorption, softness, and durability." She blots her eyes, sniffs, and tries on a smile I know is for my benefit. "Grief humor is a strange thing."

I don't have a reply for this, so I just nod as she takes the first bite of the salad and wait for her report. Her approving *mmms* boost my confidence dramatically, and I'm not sure if I'm more elated over the idea that she enjoys something I made or being able to tell Joel that she ate a nutrient-rich dinner tonight. Even if her bites are baby-sized at best.

If I had to guess, I'd say Wendy's weight loss since the funeral is somewhere in the ballpark of forty to fifty pounds—on a frame that could only stand to lose half that without appearing unwell. I try not to think about how waif-like her arms and chest bones look as they peek through the periwinkle V-neck she wears while I indulge in a few bites of my own salad.

We share a moment of silence as my eyes sweep across the yard again at all the projects waiting to be started and finished and all the beauty waiting to be created. She'd told me that it started when Stephen placed an old workbench at the curb she could view from her bedroom window. And how surprising her indignation had been over the discarded object she'd seen him use in his shop countless times. Even more surprising was that it continued to poke at her all day until finally, she brought the bench into her garage where it sat for a week untouched. It was only after a beach walk where she collected more than her usual share of ocean tears that an idea sparked. She claims the first piece she worked on was nothing more than a hodgepodge of trial and error. It was the result of a dozen YouTube videos explaining the correct formulas and techniques she'd eventually need to create the art she envisioned in her mind.

"Do you have any plans for these pieces once they're finished? Will you sell them?"

As Wendy sets her fork down and wipes her fingertips on a napkin, I can't help but glance at the remaining half of her uneaten food on her plate. "I lived the better part of this year without vision for much of anything, much less a future, so I think there's still a part of me that doesn't want to place too much pressure or expectation on how long this project will last or even what it might grow to become. I'm simply trying to focus on having faith enough for today. And for today, this broken, recycled art is what God's using to repair the broken pieces of my heart."

At her honest reflection, something expands in my chest, and I'm suddenly unable to hold back the words I wanted to say when I first saw her in the hotel basement. "I'm sorry, Wendy. I should have come sooner to check on you. Cece would be so ashamed if she knew I waited ten months to—"

"No." Wendy lays her hand over mine, gives a soft shake of her head. "Cece wasn't naïve to your pain, Ingrid. When we made the final decision to go ahead with her surgery, we discussed the different scenarios and outcomes at length. Apart from me, it was you she worried over most. She knew, given the circumstances, that it would be extremely difficult for you to come back here without some real hope to hold on to. She never wanted to add to your trauma of losing your father the way you did."

At her words, my mind slams to a complete stop and then slowly begins to crawl backward. I wait until I can form a question without any trace of accusation in my voice. "I'm not sure what you mean by the final decision to go ahead with her surgery. Did *you* . . . know the odds she was facing beforehand?" In the letter Cece had prepared for her lawyer to read to her closest friends and family after the services, Cece took full ownership and responsibility of the decision to go ahead with the surgery despite the heightened risks many of us knew nothing about.

Wendy exhales through her nose and seems to consider her next words carefully. "Yes, I did." She eyes her uneaten plate of food. "And even now, only a small handful of people know the details of those last few days. Everything happened so quickly."

"Joel?" I ask, terrified of the answer, of learning that once again he'd kept vital information from me. "Is he one of them?"

"No, no. Not Joel. Although I owe him a sit-down much like this one in the very near future. I made a commitment in my prayer journal to talk to him after this last weekend was over." She doesn't expound on that statement any more, but it's not hard to connect the dots for myself. Joel would have been devastated to learn there was counsel over this decision he wasn't invited to. "Just my brother and Patti and the neuro team. And now a couple of trusted girlfriends in my grief group know the details, but only after the fact. That's actually why I started attending group in the first place. The guilt I had over that last week of her life was . . ."

Her sentence trails off, but my mind doesn't want to fill in the blanks this time. I'm still too lost, still too rattled to assume anything on my own. "What happened?"

Wendy takes a moment as if trying to decide which path to take, and I'm begging her with my eyes to take the one I need most: the truth, even if it hurts.

"Please," I say. "I want to understand."

"When Cece first told you about the migraines and her initial diagnosis, we were all very hopeful about her prognosis. The tumor seemed to be growing slowly and her surgeon was optimistic about the procedure and her recovery, despite the odds associated with any brain operation."

I nod, remembering when I'd met Cece in Oregon at the cabin where she'd told me of her prognosis. My shock. My fear. My utter helplessness. Though she'd kept me updated on her prescriptions, appointments, scans, and eventual surgery date, I'd spent hours researching everything I could about her specific tumor—the grade and placement in particular, and then matching her case to the testimonials of people who not only survived, but thrived after recovery.

I was in no way prepared to hear Joel's voice on the phone that September afternoon.

I was in no way prepared to hear the same words he'd spoken to me four years prior.

Wendy continues. "Early on, back when we thought her headaches were regular migraines, she could go weeks without having an episode—noticing they'd come on more often when she worked on screens and her eyes were more strained. Her doctor said it likely had to do with the light." She exhales slowly. "But the closer we got to her surgery date, the migraines were coming on far more often, and when they did, they were debilitating. It's why she eventually moved in with me again."

I knew Wendy had been helping her quite a bit, but I certainly hadn't known she was living here. Our video calls had become less and less frequent as Cece preferred the ease of voice texting, saying she was too tired or too homely-looking to be on video. But I'm guessing there was more to it now. *Ingrid, there is nothing new to see. I'm the same, just paler than usual with frizzier hair.*

"In the countdown of those last two weeks," Wendy continues, "she spent more time in the recliner in my living room than anywhere else. She could angle herself however she needed to in order to relieve the pressure in her head. It's where she often chose to sleep, too—when she slept, that is. But many nights all she wanted to do was walk, be outside, write. I'd worry about her, of course, but you know how she was." She huffs a half-laugh. "She needed to explore and imagine. Sometimes she'd walk all the way to her cottage with her notebook in hand and then call me to come pick her up when she was ready to come back." Her smile slips, sobers. "Sometimes it was hard to remember she was as sick as she was."

The revelation causes the tip of my nose to tingle. I know what she means. Cece was sending me ridiculous memes just twenty-four hours before she was rolled into that operating room in Seattle. Only an hour after our final text exchange, I'd paced my office, too distracted by the clock to be productive in any way for the next seven hours. I hadn't wanted to sit at home alone. But the office wasn't exactly a comfort, either. Barry and Chip had popped their heads in on the half hour, asking for news, until the last time when Barry came in to find me crumpled on the floor, unable to breathe.

I push the dark memory aside and focus my attention on Wendy.

"Just four days before her surgery, during her final scans, everything changed."

I press my fingertips to the icy condensation of my water glass, having no intention of drinking from it.

"The aggressiveness of her tumor since her previous scan was a shock to her neuro team. It's possible it had something to do with the medicine she was receiving to shrink it prior to surgery, but no one really knows for sure." She clears her throat, swallows. "But what they did know was that a difficult procedure had now graduated to a nearly impossible one in only a matter of weeks. Her team sought other opinions, of course, but the consensus was the same: The tumor needed to be removed, not only to relieve her migraines and save her gross motor skills, but her life." She lifts her glass to her lips, her voice trembling. "There were limited trial drugs available if we waited, but there was no guarantee, and if we waited much longer, the tumor would be inoperable. We were given four days to decide."

I knew from my many dates with Google that the odds of survival were affected by grade, placement, and the aggressiveness of the tumor, but I hadn't been told those stats had changed. I hadn't been told she was making the most difficult decision of her life during those last four days. "You wanted her to wait."

"I did." Her cheeks glisten. "I wanted to believe there would be a new trial or a new drug or . . . a miracle."

My own tears climb and climb and climb until they're forced to teeter over the edge of my lash line and fall. I have no words. No thoughts in my head other than one: At the age of twenty-six, my best friend had an impossible choice to make. But it was hers to make.

"She made me promise not to share our most recent information with anyone outside her aunt and uncle, and that was only because she knew how much I'd need their support in the days leading up to the surgery. And I did. I still do." The last sentence hitches on a sob, and I know it's only right for me to reel this conversation back in, protect her fragility, and honor Joel's request to keep the light inside her from extinguishing. But my tongue feels as if it's forgotten how to form words. "She didn't want this decision to be pinned on anybody but herself. Nor did she want this diagnosis to define her life or her relationships." Wendy releases a quivering breath. "And she certainly hadn't wanted the media involved. Unfortunately, there was no controlling them."

I think back to the news stories, to the click-bait articles, to the independent YouTuber who went viral with nearly every fact wrong about her life when he reported from the beach under her cottage. But by the way Wendy remains quiet, I know there must be more to it than what I knew from living nine hundred miles south.

"Cece and I went round and round on what to do, asking hard questions to medical professionals and seeking counsel from our pastor. All the while, my daughter's odds of surviving weren't getting any better, and I could do nothing to change them. . . ."

Wendy is crying openly now, and I'm the one who takes her hand in mine this time. I'm the one who squeezes it gently the way she's done with me on dozens of occasions. And somehow, when I open my mouth, the words are there, waiting for me. "You honored her,

Wendy. It was an impossible decision. And . . ." I close my eyes, shudder a breath. "It was hers to make."

Wendy lifts her head to meet my gaze. "That's one of the things I repeat to myself every morning after my prayer time on the beach. It was hers to make, mine to support, and God's to control." She unlocks our hands and reaches for my face, holds my chin. "If you could only know how much she wrestled over what to say to you, and how and when she should say it . . . I promise you'd never doubt her intentions for you. You are her sister in all the ways that matter, Ingrid. She wouldn't be ashamed of you coming up here when you did, she would be proud of you."

My face starts to crumple, but Wendy's grip holds firm. "In the same way I wouldn't have been ready to see God's promise to me by turning His collection of ocean tears into art three months ago, I'm not sure you would have been ready to visit me any sooner than tonight. You needed time. We all did. So if you can forgive me for not telling you all the facts of her surgery sooner, then I think we should both practice letting go of the guilt that's not ours to hold on to."

A foreign feeling begins to build inside me. It's different than love, but it spreads a similar weightless warmth throughout my ribs and torso. *Hope,* I think. This is hope.

"I'll try," I manage to whisper.

"Good." Wendy blots her cheeks and pushes out her chair. "Now, how do you feel about sorting and polishing a fresh bucket of ocean tears with me while we listen to some Carole King? I'll clear our plates if you do the heavy lifting and maneuver that bucket out there closer to the table. I've developed a bit of a system over the last couple of months." She stands and then stops abruptly, turning to me as if she's just recalled something important. "Unless you're needing to return Joel's car back to him tonight? I certainly don't want to hinder any plans the two of you may have made together." She makes no attempt to hide the interest in her voice.

"No plans," I try to answer as nonchalantly as possible. "He's picking the car up from me in the morning."

The creases around her eyes soften like her tone. "Talk about a person who's worn guilt like a second skin . . ."

Of all the topics we've discussed this evening, this is the only one I'd like to avoid completely, but Wendy's gaze has turned maternal again and I know my wish is in vain.

"I know why you felt you needed to leave Port Townsend, Ingrid. The same way I know why you felt you couldn't come back. But I'm living proof that life can go on, even when everything in your world seems to be pointing to the contrary. I'm also proof that moving forward doesn't have to mean leaving everything I loved behind. I pray you both can find the freedom you're looking for."

"Joel and I are completely different people than we used to be," I appeal without the usual defense in my tone. "Too much has changed."

"Your worlds might be different, but your hearts have always matched. They still do."

Wendy pats me on the shoulder and then moves to collect a stack of plates as if to tell me she's finished with this topic for now and immediately, the tension in my shoulders eases. Over the next few hours we sort through a mountain of red, yellow, green, and blue sea glass. But all the while her words circle my heart like a permanent marker, and I can't stop picturing the way Joel stared at me in the library earlier today. If I'm honest with myself, it's the same way he's been staring at me since I arrived.

"Oh, goodness, Ingrid," Wendy blurts as she checks her watch. "I've kept you so late." She yawns as I help her shut down her house for the night. "It's easy to lose track of time doing this, isn't it? I just love watching the colors come to life underwater."

"I enjoyed every minute," I say. "It's been a long time since I've felt that accomplished."

Back in the living room, I initiate a hug that feels like the most natural comfort in the world and promise Wendy I won't be a stranger in the time I have left here.

I pass by the bookshelves in her living room on the way to her front door and notice the recliner Cece must have sat in during her hardest days and nights. As if it's beckoning me to come closer, I move toward it and skim my fingers along its broad leather back, trying to picture her during our text exchanges when I'd believed she was in her office or out on the beach or sitting on the hotel dock. I work to reframe the memories to this chair in her mother's living room. Try to picture her here writing . . . and then my eyes snap open wide. I stare down at the chair again and then up at Wendy.

Adrenaline whooshes through my veins. "Wendy? You said Cece wrote here, even after she'd moved into your house?"

"Yes, she did."

"But the laptop screen was too triggering for her migraines—correct?"

"That's right. She stopped using it months before she moved in, but I almost never saw her without one of her notebooks. Like the kind she used in high school. Why?"

Awakening blooms in the center of my chest. "Do you happen to know *what* she might have been writing in those notebooks?"

Wendy's eyes round as if she's only just now realizing the gravity of her answer. A hand flutters to her mouth. "Oh, Ingrid. I'm so sorry, I never once thought about that until right now—"

But I don't allow her to finish that statement before I've wrapped my arms around her. "It's okay, it's okay. No guilt, remember? You had way more important things going on than keeping track of a book." Her hold on me tightens and out of my mouth comes a sentence that implies so much more than I have capacity to process. "Maybe it was supposed to happen this way. Maybe I wasn't meant to know what I was looking for until now."

It's late when I arrive back to the cottage, still in a bit of a daze over my discovery tonight. Despite how I tried to assure Wendy that her lack of mentioning the notebooks was understandable given all she'd gone through this last year, I can't help but feel like an idiot for not having thought of it as an option myself.

I carry my phone with me like a security blanket as I enter Cece's bedroom and flick on the bedside lamp. I perch on the edge of the mattress and try to imagine my friend staying up late and writing the last of her best-selling series in a set of composition notebooks she probably picked up from the corner market, in the lone aisle dedicated to office supplies. The same way she did when we were girls.

I kick off my shoes and slip my cold feet under the fluffy down comforter. Tomorrow morning I'd start my treasure hunt for the notebooks, but in the meantime, there's another story I'm feeling more and more attached to continuing. Or maybe it's my reading companion I'm feeling more and more attached to.

I squash the thought before it has a chance to multiply and tap on my darkened phone screen, hovering a finger over Joel's contact and debating between a call or a text. My cowardice wins out.

> Ingrid
>
> What time were you wanting to pick up the car in the morning?

His reply is immediate.

> Joel
>
> Depends on what time you usually drink your coffee. I've always been a fan of Cece's fancy espresso machine.

I smile.

> Ingrid
>
> I'll be up and showered by seven. But you're on your own with that machine. I have no clue how it works.

> Joel
>
> I've got you covered. Seven it is.

Ingrid

What's the probability of knocking out a couple chapters before you head off to work?

Joel

After a couple shots of espresso? I'd say high. My morning is more flexible than my afternoon.

Ingrid

Good. Because my day is going to be filled with treasure hunting.

Joel

You find one of Cece's old scavenger hunts? I thought I burned all those.

My fingers are practically shaking with adrenaline as I type.

Ingrid

Nope. But I did find out why Cece's manuscript wasn't on her laptop!

A string of question marks follows, and I'm giddy over his interest.

Ingrid

Drumroll please. . . . Cece wrote *The Fate of Kings* in notebooks! By hand.

The phone in my palm buzzes immediately and my stomach flips over.

"Hi," I say in a pitch three times higher than my regular voice.

"You're serious?"

I laugh, though I'm not totally sure why. It's like my body has forgotten how to attach the appropriate response with the appropriate emotion. "One hundred percent serious. Wendy said the blue light on the screens was giving her migraines and—"

"You asked Wendy about it?" His voice isn't exactly firm, but it's not exactly friendly, either. I rush to fill the gaps. The last thing I need is for Joel to think I went behind his back to interrogate his aunt. I'd cuto off an appendage before I'd willingly hurt Wendy.

"It actually came up in a roundabout way. She was talking about Cece's last few weeks and months and I pieced it together from a few things she said."

He makes a thinking noise. "I can't believe I never thought about her writing it in notebooks."

"None of us thought about it."

"What do you know about them? Color? Size? Possible storage locations?"

Again, I feel an almost giddy wave of delight at his curiosity. "I don't know much yet. Wendy said they resembled the ones she used in high school, but she didn't mention color. Oh, she also said you're supposed to give me a spare house key to her place so I can search when she's working on her projects. But my first mission will be to search the cottage in full. Wendy mentioned her writing here, just like Allie did. I'll check the storage unit, too."

"Wow. Well, congratulations. Those are some big leads to come from a single night. No wonder you're excited."

There's a long pause, and I wonder if Joel's realizing the same thing I am: that the sooner I find the notebooks, the sooner I'll be leaving town.

"So are you going to be able to sleep tonight?"

I frown, trying to guess at his meaning. "Because of all the excitement?"

"No, because of my clown reference from earlier. I was hoping you weren't still traumatized and picturing red balloons."

"Well, I am now," I squeal. "Thanks a lot."

He laughs, and I smile reluctantly.

"Will it help if I assure you there's nothing to worry about when it comes to that shower drain—"

"Joel! Stop!"

"Okay, okay," he chuckles. "But you do know you can call me if you need anything. Although, you do have my car so . . ."

"So I suppose I'll have to play the hero of my own story, then."

"I'm not sure you'd be willing to let anybody else play it even without a car in your driveway."

When we fall silent, I struggle to reach for a topic of conversation that will lead us back to the light, impromptu banter we—

"I'll see you at seven for coffee and reading," he says.

"Okay."

"And I do, sincerely, hope your dreams are as sweet as they are clown-less."

"Joel—"

"Good night, Indy."

15

"When the Party's Over"

In a small seaport town with only one public high school, there were only so many occasions worth getting fancy for, which was exactly why the annual staff dinner hosted at Cece's aunt and uncle's mansion in spring felt like Prom 2.0. And given her best friend had never attended a formal event in her life due to her unconventional upbringing and schooling, Cece was determined to make sure Ingrid's night was incredible—starting with a makeover courtesy of the CVS cosmetics aisle and her mother's hair tools.

"Close your eyes." Cece aimed the hair spray bottle at Ingrid's long, beach-wavy hair for the second time in five minutes. It had taken her nearly an hour to figure out how to get it to curl like the girls they saw in the magazines, as she was probably less skilled with a curling iron than she would be with a sword. But just like in her writing, she improvised well. Ingrid's hair looked better than a Disney princess at a royal ball, if she dared say so herself.

Ingrid tugged awkwardly at her gown, the way she'd been doing since the minute she put it on. "That's okay, I don't think I need any more of—"

"Eyes!" Cece bellowed just as a cloud of aerosol shot from the canister and coated Ingrid's luscious locks.

Ingrid gagged and waved her hand through the thick air in Cece's mom's bathroom, nearly tripping on her hem as she stumbled into the hallway for clean oxygen. She'd better figure out how to walk in those heels soon, because the clock was ticking.

"Please don't spray any more of that. My hair won't move for a week as it is." Ingrid coughed again. "This is a dinner, not a wedding."

Cece grinned. "Pretty sure that dress could fast-track a wedding if you wanted it to."

"It's not—we're not—" Ingrid clamped her mouth shut, seemingly flustered over her inability to tell a decent lie, especially when it came to Joel.

"*It is* and *you are.*" Cece batted Ingrid's hands away from tugging at the jewel tone, floor-length gown they'd picked up last weekend from the formal wear consignment shop in Oak Harbor. The front swooped low in a gathered, cascading fabric, while the back laced together with thick pieces of satin ribbon. It was quite literally the prettiest dress Cece had ever seen on a real life human and not just a store mannequin. "Stop fidgeting. You look beautiful, and I guarantee I won't be the only one to say so."

Ingrid rubbed at her bare arms. "I wish you were going with me. It feels weird dressing up alone."

"*I am going,* just not as a guest. That honor is only reserved for non-family hotel staff tonight. And honestly, as fun as it is to dress up, I have a feeling that watching Joel play waiter while you're at one of the tables is going to be the best entertainment of my whole year. Mark my words, he'll make sure he's the server at whatever table you're seated at."

The doorbell rang, and Cece could hear her mom pad across the living room to answer it. She tried to keep her face neutral.

Ingrid crinkled her brows. "Why are you making that face?"

"What face?"

"The face you make whenever you're trying to hide something from Joel."

Cece was still searching through a mental database of lame excuses when Wendy called for them.

"What did you do?" Ingrid hissed right before Cece shoved her friend down the four-step hallway and into the living room . . . where Captain Hal stood waiting with a single red rose.

"Dad?" Ingrid gasped, and Cece couldn't help but gasp right along with her.

Never once in the last two years had she seen Captain Hal without his red stocking cap on. She would have believed he slept in the thing—one of his many fisherman superstitions or something. But here he was, his hair combed and gelled to the side and his rust-colored beard trimmed and tamed into something other than a wiry, windblown mess. His yellow rain slicker had been swapped for a gray sports coat that looked a size too small and resembled one a certain uncle of hers had donned a time or two around the hotel. Even still, Hal was a rugged kind of handsome when he wasn't gutting a fish or wearing a Viking helmet. It was really too bad Ingrid had put a stop to Cece's matchmaking plans between their parents a year ago. Captain Hal was a catch.

"Elskede," Hal whispered to his daughter as if nobody else was in the room. "You . . . you look like your mother. Beautiful."

Ingrid moved toward him. "You said you didn't want to come tonight."

He winked. "I was hoping to surprise you."

"You did," Ingrid all but giggled. "You definitely did."

Hal glanced above his daughter's head and tipped his chin to Cece. "You can credit Curly for that. It was her idea."

Ingrid spun around, and it was only then that Cece saw the tears gleaming in her best friend's eyes. Happy tears, the best kind. Ingrid reached for Cece and pulled her in for a tight embrace. "You're the best."

"Nah. But I might be pretty close." Cece pulled back. "And look—now you don't have to sit alone. All problems solved."

Ingrid smiled as she stepped onto the porch with her father, taking his arm to steady the wobble in her high-heeled stride as they strolled the short path to her uncle's front door. Cece could feel her mom's unwavering gaze on her back as she waved them off to the pre-dinner greeting and photo ops, assuring Ingrid she'd be over as soon as she pinned her hair up and found her work apron.

The instant she closed the front door, her mother opened her arms up wide in invitation, and unlike the many times Cece had pushed her mother away during the angry years of her early teens, this time she collapsed into them. And unlike her friend, the tears she cried onto her mom's blouse were not of the happy variety.

"My sweet girl." Her mom smoothed her hair and held her close, releasing a deep sigh. "Oh, how I wish I could take away the pain he's caused you. I'm so sorry."

The condolence made her stomach clench. It had been years since her mom had mentioned *him*. But that was the thing about loss, even when you didn't make room for it, it showed up anyway, usually unannounced.

"I *hate* him for leaving us," Cece wept. "Don't you?"

Her mom loosened her arms and took hold of Cece's chin in her hands. "No, I don't."

"How?" she asked, bewildered. "He threw us away like trash, Mom. It's like neither of us ever meant anything to him at all."

When Cece looked up at her, the creases around her mother's eyes deepened, and for a moment, she wondered if she'd gone too far. "I promised God long ago that I would look for the good in every season of life He gives me, even the hard ones. And right now, I'm looking straight into the eyes of the good that came from the season I shared with your father." She pressed a kiss to Cece's forehead. "If you waste your heart on hate, you'll miss the good life has to give. Don't miss it, sweet girl."

Cece's mother had encouraged her to take a few extra minutes to freshen up before she arrived at the staff dinner. Each year there was a skeleton crew of employees who volunteered to stay behind and manage the hotel while everyone else came to the Campbells' Queen Anne mansion. Even though it was up to the members of the Campbell family to serve all thirty of this year's selected staff, it was a local Italian cuisine restaurant that catered the appetizers, salad, soup, fettuccini, and award-winning tiramisu. Likely, they were still enjoying the course of bread and caprese set on the tables.

Though there was a definite agenda to the special evening her aunt and uncle planned each spring, neither of them was a fan of rushing through any one course. There was a purpose for each, and by the sounds of it, the purpose of the first course—fellowship—was well underway.

After washing up in the kitchen, Cece checked in with her mom and aunt and quickly followed their lead, balancing salad plates along her forearm to serve to their guests. If there was one thing she knew well, it was how to waitress like a pro. Seconds before she slipped into her aunt's transformed Victorian dining room, she powered her smile to the highest wattage.

She'd spent most of the day setting up these dining tables with her family members, adding lights and centerpieces, and as her uncle said, "Wendy-fying" the place. Her mom definitely had an artist's eye. Maybe one day she'd put it to real use and create the kind of art Cece was certain stirred in her soul.

Greeting each of her hotel colleagues by name, Cece served the salad course, making sure to take inventory of who was seated where and which plus-one they'd invited for the evening. Ingrid and Hal's table was closest to the kitchen door, and by the looks of it, she hadn't been wrong about Joel. He was currently serving their table, and even while he poured the ice water, his gaze rarely strayed from Ingrid.

When it was time to begin bussing the empty plates, he nodded at Cece from across the room and then halted. He squinted at her as if trying to zoom in on her face. *No, thank you.* Cece made a quick diversion by offering to refill a few extra glasses of water, placing her back to him. She had no desire to rehash her little breakdown from earlier. It was over; she was fine now. Soon her uncle's talk would be the focal point of the evening, and then the real fun and games would begin after dinner.

When she'd suggested to Hal that he be Ingrid's plus-one tonight, she made sure to tell him all about the board games that came as soon as dessert finished and how there were prizes for the champions and how the evening's music selections were drawn out of a bowl. She knew Hal liked cards; she'd seen him do a few tricks on the cruiser, and once he'd even told her about the time he'd nearly won a sailboat in a poker game a few towns over. Regardless of her uncle's feelings about gambling, she'd been so impressed!

Cece spotted her friend's table, noting the way Hal was tugging at his shirt collar, and wondered how long he'd last in that stiff sports coat. The taut shoulder seams didn't look like they'd hold together for another minute, much less another couple of hours. Hopefully her uncle wasn't planning on the loaned garment being returned in one piece.

As soon as the chicken and shrimp fettuccini had been served, her uncle took the floor. The employees tapped their glasses with their forks and the room quieted. Though she'd heard this particular speech multiple times before, she looked forward to it as if it were the first time.

"As much as we want tonight to be about good food, fun, and fellowship, it's also meant to be a tremendous thank-you from our family to yours. We couldn't do what we do without your faithful dedication and service to our team. When Patti and I left Seattle a decade ago to invest in a rundown building built in the late 1800s, we never could have imagined the rich return we'd receive from our investment." He opened his hands to gesture to the room where there wasn't a single unsmiling face to be found. Even Hal seemed to be grinning, sort of. "And while many of you know the key principles we're founded upon, I always like to take this opportunity to share the more intimate details behind our family's story, especially when we're welcoming a few new employees to the mix each year." He tipped his head to Ingrid and Hal.

Cece pressed her back into the far dining room wall, content to listen to her uncle and fully decompress for a few minutes.

"Why are your eyes puffy? Were you crying?"

She immediately shushed her presumptuous cousin, who flattened his back to the wall beside her. "Don't be rude. Your father is speaking."

Joel side-eyed her. "You've heard this story as many times as you've heard the Christmas story."

"And I want to hear it again."

"Fine." He crossed his arms over his chest as if settling in for the long haul just as her uncle was getting to the part about the years of miscarriages he and Aunt Patti suffered through before Joel came along, and then all the experimental treatments they started a year after Joel was born to try for a second child. But having her cousin right next to her, breathing out his too-loud exhales, was cramping her ability to concentrate.

175

"Why aren't you standing over by Ingrid's table?" she hissed.

The flush in Joel's cheeks was immediate. "Hal makes me nervous."

She had to catch the laugh in her throat before it could bark from her mouth. "*Why?*"

"Oh, I don't know, maybe because he always looks like he's trying to figure out the quickest way to dispose of my body."

"Nah, that's way too easy. He knows he'd only have to push you overboard at night and leave you for the sharks."

"You're hilarious," he deadpans.

"Come on," she whispered through a smile. "You know he's harmless."

"I'm not so sure I do." His undertone of fun had shifted to something she wasn't sure she liked.

"What do you mean?" She tracked his gaze to Hal, who was still tugging mercilessly at the top buttons of his collared shirt.

Joel hiked an eyebrow at her. "You gonna tell me why you were crying?"

She stared him down, ultimately deciding his game wasn't worth it. "Allergies." She flattened herself to the wall again. "Now be quiet, I want to hear this part."

She worked to tune out Joel's heavy sigh and pull her uncle's testimony forward.

". . . the ups and downs at home became too much, and I found myself spending more and more time in my downtown office. First, it was one extra-long evening a week, but soon enough it became five extra-long evenings, and then I started showing up on the weekends, too. To escape the pain I couldn't figure out how to manage at home, I justified the extra office hours because of the money we needed for fertility treatments. But the truth was, I'd become a full-fledged workaholic. Work was why I woke up in the mornings and why I only slept three to four hours each night. I'd heard the term *workaholic* spoken with pride among the men in my peer groups, but it wasn't until a couple of brave souls pulled me aside that I saw the critical flaw in my logic: My quest to build my family was actually destroying it. My absence had deeply hurt my marriage, and I hardly knew my boy. It was the intervention I needed to save my family and make some pretty extreme changes. For a long time, I believed God didn't see my suffering, that He remained invisible during my time of greatest need, but the truth was I simply didn't know where to look for Him. It's been my experience that God is often made visible by the hands and feet of the people He places in our lives."

Uncle Stephen winked at his younger sister, and Cece never failed to feel a rush of affection for her mom whenever he got to that part of the story. Despite being deep in the trenches of her own struggling marriage at the time, she'd been one of the voices to steer her brother back in the right direction.

Cece admired her uncle's bravery in sharing the next pieces of his testimony—how he'd humbled himself to ask forgiveness from his wife and his son. And then, how instead of becoming a partner in the brokership he'd invested decades of his life and finances into, he'd cashed out every stock fund and asset he and Aunt Patti had owned to take a huge risk, one that would create a steady, more sustainable, more purposeful existence for his entire family.

"The day before we received our occupancy permit during the remodel, I clearly remember praying with Patti in the lobby about managing this hotel in a way that would prioritize people above business and our faith in God above our own agendas. We've continued to apply that relationship principle to every decision—big and small—as well as to every employee we hire." Uncle Stephen beamed across the room at his son. "Each of you have become a part of the legacy of our hotel because each of you has become a part of our family. Thank you for a decade of love, loyalty, and excellent service to our community and guests."

A single clap soon morphed into a thunderous applause, provoking whistles and cheers to erupt around the room. As soon as Uncle Stephen transitioned the floor to Aunt Patti so she could explain the dessert and game portion of the evening, Hal pushed back from the table and strode toward the rear of the dining hall. There was only a small archway that led into the living room from back here, and given Joel's earlier confession about his nerves around Hal, Cece figured it would be best if she was the one to point him in the right direction. None of the three bathrooms on this main floor were easily detectable.

But as she stepped into the living room it was as if he'd vanished. Brows crinkled, she walked toward the foyer and then toward the staircase leading up to the bedrooms. No trace of him. She was just about ready to rejoin the group, thinking that perhaps he'd found the restroom on his own after all, when she popped her head around the corner of the dim hallway between her uncle's study and the restroom she'd coined the grape bathroom on account of her aunt's affection for grape wallpaper.

She studied his broad back, noting the way his chin tipped north toward the ceiling for several seconds before he stuffed something shiny back into the pocket of his sport coat.

"Captain Hal?"

The speed at which he straightened his coat and twisted around caused her to question what she'd actually seen when he tapped the inside of his breast pocket. "Oh, Curly, it's you."

"Hi, uh, sorry. I wondered if you needed some directions? I always say my uncle and aunt's house should come with voice-activated GPS."

He flashed a grin. "Was just looking for a restroom."

Only, he was literally standing in the hallway three feet away from the unoccupied, grape-wallpapered guest bathroom. She felt strange pointing it out to him, but what else could she do? "There's one there on your right and another on the far side of the kitchen."

He nodded. "Much obliged."

"Sure," she said, willing her voice to sound normal. "Are you having a good—"

"Cece," Ingrid called, walking through the living room toward her. "We're choosing teams for Catch Phrase right now. Have you seen my dad?"

"Catch Phrase—that's great!" Cece exclaimed in a pitch far too upbeat to be considered anything but weird. "And huh, your dad?" For reasons she didn't quite understand in the moment, she angled herself away from the hall and glanced in the opposite direction. "Could he be using the restroom or—"

"I'm here, kiddo," Hal cut in, stepping out of the shadowed hallway. "I think I'm going to call it a night. I have an early morning on the water."

Ingrid's expression fell at his words and Cece couldn't help but notice the way she seemed to be examining her father. "But you'll miss the games, that's the best part of the whole night. Patti just showed us the prizes and—"

He shook his head. "You'll have more fun with your friends than with your old man. I'll see you at the hotel tomorrow." He clamped a hand to Ingrid's shoulder, effectively ending their discussion. Only Cece could tell Ingrid had a lot more she wanted to say. By the time Joel rounded the corner into the foyer, Hal was already out the door, walking down the cobblestone footpath.

"I should probably go with him," Ingrid said, reaching for the door handle. "I'll catch up with you both tomorrow."

"Wait, what?" Cece questioned, placing a hand on Ingrid's arm. "You've been waiting for this night for weeks, months even."

But she doubted Ingrid had even heard her, she was too busy studying her father's retreating form from the window. "I don't want him to be alone."

"Sounds like he has to get up early. Besides, not everybody is a game person. Maybe he only likes to play cards. You should stay and win some prizes for him. I'm sure he'd like that," Cece said, even though she still had an odd sensation rolling around in her gut. "It was super nice that he came for the dinner part." It was way more than her own dad would have done, that was for sure.

"Hey," Joel said, reaching for Ingrid's hand. "If you really want to leave, then I'll drive you home, but the after-party really is the best part of the night. I've been looking forward to beating you at Scrabble for weeks." He smiled at her. "You were already planning on staying over at Aunt Wendy's tonight, weren't you?"

Ingrid nodded.

"Then it's up to you. If you change your mind at any point tonight and want to leave early, then I'll take you home."

"Thank you. I appreciate that." Ingrid's shoulders visibly relaxed as she released a deep breath. And then she leaned in close enough to whisper, "Can I ask you a question?"

"Of course."

"Do you have a sweatshirt I might be able to borrow from you?"

If Joel was trying to be discreet about the way his eyes drifted over

Ingrid's figure, then he'd failed miserably. "You mean to wear right now? Over your dress?"

Ingrid nodded again, her hands rubbing up and down her arms as if someone had blasted the air-conditioning. Only, there was no air-conditioning, and if anything, all these extra bodies in the house had made the room overly stuffy.

"Sure thing. I'll be right back."

Cece hooked an arm around Ingrid's shoulders. "You'll be happy you stayed tonight, I promise." And then she scrunched up her face as an idea hit. "Quick—while Joel's gone we should make up a secret code so we can gang up on him during all the games that require clues."

"I don't think cheating was really the spirit your uncle was striving for tonight."

Cece laughed. "Fine, then let's at least go hide his plate of tiramisu and tell him there's none left."

"You're a terrible influence," Ingrid scolded, but at least she was finally smiling again. Exactly as Cece had predicted.

The rest of the night had gone according to plan. They'd laughed and snacked and teased each other mercilessly, all while Ingrid had worn Joel's favorite gray zip-up hoodie over her gorgeous ballgown. And once all the party guests had gone home for the night and the three of them had finished cleaning up the aftermath, Joel had walked them across the lawn and over the short cobblestone path that connected Cece's house to his. There'd been no more talk of Hal's early departure or of Joel driving Ingrid home.

When they reached the lighted porch steps, Joel fist-bumped Cece, then reached to pull Ingrid in for a hug.

"Oh, here." Ingrid began to tug the zipper down. "I almost forgot to give this back to you."

"Keep it," he said.

"I can't. It's your favorite."

"Which is why it makes sense for you to have it, since you're my favorite, too."

Cece huffed a groan, indicating that she had no desire to hear whatever ridiculous thing her cousin might say next. She walked past them and then through the front door into her living room. However, she chose not to flip on the living room light, as *light* made it far more difficult to spy into the night. Truth was, just because she didn't want to hear them didn't mean she didn't want to *see* them. She angled her body to fit discreetly between the front door and the living room window.

Joel hugged Ingrid one last time, this embrace lingering for nearly a minute before he whispered something in Ingrid's ear that made her smile. Eventually, she turned away and started for the porch. And it was right then, in the short span of time between their last embrace and Ingrid walking through the front door, that Cece caught sight of Joel's hand as it moved to hover over his heart . . . and then she saw his fingers thump his chest three times before he, too, turned away.

16

Joel clears his throat as he finishes our fifth chapter of the morning but avoids making eye contact with me. I wonder if he's wishing he could go back in time and take a red pen to that entire last page, cross it all out before it has the chance to go to final print. Because we've both learned the hard way that falling in love is far simpler than staying in love.

Gone is the sociable mood from earlier when we sipped on highbrow coffee from Cece's fancy espresso machine and laughed at her bright and somewhat irreverent memories of our daily grind as hotel staffers and the mischief we shared in our off-hours—most of which was in the name of *book research*. But our laughter dulled during the retelling of the annual staff party. The atmosphere had slowly shifted from nostalgic and congenial to downright uncomfortable by the close of the chapter. And it's clear by Joel's reticence that he wasn't a fan of that particular eyewitness account. Not that I can blame him. Some private moments, even those captured by our closest, most well-meaning friends, should have the right to remain private.

Despite the raw history that tethers us—the trauma, the loss, the devastating omissions and violated trust—I wouldn't wish this kind of forced exposure upon anybody. Especially when that exposure shone a giant spotlight on an innocent teenage boy who simply wanted to believe love was enough to conquer all.

Empathy coaxes me to say something, to tell him it's okay, that we were young and naïve and that nothing he read today needs to change this new rhythm of civility we've found . . . and yet the words in my head are nothing more than a jumble of disconnected starts and stops. I wish I had Chip's magical ability to create relatable small talk out of thin air, but I'm still stuck on trying to interpret the root emotion behind Joel's disquiet. Humiliation? Regret? Frustration?

A compelling case can be made for them all.

"It really was a fun game night," I say, tossing something out at random. "I remember your insane Scrabble plays."

"Couldn't have been too insane—you beat me," he amends.

"Only because you let me."

"Guess we'll never know for sure." And then, before I can continue this meaningless exchange, he gestures to the kitchen. "I should probably be going."

"Right, okay."

I watch him from the corner of my eye as we pick up our coffee mugs and breakfast plates and set them in the sink. Joel gathers the memoir and slides it into his backpack while I place his borrowed car keys on the sofa table beside him. We're a wordless kind of polite, a functional, transactional kind of coexistence, which I suppose is an upgrade from some of our more heated exchanges. But then again, maybe it's not. Maybe this bottled-up tension is worse, a step backward.

Like a well-mannered hostess, I trail behind him through the living room and eventually into the arched entryway. An instant before his hand connects with the doorknob, he draws it back, and I'm hoping his good-bye will release the vent on this pressure cooker we're in and take us back to where we were earlier this morning.

He opens his mouth and—

His phone rings.

If it were me on the receiving end of such a perfectly timed interruption, there's no doubt I would seize the moment and hightail it out of this uncomfortable situation. But this is Joel, and he's never been afraid to face the hard things head-on. He glances from his phone screen up to me.

"This should only take a second."

I nod as if he's asked for my permission, which of course, he doesn't need. It's not until he swipes to answer that I realize how close we are, the two of us standing on opposite sides of the same Welcome Home mat. The irony isn't lost on me.

"Hey, Brian." Pause. "Yes, it's set for three o'clock today, why?" Pause. "What about Danny, then?" Pause. "Chris? Adele?" Pause. "Okay, well, has anyone called Allie?" Another pause, followed by a long sigh. "I know she doesn't, but at this point, I'd take a warm body over this late of a cancellation." Joel rubs a hand down his face, and I realize only then that I've made no attempt to give him privacy or even pretend to look away. Whatever the issue, Joel's disappointment is etched in the deep V of his brow. "No, I understand. Thanks for trying. I'll call them and cancel myself." He taps the screen and lowers the phone.

"A warm body?" Out of everything I just overheard, these are the eloquent words I lead with. I try again. "Sorry, I realize it's none of my business."

"No apology necessary." He rakes a hand through his hair, and from this close, I can count the handful of silver strands at his temples, easily picturing how they'll duplicate in another decade or two. Easily picturing how his arresting features will continue to mature with time. He huffs an exhale. "I made a commitment for this afternoon that it appears I won't be able to keep. It requires a . . . specific skillset not all our employees are trained in, and we're short-staffed at the hotel tonight as it is."

I try to imagine what kind of specific skillset he might be referring to. The Campbell employees are thoroughly trained in every facet of hospitality and guest services, so I come up short in my guesses and throw one out to left field instead. "You running an underground fight club in the hotel basement?"

He cracks a smile that threatens to expand my own. "Doesn't

answering any questions about Fight Club violate the first and only rule of Fight Club?"

I shrug. "Obviously my experience in such matters is limited."

He laughs and I'm surprisingly grateful for the sound. "I was actually supposed to give a private tour today for a couple who booked an anniversary package with us—it's their forty-fifth wedding anniversary this week."

My mental gears spin on the words *private tour*, imagining Joel driving a hotel van in a town that isn't even eight square miles. Perhaps he's created a route to showcase all three hundred of the original Victorian homes and the tales that go along with them for any visiting history buffs?

"We've retired our charter fishing excursions for the time being and replaced them with sightseeing tours that include a pre-prepared meal, drinks, and binoculars for whale-watching."

I slow-blink and try to process. Not a private van tour, then, but a chartered *boat* tour. A *replacement* boat with a *replacement* captain. "Who's at the helm?"

A beat passes before Joel says, "I am."

I'm too stunned to acknowledge any one of the questions whipping through my brain at this revelation, and yet my curiosity is too piqued not to try. "You have your captain's license?"

"I do. It's not often I get the chance to take guests out, which is why we also have a small rotation of captains we contract with, but I enjoy saying yes to a booking when everything lines up and I have a first mate. Unfortunately, this time I don't have the available personnel."

It's impossible for me not to picture my father in his favorite red beanie and his yellow rain slicker with the Campbell family logo stenciled on the back. But of course, my father hasn't captained a boat for Joel's family for over five years now. Sometimes, during restless nights, I allow myself to wonder about the replacement Stephen Campbell must have hired after my father's shipwreck. I've wondered if the faceless man is the kind of captain who will take young families out during Christmas break and wrap the deck with festive lights and tinsel. If he'll tell the children to keep their eyes peeled for signs to the North Pole. If he, too, will hand out hot cocoa in Styrofoam cups and belt out "Santa Claus is Coming to Town" in a horrendous, tone-deaf baritone that's sure to break even the most stoic of passengers.

But never once in any of my imaginings did I picture Joel at the helm.

"Don't cancel on the anniversary couple. I can help." The words pass over my tongue before they've even had a chance to check in with my brain. And yet, they feel right. Like being handed a compass after being lost for days without any real sense of direction. "What time do you want to depart?"

"Ingrid," Joel murmurs in a tone that causes my stomach to swoop. "I would never expect you to—"

I straighten my spine. "Are you headed toward Victoria or Marrowstone?"

"They've actually lined up a driver to meet them in Port Williams. They're headed to the lavender fields in Sequim for a picnic dinner and then an overnight at the inn. I was going to head west around the point and then return to the marina—about a four-hour venture."

"So what time were you planning to depart?" I ask again.

"They're supposed to meet me at the marina at three."

I pull on a smile I can almost feel. "Then I'll be there at two-thirty for prep."

He studies me quietly for several seconds before he asks, "You're really sure about this?"

I'm not even on the same planet as sure, I think to myself. "Absolutely."

As I step onto the deck of the unfamiliar, fifty-foot flybridge charter yacht, my brain switches into a mode it hasn't needed in a long time, one I've been too afraid to access for just as long. The finishes on this gently used seacraft are as stunning as the three private staterooms and head compartments below the expansive salon and dinette area of the main cabin. It's clear to see the trade-off of chartering fishing tours to sightseeing pleasure rides has afforded a far more luxurious form of sea travel. Unlike the forty-foot cabin cruiser my father captained for the Campbells, the emphasis of this vessel is all about passenger comfort for guests who want to relax in style. Absent is the large utilitarian deck suitable for tourists and deckhands reeling in their catches . . . or for a romantic dance under a midnight moon between two fictional muses. I push that last thought aside and focus on why I'm here.

Joel starts out in the flybridge cockpit over the main cabin. The deck up top is a third of the length of the boat overall, with benches and chairs and an unsurpassed view of the sea, but he doesn't stay up there for long. Unlike the unease that passed between us after the reading this morning, now we're a united front, readying the boat for our arriving passengers together. I work through a departure checklist I memorized by the time I was eight years old and find it takes no effort at all to slip back into the role of first mate. And instead of the anxiety I'd anticipated upon boarding, there's a strange kind of comfort in working around dock lines and stowing hatch covers again. Oddly, the comfort deepens when I observe Joel verifying the operation of the twin diesel engines and double-checking our intended course on his GPS.

When Wayne and Jan—a sweet couple from west Texas in their mid-sixties—board the yacht, I get busy wrapping cables and retrieving bumpers. As soon as Joel gives me the go-ahead, I leap off the deck to release the dock lines. And though my jump back on board is out of practice and less than lady-like, Jan applauds me, and I'm smiling when I give Joel the all-clear to navigate us out of the harbor.

Once at sea, I slip on the hotel apron and head inside the salon, where Wayne and Jan are cuddled on a white, L-shaped sofa directly opposite the cabin cockpit where Joel is positioned. While he points out landmarks on the Salish Sea and tells some history about the ports around the peninsula, I set the prepared snack boxes— courtesy of the hotel kitchen staff—on the sofa table in front of our guests. I congratulate them on their special anniversary.

"This is all just beyond extraordinary," Jan exclaims with un- bridled joy. "Thank you both—this is such a treat." Her cropped silver hair frames her slender face and highlights her sky-blue eyes. "Port Townsend has been on our radar since the early 2000s. One of Wayne's staff pastors performed a wedding out here years ago, and when we saw the pictures, we added it to our retirement list straightaway."

Wayne slips an arm around his wife's shoulders. "Don't let my bride's romantic talk fool you. She's really only here to see a whale— orca, humpback, gray, doesn't matter. It's a good thing I'm not the jealous type, because I'm third in line after Jesus and marine life."

Jan elbows him in the side, and when the two laugh, Joel catches my eye and neither of us can keep a straight face.

Jan works to unfasten her binocular case, and I encourage her to keep her focus starboard as the pods tend to stay west this time of year. She thanks me, and I decide to stick close in case she needs any more pointers. As we roll over the sea at a leisurely pace, I'm all too aware of Joel's presence at the helm. His technique is smooth and relaxed, as is the way he converses with our passengers about how the pods are tracked and named and how they're known by all the whale-watching boats who frequent these waters.

While Wayne asks dozens of questions about the area, I assist Jan with the binoculars again, showing her how to focus them and giving her tips on how to sweep the waves in search of marine life. It's a bit too windy for her out on the deck, so she uses the viewing window inside and braces herself against the back of the sofa like an eager child.

Once she gets the hang of it, I do another refill on drinks, retriev- ing a Sprite from the fridge for Joel. He tolerated Cece's lemonade slushies, but a cold soda has always been his favorite summertime beverage.

Our fingertips brush in the handoff, and despite the chilled can a hot *zing* zips up my spine. "You should come sit down with us, Indy," Joel invites. "I can help with the other tasks once we're docked."

"Yes, come join us, there's no shortage of space," Wayne says, scooting over to give me the end of the sofa, just across the narrow aisle from where Joel sits at the helm. "You can take my seat if the two of you want to—"

"Oh no, that's all right. I'm keeping my eyes peeled for whales. I have a better vantage point if I remain standing."

I post near a window behind Joel's bench, searching the vast waters while my ears remain open to Joel and Wayne's conversation.

The retired pastor takes a sip of his Coke. "I noticed the sign outside the dining room of the hotel referring to late-brunch Sundays as well as the list of local churches and worship times they provide in the area. Sure makes checking out the competition easier." He winks at me and slides into a deep southern drawl. "You can take the preacher out of the pulpit, but you can't take away his desire to critique a good sermon."

Joel laughs. "My folks have always given our kitchen staff Sunday mornings off so they could attend church and enjoy time with their families. We try to keep as light a crew as possible that day."

"That's rare in today's world," Wayne replies. "It's a blessing to have a family whose principles are backed by a strong faith. Keeping faithful habits and traditions in our lives is what helps us stay afloat when life goes topsy-turvy."

"I suppose there's truth to that," Joel says in a contemplative tone. "Although I think even the best practices aren't enough to sustain someone through a real crisis. At least, it wasn't that way for me."

Wayne regards Joel with rapt interest, and I find myself doing the same. I've never heard him speak a contrary word about practices of faith, much less the church he'd attended for decades. Joel's family has been longtime members of Lighthouse Community Fellowship.

He'd been the one to invite me nearly every Sunday for close to a year before I finally worked up the courage to say yes. Cece had attended as well, but her snooze button often took precedence over the start time during a good portion of her teen years. It was Joel who'd accompanied me most.

"Call it an occupational habit, or simply an old man being nosy, but I hope you're planning to unpack that statement a bit more."

Joel motions to the open water, to the mountains, to the cloudless patch of sky overhead. "I'd hate for you to miss the sights. We'll be to Port Williams within thirty minutes."

Wayne waves him off with a chuckle and gestures lovingly to his wife, who hasn't lowered her binoculars once. "Consider theological discussions my personal whale-watching obsession." His grin is contagious as he slides his gaze to his wife's back and says in a purposeful whisper, "It's probably not hard to tell which of the two of us is more holy."

"My eyes might be focused on the water, Wayne, but I promise you my ears work just fine. You best behave yourself."

Once again, we all laugh, and then Jan jolts straight up.

"Look there," she points. "There's a cruise ship coming right at us!"

"Objects are closer than they appear, dear." Wayne taps her binoculars and she lowers them and squints, but to her credit, the ship isn't too far off.

"Ingrid," Joel says, craning his neck to find me. "I'll need to get over this wake quickly."

"Right." I nod at his meaning and ask the sweet couple to secure their seats for a few minutes so Joel can maneuver the boat around the wake. As I take a seat directly behind him, my right shoulder grazes his back and he twists his neck again so our faces are close.

"Thank you for being here," he murmurs just loud enough for me to hear, and something warm glows bright in my chest.

He accelerates to exit the wake quickly, and the whir of the engines and the movement of the wind and the waves put an end to any and all discussions. To converse at sea, you have to be intentional. It's why my father trained me in hand signals at the same time my mother was teaching me how to read. I'm sure most were standard but others were ours alone—how he'd tap his cap twice to tell me to stay alert to our surroundings. How he'd open and close his fist in a blinking maneuver to indicate an approaching lighthouse—my *favorite* sight on the water. Or how he'd pat his right shoulder with his left hand before touching the tip of his nose and pointing out to sea. It was my father's original way of saying, *The best life is one spent at sea.*

I notice when Wayne cocks a persuasive eyebrow at our captain as if to suggest he's ready to listen whenever he's ready to speak. If Joel is bothered by the retired pastor's forthrightness, he doesn't show it. He simply taps the throttle until the engine slows to a low hum and takes a full breath.

"I've been somewhat of an overachiever since birth," he begins. "A natural problem-solver like my dad. I prided myself on fixing potential conflicts before they ever had a chance to surface." At his hesitation, I see the span of muscles constrict in his upper back through the thin white cotton of his shirt. "But that was before a problem I tried to solve hurt someone I cared about very much . . . and there was no reversing the part I played in it."

In the quiet seconds that follow, a barrage of images flood my mind, starting with the torment on Joel's face that night on the dock when I told him I wasn't coming back from California after graduation like we'd planned. I can hear his pleas for me to stay, for me to forgive him, for me to allow him to be the one to comfort me through the dark days of grief ahead. But it's the strength of his embrace I swear I can still feel when I close my eyes. The way his arms tightened around my waist for a final time, holding me as if he thought he could keep me from leaving.

Or maybe because he knew he couldn't.

"It only took one night for me to question everything I ever believed about God," he continues, "and it took years for me to find the answers I needed most. You were right about my parents having good principles, but their faith alone wasn't enough to save me when I was drowning. I had to be the one to reach for the life raft."

Wayne nods solemnly. "I think it's the single most important reach we can make as humans. It's especially difficult to make when we're suffering."

Joel doesn't speak for close to a minute before he finally offers, "It's even more difficult when the people you love continue to suffer."

My heart is caught between my chest and my throat, and I have to glance toward the salon to keep the tears from rolling down my cheeks. Suffering isn't a word I've ever allotted to Joel Campbell, yet what right did I have to assign any kind of emotion to him when I'd been the one to walk away six weeks after we'd buried my father?

Before my thoughts can linger much longer in this altogether new territory, a piercing cry splits the air, causing all of us to leap from our seats. Joel kills the engines as Jan flails her arms and laughs. She points toward the water but her only words are a broken kind of gibberish. We look in the direction she's wildly gesturing toward and discover a pod of three or four orcas.

I immediately reach for my phone and take a video of Jan and Wayne as they share the binoculars and exclaim over the discovery of such a wonder. I zoom in on the whales just in time to see one of the orcas breach the water and smack the surface with a huge splash. It repeats this performance several times over, and Jan is beside herself, her countenance overcome with joy. Finally, when the pod heads north, Wayne takes his wife in his arms and plants a kiss on the top of her head. "Happy anniversary, sweetie."

My eyes well at their tenderness, and I can't help but study the two of them with wonder at all they must have experienced in a marriage spanning forty-five years. What kind of hardship had they overcome during that time? What kind of tragedies and regrets had they navigated?

I twist to find Joel's eyes on me, and his expression seems to hold his own set of ponderings before he takes on the role of captain once again. "We'll be in the harbor in five minutes."

For never having docked a boat with Joel at the helm, there's a seamlessness to it I can't explain. We're a synchronized dance of bumpers, ropes, cleats, and knots. By the time we're positioned in the seaweed-coated slip, Jan and Wayne have gathered up their belongings and given us both farewell hugs and well wishes. I send them the whale video I captured and encourage them both to buy the lavender soap and hand lotion from the farm.

Once they've met their driver at the end of the dock and Joel and I are left standing alone on the deck, Joel begins to reel in the back bumpers.

"I think you've forgotten your place at that fancy helm, Captain," I tease. "Bumper retrieval is my job."

The mischievous glint in his eyes when he turns is so surprising that I don't register what's happening until it's much, much too late.

Before I can even think to shield myself, Joel peels a giant piece of wet seaweed off the bumper and flings it at my bare legs. It slaps against my kneecap and sticks.

My mouth drops open, and his laugh is one I haven't been privy to in years. "You did not just do that."

His lips pull to one side. "Pretty sure I just did."

"Joel Campbell. We are too old to engage in seaweed wars." But even before I'm finished speaking, I dash to the edge of the deck and jump onto the creaky dock in search of suitable retaliation. I scan the water for the first patch of kelp I can lay eyes on.

His white shirt is starting to look a bit too white.

He bounds down the long dock after me, but I pay no mind to his apologies or to the speed at which he's approaching. My eyes are locked on my target at the end of the marina. In a quick maneuver I doubt I could repeat a second time, I drop flat onto my belly and grip the briny, soggy stalk of sea kelp floating near the shore. And much like a cowgirl lassoes a rope, I swing it in a wide circle and let it fly.

He hollers as it wraps around his middle and smacks him square in the chest. I'm still on my haunches, barely able to catch a breath from wheezing in delight.

He holds out his once-clean shirt and looks down at the kelp-imprinted design. "I've always wanted an Ingrid Erikson original."

I laugh until my cheeks hurt nearly as badly as my hamstrings. "Glad I could provide one for you then."

Joel reaches his hand out to me. "Truce?"

"Not before you admit defeat."

"Ingrid, you won long before you even knew there was a race." He pulls me up and then removes something green and wet from my shoulder. "But I don't think seaweed makes for a very good trophy."

"I agree," I say a bit breathlessly.

He stares at me a few seconds too long to be playful before shifting his gaze to the horizon. "We should probably head back. We still have two hours ahead of us and the sunset isn't too far behind."

We walk the length of the dock together in companionable silence, and I breathe in the briny sea air like a rare perfume. Somehow the scent is different here in the Sound than in the San Francisco Bay, more pungent and decipherable. More familiar.

By the time we've finished prepping the cruiser for our course, the sun's golden reflection on the water is as blinding as it is mesmerizing, and I drag my gaze away from it. I'd forgotten this. I'd forgotten so much of everything that used to be my normal routine.

"Want to join me on the sky bridge? It's the best spot this time of night."

I glance at the stairs leading to the second story cockpit. Nerves shimmy up my spine as if his invitation to be out in the open air with him is somehow more intimate than when he was navigating from the helm inside the cabin. But there's no use trying to reason with logic; I'm too acquainted with the alluring nature of the sea to be innocent to its charm.

I'm halfway up the steps before I remember to answer him.

Joel sits at one of the two white swivel chairs facing a navigation system any experienced seaman would covet. There is little about this vessel that reminds me of the one my father was hired to captain for the Campbells all those summers ago. But this spot, this bird's-eye view of the open water and surrounding islands and mountain ranges, these rocky shores and beaches where I used to read the day away in between shifts at the hotel and charter bookings with my father . . . these are the moments that swarm my heart with something that feels too much like homesickness. I rub at the fabric that covers my heart, hoping to ease the ache building beneath.

When I reach Joel, he gestures for me to take the seat beside him.

"Thank you for—" he starts at the same time I say, "You did a—"

He chuckles. "Ladies first."

"You're a good captain."

He follows my honesty with a hesitant expression. "You can't possibly know what it means to hear you say that."

His arresting tone holds me hostage until he reaches across his chest with his left arm, taps his right shoulder, tweaks his nose, and then points out to sea.

I suck in a sharp breath as realization dawns.

His smile is half-mast as he answers my unasked question. "Your father apprenticed me for my captain's license. Eighty hours in total. We started the summer of your sophomore year of college."

I think back to our constant texts and video calls during that season and shake my head. "But how is that possible? How didn't I know?"

"It was supposed to be a surprise, for when you came home from school."

My throat grows uncomfortably tight as his meaning solidifies into a timeline of events I can't possibly forget, starting with a phone call about my missing father, and then to a confession, and then to a funeral, and then finally to a breakup.

Joel sobers. "He talked about you a lot. Your mother, too, but mostly you. He told me so many stories about when you were young—how you took your first steps on a barge off the coast of Oregon, how you told him crabs would be nicer if only their claws weren't so heavy, how you never went to sleep without a book tucked under your pillow, how he wished he could go back in time and change so many things about—"

"*Joel.*" His name is a shaky whisper on my breath.

With one hand still guiding the helm, he uses his other to capture mine. "He loved you, Indy. I know his death is complicated, and I know I'm the last person you want to hear this from, but you need to hear it. Even more than I need to say it to you." He swallows. "I spent eighty-plus hours with your father alone on a fishing boat and never once did he fail to ask me the same two questions each time we docked in the marina." The pinch in his voice causes my throat to burn. "The first was always, 'She's happy at school, isn't she?'"

My chin trembles slightly as the pain in his gaze shifts to our joined hands.

"The second was, 'You'll keep her that way when she comes home, won't you?'"

I cut my misty gaze to the sea, trying to reconcile the image of my burly, overconfident father asking Joel about my happiness. It certainly wasn't my happiness he'd been thinking of that stormy night when he stole the Campbell's fishing boat, never to return.

It's difficult to swallow against the wind and even more so against the throbbing in my chest, but as soon as I slip my hand from his, my composure returns, and I find my voice. "I'm sorry, it wasn't his place to ask that of you."

"I'm just sorry my answer couldn't be yes."

17

My original plan for Operation Find Cece's Missing Notebooks was to keep a structured inventory of each area, closet, and bookshelf I searched inside the cottage. But that was all before I'd held Joel's hand on a boat during sunset as he spoke in hushed tones about my father.

Now there's not a single organized thought to be found in my head.

Hundreds of books have been pulled off the shelves in Cece's living room, and it's fairly obvious that my only goal is to leave no possibility unturned. Cece was forever stuffing bank receipts, pictures, cards, and important mementos inside and behind the books she loved most. It was her own version of an under-the-mattress savings account.

Unfortunately, Cece was always far better at hiding treasure than she was at finding it. Probably why she was so phenomenal at drawing out her pirate maps as well as the scavenger hunts she'd leave for Joel and me to find at random. But Cece herself once lost a two-hundred-dollar cash tip in what she swore was her leather-bound edition of *Pride and Prejudice*. We found it a year later tucked inside her favorite thriller novel. For all I know, her giant hardback of *War and Peace* might actually be a hollowed front, hiding all six hundred handwritten pages of *The Fate of Kings* inside it.

All I know for sure is that it's been five days and I've discovered nothing of significance. SaBrina will likely be posting a job opening for the position I currently hold very soon unless I can provide her with a promising lead, or better yet, a first draft. Whatever the case, I need to pick up the pace. As good as last night was, I'm not a first mate playing house with a part-time captain. I'm an editor, one whose future is not here.

Due to Joel's long hours at sea yesterday, he'd texted to say he'd be landlocked at the hotel today and most of tomorrow, too—a fact that should make me grateful for the extra hunting time. But of all the confusing and downright contradicting feelings splashing around inside me, *grateful* doesn't even make the top five.

Sometime in the late afternoon, I sit back on my haunches and jam my palms into my eye sockets. The chaos I've created in this room is abysmal, and I don't feel a single percent closer to finding the notebooks or going home. There has to be an easier way of going about this, but how does one search for something they have so little information about?

My legs have fallen asleep from sitting in the same position for too long, and I grab ahold of the back of the sofa to haul myself up to standing. I'm too young to be making the kinds of noises that escape me, and yet, here we are: twenty-seven going on seventy-seven. On my way up, my hip nudges one of the book piles a tad too hard, causing a Jenga-style topple. A miniature-sized Polaroid skitters out from the hardback copy of *Breaking Dawn* and spins in place on the floorboards.

I recognize the snapshot immediately. It's from the night Joel read to us yesterday morning—the annual staff party at the Campbells. Only this picture had been taken at the end of the night, when all of us looked a bit worse for wear. Thanks to Cece's obsession with hairspray, my beach waves looked like a solid piece of petrified wood. My gaze lingers on Joel's dashing, youthful face, and I think again of the claim Cece made about Joel that night outside Wendy's house, of what she saw in the shadows before he turned away.

I try and convince myself that none of it matters now. How could it? I heard what Joel said to Wayne yesterday, how the struggles he'd faced after I left town had taken him years to resolve. But even still, he'd resolved them.

If only I could be so lucky.

I scan our three smiling faces once more, shifting my focus to land on Cece's goofy, lopsided grin. Grief sweeps low in my belly. We were only kids back then. None of us would have guessed what only a few short years would bring.

The sound of a key turning in the lock jolts me from the question, and I shove the photo into the back pocket of my high-waisted daisy shorts. Cece would have approved this Walmart purchase.

"Ingrid? You here?" Allie's voice sails through the kitchen. "It's kind of hard to tell when there's nothing parked in the driveway."

"Hey, I'm in here, Allie," I call from the rubble. "Come on in."

I can hear her kicking off her shoes before she makes her way through the kitchen and dining room. She slams to a stop the instant she reaches the living room.

"Whoa." Her eyes round at the sight of the floor. "Is this a crime scene? Have the police dusted for fingerprints yet?"

"Afraid they'd only find mine if they did. I've been working on a . . . project."

Allie says nothing as she circles the mess and assesses the "project" that looks more like the aftermath of an earthquake.

"Ya know, I'm pretty good at organizing if you need some help."

The casual way she suggests this, as if seeing a hundred-plus books in random stacks—one that's recently been toppled—is just a normal part of her day, makes me laugh.

"Don't you have other jobs to get to today?"

"They're almost done. Besides, dusting this bookshelf is technically one of my weekly tasks at the cottage anyway."

"I think this qualifies as more than dusting." I laugh again and move to the end of the shelf and riffle through the last ten books.

"How were you hoping to organize these?" She maneuvers the

ottoman in front of the bookshelves, and I'm instantly envious of her genius. There will be no needle pricks of death for her long legs. "We could sort by book size, color, or genre? Or of course the library standard of alphabetizing by the author's last name?" She digs into her pocket. "Ooh, there's actually some book reviewers I follow whose shelves look like works of art—here, let me show you."

In less than six seconds, she's swiped and tapped and flipped her phone around to show me a bookshelf in the color scheme of a rainbow, and she's right—it looks like a mural I'd see on the side of a used bookstore in my city. She continues to tap on new images via hashtags, and I'm in absolute awe at how quickly she's finding these things and how old I feel that I know so little of this world. And it's then my brain does some clicking and swiping of its own as I recall that Miss Allie Spencer here is not only a loyal employee to the Campbells but an admin for Cecelia J. Campbell's Memorial Page. As well as countless other such pages. I stare at the books on the floor again and then back at Allie on her phone. Perhaps the easier approach to my book hunting is sitting right in front of me.

"Allie?"

She types in a new hashtag and shows me a pic of a mountain pattern and sky pattern and then one more of a tree-like shelf made entirely of books. "Cool, huh?"

"Yeah, super cool." Gingerly, I sit on a stack of hardback books across from her so we're nearly eye to eye.

She looks up from her phone and seems to register something in my eyes. "What? Did you think of a pattern you want to try? There's lots of color in these stacks so there are tons of options."

I shake my head. "I don't have a pattern in mind, but I do have something else I'd like to ask you about."

She leans in, elbows on her knees. "Okay, shoot."

"Let's say I wanted to search for something specific, across every social media platform out there—a specific type of picture, with a specific person in it, during a specific time period. Would that be possible?"

She nods slowly, as if still waiting for me to get to the hard part. Only for me, that is the hard part. I don't have the first clue about filtering details through social media posts. "Sure. So if I heard you right, you're wanting to find something . . . specific?" She smiles.

I pick up the nearest book, which just so happens to be a thriller spy novel from the early 2000s I never read. "What would you think about doing some online investigative work for me?"

Her entire face cracks wide open. "I'd say absolutely. Just tell me what you need."

I glance around the house. "How often are you supposed to tidy up this place?"

"Twice a week, at about an hour each time. It's mostly light cleaning and airing out the rooms and stuff."

"What would you say if I offered to do your two hours of cleaning inside the cottage in exchange for you doing two hours of online detective work for me—plus, I'd pay you an hourly wage for whatever time you can give me above and beyond that."

Her eyebrows jump to her hairline. "You want to *pay me* to search some stuff on social media for you?"

"Yes." I pause, debating how much I should tell her about the search itself. "It's important work—confidential, even. But if you can help me find what I'm looking for, it would mean a great deal to a lot of people. Myself included."

She sits back and sucks her bottom lip between her teeth. "I'll do it," she says, "but I don't want you to pay me." A full three seconds go by before her heel jitters on the floorboards. "I'm wondering if we might work out a different kind of trade instead? It's totally okay if not, though. I don't really know how this kind of thing works. It's part of why Cece agreed to come to my writing club at school—she was going to talk to us about the process of publication and such." She shakes her head, as if realizing I'm not tracking with her. "I know you're like one of the best editors in the entire world, and I have no business asking this of you, but—"

I reach my hand out and place it on her knee, finally understanding where this is going. "Allie, do you have something you'd like me to read?"

Her nod is reluctant. "It might be really awful though."

I smile and think back to how many times Cece started off her chapter readings to me by saying just that. "Why don't you tell me a little about it—it's fiction, I presume?"

She nods and exhales a deep breath, and then launches into a fantasy premise about fairies and trolls and humans all coexisting inside a story world that wedges itself deep into the folds of my heart. Her passionate voice creates images that rise to life and waltz across my mind's eye. I'm not prepared for the movie reel she awakens from inside the black cave of my hibernating imagination. Goosebumps trail my arms and neck as she describes an unjust moral system which begs for mercy. Her voice quakes with the heartbeat of characters who revive an instinct inside me I believed dead until now.

When she finally breaks long enough to inhale, I'm barely able to blink my tears away in time before I say, "Send it to me, Allie. I'd love to read it."

It's nearly seven when my phone rings, and I pause before I reach for it. Joel predicted his last meeting would end around seven—not that I've been keeping track of the time since he texted two hours ago to ask about dinner plans—but the bag of microwavable kettle corn I shared with Allie won't tide me over much longer. And since Joel mentioned picking up takeout for us, I've been avoiding the siren's call of the pantry ever since. By cleaning.

I flip my phone over. Not Joel.

I swipe to accept Chip's call.

"Hey," I say, opening the dishwasher and positioning my face in the steam. It's the closest I've come to a facial since Cece's twenty-fourth birthday at a spa in Denver.

"Hang on," he says, "my voice recognition software isn't a hundred percent positive it's really you. Is this *the* Ingrid Erikson of Fog Harbor Books, winner of the prestigious Editor of the Year Award? If so, I'll need you to authenticate."

I can't help but smile, but I suppose it has been a bit strange that most of our interactions have been subject to text as of late. "Hmm, let's see. I once wrote you a three-by-five card of approved pick-up lines for your favorite pink-haired barista. How's that going anyway?"

He sighs.

"Uh oh." I set the mugs on the open shelving to the left of the sink and arrange them with their handles facing to the right. "I thought you were asking her out this week?"

"I thought so, too. But new evidence suggests she has a boyfriend."

"What kind of new evidence?"

"I saw her kissing a Seattle Seahawks fan by the milk steamer on Monday."

I gasp. "Noooo."

"Yep. I really thought she had better sports judgment than that. It was devestating on multiple levels."

"I'm so sorry, Chip."

"Eh, I'll live." He clears his throat. "Anyway, do you have a chance to check your email? I'm getting your pitches ready for the sales conference next week, and I was hoping you could look them over for me. I could ask SaBrina but . . ." He trails off, and I understand every ounce of his hesitation.

I set the last glass from the top rack of the dishwasher into the cabinet and admire a mug on the top shelf in the shape of a puppy that looks uncannily similar to Rontu. "Give me just a minute, and I'll look them over."

"Sure, I'm not going anywhere for a while."

"Wait, are you still at the office?"

"Headed to the break room as we speak to scavenge for food. I'm starving, but I still have to prep for a couple of meetings tomorrow—

one with the cover design team and another to go over a proposal for a new production schedule timeline, and then one on the sales conference."

All things I would be doing if I were there. Guilt dulls my own hunger pangs. "Chip, I'm sorry. I feel terrible you're stuck doing all that on your own when—"

"Nope. That was not a you-should-feel-guilty-for-not-being-here comment. You've needed a break from here, I just wish you weren't stuck in the last place on earth you want to be." I feel a strange urge to correct him when the slamming of cupboard doors in the background causes me to pull the phone away from my ear. I set it to speaker and place it on top of the microwave so I can finish cleaning the kitchen.

"You know what this office needs?" Chip continues as another cupboard door slams. "Someone who will police the snack inventory and expiration dates inside this break room."

"Can they also police how hard you're closing those cupboard doors, too? My eardrums are about ready to file an official complaint to HR."

"Sorry about that. Had to put you on speaker. Need both hands to peruse this sad collection of party crackers."

"You're on speaker here, too." I tap my phone screen. No new texts from Joel. Once in the living room, I set it down on the arm of the sofa, then reach for my laptop. "Okay, I'm looking over the email now, Chip." Using track changes, I make just a few edits to the pitches and a couple more on the structure, but overall he's done a great job.

"*Jackpot!* Guess who just found a half bag of Taco Doritos."

The distinctive sound of a chip bag unfurling has me reaching again for the volume control on my phone. I tap it down but not in time to avoid the sound of him munching, and my stomach roils. "Chip, you can't seriously be eating those."

His chomping makes me cringe.

"Honestly, this is far from the worse thing I've eaten at the office."

A text flashes on the screen next to me, and Joel's name mutes all crunching and commentary from Chip.

Joel

Indy—sorry to keep you waiting. Discovered a blown breaker thirty minutes ago. An electrician is on his way over. Looks like I'll be stuck here for a while. Can we reschedule for tomorrow afternoon? I'll bring the memoir.

I think on my reply—starting it twice before landing on something safe.

Ingrid

Tomorrow afternoon is good for me. Hope everything goes well tonight.

Joel

Thx. I'll call you tomorrow.

". . . although, in my opinion, the Green Salsa Verde ranks below Taco. I wonder if anybody has ever taken the time to officially rank Doritos by flavor?"

Hoping Chip's Dorito flavor ranking question is rhetorical only, I jump in with a topic change. "These pitches look great to me. Feel free to send anything else for me to review before the conference."

"Wait, conference isn't until next month. You'll be back by then, right?"

"Of course I will," I say with all the confidence I can muster, though we both know my answer hinges on a certain discovery that is still MIA.

"Okay, good. I was hoping I wasn't missing something."

Only I know he is missing something, maybe a couple of somethings, and I don't want to get off the phone without clearing them up. "I don't hate it here, Chip. It's not a tropical vacation or anything, but it's not all bad." I think of my time at Wendy's and then with Allie today. I smile as I recall Rontu's wagging tail and my sunrise walks on the beach. And then I picture Joel at the helm of a boat last night as he took my hand and shared a kindness with me I won't soon forget and certainly hadn't deserved.

"Oh . . . well, that's good. Does that mean things are less complicated than you thought?"

"Hardly." I breathe through my nose and feel a tingling in my lips to tell him what I've been holding back since the day after I arrived. "If anything, they're even more complicated now."

I think of the critical findings Allie helped me discover today, the ones I haven't even had the chance to tell Joel about yet. A mix of elation and anticipation buzzes in my chest. I click out of my email browser and into the online spreadsheet we're using to track every post that mentions a location Cece visited or was tagged in during the last year of her life. We tracked patterns, activities, hashtags, fan visits, and most importantly, any clue involving *The Fate of King* and her notebooks. Another confirmation: It's definitely more than one notebook, like I suspected. One wouldn't be enough. She'd have needed multiple. No wonder Wendy couldn't pinpoint an exact description. We tracked the posts from December to early August—the last month Cece was online. We spotted four unique composition notebooks in total—similar to the ones she used in high school—in yellow, blue, red, and black.

"This can't go beyond you and me, Chip, but there is something I haven't told you yet."

All sound in the background stills, and a strange blend of foreboding and excitement brews inside me as his silence encourages me to continue.

"The package I picked up from the attorney's office last Friday—it wasn't *The Fate of Kings.*"

"Y-e-a-h." The word is drawn-out, confused. "You told me that already, remember?"

"Yes, but what I didn't tell you then was that the package did actually contain a manuscript. One Cece wrote for her cousin Joel and me. It's a retelling of our childhood friendships, of our lives together in Port Townsend. We've been reading it like she asked us to and . . ." The hair on the back of my neck rises as I recall my conversation with Wendy. "And despite it not being the manuscript I wanted, I can't help but think there's a bigger purpose for why she gave it to us, you know?"

Chip's breathy swear is so muted I barely register it. "So you're telling me that Cece wrote a manuscript you had no idea she was writing?"

"Yes."

"And then she left it to you?"

"And to Joel, yes."

Another curse. "Sorry, that's just *a lot* to process."

"Which is why I needed some time before I said anything to you about it."

"Understandable." A long, pensive silence stretches between us before Chip speaks again, his tone far more serious than it had been a moment ago. "Ingrid? You haven't told anyone else about this right?"

"Just you. Well, and Allie."

"Who?"

"Allie Spencer, she's been helping me search for the manuscript, as well as keeping the cottage organized, the groceries stocked, and my transportation needs sorted."

"So she's basically the Washington version of me."

"Actually, in a couple years after she graduates she might be exactly you."

"Okay, well, I don't think it's a good idea to mention the contents of that package to anybody else." There's a warning in his tone that sobers me. "It's just, if the wrong person was to discover there's an unpublished manuscript written by Cece Campbell in your possession . . . I don't even want to imagine the media circus that would ensue."

I picture the pages tucked away in Joel's backpack. "It's safe, Chip. I promise. You don't need to worry."

"I really hope you're right." He pauses again. "People do crazy things for treasures far less valuable than the one in your possession."

18

I've circled the living room coffee table where my laptop sits open four times now. And all four times, I've found a reason not to click on the file Allie emailed me roughly thirty minutes after I arrived back from conducting a thorough manuscript hunt at Wendy's house. I've braided my hair, spot-cleaned my daisy shorts for a second-day wear, retrieved a bottle of water from the fridge, and applied a thick layer of sunscreen to my arms and face for the on-location reading excursion Joel planned for us in t-minus ten minutes.

My palms are damp as I drop to the edge of the chair and pull the laptop toward me. Never in a thousand lifetimes would I have thought I'd ever be scared *to read a story*. Then again, never in a thousand lifetimes would I have imagined many of the events that have taken place over the past five years.

When I offered this trade to Allie, I felt confident, as if I'd left all my reading issues behind me in California. I'm not so sure anymore. Light editing on the pitches Chip sent me last night is not even in the same stratosphere as reviewing a piece of fiction.

I hold my breath and double-click on the file.

It opens immediately.

Allie's youthful font choice tugs at the corners of my lips, and the pressure inside my chest eases considerably. I re-envision the imagery and world-building her words created in my mind yesterday and try not to think of the next few minutes as a test. I scroll past her working title—*The Faerie Huntress*—and engage my cursor on the first line. *Only the first line,* I coach myself, *and then the first paragraph. Focus. Focus. Focus.*

In my experience, most humans define the *fae* as a flock of flirtatiously clad Tinkerbells with pockets full of pixie dust. Millions of trusting parents read bedtime stories to their children, marveling at the illustrations of mystical gardens and magical streams where fairies grant wishes for nothing more than a smile. But in my line of work, I find most humans to be irresponsibly naïve. They do not fear the veil that divides our worlds because they do not seek to understand our world. Not as it truly is. And therefore, they understand nothing.

I pause and review the words in my head, rolling them around in my mind's eye to make sure all are accounted for. That none have defected.

To my shock, they're all here.

I continue on, the assertive voice behind the narrative tugging me forward until I lose myself in the action.

After a person is forced to watch their soulmate plead for life as the hand of evil mercilessly steals their last breath, one's moral compass shifts. Four hundred and thirty-two days ago, I experienced such a shift. I sheath my weapon and step into my boots, glancing once more at the sketch taped to my wall: a face I've vowed never to forget. Or to forgive.

I manage to read all the way to the end of the paragraph before the fatigue hits like a brick wall.

And then, just like that, the film reel in my head clicks off and ejects.

It's as if a director in a different hemisphere of my brain has just called *cut!,* banishing all actors from the set despite my internal screams for them to stay. I slump against the padded chair and stare out at the tide slipping away. Nothing has changed. Whatever progress I thought I'd made yesterday hasn't translated to the page. I'm still just as broken here as I was in California.

Before I can feel the full weight of this revelation, I slam the laptop closed and stand, giving my daisy shorts a swift tug south before tightening the tie at my waist. Then two shrill rings coming from the direction of the driveway pull me through the kitchen to the door.

The instant I step onto Cece's porch, I stop at the sight of a seafoam-colored bike propped on its kickstand in the middle of the driveway. Joel is just a few steps behind it, unloading a slate-gray version of the same bike from the back of the hotel's utility truck. He sets it down next to the first and rings the bell on the handlebars. His lazy grin coils around my insides and in an instant, I'm picturing his fingers wrapped around mine the way they were last night.

"Thought we could try these out." He points to the cruiser closest to me and slips on his backpack. "Take a test ride to the lighthouse. This one's yours."

The sleek, trendy design captivates my full attention. There's not a single scuff on the paint, and the fat black tires show no sign of tread wear. It's brand-new. I walk around it, grazing my fingers along the broad chrome handlebars and the woven basket that sits sweetly behind the wide leather seat. It's then I see the black rectangular box on the adjustment bar just below where I'm to sit.

"Is that a motor?" I lift my eyes and meet Joel's studious gaze.

"Yes. It's electric with a pedal-assist option so you can utilize the motor as little or as much as you want. We have a dozen or so on order for next summer. Our plan is to offer them as day rentals for our guests who want more of a true beach-town experience."

"That's a really smart idea," I say, imagining the appeal for tourists.

"I think so, too. Although I can't take credit for it."

And just by the way he says it, it's not hard to conclude where such marketing brilliance might have come from.

"Madison?" I guess.

He confirms with a nod.

"Then shouldn't she be the one to do the test ride with you?" Seems only fair of me to ask, not that I suddenly believe in the idea of fair. Or that I suddenly like the idea of Madison alone on a beach with Joel. Then again, perhaps people who live outside of a nine-hundred-mile radius shouldn't get an opinion on such matters.

"Madison owns one," he concludes easily, though now I'm left to wonder just how many sunset rides the two of them have shared together.

He shoves his hands into the pockets of his cargo shorts. The muscles in his biceps flex and release, and I notice the contrast of sun-kissed skin against the lightweight aqua tee he's wearing. I divert my gaze from the ink that spirals up his right forearm. "I thought you could use a better way to get around town." He smiles. "Consider this yours for however long you're here."

I've never understood how kindness can sometimes feel like a fresh cut, how the sting intensifies the longer it remains in open air, how even after the wound is cleaned and covered, the tenderness can linger for days.

But as I look from Joel to the bike, I feel the raw, warring sensation anew. "Thank you."

"My pleasure."

My cheeks prickle at the warmth of his voice, and I smooth my hand over the bike seat. "Chip has an electric bike, too, although this is a different style than his."

"Ah, Chip," Joel says in a tone that definitely doesn't scream friendliness. "Is this the same Chip that called you during our brunch?"

I tilt my head and squint to see his face despite the blinding sun behind his head. "I only know one."

"And he's . . . ?"

"A super great guy," I fill in, letting the assumption dangle a few seconds too long—but honestly, if I have to imagine sunset bike rides with Madison the Model, then is it really so wrong of me to let Joel wonder for all of three seconds that someone out there might still find me desirable?

I clear my throat. "He's also my assistant, one I trained when he was a college intern." This feels like an important detail to mention, as does, "He has a crippling phobia of seaweed, leads a gamer squadron with the IT guys at the office called the Nerd Herd, and named his bike Eugenia." There, in case there was any doubt who Chip is to me, all confusion should be cleared up now.

Joel quirks an eyebrow. "Your assistant named his bike?"

"Is that really the quirk you find the weirdest out of that list?"

He laughs. "Why seaweed?"

"Trust me, you really don't want to know." I pull on the helmet he gives me and fiddle with the adjustments on the straps, missing the buckle connection multiple times over. Despite what Joel may think, I'm far from a biking expert. A Peloton rider I might be, but I haven't ridden an actual bike in many, many years.

"I should confess, I haven't done this for a while."

I anticipate a round of jokes about my stationary bike, but Joel simply steps towards me, slips his fingers under my chin, and connects the two parts in a single try. "You'll remember." He grips the handle of my bike and releases the kickstand, holding it upright for me. "Let the bike do the work for you until you're comfortable. It's easy to make adjustments along the way." He sets a spare water bottle in my basket and then wakes the display screen mounted between my handlebars. The numbers and arrows are bright and clear—speed, mileage, weather, battery strength. "The throttle is here, and the handbrakes work the same as on a regular bike." He climbs onto his seat and inclines his head for me to take the lead. "I'll stay close until we get off the main road."

And with that, I pedal and slowly engage the throttle to exit the driveway. Joel's right, the muscle memory is there. Right where I left it.

We're halfway up the hill and moving too quickly for me to interpret Joel's expression, but I file it away with so many other details about this afternoon—the cotton-white clouds, the hint of salt in the air, and the lack of car horns, smog, and crowds.

I pause my pedaling for a few rotations and hold my face to the sun.

"You approve?" Joel asks.

"Not sure I'll be able to ride in my office ever again."

I hear him chuckle. "That's good enough for me."

I hunker down, tap the up arrow until it reaches max speed, and leave Joel in my dust. I pedal until my lungs burn as if my menial efforts might push the limits of a bike that is likely more advanced than my laptop. My sneaky head start serves to keep Joel in my periphery for approximately sixty seconds. But even still, the rush that comes from gaining ground, even if only in a bike race, is one I haven't felt in some time. I've been playing catch-up in life for too long.

"Brake, Indy! *Brake!*" Joel hollers as we approach a four-way stop that wasn't there five years ago. I react immediately, not prepared for how quickly the brakes respond to my touch.

I'm still panting when Joel pulls to a stop beside me and reaches for my handlebars, pulling me in the way he did years ago after he lost to Cece in a bike race he never planned to win. Only this time, he doesn't lean in close to whisper in my ear. This time, his expression darkens as he fixes his gaze on something in the distance.

"What is it?" I follow his glower to the beach where a lone news truck is parked. "The news truck?"

"It's fine." But by the way his jaw is clenched, it's clearly anything but *fine*. "You good to ride again?"

I nod and soon we're in motion again. Neither of us engage our motors as we ride in silence toward the shadowy, scenic trails of Fort Warden State Park. We weave our way through colonial-style military buildings and the old bunkers we used to explore when tourist season was over and we had full rein of the meticulously maintained grounds. But I doubt Joel took this detour for nostalgia's sake.

As soon as we exit the park, his shoulders relax. "I'm not a fan of the media."

And the way he says it reminds me of a similar comment Wendy made at dinner the other night. "How long did they stick around after the funeral?"

"Too long." He doesn't bother to mask the disgust in his voice. "All sharks on the hunt for blood, especially when it came to Aunt Wendy."

At his biting words, the madhouse of media surrounding the church and funeral procession last fall materializes in my mind, as does the security detail hired to keep them away. I'd known the rising popularity of Cece's books had turned many of her fans into tourists, but the crowds gathered during that weekend were recordbreaking.

For the most part, readers had respected Cece's privacy and her private residence. They took pictures of her town, her beaches, the arbor and reading benches she'd donated to the community library, and whatever other landmarks she highlighted on her social media pages. And if one was lucky enough to find her, she was always approachable, never one to turn down a selfie or an autograph. But Joel was right, the media was a different breed. They weren't loyal fans; they were cutthroat opportunists.

"In the early days after Cece's death, Aunt Wendy wanted to keep her work hours at the hotel the same," Joel continues. "She was afraid of spending too much time alone, I think." He blows out another hard breath. "But she kept getting ambushed at the hotel. Fake event meetings that would turn into a surprise interview. Reporters waiting in the parking lot, in the lobby, at the restaurants she'd get takeout from. And that was far from all their stunts."

"I imagine your father didn't take too kindly to that," I say, sticking close to him, our speed barely reaching five miles an hour now.

"You're correct. We hired extra security and even had the chief of police post a warning at the hotel. But when they started following her on her morning beach walks and into the grocery stores, it became much more serious. One idiot even knocked on her front door when my folks were gone."

"No," I gasp. "That's horrible."

"That's when her panic attacks started. We've taken her to the ER more times than I can count. Thankfully her last one was months ago now, and she has medication to help when she needs it."

I shake my head. "That explains so much." Her extreme weight loss, her fear of social gatherings, her exit at the hotel . . . and the recycled art that has given her some much-needed purpose. "What were they even hoping to gain from a grieving mother?"

"They all wanted the same thing—an exclusive story that none of us were offering, as well as the publishing date of Cece's final manuscript. There was so much coverage already, so many articles based on assumption, but we'd agreed early on as a family that Cece's personal life was off-limits. The public has her books, her social media pages, her interviews, and maybe someday her movies, too. But we refused to give them anything more." The breeze ruffles through his hair like fingers. "Aunt Wendy didn't lose a best-selling author; she lost her only child."

The pain of that truth zings through every nerve ending in my body as I picture Wendy's grief-worn face and hear her vulnerable confessions about Cece's last weeks all over again. "You were right to protect Cece and your family."

His gaze rests on my profile. "You didn't give them an exclusive, either."

"Never," I say firmly. "And I never will." Thankfully, Chip had taken care of most of the annoying emails and voicemails from badgering media representatives. "It's like you said earlier, there are some parts of Cece that are too sacred to share with strangers. And I think we've shared enough of her with the world already."

When he nods, the intense green of his eyes glistens in the sunlight, and it's almost enough to shock me into believing we're a team again. *Almost.*

After we round the last sand berm, there stands Point Wilson Lighthouse like a loyal sentinel guarding the western entrance to the Admiralty Inlet from the Strait of Juan de Fuca. My breath catches the way it always used to when I was a girl, and a memory comes as swift as the breeze, carrying my father's voice with it. *"Looks like a perfect place to start over someday. Rich people are always looking to rent a day at sea with a bearded captain."*

He'd slung his arm around my shoulders, pointing it out to me as we motored by in the charter boat we'd owned before my mother died. I begged him to stop at the dock, to eat an ice cream cone with me on the harbor and explore such a pretty place for just a few hours, but we always had somewhere else to be, some shipment to drop off, some contact to meet on a timeline that was never ours to change. *"One day, Elskede. One day I'll give you a life where we can start over for good and leave everything else behind us."* It was the promise he came closest to keeping. We'd visited Port Townsend a handful of times before opportunity finally struck, when we could finally make a new life.

Joel downshifts his speed, and I follow his lead. Surprisingly, our tires make a flawless transition from pavement to sand as we navigate our way to the lightkeeper's quarters. The wind is always chillier at the Point. Something about the air pressure colliding as the two bodies of water meet makes this spot considerably windier, too—a natural air-conditioning, my father used to say. It's where the locals come when the summer sun burns too hot on the beaches closer to town.

As we park our bikes and traverse the sandy path on foot, a hundred snapshots flood my brain at once—of the nights we snuck in through the faulty door lock. But even though we were chronic trespassers, we were always careful to obey the same rules the tourists were given: no food, drink, or trash left behind.

Joel makes his way up the sand-blown sidewalk and stops at the door. "Shall we? I figured it might be a safer place to read. Too breezy to be holding loose paper."

At the thought of losing even a single page of Cece's words, I recall my conversation with Chip last night and his warning to be careful. I stare down at the thick grouping of papers in Joel's grasp and spot the wrinkled edges and folded-down corners.

"Probably a good idea," I conclude. "This is the only copy we have."

I notice the lock on the door has changed from a janky deadbolt requiring a key to a coded lock box, which Joel is apparently privy to. He taps in a sequence of numbers, then meets my questioning gaze.

"Old Harry gave me the code when I called him this morning." He glances over his shoulder at me before he pushes the door open.

The space is dim when we enter, though the sunshine illuminates dozens of framed maps and black-and-white pictures of the lighthouse and its keepers through the years. A donation box sits on a table near the back wall. Looks like the tours are still free, but donations are highly encouraged.

Our footsteps echo in the rectangular room until Joel reaches the door leading up the spiral staircase to the lantern room and gallery deck. There's a large red sign chained across the opening: "Restricted Area. CLOSED for touring."

"Henry approved this area, too?" I ask as Joel releases the chain from the doorjamb and nods.

"The lighthouse is under a phased restoration plan, so they've closed sections off to the public so they can work without disruption. The lantern room will remain off-limits for roughly a year until it's completed."

"I feel like a VIP."

He laughs. "As long as you're free of all sticky drinks and snack foods, then you can be whatever you want to be up here." He waves a hand for me to go first. "After you."

It's a nerve-racking climb up the tower of the lighthouse, though admittedly I didn't think twice about trespassing these steps when I was seventeen. Life felt simpler back then, and consequences felt far out of reach. But as we near the top of the tower, a sinking reality presses in. While the rules have remained the same up here, everything else is different.

There's no Cece bounding up the stairs after us, demanding we sit opposite the rusty iron door off the lantern room. She loved to sit with her back against the steel wall, her feet touching the rail encircling the active lens used to guide thousands of sailors and fishermen safely to shore for over a hundred and twenty years. I grunt when my rear meets the cold, unforgiving steel. The gap between the lens and wall feels noticeably tighter, and by the way Joel struggles to stretch out his legs fully, I can tell he's thinking the same.

The air is musty and a bit too overheated for comfort, but the sun is high enough in the horizon for both our faces to be shaded by the half wall that's divided into windows on top, steel plating on bottom. And though we can only see blue sky from our vantage point down on the floor, I know the view is spectacular from the other side of the stairs. But for Cece, I want to save it for the end of our time here, the way she always did.

Seated to my right, Joel twists his head, his breath sweeping the side of my neck as he asks, "Do you want to try reading a chapter today?"

I clasp my hands on my lap and recall my failed attempt at reading Allie's manuscript back at the cottage. "Not this time."

"All right," he says. "Just say the word if you change your mind."

I nod, close my eyes, and prepare to sink back into another memory that feels as real as the lighthouse we're inside. Only as he begins, I realize there's something Cece left out in the timeline of our friendships. Not because she was neglectful, but because there were some things I was never brave enough to put into words. Not even for her.

Sometime after the summer I officially became a Campbell employee, saving every penny I made for whatever my college scholarships wouldn't cover, there'd been a shift between Joel and me. Something unspoken, but certain. Something too special to be defined in casual terms. Something that had caused me to hope in a way I'd never allowed myself to hope before. Then again, before Joel and Cece, hope wasn't a gift I understood much at all.

19

"Fall Is Hardly the Best Season of All"

Contrary to what most women in Cece's age group fancied about "the season of pumpkin spice," she had little affection for fall in the Pacific Northwest. She wasn't made for the cold, wet, and the dreary. If she had her choice, she'd hibernate straight through Halloween and set her alarm for Christmas Eve. At least winter boasted a holiday she cared about. Which was why Joel's agitated state as he paced her living room did nothing but grate on her perpetually sour mood.

"Chill out, Joel. You're going to give yourself high blood pressure before you're even old enough to buy a beer. She'll be here soon," Cece said, closing her eyes and listening to the rain beat against her mom's roof the way it had for weeks. With weather like this, it left their trio little option in the way of weekend entertainment. They could catch a movie at the theater, but did she really want to endure another two hours of Ingrid and Joel making not-so-secret heart eyes at each other over a tub of popcorn? She might as well just change her name to Third Wheel Cece.

It was a strange thing to want nothing more than for your two best friends to finally confess their obvious-to-everybody-with-eyes feelings to each other and also to want nothing about her current relationship with either one of them to change. But change was coming; she could feel it the same way she could feel her seasonal depression creeping in every late September since she first moved to Port Townsend.

"She's never been this late," Joel grumbled, standing by the front door and checking his watch like a worried father. But Ingrid already had a father, one who doted and bragged on her often. She hardly needed another one.

Joel turned and pelted her with a stare. "Are you absolutely positive she said she'd meet us here, at your house, at six o'clock?"

"Yes, *Dad*, I'm *positive*." Cece rolled her eyes. "After our shift she said she needed to run home and grab her laundry bag so she could wash a couple loads here this week. And as per usual, she didn't want me to tag along." A sore point in their friendship for sure, but one Cece was doing her best to ignore. "She probably just lost track of time." But even Cece was struggling to believe that the longer the minutes ticked on.

Ingrid had only recently purchased a cell phone, but the plan was almost as awful as the coverage. Joel had mentioned wanting to buy her a better data package for her birthday so she could text and call however much she wanted to, but seeing as it was the end of the month, the minutes were long gone and her birthday wasn't till spring. In the meantime, they all knew each other's work schedules, and their weekend plans were so routine at this point they were rarely disrupted—including Ingrid's overnights at Cece's. Her mom had already made up the sofa bed for Ingrid with fresh linens, pillows, and blankets. At first, Ingrid only stayed a night, maybe two a week. But last week she'd stayed five. The increase might have something to do with the fact that Joel's house was only a backyard away.

With one last glance at his watch, her cousin yanked open the front door. A blast of wretchedly wet air swooped through the living room, scattering her mother's art magazines to the floor. "Hey, close the door!"

"I'm going out to look for her."

Cece bolted to her feet and hurried to toss the stack of magazines back on the table. "Not without me, you're not."

Joel gave Cece a hard look, as if calculating how he might get away without the use of duct tape to restrain her.

"Fine," he conceded. "But I'm not waiting for you to change your clothes another five times. Grab a coat and let's go."

She was already snapping up her mom's new red and white polka dot raincoat. It wasn't her style, and it was too thin to bring any kind of real warmth, but it beat having to look through the jam-packed hall closet for a real jacket—she feared Joel would leave her behind if she attempted to open that door. "Do you think she stopped at the marina to help her dad tidy up the boat?"

Joel shook his head and marched into the horizontal rain, leaving Cece to race after him once she'd locked up the house, knowing her mom wouldn't be home for at least another couple of hours. There was a private event at the hotel tonight; some fancy outdoor gear company from California had rented out the entire place for the weekend. They were perhaps the only guests crazy enough to buy the fishing excursion package and take a tour with Hal when the skies hadn't stopped leaking for longer than ten minutes. At least she'd made some great tips serving them appetizers and drinks last night.

Once they were both inside Joel's car, he said, "She's not at the marina. Hal was off today."

"No, he wasn't." Cece scowled at him. "He took the boat out this morning, with all those men in waders. The storm probably gave their fishing gear a good run for their money, too. I bet they only got back an hour or so ago, so they'd have time to get ready for the dinner thing tonight."

Joel started the engine, his voice nearly too low to be heard. "That charter trip was canceled."

"And how do you know that?" But the instant it was out of her mouth, she felt like an idiot. "Oh." Joel's newest role was playing chauffeur to the guests who purchased excursion packages through the hotel, including boat guides, fishing tours, and private parties. Captain Hal was a sought-after hire, and her uncle often said their bottom line proved it.

Joel took a hard left out of their driveway and cruised downhill at a speed Cece didn't realize he knew how to drive. He was usually a grandma behind the wheel. A great-grandma most days. But not this night. His eyes were like two focused lasers beaming through the quick cadence of the windshield wipers.

She double-checked her seatbelt. "Where are we going then, Joel?"

"To Ingrid's."

Her gaze snapped from the dark road back to his profile. "You know where she lives?" Something like hurt wiggled its way up through her diaphragm. Had Ingrid invited Joel over to her boathouse and not her?

His long pause only heightened the burning sensation all the more until he added, "I know, but Ingrid wasn't the one who told me."

A thousand questions traveled through her mind at once, all pleading for answers. When Joel turned down an unmarked road she'd never noticed before, he slowed his speed considerably, dodging trees and debris. Even still, branches pawed at Joel's car like a horror movie, scraping the windows and doors like long, grotesque fingernails as gravel turned to dirt and then eventually to rocky sand. Somewhere in the distance she could sense the water, could *feel* its looming presence. Only this water wasn't the Sound. The smell was all wrong, as was the direction of the wind.

This was some kind of isolated inlet.

A slough.

"This can't be right." Cece's whisper sounded more like a plea as Joel parked and flipped off the headlights. "She lives on a houseboat with her dad. You must have taken a wrong turn."

But all he said in reply was, "Lock the doors as soon as I'm out and wait for us to return."

"No way," she hissed. "If you go, then I—"

"I'm serious, Cece. If I don't come back in ten minutes with Ingrid, then—"

"Stop it, you're scaring me." She peered hard into his shadowed face. "What aren't you telling me?"

He released his seatbelt and gripped his door handle. "Hal's . . . he's been suspended. He no longer has access to the charter boat, and he's not allowed on Campbell property. At least, not until he's willing to have a truthful conversation with my dad."

Ice crystallized in Cece's chest. "About what?"

He huffed an exasperated breath. "I don't have time for a full Q&A right now. I need to find Ingrid." His expression was stern, but she could see the fear building behind it. She could hear it, too. "Please, just . . . stay here."

And then he was out of the car. But even with his use of *please*, there was no way on earth Cece wouldn't follow him. She'd watched and read enough espionage to know she'd need to keep her distance and walk on the sides of her feet, rolling her steps inward as to not upset whatever loose debris could be underfoot. Darn the reflective vinyl of her mother's bright red raincoat. She certainly wasn't in suitable gear for such a task.

She could hear the isolated shore to her left through the thick forest of trees, but it was too dark to make out anything more than the reflective strips on the heels of Joel's Nikes. At least the rain had subsided—for the moment. She followed him up a sandy embankment and stopped short at the hazy light coming from what looked like a relic of a tugboat. It was half in water, half beached on the shore like a bloated, white whale. Even bathed in reflective, silvery moonlight, the rust, chipping paint, and at least one missing window turned Cece's stomach inside-out. *Please, God, don't let this be right.* Perhaps her cousin had mixed up whatever directions he'd been given, because Ingrid couldn't live anywhere near this dilapidated heap of metal. The thing didn't even look seaworthy.

A ray of golden light shone from the bow, making Joel into a shadow puppet against the side of the vessel. She hissed his name. He didn't respond. But then another sound cut through the darkness. Raised voices and odd banging and clanging.

"I said go secure your things!" a sickeningly familiar baritone shot into the cold night like a dart. *"We're leaving."*

Cece heard Ingrid's voice but couldn't catch every word. She strained to string them together as she pushed closer. "This boat . . . not safe . . ."

"It will be as soon as you help me lighten the load."

"Is that why . . . all over the floor?"

"This boat will last us until I can secure another charter," Hal said. "I have a contact with a lead."

As Cece grew closer, her friend's voice sharpened, the words crisper than before. "A contact or a gambling buddy? You can't win back the boat you lost, Dad. It's gone."

Hal's volume dropped too low to hear what he said next, but whatever it was sparked a fire in Ingrid. "But you promised. You *promised* we could stay here, that we could make a life here and start over!" Silence descended until Ingrid's voice quaked. "What did you do, Dad?"

"The world is far too big for you to think so small. There are plenty of places left for us to see—"

"Just tell me what happened!" The urgency in Ingrid's tone raised the hair on Cece's neck. "Whatever it is, I'm sure it can be fixed. The Campbells are reasonable people, *good* people. Maybe if you just talked to them, they would—"

"What have I told you! There are *no good people*!" Hal barked. "Talking about your problems never fixes anything."

"And running away does?" Ingrid's question broke on a sob. "This does?"

A sharp shattering of glass cracked through the forest like a whip, causing Joel to break into a hard sprint toward the boat. Cece didn't bother to keep up the spy charade now; all she could imagine was Ingrid being hurt by a man three times her size. She ran after Joel until she felt she might vomit, but whatever was going on inside that tugboat was too big for Joel to manage on his own. He needed to be *smart*, not try to be a hero!

Not caring how loud or obvious her mother's red jacket was streaking across the dark shore, she pumped her arms and hissed his name over and over. It was only when he stumbled over a piece of driftwood that she caught up with him. Only steps away from the deck, she yanked him back, nearly taking them both to the ground.

"Wait!" she hissed. "Just wait a second—*think*!"

When he spun to face her, his eyes were too wild, too frenzied, too ready for a fight she was sure he wouldn't win.

She gripped his arm even harder, shaking him until she saw a glimpse of her level-headed cousin return. "*Be smart*, Joel. You can't just barge in there unannounced. You need to assess *first*, plan *second*. And then act." She pointed to the cracked window closest to them as if she were the skilled detective and he was her rookie. She waited for the blazing heat in his eyes to cool before she gestured him toward the window as the argument between Hal and Ingrid escalated.

Joel peered through the gauzy fabric while Cece held her breath as she watched her cousin assess the scene and make a plan she knew he'd execute when the time was right. After a hard exhale, he rotated to face her again. His adrenaline spike seemed to have stabilized, at least for the moment.

He pointed to the chest of his sweatshirt and gestured that he was going in from around the deck and that she was to stay put and watch from here. For once, she didn't protest. For once, she was too afraid to rebel.

With one last look at her, his eyes communicated everything his silence could not. *If things go poorly, you get out of here.* This time her nod came slower. When he turned to walk away, she threw both arms around his back, squeezing his middle tight. He twisted quickly to press a hard kiss to the top of her head, the way he'd done since they were toddlers, and then he was gone, the night swallowing him up whole.

She raised up on her tiptoes to peer through the same threadbare curtain Joel had only a minute ago. Her stomach lurched at the sight before her. She barely made it three seconds before she clutched a hand to her mouth to keep from crying out.

Surrounded by broken glass, pots and pans, and a random mix of household items, was Ingrid. Her splotchy cheeks were tear streaked, her knuckles white against a broom handle that remained motionless. It was as if an entire kitchen had been dumped onto that galley floor, and given the empty cabinets behind her friend, she likely wasn't too far off.

Cece's gaze roamed the rest of the tight space—wood-paneled walls with brass finishes that reminded her of the vintage photographs her mother kept of the 1960s. Her breath caught when she spotted Captain Hal shuffling into the galley, blathering on about lightening the load so he could pull anchor. He lifted a steel pot off the floor and tossed it off the deck into the night. The clatter was deafening, and much like the sounds she'd heard earlier on her run through the forest. The sight of his disheveled state made her want to squat down, cup her hands over her ears, and pretend this was all just a terrible, terrible nightmare.

How could she have been so wrong about him? Guilt tugged at her conscience over what she'd convinced herself she hadn't really seen at the staff dinner: Hal, drinking from a silver flask he'd been hiding in her uncle's sport coat.

"Stop throwing things! We're not pulling anchor tonight," Ingrid shouted. "You'd kill us both before we even got out of the harbor. You can't even hold still for longer than five seconds. Please, just go to bed. You've made a big enough mess for me to clean up already."

Cece could see the faint outline of Joel standing just beyond view of the open galley door. He was on the deck now, feet poised and ready to enter whenever he deemed it right.

"I am a *captain*!" Hal's voice resonated with machismo. "I can sail through any storm, any darkness, any danger! It's in my blood." Hal slapped a hand to his chest, which threw his entire body off-balance, causing him to smack into a small table. An open bottle of amber liquid was catapulted to the floor but didn't break. Neither did the wooden table beneath Hal's formidable weight.

The captain pointed at Ingrid through narrowed eyes, his hand swaying in the air. "Good daughters don't speak to their fathers with such—such—vulgarity."

He bent to right the fallen bottle, which hadn't seemed to lose much of its contents. Cece gasped when he brought it to his mouth and took a deep swig.

Ingrid's humorless laugh was sharp and erratic. "And good fathers don't drink themselves into oblivion every time something goes wrong and then expect their daughters to clean up their mess. Well? Maybe I won't this time." She dropped the broom to the floor. "You hear me, Dad? You can clean up your own mess."

Ingrid crunched over the random glass and debris on the floor, but before she could pass him, Hal set the bottle down and slumped his large shoulder against the cabin wall.

"Elskede, wait, please," he croaked. "Don't leave me."

Ingrid stopped but didn't turn around.

Hal reached his meaty hand toward his daughter, but she simply stared straight ahead without reaching back. "You're right. I am a mess. Your mother was so kind, so patient, so gentle, so pure of heart. I never wanted you to grow up without her love and care" came a weepy baritone Cece hardly recognized. "I never wanted you to be stuck with a brute like me."

Ingrid wiped her nose with the heel of her palm, refusing to look at her father.

"You are my reason for living. My Elskede. The lighthouse in my dark world. Don't be mad at me." A wobbly smile curved Hal's lips. "I can live anywhere as long as I have you. People's opinions . . ." He puffs out a *tfffp* sound. "They don't matter. You and I together are the only thing that matters."

It was then Joel made his entrance. His steps were cautious but purposeful. "Evening, Mr. Erikson. Ingrid," Joel said with such chilling clarity and calm, Cece's breath seized in her chest.

Hal's eyes darkened, his words slurring considerably more than a few minutes ago. "What are you doing here?" And then to his daughter, he asked, "Did you invite him, Ingrid?"

But Ingrid stood motionless, her eyes round and unblinking.

Joel locked gazes with her. "No, sir. I wasn't invited."

"Then go home."

"I'm afraid I can't do that." Joel's gaze skimmed over Ingrid before turning his dark eyes back to Hal. "Not until we have a conversation."

"I don't owe you or your family anything."

"No, you don't. But I'm hoping we might figure out a solution together. One that works for everybody. One that doesn't mean leaving Port Townsend."

Hal assessed Joel for an immeasurable amount of time before he turned back to his daughter. "What did I tell you before? Rich boys like him live to be the hero, but their promises are empty."

"You don't know anything about him." Ingrid's voice was barely audible.

"I know enough." Hal leaned forward in his seat, a smirk dancing on his lips as he pressed his elbows to the table and dropped his head into his hands. "I'd offer you a drink, but we seem to be having a bit of a housekeeping issue tonight."

Joel stayed where he was, his body positioned between Ingrid and her father. "My dad will help you."

Once again, Hal seemed to consider the young man before him. "I don't need your dad or his charity. I can find other work."

"You're a captain without a boat; seems like you might need him more than you think you do."

Captain Hal huffed. "We'll be just fine. Won't we, Ingrid?"

When she didn't answer, Joel's expression softened, and Cece could tell he was searching for the right words. Maybe even praying for them. He took a single step toward the table. "Everyone has things they regret from their past—my father included. But he always says we can't change the time we've spent, just how we choose to spend the time we have left." Joel eyed Hal's fingers choking the rum bottle. "You might have more options than you think you do right now. But you have to talk to him. You have to be honest about what's really going on here."

A minute passed before Hal spoke again, his voice disarmed and almost wistful. "I had a beauty of a boat once—named her after my wife, Skylark. She changed my life, made me into an honest man. Gave me dreams, hopes. We were supposed to sail the whole world together in that boat." His chest heaved as an unexpected sob broke from his throat. "Her initials carved into my ax are all I have left of her now." His nose dripped into his wiry beard, but he made no effort to wipe his face. "And my loyal daughter."

At Hal's pronouncement, Ingrid closed her eyes.

"I'm going to get another boat someday and name it after both my girls," Hal said, his words are as droopy as his eyelids. "The *Ingrid Sky*."

"I hope you do, sir."

Hal's eyes closed as his body swayed hard to the right. He bumped against the wall as if ready to call it a night right then and there.

Joel twisted to look at Ingrid and asked, "Where's his room?"

She didn't budge.

"Ingrid," Joel repeated. She blinked and met his gaze. "Where's his room?"

"Back cabin. Portside," Ingrid responded as if coming out of her self-induced coma. "But he won't let you touch him. I'm the only one who can handle him like this." She jerked her dad's shoulder back and forth as if she'd done this routine many times before. "Time for bed, Dad. Let's go."

Hal only grunted in response, and Ingrid shook him again. This time Hal's eyes popped open and stayed wide.

"I'm taking you to bed. Stand up."

Ingrid hooked her arm under Hal's and shook her head at Joel when he reached to do the same on Hal's other side. He backed off as Ingrid escorted her father to the back of the boat alone. The whole ordeal took less than a minute or two, and then she was striding back through the main cabin. Only Ingrid didn't return to her place among the kitchen rubble, she bolted through the open door and into the freezing, damp night. She wrapped her arms round her chest, covering the Team Edward design on the *Twilight* tee she'd purchased with Cece last summer in Forks. Joel was hot on her heels, careful to avoid discarded cookware and trash in the darkness.

Cece pushed away from the boat wall and headed straight for them, stopping short at the sight of her cousin reaching for Ingrid's upper arm before she ripped it out of his grasp. "You had *no right* showing up here tonight. I had it handled!"

"You had it *handled*?" Visibly shocked, Joel made no attempt to move toward her again. "I was worried about you, Ingrid. When my dad told me Hal had been caught drinking on duty and then you didn't show up tonight, I—"

Her laugh was tight, cold. "Is that what all this is about? His *flask*?"

"A passenger reported him drinking from it multiple times yesterday on the excursion, pouring it in his coffee and soda. They even took pictures for proof."

Ingrid peered at Joel as if he'd lost his mind somewhere between the boat and the forest. "My dad's been drinking from that flask longer than I've been alive. He's not a threat."

Disbelief settled over Joel's face. "There's a clear no-drinking policy for any active crew member aboard that vessel. Your dad signed the contract. He knows the rules." He hesitated, as if waiting for her to acknowledge what he'd just said. But she only crossed her arms over her chest. "He's been in charge of a half-million-dollar fishing charter, Ingrid, not to mention all the lives he's been putting at risk each week, including *yours*."

"Not everything is so black and white in this world, Joel."

"But there is plenty that is." He stared at her a long moment before lowering his voice. "He lied on his resume. I'm not sure if you know this, but . . . he has a felony. He served time in his early twenties for smuggling and possession before you were born."

There was not an ounce of surprise on her face. "Do you really think someone like your father would have hired him if he *hadn't* lied on his resume? Do you think your father would have focused on the three decades of solid sailing experience my dad has under his belt—which more than qualified him for the position, I might add—if he'd known about the priors? No. He would have taken one look at the ugly truth of his past and dismissed him like everybody else always has." She shook her head. "My dad's not the same guy he was back then."

Joel edged toward her cautiously. "Is he the kind of guy who would hit you? Because he certainly didn't seem to be in control of himself in there."

"*What?* No."

"Ingrid," Joel pressed. "I need you to tell me the truth. If he's ever laid a hand on you then—"

"Never one time!" She snapped her neck around so quickly her damp hair stuck to her shoulder. "He'd hurt himself long before he'd ever hurt me in that way." The pronouncement bellowed through the thick forest and Cece had to swallow back a sob of relief, but Ingrid wasn't finished yet. "You don't know him the way I do. He's not dangerous. Bullheaded and impulsive, yes—but *not* dangerous."

"And all this time, you've just been out here with him, *handling* things on your own."

"What other choice do I have? My mom isn't here anymore. It's just me. Now you see why I can't ever leave him—not even to go away to college. He needs me too much."

The wind gusted hard and Cece trembled in the shadows, wrapping her arms around her middle.

"So he's never been . . . sober?"

"Not since before Mom died."

Cece could tell Ingrid was trying to be nonchalant, but she was shaking so violently now that her words came out in a choppy, breathy staccato.

Joel rubbed at his temples before pointing to the boat. "Ingrid, this isn't okay. What I saw in there tonight—"

"What you *saw* in there tonight is a man who feels like a failure. Who couldn't bear to tell the only living family member he has left that he messed up again, so instead he drank a fifth of rum and started cleaning out the cupboards, looking for a way to make sense of something. To fix something he could control. What you *saw* is a father who is too ashamed to ask his daughter to leave the only town she's ever loved because he doesn't know another way around it." Her lips quivered. "And neither do I." She stared at the ground. "My life isn't like yours and Cece's. I don't have parents who go to church on Sunday and pray before meals and buy matching sheet sets for their guest rooms. But I do have my dad. And as rough around the edges as he is at times, he's mine." She began to cry openly. "He's all I have."

Joel didn't wait for permission before he crushed Ingrid to his chest and wrapped his arms around her. She sagged against him without a fight. He held her close and pressed his lips to her temple. "You have me, too, Indy. I promise, you will *always* have me."

Slipping off her mother's red raincoat, Cece moved toward them, wrapping her jacket around her friend's soaked shoulders like a cape as Joel opened his arms to allow her into the sacred space. She looped her arms around Ingrid's waist and hoped she was giving as much warmth as she was taking.

"You're ours for keeps," Cece whispered into the huddle. "We'll never let you go."

20

I'm numb as Joel pins the remaining memoir pages under his backpack and stands without speaking a word. He exits the lantern room through the steel gallery door and walks several paces onto the deck to my right. But seeing as the lantern room is one large circular window without obstruction, I can see him as plainly as if he was standing directly in front of me. He bends at his waist and rests his forearms on the railing as if something in that great beyond holds the power to heal the gaping hole this last chapter ripped open in our chests.

I've tried to forget that night so many, many times. Tried to lock away the multitude of feelings surrounding it, to no avail. I'm convinced milestone memories are the hardest to erase because they wedge themselves deepest into the soul.

Joel and Cece not only uncovered a lifetime of secrets that rainy fall evening, but their insistence on spending the next several hours cleaning up the mess my father had made inside that weary old tugboat left a permanent mark on me. I'd been terrified for them to see the world I really lived in, one so unlike theirs. Yet when they had, they hadn't abandoned me to it . . . they joined me in it.

Within a few days' time, Stephen had arranged a follow-up meeting with my father and the president of a faith-based rehab facility in Seattle, offering him something nobody had before: the chance to truly start over fresh. It was his choice. If he said yes, his chartering contract with the Campbells would be waiting for him upon his return. And if he said no, there would be no future for us in Port Townsend.

I had just arrived at the hotel for the start of my lunch shift that Tuesday morning to find my father waiting for me, his favorite crimson sea cap folded in his meaty hands. I tried to dissuade him from standing in the middle of the main dining room, knowing that at any moment the hotel's clientele would be looking for a hostess to seat them. But my father was as immovable as a dry-docked battleship. His watery, expressive blue eyes held mine for several beats, and I knew he'd come to a decision. *"I'm leaving for Seattle tomorrow. I'll be gone sixteen weeks, maybe more. Stay with your friends. I know they make you happy."* He'd paused and then reached for my face. His calloused fingers cradled my chin the way he'd done since I was a girl. *"You are strong, Elskede. Brave. You will be okay without me."*

Only I'd just wanted *him* to be okay.

My father had mentioned sobriety before, but this was the first time the conversation was motivated by something other than a hangover confession. And maybe that was the reason I allowed myself to hope for a miracle from a God I so desperately wanted to believe had heard my prayers. *"Wendy said I could stay with her and Cece. Until you come back"* was all I could choke out in response, too afraid to jinx the moment. Too afraid to show my father just how much I needed him to follow through for me. How much I needed him, period.

He'd pulled me in for a brisk hug that left my entire body wrought with hope and confusion. And when he'd strode out the lobby doors that day, leaving me to seat my first customers, it wasn't the list of lunch specials I recalled as I'd handed them their menus and lifted my eyes to the street. It was the parting words my father had spoken in my ear. *"Maybe the Campbells are exactly who you say they are."*

It's an effort for me to slow my mental highlight reel from going too much further. I cut it off at the strong, healthy version of my father upon his return home from the inpatient treatment center, the sober man who claimed he'd found faith in the same God the Campbells trusted in. The same God I'd come to trust in, too.

My cloudy gaze focuses on Joel through the viewing window. I watch the way his shoulders tense and contract on every inhale-exhale exchange. I watch the way he clasps his hands in front of him and the way the breeze teases the hemline of his shirt to expose the defined muscle beneath it.

I watch him until I can't watch him anymore, at least not from in here.

My stomach is both fire and ice as I step onto that deck, each sensation warring for their rightful place, and I don't know which will win—the frost that's kept my heart safe for so long, or the fire that burns hot whenever I'm within arm's reach of this man.

I'm silent as I grip the sun-warmed rail beside him, aiming my gaze to the endless horizon.

"I could have read that entire last chapter with my eyes closed." Joel's voice is so hoarse it blends with the wind. "I've replayed the details of that night almost as many times as I've replayed the details of . . ." His tortured gaze ignites my fear. "The last time I saw Hal alive."

"Please," I struggle to speak. "I don't want to talk about that night."

He pushes off the railing, his focus shifting down to me. "Of course you don't. You never have. But you're not the only one who suffered a loss that night, Ingrid. You're not the only one whose future was demolished by the choices of a man who put his addiction before everything else in his world. Can't you see that?" he pleads. "Can't you see that I needed to talk?"

By the fervor in his voice, I know exactly where he's headed next. Not to the night when he found my father drinking in a bar thirty minutes south of town with his sponsor, or to the night of the shipwreck. But to a night six months after the Campbells paid for a headstone to be placed in a gated cemetery on the fancy side of town. To that breezy fall evening when I met Joel on the hotel dock and told him I couldn't stay here any longer.

"We did talk," I say warily. "It's why I came back after fall semester. To talk to you in person."

"No." He laughs gruffly. "You came back to give me some lame excuse about how your internship had turned into something more. That you'd said yes to the editorial assistant job because you were unsure of your future here—of *our* future here together." He steps closer, shakes his head. "And even still, I couldn't—wouldn't—believe it was over. I fought and I waited and I prayed because I've known you were it for me since I was seventeen years old. You're the only woman I've ever wanted to spend my life with." He grips the back of his neck, making it nearly impossible not to see the ink printed on his forearm. "I promised you my grandmother's ring after graduation. We circled our wedding date on the hotel calendar for the following summer. I was saving up for a down payment on a home for us, and you threw it all back in my face because you were too afraid to just *talk* to me!"

"Talking about problems doesn't fix them!" My father's words explode into the space between us but Joel doesn't so much as flinch.

"And *not* talking about them will kill you."

"Fine!" I shout. "You want me to tell you how it really was for me? Every time you looked at me, every time you spoke to me, every time you reached for me, all I could feel was the knife blade of your omissions plunging deeper and deeper into my chest. You promised that if I left for college you'd watch over him! You promised you'd keep him out of trouble! And instead, you hid the fact that he'd relapsed long before the night he boarded your father's boat for the last time. You were the last person to see him alive, and yet nothing about his death makes any sense!" I scream into the blustering wind as a sob cracks inside my throat. "He drowned on *your* watch, Joel!"

"You're right. Is that what you need to hear me say? That I made a horrible judgment call when I decided to delay telling you about your dad's relapse until after your finals were over? Okay, I'll say it. I'll say it however many times you need to hear it. I was wrong, Ingrid. And there's not a single day that goes by that I don't regret not telling you as soon as I found out. If I could go back, I would. If I could change it, I would." His voice dips low. "I only ever wanted to protect you."

"I wasn't the one who needed to be protected."

"Of course you were." His words reverberate in my ears. "*You* were the child, Hal was the parent, the father. It was never your job to protect him. Please tell me you can see that now, Ingrid. Tell me you can see the way your whole life stood still for his. How the dependence he created on you robbed you of your childhood, of the future you wanted . . . of the future we both wanted."

"That future died the minute my father's body was recovered in the middle of the Pacific." I summon the frost to come back, to protect the last thawed piece of my heart. "Relationships aren't meant to survive that kind of trauma; *we* never could have survived it."

"You can't possibly know what we could have survived. You never even gave us the chance to try!"

Before I can fight back, a strong wind gust whips between us and funnels into the lantern room through the cracked deck door. A chaotic rustling sound follows as our attention is captured by the funnel of loose pages circling the room inside the lighthouse and several more sailing over our heads toward the beach.

"The memoir! *Close the door!*"

I race inside where hundreds of pages soar and swirl above my head, and I jump to collect as many as possible before they're lost to us forever. Joel hurtles past me down the spiral staircase and out onto the beach. Against the wind, I yank the gallery deck door closed, and the hollow boom that follows is like the quick snap of a magician's fingers.

In an instant, the pages freeze mid-air and float to whatever surface they're closest to. With frantic starts and stops, I continue gathering the pages, combing over every inch in the lantern room, desperate to salvage every lost word. It's an overwhelming task as the pages are bent and scattered in random clumps, so unlike the stacked pile of pristine paper we were handed last week. I can only hope Joel caught the few that escaped to the shore before they hit the water.

I'm on my knees, stretching my fingers toward a single page underneath a display case, when I hear Joel enter the foyer, breathing hard.

Winded myself, I slump back on my haunches, adding page ninety-six to the others I've retrieved and organized into numerical order once again. I skim the opening paragraphs of the next chapter just long enough for the keywords to stir a memory that's branded on my body as much as it is on my heart. Only I don't want to be here for that. I don't want to relive one more page of this memoir.

"How many pages were there in total?" Joel asks.

"I'm not sure, I never checked." I get to my feet, dust off my shorts.

"Neither did I. But I think I caught the ones that escaped off the deck."

I shuffle through the stack in my hands and count the missing pages. "You have twenty-two, twenty-three, forty-eight, and fifty-five?"

Joel studies me from across the foyer and holds up the wrinkled, sandy pages. "All present and accounted for."

The cautious way he watches me is a reminder of where our conversation left off on the balcony before we nearly lost the last pieces of Cece we have left.

Silently, I take his offering and insert each page back into the stack where they belong before handing the weathered manuscript to him. His voice says *thanks*, but his eyes seem to be saying something else entirely. Something I'm not sure I can hear.

As he secures the written ledger of our youth inside his backpack, I wait to feel the kind of relief that only comes after you find something you've deemed lost forever . . . but it never does.

I'm several steps outside the lighthouse, down the sandy path and headed across the bluff to where our bikes are parked, when Joel's voice smacks me from behind.

"The morning you came to me second-guessing your scholarship at Berkeley, I swore to myself I'd do anything it took to get you on that plane." I stop walking, the wind blowing hard against my back. "You'd already pushed your school plans off for an entire year so you could ensure your dad reached the twelve-month mark on his sobriety. But you were still fighting harder for him than you were for yourself. You were still playing the role of a guardian, putting his needs above your own. But we both know he was stable when you left. His job was secure. His sponsor was dedicated. And my family was here to help in whatever capacity we could." Slowly, I rotate to face him as he says, "I loved you too much to watch you abandon everything you'd worked so hard for—every test you took to prove your academic competency. Every essay you wrote. Every tip you saved." His voice breaks with conviction. "And then later, after . . . I knew you couldn't look at me without thinking of your father, without wondering if you could have done something to stop him from boarding that boat and motoring into that storm. I don't have those answers, either, but if I did, I'd give them to you. I've told you everything I know. . . ." His voice strains and cracks. "I know why you needed to blame me. For years, I blamed myself, too. But Hal was a grown man. He made his own choices that night." His gaze holds mine, his eyes reaching for me in a way that sucks the breath from my lungs. "I couldn't have saved him from himself, and you couldn't have, either."

Though I'd heard the same admonishment from Dr. Rogers during our therapy sessions, the truth cuts deeper when Joel speaks it.

"I kept hoping, that with enough time, you'd come back," he continues. "That you'd remember who we were together. That you'd . . . forgive me." Tears glisten in his eyes. "Cece was the only real link I had left to you, and when she died, it wasn't only the loss of my cousin I grieved. It felt like I lost you all over again."

The raw admission stuns me as I recall the devastation of that second cyclone of grief. It had struck with so much force and intensity, obliterating the progress I'd made from self-help books on childhood trauma and creating healthy boundaries. Once again, grief had knocked me down flat, nearly taking me out completely.

As I stare into Joel's eyes, I hate that my silence caused him even an ounce of suffering. I wouldn't wish that on anybody.

"I'm sorry, Joel. I'm sorry I hurt you." My apology is stripped of pretense but not of perspective. Loss clarifies even the muddiest of circumstances. "But I'm not sorry I left when I did. Staying here would have made things worse—especially for you."

"I don't believe that."

"You should." I rub my lips together and glance at the spray flinging over the cliff. "I won't deny the pain you've walked through, but neither will I deny all the good things I can see in your life now, proof you can move forward as you should." My confidence wanes as he studies me. Nervously, I begin to name the random few that come to mind first. "Your promotion to hotel manager, that fancy new car you now drive, that adorable puppy you share with an even more adorable strawberry blonde whose eyes are practically heart-shaped every time she looks at you."

"That promotion," he begins undeterred, "has been in the works for fifteen years—you know that. And that fancy car? Believe me, if there was a way I could return it back to sender, I would. Cece left it to me in her will without explanation. And Madison? I can't speak for how she may or may not feel about me, but she knows exactly where I stand with her." He doesn't blink as he says, "She's a friend. Nothing more."

Instead of the relief I long to feel, his explanation only serves to stir the empathy brewing inside me. There are no winners in grief—only survivors. And I realize, in our own separate ways, that's exactly what Joel and I have done these last five years. We've simply survived.

Only now, surviving doesn't feel like enough. I want more than that for him, even if I don't know how to want that kind of more for myself yet. Joel shouldn't have to be a prisoner to this part of our story any longer, which is why I extend the only thing I can: the release I should have offered him years ago.

"Maybe she should be," I reply softly. "Maybe Madison should be something more than a friend to you." I swipe at the flyaway hairs batting against my cheek at every crosswind. "You deserve to be happy with someone like her. She's sweet and uncomplicated; kind and upbeat." *Innocent and undamaged.* "She's a good person. It's easy to see that." My heart kicks hard in my chest as I fight to get the words out. "The two of you would be a good match for each other." In all the ways I wished I could have been for him.

"Don't do that," he says as he moves toward me, sand scattering over our feet as the tide breaks hard against the edge of the bluff. White sea-foam sprays the rocks surrounding us as he slips his backpack from his shoulders and drops it to the ground without taking his eyes off me. "Don't give me permission to love someone else."

"I'm telling you it's okay to move on. To let go of what we had when we were young so you can be free—of all this." *Of me.* "I was wrong when I said *we* couldn't have survived the trauma of my dad's death. I'm the who couldn't. I'm the one who wasn't strong enough. Not you."

I watch the muscles in his neck constrict twice before he speaks. "I never needed you to be strong enough. I only ever needed you to be here."

My resolve begins to swirl like the papers inside the lantern room only moments ago. "Joel," I manage to choke out as his gaze travels in a slow circuit over my face, moving from my eyes to my lips and back again.

He reaches for me, his thumbs grazing across my jaw, his fingers laced at the nape of my neck. "You know I don't want the kind of freedom you're offering me. You've known it since the day we first met inside the hotel library, just like you knew it the minute you saw me in your office last week. I've never wanted freedom from you, Indy. I've only ever wanted freedom *for* you."

I'm shivering in a way that has nothing to do with the sea mist swirling around us, and behind my clamped jaw are the words I'm desperate to shout: *I don't know how to find that!* They beg to be released, but I keep them in, keep them trapped. With a single step back, I break away from his hold and turn to stare at a horizon that feels as unreachable as my heart.

I expect him to leave me there, to abandon me the same way I did to him all those years ago. It's what I deserve. It's what I know best.

But Joel doesn't leave me there alone. Instead, he joins me. And this time, in a silent invitation I have no desire to resist, he wraps me in an embrace so tight it's both an undoing and a remaking. Because here, in these arms, is the closest thing to whole I've felt since the night I walked out of them.

21

T he following morning, I wake to a text that immediately causes my stomach to clench:

SaBrina

It's been a week. I need an update on your search efforts ASAP.

I start approximately seven text replies before one finally sticks and I'm brave enough to tap *send*, but basically, there's no good way to tell your boss you haven't completed the task they assigned you, especially when said task determines your future.

Ingrid

Making good headway. Following up with some leads today. Will update.

SaBrina

What leads?

I worry my bottom lip, trying to think of a way to spin the truth in my favor. The truth being that there are only two places left on my list to search before I'm out of ideas and back at ground zero again.

Ingrid

Two promising locations.

There's a long pause.

SaBrina

Where specifically, and who told you they were promising?

I frown at the screen. Why does it matter to her where or who tipped me off? It isn't like SaBrina knows this town or any of Cece's family members other than by name. Then again, she had been the one to send me on this mission, just like I'd been the one who'd begged her for a chance to redeem myself as a reputable editor. So of course she's micromanaging me, why would I expect anything less?

Ingrid

A garage and a storage unit. Cecelia's mom encouraged me to look there.

SaBrina

Is that all? No other updates to report?

I crinkle my brow and reread the exchange over before replying.

Ingrid

That's all for now.

To drown out the fear building inside me at the thought of what SaBrina could do to my professional reputation after she fires me for non-delivery, I pop in my earbuds, crank up my workout play-list, and tackle Cece's garage as if I've been commissioned to do so under penalty of death. Not too far from the truth. SaBrina is hardly a lightweight when it comes to communicating her demands.

Much like inside Cece's cottage, the garage is full of books. Only these books are tucked inside boxes marked either with *To Be*

Donated or *For Storage Unit*. The heavy content explains why the boxes are not stacked but shoved against the perimeter of the garage walls.

As I work my way through them, my gaze continually catches on the seafoam bike charging in the outlet, stirring up the mass of indistinguishable emotions I've been failing to sort since I rode back to the cottage with Joel yesterday. He hadn't asked to come inside or even alluded to a follow-up conversation. He'd simply plugged in my bike and said he'd call me later.

I'd watched him leave with a substantial question mark hovering above my heart, knowing we both needed time to process what had just happened at the base of the lighthouse. It was clear neither of us had planned or expected it, and yet . . . it was also clear there had been a significant shift in us both because of it.

I pause my playlist on my favorite NF song and pull my phone from my pocket to check the time. Five missed notifications are waiting for me. All from Joel. My stomach muscles constrict as I click into his text thread and then immediately relax on an exhale.

Joel

So you know how you like dogs? 🐶

Missed call.

Joel

Okay, so that was a poor lead-in. How about: What would you say to dog sitting for a few hours this afternoon? 🙏

Missed call.
Missed call.

I check the timestamp on his last message—sent seventeen minutes ago. I don't have to think about my answer for longer than two seconds, seeing as there's no actual choice to be made between digging through dusty boxes in a garage or playing with a puppy. It's the easiest decision I've made since I arrived in town.

Ingrid

> Hey, sorry I missed you. Happy to take Rontu for the day. Do you think he'll fit in the bike basket? I can be there in thirty or so.

I would need a quick shower before I'd be suitable for the public eye as I currently resemble a character from Whoville. Messy buns are no longer considered trendy after they've been slept in, worked in, and dusted by cobwebs.

And if possible, my walking fashion disaster look is actually worse from my neck down.

Joel

> It's actually for Rita. I was thinking I'd be home to take her by now, but I had a few meetings pop up and Madison is going out of town for the evening.

It's impossible to see her name and not remember the conversation from yesterday. *"I can't speak for how she may or may not feel about me, but she knows exactly where I stand with her. She's a friend. Nothing more."* I delete my first attempt at a reply and try again, this time with an exclamation point as if it can erase the awkwardness I'm not sure how to let go of when it comes to her.

Ingrid

> Sure!

Joel

> Great, thank you. Two fur balls in this office is two too many. I'll ask M to drop her off at the cottage. She's probably already en route. I'll call you in a bit to check in.

> Also, how about I make you dinner tonight—fish tacos? I can pick you and the pink princess up at five-thirty. That work?

My brain short-circuits as I realize Joel's text means that Madison the Fashionista is on her way here—to *this* cottage—in mere minutes. I stare down at the dusty knees of my pj pants and then at my braless sleep tank and hightail it across the open driveway through the kitchen door. I'm yanking the sad bun from my hair at the same time I'm brushing my teeth over the bathroom sink when I hear the electric security gate slide open out front. *How did she get here so quickly?* I barely have time to pull on a sports bra and a clean pair of jeans before the doorbell rings. I open Cece's dresser in search of a clean T-shirt but the drawer is bare. I try a second one, and a third, and they're empty, too.

I swipe the zip-up hoodie I discarded onto the corner chair after my last beach combing excursion and tug it over my head before racing down the hall to pull the door open. A smiling Madison is waiting on the other side in a short denim skirt, a red flutter-sleeve blouse, and trendy tan wedge sandals. Naturally, she's adorable. Rita is not dressed in human clothing today, but she is wearing a rhinestone collar that should come with a warning that reads: Retina Protection Required.

"Hi, Ingrid." Madison smiles sheepishly with her puppy clutched to her chest. "I'm sorry. I really hate to intrude on you like this. My mom's allergic to dogs, and Allie is still in Port Angeles on a restaurant supply run. Are you really okay with this?"

And just like that, I remember how much I like her again. The Spencer sisters are nothing if not completely disarming.

"Of course, happy to help. Come on in."

"Actually, if I can just hand Rita off to you, then I can bring in her sleepover stuff."

"Right, sure thing." I take a very happy Rita from her dog mom and watch as Madison dashes back to her Mini Cooper for a monogrammed pink duffle bag and a pink plastic dog pen. It's an effort to press the smile from my lips. Madison's love for Rita is next level, and it's far more endearing than I would have expected.

She slips past me into the kitchen and begins to set up the doggy daycare center she's carried into the living room. Rita whines in my arms for me to put her down.

"Oh, that's her potty whine," Madison says matter-of-factly as she snaps together a miniature corral. "Her leash is in the side pocket of her duffle there. Once you walk her out to the grass, she'll do her lady business quickly for you."

I take Rita to the grass and find Madison's assessment of her puppy's potty manners to be accurate. By the time we're inside the house again, Madison has laid out a dog bed, food and water dishes, and set a few toys in the pen.

"There we go. I've measured her food out in bags for tonight and tomorrow. Also, she should be pretty content to play in here, so don't feel like you need to entertain her or anything. This is how I take her with me to the shop, too. Although, it's rare someone isn't carrying her around like a baby."

I'm beginning to suspect Madison is the *someone* as she kisses Rita's head and then sets her down in the pen. After commenting on the cuteness of Rita as she cuddles with her favorite stuffed squirrel, Madison worries her bottom lip and glances up at me with a curious look of uncertainty. "If you're all good, then I should probably get on the road. I'm headed to Seattle, and you know how bad traffic can be the closer you get to rush hour."

I eye her fidgeting hands and wonder if she's nervous about leaving Rita. "We're all good here, really. I can text you though if—"

"It's a date."

I blink. "What?"

"What I'm doing, the reason I'm going to Seattle. It's a new thing. Well, an old but new thing, ya know?"

No, I definitely don't know, but I smile at her encouragingly because Madison looks on the verge of passing out, and puppy sitting isn't really on the same page as giving mouth-to-mouth to an unconscious acquaintance. "Would you like a glass of water?"

"Actually, yes, that would be nice. I'm just . . . I'm nervous."

I move to the sink and fill up a glass with tap water. She accepts it with a grateful smile.

"His name is Carter. We met years ago when I was on a West

Coast summer dance tour—it was pretty casual back then since we technically weren't allowed to date anyone on our production team." She shrugs. "He ran the show lights. But he found me online a few months ago and we've been talking on and off ever since. I'm going to meet his parents and his sister tonight—they have tickets to *Wicked* and invited me to stay overnight at their farm afterward."

"Sounds like a great date. I hope you have a really nice time."

"Me too." She turns the glass in her hands. "I guess . . . I guess I also wanted to tell you so you knew I wasn't after Joel."

Stunned at her bluntness, I start my own nervous stammer. "Oh, I wasn't—I mean, I didn't think—"

She laughs and holds up a palm. "Of course you did. I would have, too, if I were you. Don't get me wrong; I'm no saint. If Joel would have shown any real interest in me other than as a friend, it would have been difficult to turn him down. But I've known about you since my first coffee date with Cece. The way she talked about the three of you was . . ." Her sigh is wistful. "It made me wish for friends like that."

My chest squeezes at her honesty, which forces me to process some honesty of my own. The three of us had been something wonderful once upon a time, sharing a bond in friendship that was almost too good to be true, but it hadn't been that way for many years now. It was death that had divided our original trio into a duo, and death, once again, that had divided our duo into two broken individuals who've lived as little more than strangers up until a week ago.

"It's obvious Joel still cares for you—a lot. And I know it's not my place to say something like that, but I adored Cece. We all did. I know she was really looking forward to having you come up and stay with her. She had plans for you and Joel during her recovery."

The erratic beat in my chest quickens. "What kind of plans?"

"She never told me the specifics, but it involved her using some kind of dictation app on her phone. I only know because I walked in on her once in the hotel library, thinking she was on a call, but she was actually recording herself talking. All she told me was that it was for a special project she was trying to finish up before her surgery."

Her explanation answers a question about the memoir I should have thought to ask days ago. The pages were typed and yet according to Wendy, Cece wasn't often on her laptop due to her migraines. The use of a dictation app that downloads straight into a word document would make the most sense. It would also explain some of the homonym errors Joel has caught during his readings. Several authors on my list choose the dictation method for drafting. Although for Cece, it wasn't a fiction tale she was drafting, but a retelling of her most poignant memories.

Prior to this conversation with Madison, I couldn't imagine asking her any questions about Cece, much less about the greater search I was on, but now it seems foolish not to. "Do you remember seeing her working in any composition-style notebooks in those last few weeks?"

Madison scrunches up her nose and peers up at the ceiling. "Hmm, not specifically, no. But I do know a lot of that type of stuff went to Wendy's storage unit a few months after the funeral. When Wendy was . . . struggling, she was very concerned about Cece's personal items being left inside the cottage while there were so many strangers and fans lurking around town. I spent a weekend helping Patti clear out most of Cece's closets and clothes and the extra books she kept in the spare room, but we left everything on her living room shelves alone." She gestures to the living room. "It felt wrong to disturb those ones. Keeping them out made it feel like she could still come back, you know? That's how I'll always remember her most, with a hot cup of coffee in one hand and a good book in the other." Her voice gives out on the last words, and she pinches her lips together.

And much like with her younger sister, I feel an inexplicable gratitude for having met her and for knowing that Cece had found a friend in her, too.

"Thank you for doing that for Wendy, Madison," I say through a quiver in my voice. "I'm really glad Cece had you as a friend."

She touches my arm with a carefulness I know is more about me than her, and in a moment so far outside the scope of my normal, I give her a hug. She wastes no time in hugging me back. "And I'm really glad I finally got to meet Cece's Ingrid."

After blowing a final kiss to a now-snoring Rita, Madison waves good-bye and takes off for her date in Seattle, leaving me plenty of time to confirm and get ready for a date of my own.

I text Joel that five-thirty will work just fine for dinner.

While Rita sleeps in her playpen, I take a proper shower, all while keeping one ear attuned to a very specific *potty whine*. After the moment Madison and I shared in the kitchen, I feel all the more obliged to give Madison a good report when it comes to her fur baby.

Wrapped in a bath towel, I pass over the fancy dress I purchased from Madison's Wardrobe and land instead on a pair of light linen slacks and a fitted black top with lace detailing at the neckline. I style my hair down, adding some loose waves with a flat iron I found in the bottom drawer of the bathroom cabinet. The discovery of the hair tool made me pause as I recalled the tedious process of straightening Cece's thick, bouncy curls the night she declared she "wanted to try a different look." Said *look* didn't last even twenty-four hours before she revived her corkscrew locks with a shower and anti-frizz gel, claiming she was too spicy for sleek hair.

I lift my face to the mirror, hearing her makeup instructions as if she were standing right here next to me: *"Don't skimp on the eyeliner"* and *"Make sure to use the plum eyeshadows—they bring out the gold in your irises."* I unscrew the sheer, petal-pink lip gloss and apply it before smacking my lips together three times afterward, the same way she always did with the cherry lip balm she was never without.

It had been Cece who'd helped me get ready for my first official date with Joel as his girlfriend. He was only weeks away from entering a new stage of life, taking remote business classes in the evenings while shadowing his father at the hotel during the days.

But somewhere in between it all, our unspoken commitment to one another had managed to find a voice all its own. And on a cold January evening, as snowflakes dusted the hoods of our coats, Joel took my hand in his and asked me to be something more than his friend. And my answer left zero room for any second-guessing.

So much of my world had changed after my father left for rehab in Seattle. Instead of the sofa bed Wendy routinely made up for me as her weekend houseguest, I became more of a permanent roommate. She'd purchased a second twin-sized mattress and box spring set to add to Cece's dollhouse-sized bedroom. It was comical the way the two of us had to shuffle around each other, as there wasn't enough space for both of us to stand in the gap between our beds at the same time. But in all those months of working together at the hotel and sharing a room at her mom's place before my father came back from rehab and I eventually left for college, we never once complained about the lack of space. If anything, the close quarters solidified our bond.

"You realize it really doesn't matter what you wear tonight, right?" was the question Cece had asked as she flung herself onto the floral duvet cover Wendy had picked out for me. She folded my pillow to fit under her chin, kicked her shoes to the floor, and scanned the three outfits laid out across her own mattress. *"If Joel can't take his eyes off you when you're wearing our Campbell Hotel polos and those hideous pleated dress pants—then any of these options could potentially send him into cardiac arrest."*

Though my stomach fluttered at the mention of his name, I'd reached for the only other pillow in the room and chucked it at her head.

"You know it's true." She'd shrugged, stacking her pillow atop mine before flipping onto her back. *"The only thing he's gonna care about is the kissability of your mouth."*

I'd gaped at her. *"Cece!"*

"Oh, please, don't you dare act shocked by that. You know the way he looks at you is a step shy of stalkerish."

"No, it's not," I'd defended. "*He's been nothing but a gentleman.*"

"*I'm positive that's because Uncle Stephen made sure of that.*" She'd shot her eyes to the ceiling.

My face had blushed a thousand shades of crimson, causing Cece to bust out laughing. She rolled up on her shoulder. "*All I know is that whether you choose the red, blue, or black sweater for your date*"— she pointed to each of my fashion choices on her bed —"*you are so getting kissed tonight.*"

Rita's potty whine pulls me out of the memory, and I'm halfway down the hallway before I realize it's the first time I don't want to push the grief away.

I want to hold it close.

Joel's house sits at the farthest edge of town, bordering the county line nearly fifteen minutes from Cece's cottage. Rita is near a complete meltdown as we exit Joel's car and step onto the driveway, and Rontu is no better. As soon as Joel swings open the front door of his single-story Craftsman, the two puppies are a tumble of fur and delight. I squat to give Rontu a few undivided seconds of my affection before he's off again.

I don't miss the way Joel's gaze sweeps over me the same way it did for most of the ride over: like I'm an apparition that might disappear if he looks away.

I smile up at him, and he reaches for my hand and pulls me to my feet, offering me a house tour that's finished before my many curiosities are properly satisfied. When he heads to the kitchen to prep for dinner, I hang back and meander through the great room for a second time, glancing up at the exposed beams in the vaulted ceiling before crossing into the open dining area. Joel's not necessarily a minimalist, but he's definitely organized and clean. A trait he comes by honestly, considering the life of hospitality he's grown up in. The paint on the walls is light, and the furniture he's selected is dark. And all of it feels right for him.

Joel's home tours like a posh real estate ad: a spacious, modern floor plan of three bedrooms and a convertible den, boasting gorgeous plank hardwoods and large wall-to-wall windows with perfect views of the grand Olympic Mountains I haven't had my fill of yet.

Maybe because that's what surprises me the most: It's not close to the water. Not a significant body of water, anyway.

I gaze out at the back patio, which is likely the best view in the house, and spot a narrow creek that runs as far as my eye can see, as does the acreage his home is situated on. The property is dotted with glorious weeping willows, spruce, and fir trees, and the beauty of it makes the tip of my nose tingle with oncoming tears.

It's like looking at a visual representation of everything I was so desperate for as a child—grounding, stability, peace.

Standing here, it's impossible not to think of all the could-have-beens if life had worked out differently. My gaze trails to the fenced-in area below the far edge of the deck. It's occupied by a dog run and some kind of canine agility course I'm sure Rontu and Rita can't get enough of.

As if summoned by my assessment of his outdoor living space, Rontu brushes against my ankle and whines. His sister follows his lead.

"Mind letting them out?" Joel asks, leaning against the open archway of the kitchen. I don't have a clue how long he's been watching me, but I unlatch the door for the pups, and they jet outside at high speed. Rontu bounds across the yard and snatches up a rope toy only to toss it into the air and catch it mid-arch. A solo game he repeats multiple times despite Rita's attempts to grab it.

"He's obviously quite shy and laid-back," Joel deadpans.

"Obviously." I don't dare drag my gaze away from the property when I say, "It's like a nature reserve out here. Beautiful."

"There's a question in there somewhere. I can hear it brewing." He prods gently.

"I'm guess I'm just surprised you didn't choose something closer to your family, to the hotel." *To the water* is what I don't say.

He studies me for a long moment. "A girl I once knew told me that a home on land was superior to a home on the water simply because you'd never have to worry about it floating away when you wanted to stay put." The corner of his mouth tips north along with his shoulder. "Guess I thought it was advice worth hanging on to."

He must see how his remembrance of something I told him nearly a decade ago affects me, because he moves to stand at my side and points to a spot just beyond the willows. "You can't quite see it from here, but that little creek out there eventually connects to Discovery Bay."

"How close is it?"

"About a half mile walk or so. We can take the dogs out that way after dinner if you're up for it."

I nod, though it's not the dogs or the bay I'm thinking about at the moment, but rather all the moments that have made up all the years where there was nothing but silence between the two of us.

Joel inclines his head. "Shall we?"

I follow him into a kitchen that could be featured on HGTV. Four swivel stools are stationed at the massive slab of white quartz Joel has directed me to sit at while he cooks. The pendant lights overhead catch the ribbons of silver and gray trailing throughout the island. But what snags at my attention the most are the memoir pages that took a beating at the lighthouse yesterday. Joel's pinned them flat with the help of weighty, hardback books. I spot a dictionary, a business textbook, and a giant Strong's Bible Concordance.

"I meant to move those earlier, sorry," he says. "I'll get my backpack out of the way, too."

"Don't worry about it. There's plenty of space for me here. Unless, of course, you've changed your mind about letting me help you with dinner?"

"I haven't." He turns, smiles, and pulls out a wooden cutting board and then the ingredients from the fridge. "A favor for a favor."

"Rita slept ninety percent of the time she was at the cottage with me. A homecooked meal hardly feels like an equal trade-off." I select a stool near the manuscript as Joel sets a Diet Coke in front of me.

"We can agree to disagree on that then."

We clink our soda bottles together and each take a sip.

"I had a good talk with Madison this afternoon," I say.

"Oh yeah? What about?"

When he reaches for his knife, I contemplate how appealing it is to watch grown-up Joel preparing a grown-up meal in his own grown-up kitchen. This front row seat which features the predominant flex in his right forearm as he chops vegetables sure does beat the late night dinner drive-thrus of our youth.

I blink and try to recall the conversation with Madison. "She mentioned seeing Cece use a writing dictation app on her phone. I think it's how she wrote the majority of the memoir. It's a common method for authors, and makes the most sense given Cece's symptoms."

Joel stills his hands, peers at me. "As in, you think she dictated each chapter into her phone?"

"I do." I nod. "And I think she'd planned to give it to us in person after I came up during her recovery. Maybe she even planned to read it *with* us."

Joel makes a *hmm* sound in his throat. "It certainly would have made chucking a pillow at her easier if she were in the room with us."

It would also make asking her one of a thousand questions easier, too.

As Joel continues to prep, I thumb through the chapters we've already read together, pausing in the place we left off. But then my eyes drag over the first paragraph. And then move on to the second.

To the third.

To the fourth.

To the fifth.

I flip to the next page, not wanting to stop now that I have some traction, but Joel's teasing tenor breaks my momentum.

"You know, it's a lot harder to follow along with you when you're reading silently." But whatever expression he interprets on my face causes him to set down his chopping knife. "What's wrong, Indy?"

"Nothing." I shake my head, emotion tightening in my throat. "I actually think something might be *right*. I just read this entire page without having to re-read a single sentence." I swallow. "This chapter's about the night of the treasure hunt." My gaze slides to Joel's right forearm again, only this time for a very different reason.

He dips his chin encouragingly. "Will you read it to me?"

I position the chapter in front of me, hoping I won't jinx my momentary win by saying yes. "I'll read for however long I can."

"Then I promise not to miss a single word."

22

"X Marks the Spot"

Cece knew how to keep a secret. Truth was, she'd been keeping secrets long before she started searching for her father online without her mother's knowledge. And long before she considered the consequences of what such a search might reveal. Maybe that was the reason she'd insisted on ending Ingrid's last day of spring break from Berkeley with a celebratory treasure hunt. Because while she couldn't change the discovery of her father's second family in Florida or the fact that he hadn't bothered to reply to *any* of her email messages, she could control the outcome of where her final clue would land Joel and Ingrid for their last night together until summer.

She sat on a hard bench outside the obscure tattoo parlor directly across from one of three liquor stores she kept tabs on while her best friend was away at college. Ingrid hadn't asked that of her, of course. It was Joel she'd entrusted her father's sobriety to, not Cece. But much like his own father, Joel was often too quick to forgive. Too willing to move on from a scandal and believe the best about people. But in these last two years since Captain Hal had returned from rehab, she'd kept her distance from him whenever possible, unwilling to get sucked back into the vortex of his magnetism. She'd been blinded by his gregarious personality and larger-than-life stories in the past, but she wouldn't fall for it again.

Hal might be collecting sobriety chips from the local recovery group, but Cece would never again see him through the innocent eyes of her sixteen-year-old self—a girl desperate for her own daddy's love. That girl had since grown up. And she'd learned how to funnel her personal struggles into her characters. The same way she'd do with this newest blow. Even now, she was plotting Ember's narrative in her head for her final chapter in book two, using her own rejection issues to strengthen her heroine's arc.

Cece had always believed the bond she shared with Ingrid was based on their mutual affection for all things fiction, but tonight, as she sat waiting for her friend, she wondered if their sisterhood had been built on something far more substantial: two failed fathers.

Determined to eradicate any trace of gloom from her mood, she breathed out a hard breath and refused to give another thought to either of those undeserving men. If she only had one more night with Ingrid before she went back to college, then Cece needed to make the memory count. And she needed to make it last. Life was too unpredictable not to make a permanent declaration of what mattered most.

The instant Cece spotted Ingrid and Joel walking hand-in-hand through the parking lot toward her, she plastered a smile on her face and jumped to her feet, every bit the fun friend Ingrid would expect her to be. "Good thing I didn't put a time limit on that treasure hunt. You two would have lost."

"It would have gone a lot faster if your clues had been better. You may know how to write pirates, but let me be the first to say your rhymes need work," Joel doled out in his usual flat jest.

"Hey, be nice." Ingrid elbowed him in the ribs and reached to hug Cece. "I think it was creative. Thanks for going to so much effort to make my last night here memorable. I'm just hoping I'm right about the last clue." When Ingrid stepped back, Cece didn't miss the way her best friend's gaze latched on to the gift bag she'd purposefully left on the bench. The one she'd decorated in old maps and a giant red X-marks-the-spot on the front. Ingrid clapped and brought her hands to her mouth, her pitch climbing in childlike excitement. "Please tell me the real treasure I've been dying to get my hands on is inside that bag, Cece."

Ingrid's enthusiasm brought a real smile to Cece's face. The once stoic, cautious girl Cece had met reading on the hotel dock years ago was not the same young woman standing in front of her now. Perhaps this was what love did to a person: It slowly turned up the temperature from within so that eventually the outside of a person had no choice but to match the warmth of the inside. The temperature of Ingrid's heart radiated through her eyes, her smile, her voice. The striking transformation was impossible to miss.

And even though Joel often kept his professional hat on whenever he saw Cece around the hotel while Ingrid was off working her way through the English program at Berkeley, Cece knew he had to be struggling. The transition from a day-to-day romance to a long-distance one couldn't be easy. Nor was the transition from sharing everything with her two best friends to being scheduled into a single weekly phone call. Truth was, she was lonely in a way she'd never been. And it scared her.

She noted the way Joel's arm casually looped around Ingrid's waist as if he couldn't help but pull her close in these final hours together. Cece wished she could freeze time right here and now. But seeing as she'd never been able to before, she simply reached behind her to retrieve the gift bag. "I know I could have sent this to you in an email attachment, but a novel feels way more legit when you can hold it in your hands—even though it did use all the ink in Uncle Stephen's printer." She cringed. "But I promised you the first printed copy of my first book, and even if nobody else ever cares to read it, this one belongs to you." She offered Ingrid the bag. "I couldn't have written it without you." A truth she felt deep in the marrow of her bones. There'd been so many plotting brainstorms, field trips, scene reenactments, and painful deletions and rewrites that went into finalizing this first draft of The Pulse of Gold. As well as a few characters who'd stitched themselves to her soul in the process. She squinted at Joel. "And I suppose I owe a fair amount to you, as well. I have a copy with your name on it, too."

Cece reached for the other bag she'd hidden under the bench seat for her cousin. Surprises were always more fun.

"Good thing," Joel said, failing to keep the smile from his face as he took it from her. "Because Merrick wouldn't be half the hero he is without my guidance."

Cece rolled her eyes. "I definitely wouldn't go *that* far."

A nervous kind of elation fluttered through her as she watched the people she loved most slip their respective copies of *The Pulse of Gold* out of their bags. Joel stared down at the ream of copy paper in his hands while Ingrid giddily hugged all four hundred and sixty-three pages to her chest.

"This has to be the best ending to a treasure hunt ever. I would have read a hundred more clues if I knew this was the ending. I'll start it bright and early on the ferry tomorrow." She clung to the manuscript as if it was actual gold. "We might be your first readers, but we won't be your last. The world needs your stories, Cece. I can hardly wait for you to finish up with book two so I can read all your revisions in order."

Cece was just about to tell her that she was only a couple of chapters away from starting her first major edit on her second book when Joel seized her in a hug that left her feet dangling off the ground.

"I'm proud of you, cuz."

Cece's eyes burned at Joel's spontaneous burst of affection, especially considering that the two of them had gone round and round over her choice to skip college in exchange for more writing time. Joel had always been degree-minded, setting his sights on an online MBA program before they'd even finished middle school. But for Cece, the idea of signing up for another four years of schooling, of her time being dictated by subjects and homework and tests she didn't care about, made her physically ill. She'd watched her mother's love of art take a back seat throughout the majority of her childhood, life's mounting pressures and responsibilities always taking first priority. It was partly due to her mother's journey, and hugely due to her mother's encouragement, that she'd decided to use her would-be college years to maximize her passion for words. It would mean living at home a little longer than her peers and continuing to collect her paychecks from the same uncle and aunt who'd employed her at sixteen, but she often prayed it would all be worth it someday.

Really, she and Joel weren't so different from one another. Both of them knew exactly who they were meant to become. But while he was set to get his degree in business this coming summer, there was no such date of achievement in sight for her. Which is why his generous words to her just now had felt like an achievement all on their own.

"Thank you" was all she could say as he placed her back on solid ground and squeezed her shoulder.

The three of them lapsed into a sort of reverent silence Cece could only stand for so long. Their night was far from over. "Are either of you going to ask about the final clue?" Cece lifted her gaze to the sign above their heads. "I mean, if tonight was just about getting these first drafts to you then I would have done it over a basket of fish and chips down on the pier."

Ingrid pulled a face. "But we found the last clue. We found you."

"There's always a *final* clue." Cece's smug face revealed nothing.

With narrowed eyes, Joel circled the area outside the parlor doors and then reached for the discarded gift bag, peeling off Cece's red X to reveal a three-by-five card he read out loud. "'You can find it with a compass, inked deep inside your chest. This place your friends call home, should be carved into your flesh.'"

Cece turned and swept the curls off the back of her neck, lowering her shirt to expose the detailed compass inked on her skin. Break waves smudged the borderlines of the nautical compass and highlighted the raised quarterdeck of a glorious pirate ship sailing toward the horizon. It was the very ship she'd been dreaming about for years now. All four masts pointed toward the heaven, sails raised high, while a single anchor trailed behind it from the stern. Etched on its arms was 48.1170° N, 122.7604° W.

The coordinates of Port Townsend.

Home.

If there was anything good that came from her childhood worship of Captain Hal—this was it. The inspiration she needed to create her own tattoo.

"Cece." She heard Ingrid gasp. "Oh my . . . it's, it's—"

A finger swiped across her skin. "It's not real."

Naturally, Joel would have to check for himself.

"Thank you, Captain Killjoy." She spun back around. "Of course it's not real. Not yet, anyway. But it will be soon. And I'm hoping you two will join me. Rupert said he has time for all three of us if we go in now."

"You're actually serious?" Ingrid all but squeaked.

"As serious as a pirate with a map."

Joel tugged at the back of his neck. "Cece," he began, glancing at the parlor windows. "I know we talked about doing this together a couple years ago, but I'm not sure this is the right time. Seems . . . a bit quick."

"And I think the timing couldn't be any *more* right. Think about it. Things are changing for all of us. Ingrid is off at school, getting leads on teaching jobs left and right, while your responsibilities at the hotel are multiplying every day." She didn't have much of a case to make for the changes in her own schedule, which still looked exactly like it had two years ago. Even still, she knew she wasn't wrong. "I just don't want us to forget."

"Forget what?" Joel asked in the emotionally clueless way of males everywhere.

"*This! Us!*" She gestured to the three of them, her pent-up fears starting to expose themselves. "Who we are to each other and where it all began."

"We don't need a tattoo for that," he said dismissively. "None of us are going to forget anything."

But while her cousin tried to rally support from his girlfriend, Ingrid's gaze remained locked on Cece, as if she were reading between the lines of her unspoken words. Words Cece wasn't ready to reveal. Not even to her best friend.

"Listen," she tried again. "I checked this place out—their reviews are solid and their portfolios are incredible. And Rupert in there, well, he recently won Tattoo Artist of the Year for the entire Pacific Northwest. Who knew we had a celebrity right here in our own little town?"

Joel furrowed his brow. "And he just happens to have three slots available tonight?"

Heat bloomed in Cece's cheeks. "I may have put a deposit down for him to hold our spots a while back."

Joel swiped a hand over his face, and she could practically hear the lecture building in his head. Too bad for him, she was *not* in the mood for mansplaining tonight.

"Fine. You know what, Joel? You're off the hook. It's not like the three of us took a blood oath or anything. But just for the record, I know you think I'm some silly little head-in-the-clouds dreamer, but I put a lot of thought into this one. I wanted us to do something memorable at the end of our week together, and I wanted to celebrate something I worked really hard on with the people . . . with the people . . ." Her words broke off before she could finish. Because outside of her mother, these two were *her* people. Ingrid and Joel. And while she wanted their relationship to advance to marriage and eventually to children, and while she rooted for each of their professions to mature into structured positions with 401(k)s and health benefits and paid vacations . . . she didn't want to be the one left behind.

Change *would* come for their little trio. It was inevitable. But she feared she'd be on the wrong side of it when it did.

The tears fell too fast for her to wipe away.

Ingrid's arms went around her. "I'm in for getting tattooed with you tonight. Did you already give Rupert our sketch-up drawings?" Cece sniffed and nodded. "Great. Then I'm all set. I love that our compass designs are unique to each of us, yet still share the same heart." She pursed her lips. "I just need a minute to figure out the placement of where to put mine."

Joel's eyes went wide. "You only need a minute to decide that?"

Ingrid rolled her eyes at him with a smile. "The design is the most important thing to me, and I've known that was right since the night we first sketched them all out after my dad left for rehab." She tipped her head to rest on Cece's. "I never understood why my dad tattooed the coordinates to Stavanger, Norway, on his arm when he hadn't lived there for so many years, but I get it now." Ingrid's voice flared with passion. "I never want to forget where my home is or the people who helped me find it."

Joel tugged at the back of his neck again and looked up at the sky for a long moment. Cece was certain he was about to tell them they were being overly sentimental and ridiculous about the whole thing. But instead, he blew out a weighted exhale and then stared her in the eyes.

"I don't think you're a silly little head-in-the-sky dreamer, Cece. I actually think . . ." He cleared his throat. "That you're a pretty incredible person." He looked between them. "And I'd be honored to share such an important evening with the two most important women in my life."

Cece sniffed and wiped her eyes. "I'm so going to tell your mom you said that."

"Then I'll tell *your* mom what you really did with her old stack of art magazines she was saving." He smiled ruefully and then moved to open the parlor door. "Come on, apparently our appointments have already been made. Let's just hope this Rupert guy isn't charging us by the hour."

He held open the door and Ingrid took the lead. She slowed to whisper something in Joel's ear before moving to sign them in at the clipboard on the front desk.

But before Cece could pass by him, Joel clamped a hand onto her shoulder. "Hey, wait a sec." Usually, she was annoyed when he tried to play the big brother, but strangely, she couldn't find a single thing that annoyed her about him in this moment. "None of us are ever going to forget where our home is. You got that? The three of us are in this together. Now, later, always. Nothing is going to change that. I promise."

Not trusting her voice to speak, she simply nodded at him, taking care to carve his promise in a place no tattoo artist could ever reach.

23

I am so focused on the reading, on the inexplicable lack of fatigue between my eye and my mind, that I'm unsure when Joel stops chopping the cabbage. All I know for sure is that we're both acutely aware of each other as I place the pages of this chapter back onto the countertop. Despite a hundred thoughts vying for my attention after Cece's retelling of the treasure hunt, there is only one that rises to the surface and warms the truth written across my heart.

Before I can speak it, Joel speaks first. "I came to find you once."

His words hover above me, unable to land without proper context. "What? When?"

After a labored sigh, he flattens his hands onto the quartz, shrinking the width of the island between us as his shoulders bear the weight of his reply. "I was tired of waiting, tired of hoping you'd find your way back on your own. Cece told me about a big publishing banquet at The Palace Hotel in San Francisco and that you'd be in attendance rooting for Barry and his Editor of the Year nomination, so I bought a ticket and a new suit and two dozen roses on my way to the venue."

My mind flashes back to the night of the publishing banquet three years ago. The year the Nocturnal Heart series exploded across international borders despite the last two books not having yet been released. It was held the same month the movie producers optioned her film rights after an extended bidding war. And during the same week that Barry promoted me to Senior Acquisitions Editor and officially added Cecelia Campbell's name to the top of my editorial list.

My boss had called me into his office two days before the award ceremony, gesturing for me to take a seat. "*In the beginning, it was a conflict of interest to have Cece on your editorial list during her initial contract negotiations, and honestly, you were still too green, which is why it was the right decision for me to be the one to oversee her projects. But I've never forgotten that you were the one who discovered her, Ingrid. It's always been your voice she hears when she edits her scenes, not mine.*" He'd leaned forward in his desk chair, his grin stretched ear to ear. "*And I'm convinced the extraordinary success of Cece's series has as much to do with your keen eye and instinct as it does her rare talent.*" I'd been taken aback by his words, but never could I have imagined what was to come when he slid an official-looking document across his desk, my name typed on the line where his should be. "*This Editor of the Year nomination belongs to you, kid. You're one of the best I've seen come through this industry, and it's past time you get the recognition you deserve.*" He'd winked at me. "*Now, go buy yourself something fancy for the gala and don't forget to write an acceptance speech. I'll be rooting for you.*"

I blink Joel back into focus again, still trying to wrap my mind around what he's telling me. "You were there that night? At the awards banquet?"

His nod is subtle, but his gaze is fire. "You wore a long red dress that swept the floor when you walked. The neckline was high but your shoulders were bare. And when your name was called from that podium and the entire room erupted in applause as you made your way to the front . . . it was the first time it hurt more to see you than it did to miss you, because I knew right then you weren't coming home with me."

"So you . . . you just left?"

"How could I not? You'd ghosted me for nearly three years—ignoring my calls and banning Cece from giving you any of my messages. The only reason I knew anything about you was because of her." He stretches his neck, readjusts his hands on the counter. "I realized that night I had no business trying to compete with the life you'd made, especially given the circumstances I'd be asking you to return to."

I don't need to close my eyes to recall the life I'd made for myself in San Francisco after saying yes to an internship that turned into a job that soon turned into my only reason to exist. My memory pulses with the never-ending traffic and the overcrowded sidewalks, the inescapable stress and fatigue of my daily workload. The constant noise that keeps me company late into the night so I never have to face the quiet I fear most.

The woman who lives there, in that tiny, overpriced apartment, may have grown accustomed to living on her own, but she's far from mastering *being alone*. And the blurred lines between the two have become more and more distinct ever since the day she arrived back in Port Townsend.

I hardly recognized the Ingrid Cece described in her last chapter. The woman whose walls had slowly been chipped away by the persistent knock of two friends who simply wouldn't allow her to hide—not at sea and not in books. That woman had found her home only after she'd been found by love.

If only for this moment right now, I wish I could be her again. I want to be the Ingrid who doesn't filter her every action through her past heartaches. I want to be the Ingrid who doesn't need all the directions before she's willing to take a step forward. I want to be the Ingrid who walks toward someone she wants to trust without planning her exit strategy.

When I slide off the barstool and move to the other side of the island, his gaze tracks my every step, much the way I imagine him doing the night of the banquet before I won a cold trophy that had no arms to hold me, no lips to kiss me, and no voice to congratulate me.

I feel the heat of his body as I draw near—and the closer I get to him, the closer I want to be. His breathing grows shallow when I reach for his arm and cradle it in my open palm. I trail my fingers along the smooth surface of the inked skin between his wrist and elbow, exploring the artwork that appears as fresh and bold as the day it was tattooed. His is of a compass surrounded by mountains, trees, and water. On the upper left quadrant, an old Victorian hotel perches at the edge of a bluff, reminiscent of the Campbells'—all of it entwined by a thick, three-strand rope that ends at an anchor. And there, carved into the crown of the anchor's arms, are the co-ordinates all three of us shared: *our home.*

The intense green of his eyes flickers as he skims my face with a silent request I need no help to interpret. Ever the gentleman, he releases himself from my hold and allows me to answer in my own way, in my own time. My nod is certain as I grant him an invitation I've given no one else.

Gingerly, he brushes my hair aside and then slides the chambray overshirt I'm wearing off my shoulder. His fingers graze along the ridge of my left collarbone until they connect with the high neckline of my black camisole. My eyes remain focused on his face as he slips the fabric low enough to expose the artwork inked on the soft flesh directly above my heart. The span of my tattoo is easy enough to cover with a modest neckline but impossible to hide wearing anything cut to rest near my breastbone.

Joel hasn't seen this tattoo in five years.

Truth is, I've barely allowed myself to look at it in nearly as long.

The shaky exhale that escapes him sounds half-pained, half-relieved. And I have to remind myself to keep breathing as his fingers trace the surging waves that break over the left half of my compass before they trail to the right. To the side where a dock stretches across peaceful waters to a shoreline masterfully shaded to resemble the illuminating light that first led me here. To the coordinates per-manently inked to my chest.

Joel presses his palm to my skin, searing his heat into my tattoo, which forces a confession to break from my lips.

"I wanted to forget," I utter into the safe space between us. "When

I left, I told myself it would be better that way. I told myself that I could control the pain if I was the only one I had to rely on. And I'd almost managed to convince myself that grief had tainted my memories of you—of us together. That they couldn't possibly be real."

With a tenderness that makes me weak, he whispers, "They are real, Indy. We are real." He brushes his thumb across the width of my tattoo. "I can't erase the darkness for you, but I can be the one to hold the light when you're ready to come home."

When I meet his steadfast gaze, Joel lifts his fingers from my hot skin just enough to tap them to my chest three distinct times, communicating in a sacred language that echoes through me like a vow. There's purpose in the way I reach for him then. My desire for Joel is as intrinsic as it is honest, as if for the first time in years I might actually be able to look ahead and not behind.

When our lips connect, it doesn't feel like the start of something new, but rather the continuation of something that began long ago. Of something that never stopped despite the distance. Of something backed by a history belonging only to us. And with every move of his lips over mine, every taste of his kiss and caress of his hands, pulling me in, pulling me close, I want it all to be real.

I want it to be as real as the truth branded on my chest.

24

Rontu hopes you slept well last night.

My eyes have barely opened when Joel's text comes through, and yet my grin feels as if it needs no warm-up time at all. I'm fairly certain it's in the exact same position it was last night after he walked me to the cottage door, brushed my hair away from my cheek, and pressed a lingering kiss to my mouth.

I touch my lips, welcoming the tingling sensation the memory brings.

Immediately, I picture all the manuscripts I've marked up over the years while donning my editor's hat. All the opening lines of chapters I've highlighted featuring giddy protagonists who rouse from deep slumbers while enjoying a mental frolic of recent romantic escapades . . .

Let's rewrite this opener, I'd type in the margins. *Can we try for something a bit fresher?* Or simply: *This is too cliché.*

Only this morning, I am the cliché protagonist. And I have no desire to be anyone else. Perhaps as long as I can stay snuggled in this bed, I won't have to be.

I pull my phone deeper into my cave of covers and text him back.

Ingrid

Please let Rontu know that I slept till 9:06 a.m. . . . and I can't decide if I should be horrified or exhilarated by this rare phenomenon?

Joel

He says as long as you woke up where you were dropped off last night . . . then he votes for exhilarated. He's a big fan of sleep.

And because I want this blissful, out-of-body experience to last for as long as humanly possible, I snap a picture of the mound of blankets covering my legs and feet, making sure to include the glorious beach scene just beyond Cece's large bedroom windows. I tap send.

Ingrid

Still here.

Joel

He'll be relieved. He was 5% concerned you might try to skip town on an electric bike sometime in the night.

Fine, he was more like 15% concerned.

Ingrid

And leave Rontu behind? Never. We have an unbreakable bond.

Joel

I think you are confusing an unbreakable bond with an unbreakable bad habit. One that started by you secretly feeding him table scraps. That's hardly the start of a healthy relationship, Indy. Don't be surprised when I send you the bill from his next puppy training session.

I'm laughing alone in this bedroom, picturing the way Joel's eyes are likely crinkling at the corners and the way his facetious grin must be pulling to one side. How I wish I could see it in real time. How I wish I could see it all the time.

And why can't I?

The question hits like a bolt of lightning when I think of the world I came from—a world that will very likely be ending in only a matter of days without the discovery of Cece's notebooks. A world that not so long ago seemed like the only thing left in my life to fight for. But maybe that's not true anymore.

Maybe there is something more to fight for . . . or perhaps something I need to stop fighting so hard against.

As if by unspoken agreement, last night held no discussions revolving around *future expectations* or mentions of the improbabilities associated with living nine hundred miles apart. Instead, we'd taken the puppies on a walk around the bay at sunset, laughing when lazy Princess Rita refused to take even one more step, whining for Joel to carry her all the way back. But there was more than longing in his good-night kiss last night; there was also a promise to *talk* tomorrow.

And now tomorrow is here.

Joel

What are your plans today?

Seeing as I already asked Allie to meet me at the storage unit this afternoon for our last lead on *The Fate of Kings*'s whereabouts, I can't exactly spend all day lounging in this bed like I want to. But that isn't for another three hours, which means I don't have to give up my cocoon of contentment just yet. I haven't had much time to process why my reading fatigue had been so much less bothersome last night as I'd read Cece's chapter to Joel, but I know the perfect way to test my luck again.

I prop myself up with pillows, reach for my laptop, then open the file containing Allie's novel.

Ingrid

I'm going to attempt to read for a while before I go to the storage unit because 1. It doesn't require me to get out of this bed. 2. It doesn't require me to put on real pants.

Joel

I will refrain from commenting on either of those points, though you should know there are many possible responses.

Ingrid

Joel

Would you be willing to entertain a dinner invitation for this evening? I happen to know a reputable restaurant in town on the water. I also happen to know there's a patio table reserved for two at 6:00 p.m.

Ingrid

Rontu will be disappointed when he finds out he wasn't invited to dinner. 😔

Joel

I don't ask him to share his favorite things with me so he doesn't get to share mine.

After we confirm the logistics for dinner, I take a deep breath and work to steady my mind on the story in front of me. My concentration is far from perfect, and my speed is reminiscent of Princess Rita right before she plopped her hindquarters on the ground for the final time last night. But my progress is steady, nonetheless. I stop a few times to give my eyes a rest and have to reread multiple sections a second time for comprehension, but the difference in my absorption rate is undeniably better. For the first time in months, I feel more than the struggle. I feel the *story,* and I can see it playing out in my mind's eye the way I haven't for so long.

In just over three hours, I manage to read and add notes to the margins of nearly thirty percent of Allie's fantasy novel. I send her an email with my initial thoughts and feedback, explaining that I'll send her a much more exhaustive report once I finish reading her manuscript.

When I finally slide my dying laptop onto the covers beside me, all I can do is stare in awe at the sunshiny walls of Cece's bedroom, trying to make sense of what just transpired for the second time in less than twenty-four hours.

For the better part of a year, I'd been on a downward spiral when it came to my reading paralysis. I feared I'd lost the one thing I've carried with me since I was a girl. But this emotion breaking through the surface of all my rationale . . . it's more than relief, it's hope.

I pick up my phone and send out a brief but somewhat ecstatic email to my therapist and then an over-the-top text to Chip saying simply, *The fog is lifting!* And then I study the contact name illuminated near the top of my screen, the only other person I want to update with such a victory: the man I'll be dining with in only a matter of hours.

I can wait.

I may not be able to articulate the how or the why of it all, but the where is obvious. Here, in the one place I'd vowed never to return, and yet now I can't imagine walking away from again.

As I ready myself to meet Allie at the storage unit, I work my hair into an inverted braid, inspired by the courageous protagonist she created in *The Faerie Huntress.* I think about the gifted storyteller she is—how her talent is raw but her instinct is beautifully uncluttered by mechanics.

More than once as I'd highlighted passages to add suggestions and feedback, my chest tingled with the remembrance of those early days in my career. The days as a young intern paid to read through the slush pile of unpublished works in search of anything worthy to pitch to the acquisitions team. It's how I was able to present Cece's manuscript to Barry all those years ago, and it's what made me believe in this industry in the first place: the infinite possibility and potential inside each new first draft.

As I ride leisurely across town on a bike I barely have to pedal, there's not a single frantic thought in my head tied to today's search. Despite this being the last known lead we have, I'm not panicked about the results. I still want the conclusion of Ember and Merrick's love story to be read by Cece's devoted fans, but I no longer feel the prick of SaBrina's claws around my neck to deliver it by the end of the week.

Though I can't imagine ever wanting a career apart from books, there are other things I know I could part with—editorial dictators for starters. I don't need a fancy title or a corner office. I simply need dedicated authors and a proverbial red pen. And Chip.

As I weave my way through a maze of tin-roofed storage units, I find Allie sitting in the hotel club car in front of unit number 199.

"Hey!" she calls out, beaming and waving at me with an energy level that just might rival Chip's. "I finished cleaning the last rental house on my list today in half the time—thanks to you."

"Thanks to me?" I ask, surprised.

Her nod is so vigorous I can't help but laugh. "Yes, as soon as I got the notification on my phone that you'd sent an email with your initial thoughts on the beginning of *The Faerie Huntress*, I stopped everything I was doing and took my lunch break right then and there, next to a dirty mop-water bucket. I think I read your notes over three times, maybe four." Her eyes grow bright and misty. "You liked it? You honest and truly liked it?"

"Honest and truly," I confirm.

And before I even have time to dismount from my bike, Allie is rushing toward me with arms stretched wide. Her embrace is more of a tackle, and I don't doubt for a minute that she's a phenomenal athlete. "I feel like I just won the lottery without ever buying a ticket." She pulls back. "Thank you. Thank you so, so much. I've only let a couple of my writing friends read it, but none of us really know what we're doing."

"You know more than you think you do. It's obvious you're a dedicated reader inside your genre. Like I said in the email, writing mechanics can be learned, but what you possess in story instinct . . ." I shake my head. "That's much harder to be taught. Your writing is sophisticated—and I don't just mean for your age. It actually reminds me of someone we both admired."

Allie falls back a step and clutches her chest as she mouths, "Cece?"

The smile that tugs at the corners of my mouth also tugs at my heart. "That's exactly who I mean."

She only blinks, her silence indicative of all that must be going on in her brain.

"Just promise me you won't give up," I encourage as I slip off the bike seat and kick the stand in place. "I think you have a lot more stories inside you if you're willing to do the work to explore them."

She nods. "I promise."

I move to the keypad on the outside of the unit and punch in the code Wendy texted me earlier.

"I'll get the door," Allie says, gripping the handle on the roll-up door and yanking it up.

The minute the unit is exposed to the daylight, it's my turn to take a step back.

"Whoa," Allie says, her cheery mood sobering. "This is . . . a lot."

There are three tall stacks of sealed Rubbermaid storage containers to the left side of the unit and several loose items on the ground I'm having a difficult time diverting my gaze from. Baby keepsakes—a dusty rocker and bassinet—along with a couple of older bikes and scooters Cece likely used as a child. Wendy has obviously been storing these things here since their move from Nevada. She wouldn't have had room for them in her little house or in her shed out back. These are the physical belongings that make up a person's entire life, not just the final year of it.

Allie meanders inside on her own, giving me a moment to reflect.

After a few deep breaths, I'm able to direct Allie's attention to the storage containers on the left. If Cece's notebooks are anywhere inside this space, it's there.

We're two dust-covered stacks in, our foreheads damp with sweat, when the corner air conditioner finally kicks on to a low whisper. Allie fans the front of her shirt and breaks the reserved atmosphere. "Do you think she had a plan? I mean, you knew her way better than I did, but it just doesn't seem like she would misplace something this important."

A thought I've had more times than I could count. "I agree."

I'm pulling off another heavy plastic lid and uncovering another box of multigenerational family pictures. With a sigh, I seal it up again and then push it aside to stretch my back.

"Do you think the notebooks could have been stolen?"

I reach for another tote, but it's far too heavy to lift on my own. Allie sees my struggle and steps in. We bring it down to the cement floor on the count of three. Dust plumes and we both turn our heads away and cough. "If they were, I don't know why they wouldn't have been pirated by now. The demand would be huge and those sites are like a fast-spreading cancer."

"Just like social media can be," Allie says. "I've seen some crazy things done by fans."

I'm about to ask her what she means when my fingers skim the top of a familiar-looking red notebook.

I jolt upright. "Allie! Look!"

Her gaze locks with mine. "That's the same brand I saw in the photos online."

I hold my breath as Allie digs for the other three. I flip open the cover and squint my eyes at a title page written in black sharpie.

Weird Happenings at the Campbell Hotel—Vol. One

Allie scoots in to read over my shoulder, and I note the date at the top. "She wrote this when she was fifteen. The year she moved here with her mom."

There are over twenty entries. Stories of weird incidents and strange guests. And by the third one, Allie is struggling not to laugh.

She taps a finger on the fifth. "Weird cat lady insists Joel brings her a specialty breakfast menu of foods she can enjoy with her kitty." Allie sucks in her cheeks. "What do you think this is all about?"

"Knowing Cece?" I shrug. "She was likely using this to build her characters."

We read on, finding quirky tidbits about townspeople, staff, and guests.

Entry 18: A widower rents room 114 every month on the twenty-first. It's booked for an entire year. What happened to his wife? Perhaps we should be offering a discount for other guests who book that room on account of a possible haunting.

Entry 23: Jeffery the bartender tells everybody he's allergic to peanuts, but I've seen him scoop handfuls into his mouth when he's doing bar cleanup at night. No EpiPen ever required. Definitely an attention seeker of the first degree.

Entry 30: Someone is stealing the butter cubes from the serving bowls in the kitchen fridge. I think it could be Verna from Guest Services, but I'm not positive yet. Will report back soon.

Allie pinches her lips together and then says, "I don't want to sound irreverent or anything, but I'd totally buy this if it was published."

Her joke catches me so off guard that before I know it, I'm laughing so hard that I'm swiping tears from my cheeks. "Thanks for doing this with me, Allie—and for all your searching online, too."

She sighs and helps me off the cement floor. "I just really thought we'd find them by now."

"Me too."

After we wedge the red notebook back into place and do a last search through the final two storage totes, I know we've reached the end of the road. I'm out of logical places to look, and I'm nearly out of time. But unlike last week, the thought doesn't create a ricochet of panic inside me.

In fact, I feel something opposite of panic.

Something impossibly similar to . . . peace.

Allie heads out to the club car, asking me if I'd want to get a black-berry lemonade slush with her before I head back to the cottage. But when I rotate to stretch my lower back, all thoughts of slushies slip from my mind as I notice an old desk protruding from the back wall. The surface of it is draped in a flat white sheet, blanketing something small and rectangular. I edge toward it, confused at why this one piece of furniture would be protected from dust when everything else of value is sitting out in the open.

I lift the corner of the sheet and immediately begin to tremble.

No, I think. *This can't be.*

Only it is.

I stare down at the ghosted shape of an object I believed to be at the bottom of the ocean floor.

With one gentle tug, my breath snags in my chest, resurrecting a piece of my family history I mourned years ago. The aged wooden chest that holds my father's most precious possession lies only inches from me. Gingerly, I reach for it, my fingertip grazing the scarred wood along the places where my family of three once etched our initials next to the lock. I'm not breathing when I slide the brass lock bar to the left and carefully lift the lid to reveal the bearded ax my father never sailed without.

"This will be yours one day, Elskede. It is our reminder for courage. To stay in the battle even when you fear you have lost. You will pass it to your children one day, the same way it was passed down to me."

I touch the blade and search my memory storehouses, needing to make sense of how this could be here. Of why Cece would have had this in her possession. Of why she wouldn't have told me that she did.

I hear Allie's footsteps behind me. "Ingrid? I think someone's trying to get ahold of you. Your phone keeps ringing."

I blink to reorient myself. "What?"

"Your phone. You left it in the bike basket with your wallet and sunglasses—here." She offers it to me, but my hands are currently occupied with resurrected history. I tell her my passcode to unlock my screen, and her eyes go wide.

"Who was it?" I ask, shifting the chest in my arms.

"Chip Stanton."

"Oh." I immediately breathe away my concern. "It's okay, he's my assistant. I'll call him back later." It's hard to even recall my ecstatic text to him earlier about my reading win while holding my father's battle-ax.

"Um, I'm guessing this isn't a call-him-back-later kind of thing. Not unless it's normal for him to call you nineteen times in a span of twenty minutes?"

Without further discussion, I hand her the chest and take my phone.

25

I watch Allie tuck my father's chest between the two seats in the club car as I return Chip's call. The phone barely has a chance to ring before he answers and launches in without a greeting.

"Ingrid, listen. I don't have much time. Minutes, seconds. I'm not sure." His words are spoken in such a harsh, reverberating whisper that I have to press the phone closer to my ear to understand him. "SaBrina knows about the manuscript you have from Cece. The one the attorney gave you—"

"*What?* No. She couldn't possibly—"

"She overheard our conversation on speakerphone the other night when I was in the break room. I swear to you, I thought I was the only one left in the building. She stayed in her office all day yesterday, and she canceled our all-staff meeting this afternoon." His strained words bounce and echo as if he's in a gym locker room, or possibly hiding out in an office restroom. The revelation causes the back of my neck to prickle. "I was caught completely off guard when she called me into her office this morning and interrogated me on what I knew about the *other* manuscript. . . . Ingrid, she asked about things you and I never even discussed that night." He goes quiet, and then his voice snags. "I—I tried my best to protect you. Please, believe that."

The icy spasm in my core spreads to each one of my limbs within the span of two heartbeats, and I brace a hand on the frame of the storage unit door. Allie steps out of the driver's seat of the club car, her fear-filled eyes likely a mirror image of my own.

"She's been on the phone since I left her office, but she's going to call you. I just wanted you to hear it from—"

A door whooshes open and closed in the background, and Chip doesn't wait to say good-bye before he hangs up. Instead, he sends an immediate follow-up text.

Chip

I'm so sorry.

Eyes wide, I stare at the phone in my hand as if it's a grenade.

"Ingrid?" Allie places a steadying hand on my shoulder. "Are you okay?"

But there's no time to answer that question, because SaBrina's call is ringing in my palm.

For all of three seconds, I contemplate sending her to voicemail, or better yet, tossing the entire device under the wheel of the club car's tire. But ignoring this won't make it any easier. Ignoring the unknown only makes things worse.

I swipe right. "Hi, SaBrina."

"Ingrid. Hello. So glad I caught you." The lack of professional undertone as she speaks is unsettling, but I have no doubt her double entendre is intentional. "I was hoping we might discuss something that's recently come to my attention. Do you have a moment, or are you too busy searching those final locations?"

"I have a minute," I say carefully, willing the pulsebeat in my throat to slow.

"Good," she says, leaving a chunk of radio silence before starting in again. "I was hoping that despite some of our initial setbacks, you and I were beginning to operate on a similar frequency. That we shared a mutual understanding. After all, we're two intelligent, innovative women who have the same goal of expanding quality literature worldwide."

Not entirely sure where this was headed, I adopt the less-is-more policy and keep my mouth shut as Allie stands guard beside me.

"Which is why I was surprised to discover that you are in the possession of a manuscript written by our late, best-selling author Cecelia Campbell." She takes a breath. "A manuscript it seems you collected the day after you arrived there." Her implication is as clear as the fake-nice voice she's still trying to maintain. "Now, as I've already assured our legal team back in New York, I know you must have a perfectly valid reason for why you chose not to disclose such a critical piece of information to me in your update reports, but I shouldn't have to remind you of the binding, contractual agreement Cecelia's manuscript is still under."

I rub my lips together once and aim to match her unassuming tone as if she hadn't just casually slipped in the words *legal team*. "I apologize for the misunderstanding, SaBrina, but *The Fate of Kings* is still missing. I don't have it."

"But you *do* have a manuscript written by Cecelia Campbell in your possession, correct?"

I hesitate. "That's correct, but—"

"Then I expect to see a copy of it in my inbox for review by the end of business today."

"I—I can't do that."

"Why not?" Her sugary veneer quickly dissolves.

There's no time to think strategically on what I should or shouldn't say to my boss. But I'm not new to the publishing industry or to the contractual agreements we initiate as an editorial staff. I've negotiated dozens and dozens of them over the years. And though each one is as individual as the authors we represent, I know SaBrina doesn't have a leg to stand on when it comes to intellectual property that has yet to be negotiated. The manuscript in question belongs to a trust, in which *only* Joel and I have named access.

"Because the manuscript in my possession is not under contract with Fog Harbor Books," I reply.

SaBrina's exhale is unnervingly long. "I wish I could believe that, Ingrid, but unfortunately, this is hardly the first time your integrity has been called into question in regards to your work ethic."

"My *integrity*?"

"How many months would you say you've been passing off your assistant's work as your own? Seven, eight? I'm sure it wouldn't be too hard for me to figure out. Chip can actually be quite helpful when the right carrots are dangled in front of him." She waits for my response, but I don't take the bait. I have no doubt the *carrots* she dangled were actually threats.

"And then, of course, there's your more recent indiscretions. I'm sure your pity-struck coworkers would be surprised to learn that your *exhaustive search* for *The Fate of Kings* this last year was nothing more than a ruse, given you've known exactly where that manuscript has been since Cecelia's death: sitting in a trust with your name on it."

A punch of air escapes me. "That's not true—"

"Which part? Hiding behind your assistant or hiding a manuscript from your employer?" Her voice is unflinching. "If your plan is to try and run out the clock on Cecelia's contract, then you're a fool. Don't think for a moment you'll be able to shop it around without submitting it to me *first*—not without severe legal consequences, which we are prepared to fight to the fullest. We've already fronted a considerable sum in advances to own the rights of the Nocturnal Hearts series, not to mention the film rights that are still pending on their completion. That manuscript belongs to us."

"I know Fog Harbor owns the rights to *The Fate of Kings*—but what we have isn't it." Panic brews inside me like a storm. "It's not even a work of fiction." The instant it's out of my mouth, I want to take it back. I don't want SaBrina knowing anything about this memoir.

"If that's true, then you should have no objections sending it over to me so I can verify that for myself."

Sickness sloshes in my gut. How many times had I thought nothing about asking an author to do that very thing—to send me the story draft they'd hemorrhaged all over by whatever date I specified, usually the week following a writing conference. I'd sit with dozens of writers over the course of a weekend, each hoping for their big break, while I knew only a fraction of them would ever make it to acquisitions.

Requesting a manuscript from an author willing to sell their soul for a chance to be published by a reputable house had become a normal part of my job. And yet the paralyzing fear of turning any of the pages in my possession over for SaBrina's entertainment makes me want to retch. I may not be the one who penned these words, but my blood is splattered on each and every page.

Right then, a detail I would have sworn I hadn't heard during the exchange in Marshall's office surfaces in my mind. I force it out with as much backbone as I can muster. "The trustees have to be in unanimous agreement before any action can be taken on the intellectual property."

"And just how soon can I expect you and Joel to make such a decision?"

I grit my teeth at her mention of Joel, at her knowledge that it's just the two of us who have the authority to make such a decision. As I work to construct an answer, I imagine again just how quickly SaBrina could ruin a reputation in our industry with no more than a single wave of her manicured hand. "I really can't say without conferring with him first."

"Well, I advise you two to come to a decision quickly. This is the kind of information that tends to leak out one way or another, and I'd hate to see the chaos that would be unleashed upon Cecelia's family for a second time if her fans find out about this *secret manuscript*," she enunciates. "As you know, many of them were extremely agitated by the way Cece left the cliffhanger in *The Twist of Wills*. But news like this would revive even the most frustrated of fans. They'd all flock right back to that little seaport town of hers—set up their candlelight vigils and share their conspiracy theories about how their favorite author staged her own death as a publicity stunt all over again. You've heard that one, haven't you? It's right up there with how Cecelia's publishing house posted a reward for anyone who brought in *The Fate of Kings*. Suppose that's what happens when teenagers are given free rein of the internet . . . their influence is power." Another pause. "Don't underestimate them, Ingrid. Secrets like this only keep for so long."

I'm shaking by the time the call drops, SaBrina's last line echoing in my brain. Was that a threat? Was she actually threatening to out the manuscript in my possession to the public?

Allie is already loading my bike into the back of the club car as if she knows what my next words will be before I speak them. "I . . . I need to get to the hotel, Allie."

She nods. "I'll text Joel and tell him we're on our way."

Allie has us out of the maze of storage units in a matter of seconds, her gaze darting to me several times. I don't know what all she heard, but it's pointless to pretend she hasn't pieced the gist of it together by now.

As we hurry down the hill, every possible landmark mentioned in Cece's chapters—the lighthouse, the marina, the tattoo parlor, even the liquor store on Fifth and Chambers—points to a memory I'd rather die than hand over to SaBrina.

I replay her final words to me. The threats hidden inside so many other threats. The resurrection of fans hosting vigils and the chaos that will ensue on the Campbell family if this secret is outed makes me unable to take in a full breath. As does the idea of having to tell it all to Joel.

I close my eyes, sick at the thought, which is why I know I can't go into this conversation blindly. I need to know what actually happened in the months following Cece's death. In the months Joel's only alluded to when it comes to his aunt.

I try to project my voice over the engine noise as Allie takes a right onto Water Street. "Do you know anything about a list of conspiracy theories involving Cece's death?"

By the way her expression distorts, and the way her foot backs off the accelerator, I know her answer even before she confirms it. "Unfortunately, yes. I do."

"How come I never saw anything pop up on her memorial page? There are hundreds of thousands of fans on there."

She slows her speed even more to allow a car to pass us. "Because the admins on that page try our best to block and report any post that isn't verifiable. Even still, a few have gotten through. We keep a record of all the offenders by taking screenshots of their posts and profiles. It's gross what some people will do for attention."

"Have you actually seen posts about a publisher's reward for finding *The Fate of Kings* and . . ." I swallow back the acid in my throat. "And then one about her faking her own death for a publicity stunt?"

She crinkles her eyebrows. "Who told you that?"

"My boss."

Her frown morphs into a look I can't quite decipher, like she's scrolling back in her mind and reading them all over again.

"Please, Allie, I need to know everything, even if you think it will be hard for me to hear."

With some reluctance, she finally nods. "Most of the conspiracy posts I've seen are related to the cause of Cece's death, assumptions on how she actually died—drug addiction, murder, rare disease, suicide, etc. But others claim to have proof she's still alive, writing in some nondescript location off-grid somewhere. And . . ."

"And what?" I ask, though I'm already dreading her answer.

"There were rumors circulating in the fan groups a while back that Wendy was the one who helped her daughter escape, and that she's also the only person who knows where Cece is hiding out and where her last manuscript is hiding, too. A group of them showed up here this spring, looking for Wendy."

I twist in my seat, gawk at her as if I can't possibly be hearing this correctly. "This spring? As in a few months ago?" I calculate the time-line. "But I thought it was the reporters who were following Wendy around. Joel said the media was hounding her for an exclusive."

"At first it was, but the media didn't stick around too long. It was everything that came later that was the real problem. Stephen said our spring tourist population was triple what it usually is—there wasn't a single hotel room available within ninety minutes of Port Townsend." We approach the hotel and turn into the staff parking lot.

"But I knew it wasn't just tourists," she continues. "I could see the online traffic in the fan groups. And for every "Wendy sighting" post or hashtag I saw and reported, I'm sure there were a dozen more just like it posted in secret groups I couldn't access. It's why Wendy stopped leaving her house and why Stephen hired security guards to park in front of her driveway for weeks at a time."

I'm as gutted by the heinous insensitivity Allie's described as I am by the ignorance and cruelty of those who claimed to love Cece's art and still dared to treat her mother this way. I can't even begin to fathom the trauma Wendy must have faced each and every time she was confronted by one of Cece's fans accusing her of hiding her daughter away. Worse, accusing her of being an accomplice in a publicity stunt when in reality Wendy was still reeling from the grief of having to say good-bye to her only child.

I tug at the collar of my T-shirt, suddenly unable to take in a sufficient breath despite being surrounded by fresh air. My mind spins with questions that throw my entire center of gravity off-kilter, because if all those conspiracies were sparked by rumors without any basis, then what will happen if the rumors of a found manuscript are substantiated? What will happen to Joel's family?

What will happen to Wendy?

The answer hits me with such force I barely have time to signal Allie to shift into park. I stumble out the passenger side door and into the only patch of green I can see. I'm braced to be sick, hands on my knees as my stomach attempts to eject itself from my body multiple times. The world blurs and shimmers, and from somewhere outside me, I can hear my name being called. Feet smack against the pavement. A dog's panicked bark circles my eardrums. But my lungs scream louder than all those sounds combined.

I claw at my chest as globs of darkness crowd out the last of my vision.

Another wave of nausea hits, and this time, it takes me to my knees.

There is no more air.

26

When my eyes blink open, two familiar faces peer down at me. One has a phone to his ear, speaking in hushed tones and answering questions about my well-being. The other holds a cool, wet rag to my forehead.

"Are you here to stay this time?" Allie asks, quirking an eyebrow.

"What happened?" I ask groggily, my head pounding.

"This is the third time you've opened your eyes and asked that same question before falling back to sleep. You're beginning to sound a bit like my great-grandma Dotty, and she needs help remembering to put her teeth in before breakfast."

"Yes, Dr. Jacobs," Joel says into his phone while his eyes rake over me with concern. "Will do. Thanks again for your help."

I try to sit up from the comfy recliner I'm stretched out on, but Joel shakes his head and moves toward me. "Easy. How do you feel?"

"Headache, but otherwise I feel okay."

"You passed out in the memorial garden," Allie supplies, sitting only a few inches from where I lay. "Has that happened to you before? It was pretty freaky."

"Only a few times." My gaze slides to Joel, who's been given a front row seat more than once now. When the Coast Guard called with news they'd recovered my father's missing body—still buckled into his life jacket not too far from the wreckage of the Campbell's charter—I lost all sense of time and place, my breath tapering off until there was simply none left to breathe. And then again with the news of Cece. The helplessness, the powerlessness of being so far away was simply too much for me to remain upright.

With Joel's assistance, I raise the back of the recliner to more of a seated position. Rontu sits close by at my feet, his eyes attentive. Just like his master's.

"Doctor says you likely hyperventilated." He untwists the cap off a water bottle and offers it to me before he sets two acetaminophens in my open palm. I take them both in one swallow.

"At least you don't have to worry about a concussion. Joel caught you before your head smacked against the pavement."

The concern in Joel's eyes is almost enough to knock the wind out of me a second time.

"Allie," he says, "would you mind giving us a few moments alone, please?"

"Sure thing. I'll go help my mom in the kitchen. She's making you up a plate right now, Ingrid." She lowers her voice. "Beware, she tends to think croissants cure everything." Allie pats the blanket covering my knees and hands off the cool rag she was pressing to my face earlier. I don't miss the way her gaze glances between Joel and me as she exits.

"I'm sorry," I whisper, wishing my mind was free enough to un-lock the details it's holding back.

He scrubs a hand down his face before pulling up a chair to sit beside me. "I'll admit, seeing you like that again was . . . not my favorite moment." He takes my hand in his, rubs his thumb over my knuckles. His voice is calm, soothing, even. "I'm just glad you're okay."

Only, I'm not okay—that much I'm sure of. I just can't quite re-member . . .

"Ingrid?" Joel reaches for the trash can on the floor. "Are you going to be sick again?"

I pinch my lips together until they hurt, not because I'm nauseous, but because I remember. I remember everything. "Something's happened."

"I gathered that when Allie said you had a distressing phone call at the storage unit. But I'd rather you take some time to catch your breath before you fill me in on—"

"No," I force out. "This can't wait." I twist my ring around and around on my finger. "My boss found out we're in possession of an unpublished manuscript of Cece's. She's demanding we turn it over to her for verification."

Joel sits back in his chair, his stunned expression muting the loud throb in my head. "Verification of what? Fog Harbor only holds the rights to Cece's Nocturnal Heart series."

"I know that, but SaBrina has reason to doubt my integrity and refuses to take my word for—"

"SaBrina," Joel scoffs. "The only integrity that woman should be questioning is her own. If not for your . . ." He stops himself, and then restarts. "She has no grounds to be making any demands on anyone."

Like piecing together the remnants of a bad dream, I recall the odd introduction between the two of them in my office, the way his eyes narrowed when she spoke to him, the telling tick of his jaw.

That wasn't their first interaction.

The tentacles of fear squeeze my chest as I push the question out. "If not for my *what*, Joel?"

He hesitates for only a second before he responds. "If not for your employment at Fog Harbor Books, I would have pushed my family to take legal action against them after I found out about SaBrina's incessant phone calls to "check in" on Wendy. At first my aunt believed SaBrina's motives for calling were pure, and because she desired to connect with anything pertaining to Cece's fiction world, Aunt Wendy didn't tell us about the calls for months. Not until after Cece's fans started showing up in droves last spring and her panic attacks wouldn't subside. I emailed SaBrina personally and told her never to contact Wendy again."

"What . . . what was it she wanted from her?"

"The same thing everyone wants from her: *The Fate of Kings*."

The throb in my temples increases, reducing my voice to little more than a whisper. "I wish you would have told me this sooner."

"I saw no reason to involve you. I knew you weren't the one behind SaBrina's manipulation." He sighs as if there's nothing more for either of us to say on the matter, only I know just the opposite to be true.

"Bottom line," he continues, "I think SaBrina is little more than a con artist willing to prey on a grieving mother for her own gain."

The blood drains from my face as I realize that I, too, have been a pawn in SaBrina's game. Her ultimatum is the reason I agreed to come, after all. I squeeze my eyes closed, willing myself to keep breathing.

"Ingrid?"

It's the worry in his voice that undoes me. "I wish I'd known all that had happened here with Cece's fans, with Wendy . . ." I swallow and start again, though I have no clue how this conversation will end. "I've loved Cece's stories since I was sixteen years old, you know that. I hope you also know that I would never willingly do anything to harm anyone in your family."

His perplexed expression only makes my confession more difficult.

"The day you came to my office at Fog Harbor, SaBrina was getting ready to fire me. My productivity since Cece's death has been subpar at best, and Chip has been covering for my slow production for months and months. But then you showed up with a birthday invitation in Port Townsend and . . ." I fail to extinguish the burn at the base of my throat. "And SaBrina told me that if I accepted the invitation and used my time here to find the missing manuscript, I could keep my job."

For close to a minute, Joel doesn't move. Not a blink, not a muscle twitch, not a single acknowledgment that he's even heard a word I've spoken. And then, in one controlled movement, he rises from his chair and crosses the length of his office, as if he suddenly can't stand to be near me.

"You're saying the only reason you agreed to come back was because of the manuscript," he calmly confirms. "Not because Cece asked you to, and not because I asked you to. But because Sa-Brina asked you to."

I want to deny it, but I can't. "I—I would have lost my job and the life I made there, my home."

"That city has never been your home."

"It's the only thing I had after everything broke."

"No, Ingrid, it's the only thing you *chose* after everything broke. There's a big difference." His gaze is pained as he takes me in. "I thought we . . ." Whatever he's about to say, he shuts it down with a hard shake of his head. "I won't be signing anything over to SaBrina for verification."

"I understand that's how you feel—it's how I feel, too, but . . ." I can barely force my next words out. "She threatened to leak the existence of Cece's memoir to the media if she doesn't get a chance to see what's in our possession for herself."

"Of course she did." He slams the base of his fist on the bookshelf he's standing beside and refuses to meet my gaze for so long I fight a true wave of nausea.

"We need to come up with a plan," I plead gently. "If the public finds out there's an unpublished manuscript by Cece floating around here, regardless of the content, it will start the chaos all over again. They'll come. And they'll look for Wendy."

He grips the back of his neck, a mix of shock and disappointment on his face.

"I'm so sorry," I say with a quivering lip.

Slowly, as his gaze connects with mine, I see the face of a man I begged to keep my dad safe, to protect at all costs. The same face I'd blamed for so much of my heartache and pain these last five years.

And now here we are again. Only this time, I'm the one who put his family at risk.

The realization guts me.

He starts for the exit.

"Where are you going?"

"Where I should have gone months ago. To Marshall's."

"Joel, wait, please." I push to the end of the chair, testing my legs. They're no longer shaking, and yet they still feel absolutely bone-less. "I know you're upset. You have every right to be. But we need to work together on this. For Wendy's sake."

His back is to me when he shoves his hands into his pockets and speaks to his closed office door. "Why did you really agree to stay after the birthday party, Indy?"

I open my mouth, try to respond, only to close it again.

He twists to face me. "You came here to save your job, but is that the only reason you stayed?"

My throat burns to tell him something other than the truth, some-thing pure and upright and noble. But I won't lie to him again. My reasons then may not be the same as my reasons now, but even still, the truth is I stayed for me. I'd set out to redeem my professional reputation, and instead all I'd done is hurt a family who'd taught me more about love and loyalty and forgiveness than anyone I'd ever known.

When my silence lingers another few seconds, Joel finally says, "That's what I thought."

27

I *need to move.*

It's the only thought in my head when I find my bike parked outside the staff entrance. Allie must have unloaded it from the back of the club car, then thoughtfully placed the wooden box into the wire basket for me to take back to the cottage. Only, I don't want to go to the cottage.

I slip onto the seat, and the instant my feet hit the pedals, my calf muscles ignite with a familiar fury, honing in on a rhythm they know well. When Dr. Rogers suggested this outlet for me, he encouraged me to fight the spirals in my mind with the spinning wheels of a bike. But this is one spiral I know I can't outride. My warring thoughts are not rooted in a past I wish I could change, but on a future I desperately want to make right.

By the twelve-minute mark, the hem of my cotton shirt is already stuck to my damp lower back as I've been more focused on the intensity of my ride than on my destination. But the minute I near the marina, the prickle of awareness in my chest becomes as evident as the sun breaking free from the clouds overhead. Its refusal to hide fuels the mission I've rejected since the first time my therapist dared bring it up. Suddenly, my destination is as dialed into my internal GPS as the coordinates carved into the flesh above my heart.

The pedals are lightning under my feet until the terrain morphs from taxpayers' asphalt to a narrow dirt path most locals wouldn't even look twice at. The fir trees are taller now, their branches fuller, but the stench of decay and rot is very much the same. This has never been a shore for seashell hunts and day-long frolics with friends.

This is the shore where hope comes to die.

As soon as the bow of the weathered vessel comes into view, heat licks my insides. It's still here, still anchored to a life that no longer exists.

In a different world, I might have been the kind of daughter who would pay her respects at a cemetery. The kind who would mournfully run her fingers along a generous epitaph etched in a smooth, marble headstone. Maybe even the kind who'd leave a vase of white lilies behind when she left. But Captain Hal wouldn't have known what to do with a fresh bouquet of flowers any more than I would have known what to do with a predictable parent.

I leave the bike at the same fir tree where I used to park my old ten-speed before the night Joel and Cece stumbled upon a truth I'd managed to keep hidden for years. The closer I get to the bow, the quicker my pulse kicks against my ribs, as if it's already anticipating my need for escape.

But I have no desire to take the coward's way out this time.

My dad did enough of that for the both of us.

When my mother was still alive, we used to go through a stack of outdated *Highlights* magazines piled on the side of her bed. *"Can you spot the differences between these two pictures, Ingrid?"* And while she'd brush my long hair, I'd scrunch up my nose and narrow my eyes on the side-by-side images of playgrounds and classrooms and ice cream parlors. At first glance, they always seemed to be identical, but then slowly, surely, the differences would reveal themselves and I'd scratch them off on the finder's key one at a time.

But as I stare now at this ugly scar of my youth and recall its lack of warmth and protection, the differences in its appearance aren't enough to scratch off any of the feelings that go along with them.

The grooved indent the hull has made into the rocky shore makes it appear as if it's been dragged against its will into the murky waters behind it. The vessel slumps unevenly to one side, the cabin door warped and exposed to the elements as it is to whatever rodents and wildlife nest inside it. Shattered windows and extensive rust tell of storms I never weathered, and yet the corrosion inside me speaks of the ones I did.

Something feral and merciless begins to chew its way through the core of me as I picture myself inside that back cabin bedroom. I remember the unwashed blankets and piles of children's books that kept me company through the long, isolated nights when my dad was too gone from drink or out buying more. I hear my childlike voice crying out for him in the darkness, begging him to *please stay awake*, to *please keep me safe* as wind and rain ravaged the black waters beyond my portside window. And then I feel the caged helplessness of loving a man whose actions rarely aligned with his promises.

But I'm not helpless anymore.

I bend at the waist and dig into the wet, pebbled earth at my feet. My nails scratch into the grainy sand as I pluck out the weightiest rocks and release the rest. Accusations wrapped in rage rush to greet me, and for the first time, I invite them in.

I line up my aim on the window nearest the galley, the cracked one Cece must have peered through the night my inebriated father threatened to pull anchor from the only home I'd ever known, and from the only people who'd ever really known me. It takes three strikes for the far side of the window to break under the strength of my pitch, and the sound of it is so addicting, I refill my ammunition and go at it again. *Harder.*

With each hit, the offenses grow, as does my ability to voice them.

"Where were you going that night, Dad?" I bellow into the forest as I pitch another rock at the rusted stern. "Why were you in that storm after dark?"

Pitch. Hit. "Why didn't you tell me about your relapse?"

Pitch. Hit. "How did Cece get your ax?"

Pitch. Hit. "Why didn't you listen to Joel?"

298

Pitch. Hit. "Did you even think about me? Even once?"

Exhaustion slows my speed, but my mind still rages ahead as I close my hand around the sharp rocks and rush toward the boat. I pummel my fist into the hard steel until my entire body vibrates with an anger I don't recognize.

"I'm the one who hid your secrets, Dad! I'm the one who fought your battles! I'm the one who refused to give up on you every time you lost a bet or drank yourself sick! I'm the one who prayed for a miracle when you were lost at sea!" A cry rips from my throat. "And still, you left! *You left me!*"

I collapse against the cold wall, my head bowed low. "Why wasn't I enough for you?"

But even as my chest heaves with the ache for truth, I know I won't find it here. My questions have never been confined to this boat. Or even to the man who anchored it here. They are bigger, deeper, weightier. And unlike the foolish girl I was for so many years, hoping for a cure that would never come, trusting in a rescue plan that would arrive too late, believing in a love that was never meant to last . . . this time, I don't have it in me to hope.

With a tired breath, I unfurl my fist and watch the last of the rocks fall to the ground. I wasn't able to protect my father, but I still have time to protect Wendy. Even if doing so means I can no longer protect myself.

It's just before seven when I text Joel.

Ingrid

I know I'm probably the last person you want to hear from tonight, but can we talk? Please.

He responds within five minutes.

Joel

I can be over in ten.

Ingrid

Thank you. I'm in Cece's office.

Reclined on a bean bag pillow, I stare up at the vivid mural of the Kingdom of Cardithia on Cece's ceiling, charting my way across the painted waters the way I've charted the conversation I'll be having in only a matter of minutes. When I hear the door open downstairs, my entire body is tuned to Joel's presence, even from a floor away.

I close my eyes and trace his footsteps through the cottage by the familiar creaks and pops of the weathered floorboards below. I hear when he drops his keys on the countertop and the thump of his backpack near the place he always slips off his shoes. And as I wait for his next course of action, I wonder if this is what it would feel like to build a life with someone: the swell of anticipation of a beloved's homecoming.

But, of course, that's not what we're doing. And that's not who we are to each other.

I track him as he passes through the dining room and note the exact location where his movement pauses. It's the same place I've stopped each time I've passed my father's wooden ax chest on the coffee table. And though I can imagine his pensive expression as he studies it, I refrain from guessing at his thoughts.

My pulse hums as he climbs the stairs, but no amount of preparation could have readied me for the defeat I read in his haunted gaze when he fills the attic doorframe. The disheveled look of his hair and the open collar of his shirt that exposes the tight cords in his neck floods my gut with shame.

I did this to him.

I push myself to a seated position and tuck my legs in close. I'm suddenly unsure if I should extend an invitation for him to do the same on the pillow across from me. Truthfully, considering what I'm about to ask of him, I'm unsure of nearly everything I felt certain of only minutes ago.

But once again, Joel surprises me as he claims the bean bag across from me and folds himself into a position that is likely as comfortable for him as the company he's been asked to keep tonight.

"Thanks for coming," I say. "Were you able to speak with Marshall this afternoon?"

"I was." He's inches from me and yet he's distant, careful even. "There's no legal action we can take until there's evidence of criminal activity, or until there's a threat made to Wendy directly."

I nod in acknowledgement. It's what I've been dreading he'd say. I lift my gaze to the mural overhead for several heartbeats before I find the courage to speak. "Did Cece ever tell you I discouraged her from painting this?"

I feel his focus shift to where mine is anchored on a single ship sailing off course into the dark waters beyond the fleet. I map the rebel ship's route in my mind and continue. "My reasons were selfish, but I feared her artistic interpretation would somehow alter the way I imagined Cardithia—that it might lessen my experience or harm my understanding of a place I'd come to love almost as much as the author who invented it."

Joel's disquiet settles over the room, but it doesn't deter me.

"But I realized today that it doesn't matter if Cece's interpretation of Cardithia was the same as mine. Because my version of it lives in here." I touch my temple. "And here." I touch my chest. "All those brainstorms Cece and I shared, all those first-draft chapters I read, all those revisions I edited . . . I'm the keeper of those memories and what happens to them. They belong to me." I work to calm the erratic thump in my pulse points. "No matter how many fans post reviews I don't agree with, or how many character sketches I've seen that don't match the Merrick and Ember I've come to know, or how many future lit teachers might try to break Cece's writing into symbolic, literary nonsense . . . none of those things get to change my view of Cardithia or the Nocturnal Heart novels as I know them. Not if I don't allow them to."

I feel the instant the slow trail of his gaze finds me. It's the same time I feel the strength in my bones vacate. "I think we should send the memoir in to Fog Harbor, Joel."

"No." It's an immediate, end-of-discussion kind of *no*. And yet, I can't allow this to be the end. We are equal in our rights to it, but we are far from equal in our responsibility.

"Please, just hear me out. If I start tonight, I could scan each page into my laptop and edit the names and location details before I sent it off. I could have the whole thing finished within forty-eight hours, and I'll do everything possible to protect the Campbell family in the revision."

"You'd edit the details," he clarifies, "as in you'd whitewash the truth."

I clear my throat. "My goal would be to revise anything even slightly incriminating to Cece's reputation or history—"

"Is that what you think I'm most concerned about? Cece's reputation, *her* history?" He leans forward, his gaze boring into mine. "It's not Cece's life she exposed in that memoir, Ingrid. It's yours."

I glance at the single floorboard separating our folded legs. "It's yours, too."

"It's not even close to equal."

It's what I hoped he might say, and yet I hadn't anticipated the distress in which he'd say it. "If that's how you feel about it, then shouldn't the decision be mine to make?"

"I can't let you do that."

"I *need* to do it, Joel." My throat aches on the plea. "Please. After everything your family has done for me over the years—for my father—I can't hurt them like this." I press my lips together to keep the quiver from my chin. "I can't."

"You're willing to expose your deepest wounds solely to keep strangers from coming here again."

"Yes."

He's quiet for so long I'm not sure if he'll respond again, but when he does, I feel the impact of his refusal like a blow to my heart. "I won't sell our story, Ingrid."

"I'm not asking you to sell it—I'm only asking that we submit it for verification, not a contract. We just need to use it as proof to get SaBrina off our backs, off the idea that we're harboring *The Fate of Kings*." But even as I speak, I hear the blaring weakness in my argument. Because the minute it's out of our hands, we'll never have complete control of it again.

"You'd trust a digital record of our lives to SaBrina?"

When I don't answer, he tugs at his shirt collar until a third button frees itself, exposing the dip in Joel's throat and a sliver of tan skin just below it. As much as I want to believe in the integrity of the publisher who gave my best friend her big break, the same publisher who took me on as an editor when I had little reason to keep going, it pains me that I can't answer a question about their confidentiality with confidence. Even with the best legal team working alongside us, there's no telling what could happen under SaBrina's direction. But just like a whispered rumor, once a manuscript is leaked into the world, it's impossible to reel it back in.

Literary pirates aren't like the noble sea bandits Cece imagined; there is no moral code of conduct for thieves of the written word.

"Think of your aunt." Desperate to hold my ground, I try a different approach. "Think of how brutal things will be for her if SaBrina's threat holds true and the secret of the memoir is splattered all over the fan groups and the hunt for Wendy is on again. Think of what Cece would want us to do for her mom."

He scrubs both palms down his face, and I hate the tortured expression he wears when he stakes his elbows to his drawn knees. But he isn't saying no, not yet anyway.

"There are so many things I can't undo, Joel, lost time I'll never be able to redeem." I swallow as thoughts of last night in Joel's kitchen surface, of the way his hands gripped my waist, of his warm, inviting mouth pressed to mine, of a freedom I so badly wanted to believe could be mine . . . ours.

My nose prickles as I think of the rocks I pelted at that old tugboat in the slough, and as I think of all the moments I was too weak, too young, too helpless to fix what was broken. "Please, let me make this right."

Empathy softens his gaze. "Giving in to SaBrina's demands won't make anything right. And it won't be the only thing she asks for in the future. She's an opportunist. She'll find a way to keep exploiting us, to keep exploiting you." He sighs and stares at the floor. "That said, neither of us are in the position to make any conclusive decisions without knowing how the memoir ends. Even with your editing skills, I'd never agree to send something of hers off that I haven't first read myself."

"Did you bring it with you?"

Joel nods. "Downstairs."

"Let's finish it, then." Grateful for the possibility of a compromise, I stand from my place on the floor, waiting for him to do the same so I don't trip over him on my way to the stairs. But instead of pushing up to his full height, he remains where he is, watching me with an intensity that grips my insides.

"This may not have the resolution you want, Indy."

And suddenly, I'm unsure of the subject matter he's discussing now: the ultimatum, the memoir . . . us?

When he finally stands in the cramped space, we're a painful kind of close, a disjointed kind of separate. One best relieved by a steadying touch or a supportive embrace. And yet neither of us reaches for the other. It's a silent statement that echoes of finality, of a second chance better left unlived.

Perhaps not all first drafts can be rewritten.

28

"Love Always Finds a Way"

Cece had never experienced the extreme divide between love and hate quite like being placed on a deadline. But writing a detailed, visceral battle scene depicting the divide between good and evil was hardly the same as writing a mind-numbingly boring series outline on four books—two of which were still trapped inside her head. A head she was ready to bang against the coffee shop window of what had to be the busiest cafe set on the busiest street in Oak Harbor.

Contrary to the advice she read on Google last night, a change in writing location hadn't miraculously changed her inability to summarize. And if she had to look at those obnoxious flashing lights on the sports bar across the street for one more minute, she might be led to drink something stronger than chai tea. But of course, she would never *actually* do that. Even if she hadn't made a no-alcohol pact with Joel and Ingrid years ago, she knew too much about the pain of addiction to ever be a casual consumer of the hard stuff.

She picked up her phone and FaceTimed Ingrid.

Her friend answered on the first ring, but instead of Ingrid's face coming into view like she expected, Cece saw a blurred highway of floor-to-ceiling bookshelves and rows of dark mahogany tables with groups of students—

Oh, shoot! How could she have forgotten? Ingrid had study groups for her upcoming finals booked all weekend at the library.

"Hey, sorry. The librarians are serious about the no-phone rule," Ingrid said into the camera as sunlight spilled over her dark hair, causing her amber eyes to sparkle like gold. Ingrid had always been beautiful, but *radiant* was a far more accurate description for her as of late. College suited her well. As did the vibrant fuchsia top she wore today. Cece made a mental note to borrow it when Ingrid came home.

"No, I'm the one who's sorry. I totally spaced that you were studying for finals this weekend."

"It's okay." Ingrid sighed, leaning against the brick building. "I could use a brain break. We've been at it for hours already. I never thought I could get tired of talking about literary devices used in the classics, but I passed tired weeks ago. I seriously can't wait for these finals to be over next week." She yawned. "Anyway, what's up there? Wait—did you finish the proposal for Barry?"

"Uh . . . I wouldn't exactly say *finished*." Cece flipped the camera around to show Ingrid the same line on her laptop screen she'd rewritten forty-two times since she plopped into the chair of this highly trafficked coffee shop. Whoever said cafe background noise helped concentration should have their freedom of speech right revoked. "Do you think it's too late for me to fly down there and join a study group for synopsis writing?"

"Seeing as I told Barry you'd have the full series proposal to him first thing Monday morning so he can prep for the publication board—yes, I'd say it's much, much too late for that. Didn't you get the link I sent with all the formatting examples?"

"Formatting is not the issue," Cece grumbled. "I feel like I'm living inside a poorly written math problem. How does a writer take a two-hundred-thousand-word fantasy novel and summarize it into a thousand-word synopsis, times four? Answer: You can't. It's impossible." Cece knew she had absolutely no right to complain, considering Ingrid had taken a huge risk by sneaking *The Pulse of Gold* into Barry Brinkman's office. She could have lost her entire internship over such a stunt, but not only had he read it, he'd also requested a proposal on the full Nocturnal Heart series! It was a dream ten times larger than Cece had ever prayed for. "Urgh, I just don't want to mess this up, not after you took such a big risk for me."

"You know I'd do anything for you," Ingrid said, cutting Cece off before she could interrupt. "*Except* write your synopses."

Cece released a dramatic groan. "I *really* suck at this."

"Yeah? Well, I suck at Professor Donaldson's tag-team speech nights, but I still have to do them in order to graduate early. And you have to do this in order to become the best-selling author we know you can be." Ingrid's smile morphed into contemplation. "I know I'm only a literary major and not an editor, but what if instead of thinking you have to shrink each book to fit your synopsis, you simply focus on the main goal and conflict of each story. No fancy writing, no interesting side characters, no extra details or descriptions. Your only job is to keep the main thing the main thing. That's it." She glanced down at her watch. "I have a call with Joel in between my last two study groups tonight, but why don't you send me a progress update in three hours, okay? I might have time to help with any loose ends if you need it."

Cece gawked at her friend. "Maybe you should consider being an editor instead of a lit teacher?"

Ingrid laughed. "There are definitely some fun perks to the publishing industry, but . . ."

"But Joel's not there," Cece finished for her.

"Or you. Or my dad. Or any of the things I miss in Port Townsend. The Bay Area is great, but it could never be home."

She was just about to ask Ingrid about Hal—specifically about when she'd last seen her father on a video call. Cece had been shocked by his appearance last time she saw him at the hotel a few weeks ago. The dark circles under his eyes and his significant weight loss had been startling. But when she'd mentioned it to Joel, he'd chalked it up to the odd hours Hal had been keeping to accommodate his late-night crabbing runs on her uncle's cruiser. Even still, the explanation hadn't sat right with her. Few things about the sea captain ever did.

"Hey, Ingrid"—a feminine voice cut in—"we're about to go over the notes on the Hemingway section. I knew you wouldn't want to miss it."

"Thanks, Emily. I'll be right in."

When Ingrid came back, Cece flashed her a big smile. "Okay. Three hours starting now. I'm gonna knock this thing out."

"Good," Ingrid said. "I believe in you."

"And I believe you're gonna kill it on your finals and graduate ahead of schedule."

As soon as the two signed off, Cece got to work. Somehow she stopped noticing the irritating lights across the street, and the annoying clamor inside the coffee shop from earlier had since morphed into an energizing white noise that helped focus her thoughts. Ingrid's pep talks about keeping the main thing the main thing had worked wonders. By the time she started on the last book synopsis, she was deep in the groove. This book would be the happily ever after her characters deserved—*finally*. It was the easiest summary of them all to write. She proofread the whole thing one last time and then sent it off to Barry with a CC to Ingrid. Wouldn't her friend be surprised at all she'd accomplished today.

Impressed with her efforts, she picked up her phone to check the time. A few minutes before six. She was definitely going to treat herself to a slice of lemon poppy seed bread and a second iced chai latte. She deserved it!

But as she stood to stretch her back, all thoughts of sugary treats vanished when a familiar red knit cap worn by a familiar Norwegian giant bobbed into view and entered the sports bar across the street.

It's a sports bar, she tried to rationalize with her overactive imagination. There were lots of things that happened inside a sports bar that didn't involve drinking alcohol . . . weren't there?

But why would a recovered alcoholic drive forty minutes from home to go to one?

For Ingrid's sake, she needed to have an answer to that question. When one didn't surface after several minutes, she packed up her stuff and then pulled on an old Seattle Seahawks sweatshirt of Joel's she'd been carting around in her trunk for close to two years. She cinched her blond curls into the hood and then jogged across the street.

This wasn't the kind of thing she could leave to gut feelings or assumption. If Hal had fallen off the sobriety wagon the way she'd suspected for some time now, then she'd need hard evidence. Ingrid deserved to know the truth about what her father was really up to while she was away at school, even if Joel refused to see Hal's decline for what it was. He wouldn't point an accusatory finger at his new boat buddy unless there was solid proof of a relapse. He'd made that point crystal clear the last time they argued over this.

Stepping inside the sports bar was like stepping into a concert hall for the tone-deaf.

No hostess greeted her; instead, there was a chalkboard sign declaring: UFC Fight Night. Seat Yourself.

A collective roar caused her to jump as she edged her way through a standing crowd glued to a jumbo screen featuring two men in spandex briefs slugging it out. Another raucous cheer assaulted her ears as she watched a mouth guard full of spit and blood and possibly teeth shoot across the ring. *Disgusting.*

Cece kept her eyes low as she searched for Hal's hat among the fight-watchers. There wasn't a single red hat to be found; no sight of Hal. She pushed farther into the hazy space, the sound nearly as ear-splitting in the back of the sports bar as it was at the entrance.

And just as she was starting to think she'd missed his exit, she spotted him at a table. His red beanie was off now, but a lanky man dressed in drab casual was seated across from him. The two were deep in a concentrated conversation.

She slinked onto the only open barstool where a twenty-something bartender with crystalline blue eyes asked to check her ID. When she handed her license over to him, it was clear he was checking it for more than her birthdate. His bicep flexed as he braced one palm to the counter and slid her license across the bar top.

"Haven't had many Cecelias brave enough to venture in here on a fight night," he said with a grin Cece would have found enchanting in any other circumstance. "But if I had, I have no doubt you'd be the prettiest one."

Taken aback by his charming yet confident demeanor, she all but stuttered her drink order of a Diet Coke with a twist of lime. It was her mocktail of choice. She'd only been twenty-one for six months, but she found that if she looked like she was drinking an actual cocktail, there were fewer questions about her stance on sobriety.

She strained to make out a single word between Hal and his friend at the table near her, but it was impossible. Between the fight noise and their lowered voices, she couldn't hear a thing. She wasn't in perfect view of his table, but if she angled her hips slightly to the right, her vantage point was less obstructed. Hal, like the other man, drank from a tall glass she was ninety-nine percent certain contained beer, but she couldn't afford to be wrong. *No assumptions.* If she was going to involve her cousin in this, then her report of the situation had to be one hundred percent accurate.

"Excuse me," Cece said, waving her cute bartender over. He slid across the floor toward her as if on skates.

"You ready for something stronger than Diet Coke with a twist of lime, Cecelia Jane?" He winked.

Weirdly enough, she had no desire to correct him on the use of her full name.

She leaned her elbows on the bar top and waved him in close, just as a rebellious curl popped free of her oversize hoodie. She attempted to tuck it back behind her ear. "I'm wondering if you can tell me what kind of drink those two gentlemen are enjoying at this table to my right here?"

The bartender cast his gaze to where Cece flicked her head and then smirked. "They're porters."

"And porters are beer, right? I mean, they *do* contain alcohol, correct?"

His grin popped two identical dimples on either side of his lips as he, too, set his elbows on the shiny bar top and leaned in secret-telling close. "That particular porter there is rated at nine percent ABV. So yes, they *definitely* contain alcohol." He tapped a fingernail to her glass. "Unlike your Diet Coke here, which contains zero percent." As he righted himself, he reached to tug on the end of her curl, causing it to boing against her cheek. "I don't think this one wants to hide in that hoodie anymore."

"Guess not, thanks." She tried for a smile, but in light of the revelation, she couldn't maintain it for long. Turned out, she wasn't as good an actress as she'd hoped. "I appreciate your help."

310

"How 'bout I mix you up a Ryker Special—on the house." He tilted his head, held her gaze. "I'm Ryker, in case that didn't come out as smoothly as I intended it to."

"I'm only a fan of mocktails, but thank you anyway . . . Ryker," she added before taking a long pull from her straw.

"Want to hear something ironic?" His grin brightened all the more. "I don't drink either, but the tips are putting me through law school." He tilted his head to Cece's drink. "How 'bout we make this drink the Cecelia Jane Special then, shall we?" One of the other bartenders called for him, and Ryker tapped his palm twice on the bar top before moon-walking to the other side of the counter. He pointed to her. "Promise you won't leave before I get back."

Flustered, she nodded before twisting around in her seat once again, determined to collect the evidence she came in for, only Hal's table was empty. The remnants of his beer and his hat were still there, but he and Mr. Insurance Adjuster were nowhere to be found. Panic seized her chest as she searched for him, angry she hadn't snapped a picture when she had the chance. But then, as if in slow motion, she saw them standing along the perimeter of the busy restaurant. Only the duo she'd been looking for had doubled to four.

Two men joined Hal and his friend near the back corner. They were sleekly dressed from head to toe, with big-city vibe haircuts and attitudes that stood out among the mass of blue-collared men sloshing beer back and screaming at the referee on the screen.

She rose up on the footrest of her barstool, squinting at them over the crowd to get a better view, catching only the tail end of a quick exchange. The passing of what looked like a folded piece of paper, which Hal opened and studied for all of two seconds before he shoved it into his jacket pocket. The entire encounter was seconds, maybe half a minute tops.

Heart pounding in her throat, Cece dropped back onto her stool, trying to make sense of what she'd just seen.

She peeked under the rim of her hoodie as Hal and his friend reclaimed their seats at their table once again and ordered another round of porters from the waitress. In a rare dip of room volume, Hal's accent bit through the crowd noise and three words found their way to her ears. ". . . at first light."

At first light. *What was happening at first light?*

311

Enough was enough. She definitely had what she needed to get Joel involved. She angled her phone under her right arm and snapped two inconspicuous pictures of their table. Then she opened up a text window to Joel.

Cece

We have a 911 situation on our hands.

It took her cousin almost three minutes to respond to her, but when he did, his response of a single question mark was an epic disappointment. Cece exhaled and tried again.

Cece

I'm at a bar in Oak Harbor and Hal is here.

Joel

What are you doing in a bar?

Cece

HAL. IS. HERE. He's drinking again.

When Hal had first come back from the rehab center her uncle had paid for, there were accountability parameters in place centered around Hal's continued employment and the use of the hotel's charter boat. Their agreement was dependent on Hal's consistent check-ins with his sponsor and his attendance at the local sobriety meetings. There was also the condition regarding his church attendance each Sunday, followed by a standing invitation to the Campbell family brunch at the hotel. Only Cece hadn't seen Hal dish up a hearty plate of bacon and eggs more than a couple of times in the last six months or so. She was careful whenever she broached the subject to Ingrid, as if suggesting that Hal could be anything other than a fully recovered, well-intentioned, church-going citizen of Port Townsend was completely asinine. Ingrid was often quick to defend the sobriety milestones her father had hit over the last three years—the chips he'd collected and documented by text—and, of course, his progress toward buying his own fishing boat.

Yet whenever Cece saw Hal as of late, she didn't think he resembled the healthy man Ingrid described in their phone calls. And Joel always had some defendable excuse when it came to his girlfriend's father. As far as she was concerned, her cousin's radar for Hal's duplicity act was badly in need of repair. Hopefully tonight would fix that once and for all.

"I haven't seen Hal at church on Sundays for a while now, or at family brunch for that matter," she'd mentioned to Joel a few weeks back when he'd breezed through the hotel lobby from logging the last of his sea hours with the captain.

Joel's expression had been puzzled by her comment, as if she was crazy for questioning anything having to do with a man who'd neglected her best friend for years, leaving her alone at all hours of the night in a dilapidated tugboat so he could keep his flask full. "He's been working hard to save up money for a boat, Cece. Give the guy a break. You'd be tired, too, if you were crabbing seven-hour circuits overnight every weekend." Nearly a year ago, Joel's father had cut Hal a generous deal—for only the price of fuel, he'd allowed Hal to use his boat in the off hours for crabbing, in which Hal was able to keep one hundred percent of the profit. According to Ingrid, this was the money he'd been saving to buy his own fishing boat.

Joel narrowed his eyes at her. "What's your deal with him anyway?"

"My *deal*," she all but fumed, "is that you're supposed to be holding him accountable, not spending all your free time listening to his farfetched sea tales."

"Save the drama for your fiction, Cece. Hal's doing great. He texts me confirmations from his meetings each week, just like he agreed to do."

Joel's text popped up, pulling her out of the agitating memory.

Joel

You're 100% positive it's him?

Couldn't he see it was him in the—*oh*. The pictures she sent hadn't gone through. She tapped the screen to resend them and watched until the task was completed.

It felt like a year before Joel responded. But when he did, Cece nearly toppled off her stool.

Joel

That's his ex-sponsor with him. Darius.

Cece

What ex-sponsor? When did that happen?? Also, for the record, he just ordered them both a second round.

Naturally, Joel didn't bother answering her questions. He was more concerned with asking his own.

Joel

Has Hal seen you?

Cece

No. But I did see him and Darius talking to a couple of guys that looked like they just flew in from a Vegas night club. They gave something to Hal, but I couldn't see it clearly.

Joel

Send me the address of the bar. I'm only fifteen minutes out from Oak Harbor. And please, do not engage them, Cece. Let me handle this for once.

Cece

I texted you, didn't I?

Joel

Thank you. Keep me updated until I get there.

Cece

She was halfway through her second Cecelia Jane Special when Joel texted her again.

Joel

Please keep this to yourself for now. Ingrid needs to focus on her finals. This can wait till after. Agreed?

Cece's last sip of Diet Coke soured on her tongue at her cousin's text. She hated the idea of keeping something so huge from Ingrid, but not as much as she hated the idea of Hal screwing up Ingrid's plan to graduate early and come home. Who even knew what kind of mess she'd be coming home to now? Anger simmered low in her belly as she eyed the man who was now tossing back the last drops of a second beer, ticking her anger up from a three to an eight. In matters of injustice, it wouldn't take long for her to reach a ten.

Cece

Agreed.

"What are you doing at say 9:01 tonight?"

It took her a second to realize Ryker was speaking to her.

"Um . . . I'm not sure." With any luck, she'd be cheering on a different kind of fight night. One involving a crusty sea captain and her overprotective cousin. This time though, her money would be on Joel. Even with Hal's weight loss, he still had four inches and a good forty pounds on her cousin, but Joel had spent the majority of these past lovesick years missing Ingrid from inside the hotel gym. Gone was his lanky, adolescent build, and in its place stood a man as dense as he was quick.

Ryker slid a napkin and a ballpoint pen toward her. A ten-digit phone number was scrawled out below a check yes or no box. Those intoxicating dimples were back. "I'm off at nine. Please let me take you out to a late dinner or dessert or to any open establishment willing to serve you bottomless Cecelia Jane Specials for however long you're willing to keep me company." He lowered his voice conspiratorially. "Can't promise they'll be as good as the ones I've made you, but I will promise no sweaty men cursing at a giant TV screen." His laugh was a cool kind of confident, and Cece made a mental note to add a Ryker-inspired character to her current work in progress. "What do you say, Cecelia Jane?" He picked up the pen and drew four arrows pointing to the yes box all while giving her pleading puppy eyes.

She opened her mouth to answer him, but the sight of her cousin snaking his way through the crowd snapped it shut again. Without an ounce of hesitation, Cece swiped the pen from Ryker's hand, checked the yes box for him to see, and then jammed the napkin into the pouch of her hoodie.

She slid off the barstool, and Ryker whooped and shouted after her, "Call me! See you tonight!"

She waved a hand in acknowledgment and wove through the herd to catch up to her cousin, who was now only a few tables away from Hal's.

"Okay," she said, with her game face on. "So what's our plan?"

"*My plan* is to take Hal home," Joel said, eyeing his target with only half as much disdain as she felt the moment required.

"And then what?"

"And then nothing." He furrowed his brow at her. "I don't want you involved in this. Ingrid will be . . ." He shook his head, but Cece knew the fill-in-the-blank for that one. *Devastated*. Which was precisely why Joel needed to be far more infuriated. "She's going to need a friend she can talk to when everything comes out, and that friend needs to be you."

"What are you talking about? What's *everything*? And last I checked, we're *both* her friends." She gestured between the two of them. "We can both be there for her."

Distress creased Joel's forehead, and the scarily hollow sound of his next words pinged inside her ears. "She'll need time to work through her anger."

"Hal's the one deserving of her anger, not you," Cece hissed. "You weren't the one to break the agreement between him and your father; *Captain Hal* did that all on his own. It's time he suffered his own consequences."

"Please, Cece. Just promise me you'll be the person she can go to when she needs support." Joel's jaw ticked twice.

"Sure, fine. I promise," she huffed out, exasperated.

His nod was curt. "Then it would be best if you were never here tonight."

Baffled, Cece remained frozen where she stood as Joel continued on alone to Hal's table. He set a hand onto Hal's shoulder and bent low to speak directly into his ear while his icy gaze locked on Darius. Cold fear licked up Cece's spine as she waited on Hal's next move. She braced for him to come up swinging, to show his true colors and reveal the coward he truly was. But instead, both seated men seemed completely in control of themselves and their surroundings. They shared a knowing glance, then slowly pushed back from the table as Joel flagged down a waitress and left enough cash to cover their bill. Darius exited through a side door without so much as a backward glance. And then, as if this was all a practiced dance, Joel escorted Hal from the sports bar and out into the parking lot.

No big scene. No heated argument. No shock of any kind.

What on earth was going on?

Cece rushed to keep up with them, indignation brewing hot in her center. Surely Joel had a better plan in mind than paying for their beers and playing chauffeur! What kind of *plan* was that? He'd just caught Hal red-handed! It was time he stopped being coddled for his crimes.

Like so many other times in their adolescence, Cece followed after Joel, ducking behind parked cars in order to keep a read on the situation. She crouched low behind a blue Mazda with tinted windows and turned her attention to Hal and Joel, willing her cousin to unleash the hellfire she knew he was capable of when he finally stopped in front of his black Honda but made no attempt to get inside the car. And she knew right then that this was far from over.

Hal spoke first. "I'm sorry, kid."

"You can save your apologies for Ingrid," Joel said without looking at him.

"Ingrid doesn't need to know about this. We can keep it between the two of us."

"No, we can't," Joel fired back. "We tried that once, remember?" His voice was strained. "What happened to you begging me to keep your relapse quiet so you could tell Ingrid yourself? What happened to calling your sponsor when you're struggling—to attending a meeting? What happened to you *staying sober?*" He scrubbed both hands down his face. "That lasted all of what? Ten days? Two weeks?"

Cece's jaw slacked at the revelation. She'd been right. Hal had fallen off the wagon, and not just recently, either.

"Life's more complicated than you know."

"No, it's not. It's actually quite simple." Joel's frustration continued to rise. "Ingrid is the only thing you should be thinking about right now. Remember her? The daughter you've been lying to for I don't even know how long?" He threw out his arms. "Do you even have a clue what this will do

317

to her when she finds out that not only have you been drinking again, but that you've been permanently suspended from chartering for the hotel? That's not exactly a secret you can keep up for long, Hal." He grips the back of his neck. "What's your plan when she shows up here at the end of the semester and you have nothing to your name again but that old tugboat?"

Without any of his usual flair for the dramatic, Hal's voice remained void of emotion. "I have a plan."

Joel slapped the roof of his car. "For you? Or for Ingrid? Because I guarantee the second your twenty-two-year-old daughter finds out you've fallen off the wagon again, she will put her school plans on hold and come running back to babysit her daddy. Is that what you want? You want her to quit her dreams to take care of your—"

"*No.* That's not what I want! I've never wanted any of this for her!" Hal's deafening bark broke into the night with a boom, but almost as quickly, he reeled it back in. "Wait to tell her—for her sake, not mine. She deserves to finish her finals without worrying about me."

Joel tunneled his fingers through his hair. "At least we can both agree on that."

Several raw moments of silence ticked by before Joel broke it, his voice a low, remorseful plea that caused Cece to peek over the hood of the Mazda.

"You're better than this," Joel said. "And even if you can't believe that for yourself, your daughter believes it enough for you both. And she'll never stop." He cleared the thickness from his throat. "Which is why my loyalty will always be to her first—always."

Cece's breath was stuck somewhere between her gut and her esophagus as she waited for the captain's reply.

"You're an honorable man," Hal finally said. "Just like your father."

Don't give in to him, Joel, Cece thought. *Don't fall for his schemes. There's more to this than what he's telling you, I feel it!*

At her cousin's hard stare, her hope buoyed only to sink just as quickly at Joel's logical reply. "Here's what's going to happen: I'm going to take you home tonight, and then first thing tomorrow morning you, me, and my father are all going to sit down together and figure out a new plan. If you go anywhere before then, your options for employment in this town will go from slim to none. And the second Indy's finals are over, she'll be included in everything we discuss. I love her too much to keep secrets from her. She deserves better than that."

Cece was certain Hal would reject Joel's proposal. After all, Joel was little more than a kid in comparison to a seasoned sailor with a criminal's rap sheet. There was simply no way Hal would just roll over and accept Joel's ultimatum without argument. But much to her astonishment, that's exactly what he did. With a resigned nod and a noticeable sag in his shoulders, Captain Hal reached for the passenger handle of Joel's old Honda and shoved his bulk inside the sedan without further comment.

Of all the perplexing things she'd witnessed tonight, this was the one that shook her the most. Hal was a lot of things, but a pushover had never been one of them.

Cece kept her distance from them on the highway home, taking the back roads whenever she could. She didn't need to follow closely; she'd know her way to the marina if she had to find it during a midnight squall. She watched Joel's car pull up to the docks from the vacant lot where she had parked across the street. A minute later, Hal lumbered up the stairs to the marina caretaker's apartment her uncle had helped secure for Hal as part of his generous sobriety package agreement. Rage boiled inside her at the thought of all the people Hal had taken advantage of over the years. All the people he'd scammed into believing his intentions were honorable. All the pain he'd caused the people she loved most—the pain he was *still* causing them.

Focusing on Joel's taillights, Cece reached for her phone.

Cece

What did he say about the two men I saw him talking to at the bar tonight?

Joel

Nothing.

Eyes locked on her phone screen, Cece waited for a follow-up explanation, but her impatience was nearing maximum capacity.

> Cece
>
> Nothing because you haven't asked him yet or . . . ?

> Joel
>
> Nothing because my only objective for tonight is to keep the main thing the main thing. And right now, that looks like dealing with the immediate repercussions of Hal's relapse.

It was crazy how that same advice on keeping the main thing the main thing in regards to her book series proposal seemed like absolute genius when it came from Ingrid, but in light of this circumstance, all Cece wanted to do was chuck her phone through Joel's back window.

> Cece
>
> You should have told me about that when you first found out!

> Joel
>
> No, I shouldn't have. I'm protecting you.

> Cece
>
> No, you're protecting Hal! And I think he's hiding something bigger than his drinking. I know what I saw tonight, and it matches what I've been trying to tell you for months—something is wrong. I feel it. We need to investigate further.

> Joel
>
> You couldn't have seen anything because we agreed you were never at that bar tonight, remember? I know you want to help, but for Ingrid's sake, your part in all this needs to be over.

She gripped her steering wheel, locked her elbows, and pressed her back as hard as she could against the seat to keep her scream locked inside.

Joel

I'm sorry.

But somehow, Joel's apology only made her angrier. He wasn't the person who should be saying sorry. Why did he have to be the fall guy for Hal's sins?

As she watched Joel pull out of the marina, Cece shoved her phone back into her pocket where a familiar napkin brushed her knuckles. She pulled it out and studied Ryker's number before checking the clock on her dash.

8:07 p.m.

If she left this lot now, she'd have time to go home, shower, and dress in something a tad more attractive than an old Seahawks sweatshirt. Ryker was cute—more than cute. He had wit and charisma and the very idea of standing him up went against every instinct she possessed. Except for one. The one that demanded she uncover whatever Hal was hiding that was worth more to him than his pride.

Okay, she thought. She'd make a compromise. If she forwent the shower and cute outfit for fifty more minutes of Hal-watching, then she'd simply text Ryker to meet her at a location closer to where she lived. If he felt even half the chemistry she did with him earlier, then he'd be willing to drive the forty minutes south to Port Townsend. For what was likely the first time in her life, she was willing to root for a hero she didn't create from her own imagination.

With her headlights turned off, she coasted across the street into the quiet marina. She was deciding on her next steps when a two-hundred-and-fifty-pound plot twist wearing a red beanie skulked out of his apartment with his bulky jacket slung over his arm and a backpack slung over his right shoulder.

"I appreciate your timely cooperation, Captain," Cece muttered to herself as she opened her car door.

Securing her hoodie over her curls once again, she watched him trudge across the marina and enter the coded gate where her uncle's boat was docked. A boat Hal was suspended from using. What was he doing? A night of crabbing couldn't possibly be worth the risk of being turned in for trespassing on a boat he was no longer authorized to captain. A boat that could easily be reported stolen, given his current employment status with the hotel.

Her plan began to come together in real time, one that didn't involve Joel. Because as previously discussed, their main objectives were no longer the same.

First thing first: She needed to get on that boat.

She made a break for the loading dock. In her Hal-obsessed teenage years, she'd participated in at least a dozen crabbing ventures with Ingrid and her father, chalking it up to book research. But all that research would prove handy now. She knew his routine well. If Hal stopped to load the crates of crab pots at the dock, it would buy her enough time to get inside the boat's cabin and check for clues on what he'd really been up to since Ingrid had been away.

As Hal trekked the length of the dock to the Campbell's slip, she sprinted through the shadowed alley separating the warehouse and fish prep stations. She wouldn't have long to crouch into position behind whatever fuel barrels or wooden crates lined the edge of the loading dock. But if Hal did what she hoped he'd do, once the cruiser was tied up and Hal was climbing off the boat to the crane to move the crates aboard the stern, she'd have close to ten minutes to hunt for clues.

But in reality, she wouldn't even need half that time.

Thanks to the nosy days of her youth, she knew every hiding spot aboard her uncle's cruiser, especially Hal's favorite spot under the sofa compartment in the main cabin. It's where he kept the Viking ax he never sailed without.

Seconds after the engine roared to life, Hal motored right toward her at the docks. *Bingo*, she'd been right. Whatever he was up to, his late-night crabbing sessions played a role in it all. Cece dashed across the paved loading dock for the tower of rusty barrels she'd been counting on. She waited for him to step down from the second-story control cockpit and tie up at the dock. Once the boat was secured, he took a quick pull from a familiar-looking flask, which fueled her suspicions all the more. What else was he hiding?

Unlike that fall night long ago when she cowered under that tugboat window, crying as she watched her friend's childhood secrets unfold like the pages of a sad novel, tonight would not go down the same way. With the courage of her hero, Merrick, and the determination of her heroine, Ember, Cece crept onto the stern and into the unlocked cabin, careful to move with the tide under her feet. Keeping low, she darted to the sofa where Hal's backpack and jacket lay sprawled across the cushions and dropped to her knees to avoid being seen through the large windows. She rummaged through the pockets of his jacket until she secured the folded piece of paper she'd seen him stash away earlier tonight. Inside the fold was a long sequence of numbers—too long for a phone number or even a combination code for a safe. She examined it closer until the puzzle clicked into place.

These were coordinates, much like the ones Cece had memorized and tattooed with her friends, only they weren't for Port Townsend.

Hal was headed much farther south.

She heard the crane engine rumble to life as she shoved the paper into her own pocket and then unzipped the backpack, dumping the contents onto the sofa without care. There wasn't enough time to care. A deluge of supplies fell out—water bottles, wallet, snacks, an extra shirt. Nothing of interest.

The boat pulled hard to the right, knocking her onto the floor as the first crab cage dropped onto the bow. Hal only ever hauled four crates filled with crab pots at one time. She needed to get moving. If there was something more to find on this boat, something that explained where Hal was going with those coordinates and why, then she intended to find it before he found her. Sickness rolled through her as she swiped Hal's belongings off the sofa and heaved the edge of the cushion upward to reveal a hidden compartment underneath.

Inside was nothing but Hal's battle-ax chest, a few spare bumpers, cables, and a collection of lifejackets. She plunged her hand to the bottom until she felt the cool fiberglass against her fingertips. There was nothing else.

One by one she tore through every other compartment in the vicinity of the main cabin, opening and closing each drawer and cabinet inside the galley before she raced to the wardrobe in the bunk room below and pulled it open. Apart from a yellow rain slicker, it was empty. As were the drawers below it.

Another crate hit the deck and she was tossed into the bedpost. She collapsed to her knees and hurried to slide the brass lock open under the bunkbed mattress frame.

Another crate dropped.

A deflated orange life raft met her gaze, but this time when she pushed it aside to plunge her hand into the depths of the compartment, her fingers didn't have far to go. She chucked the raft out of the way and uncovered what had to be a thousand sealed, clear bags of white pills.

Pulse pinging against her eardrums, she plucked two from the mass and nearly tripped as the fourth and final crate crashed onto the bow. *She had to get off this boat!*

Hal was already walking toward the stern of the cruiser as she raced out the cabin door and leaped onto the dock. It didn't matter if he saw her now. She had all the evidence she needed to send him away and give Ingrid the freedom she deserved.

"Hey! Stop!" he barked, leaden feet charging after her on the dock. "Stop!"

Cece obeyed only to whirl around and hold her two bags of stolen loot over the lapping water. "No, *you* stop!"

Instantly, Hal's hands went into the air as his feet halted. And then he squinted into the dusk. "Curly?"

"Don't call me that." She reached for the seal tab on the first bag. "But I do suggest you start talking soon because if I don't get the answers I need the contents of these bags will go directly into the Sound. And I'm guessing every single one of these pills has already been accounted for." She shook the bag. "You believe me?"

Slowly, he nodded. Backlit by the lights on the cruiser, the whites of Hal's eyes shone with the kind of fear she'd expected to see when Joel found him at the sports bar, but there had been no fear in him then. Because Hal had still been playing the game.

This was the real Hal.

"Who were those men at the sports bar, and why did they give you co-ordinates?"

"What men?"

"Try again or this bag will spring a leak." She reached for the tab seal.

"No, don't! You don't know what you're doing. This isn't a game."

"I know way more than you think." A bluff she hoped would speed up the process.

With his hands still raised in front of him, he dropped his voice low. "They're my stateside contacts. They . . . tell me where to make the drops after they secure the goods from Canada. Location changed last minute due to bad weather. There's a storm brewing in the east."

"Why not just send you the coordinates in a text?"

"I'm old-fashioned. I only work with contacts I can see."

"How long?" she demanded.

He shook his head quizzically as if needing more of a prompt to go off of. She was happy to supply him with several.

"How long have you been using my family's resources to smuggle drugs, Hal? How long have you been cheating us? How long have you been lying to your daughter about living the straight and narrow life?"

"*Please*, keep your voice down," he hissed.

She held the pill bags steady over the water. "Then you better tell me the truth."

"I—I don't know. Seven, eight months, maybe? But it's not how it looks."

She actually laughed. "I'm not a stupid little girl anymore, Hal. Your big stories won't work on me anymore."

"I was on the wrong side of a bad deal—I'm paying off a debt."

"What kind of debt? Gambling?" Yet another no-no on her uncle's list of continued employment stipulations for his favorite charter captain.

He twisted his neck and searched the marina before answering this time. "I lost a few big hands and borrowed money from the wrong people. Darius introduced me to someone who could help me out." He huffed a heavy sigh. "I only agreed to take one run for them. I thought I could make enough to pay back my loan debt and then be done with it all—I never wanted this kind of life, it was a mistake. But that's not the way these guys do business. I couldn't get out." He stared at her unblinking. "Tonight's my final run."

"Why should I believe you?" Cece's bicep began to shake, and she did nothing to hide it.

"I swear to you on my wife's grave," he chokes out. "After this run, my debt will be paid, and I'll have enough cash to buy a boat of my own and then I'll be out for good. You and your family will be free of me."

"Meaning what? You just take off? Leave as if there's no consequences for smuggling drugs and abandoning your daughter?"

His refusal to answer was answer enough.

Anger seethed within her. "What kind of pathetic excuse for a father leaves his child in the middle of the night to let her second-guess her entire existence for the rest of her life? You don't deserve her! *You've never deserved her!*" At her words, a spasm of pain twisted his face, and Cece relished in it, in the chance to inflict the same wounds on Hal that she'd never get to inflict on her own good-for-nothing dad. "You are nothing but a coward and a con man, and if you think for one minute that I'm just going to let you walk back onto that boat without turning you into the police then—"

"You don't understand, I don't have a choice."

"You have always had a choice!" Cece's voice broke on a sob. "Your choice was to *choose your daughter!*"

"I *am* choosing her!" His ferocious growl rumbled through the salty night air. "These men, they know about Ingrid. They know where she goes to school, where she lives, where she eats, where she interns three days a week, and who she spends her time with. If I defect from their plan in any way, she dies."

Cece swayed on her feet, her arm falling limply to her side, the bags nearly slipping from her numb fingers. *"No."* The syllable was no more than a squeak, yet it stole every ounce of her strength. "You're . . . you're lying."

With one hand still stretched outward, he reached into his pocket and took out his phone. He tapped on it and then flipped the screen around for her to see. "This picture of her was sent to me today. They send me a current picture of her before every run, a reminder of what I'll lose if I don't stick to the plan."

Cece's knees no longer felt sturdy enough to hold her as she saw the same bright fuchsia top she'd been admiring during their FaceTime call this afternoon in the picture on Hal's phone. Recognition continued to dawn as she matched the brick background to the university library.

Someone had taken that today—this afternoon, even.

Hal wasn't lying.

"I may be a drunk and a cheat and a pathetic excuse for a father like you say, but I'm not a coward. I love my girl too much to let her die for my sins."

The choke hold around Cece's throat was too tight for her to speak much louder than a whisper. "You have to make the drop by first light?"

He nodded solemnly. "I'll have your uncle's boat returned to the marina before Joel knocks on my door tomorrow morning."

"And then what? You just sail away, never to come back? You just cut Ingrid out of your life forever?" The pill bags hung limp at Cece's sides now, their true weight pulling heavily on her conscience.

"The longer I'm away, the better off she'll be. The safer."

Only a few minutes ago, she'd believed the same. Now, she wasn't so sure.

His expression shifted as he glanced over his shoulder at the boat again, and he seemed to make a decision. "Wait here." Hal turned and ducked back inside the cruiser, returning a moment later with an antique wooden box she knew well. He opened it to reveal the battle-ax handed down to him through generations. "This is more than my word; it's my blood. The only legacy I have worth anything to pass on to my daughter in the future." He paused. "You and I will do a good faith trade. Those pills for my ax." He kissed the carvings next to the lock and then held it out to her. "I trust you to hold on to it until the time is right."

Cradling the pills close to her chest, she analyzed his suggested trade. "And when is that? What am I supposed to tell her after you're gone?"

"Nothing." Hal's gaze twisted into something hard, unyielding. "Swear to me you won't ever tell anyone about our conversation—especially not Ingrid. Let them assume I've abandoned my daughter for my freedom. It's safer that way. For everyone."

"You can't just let her believe you've deserted her." Bile rose in her throat. "It will destroy her."

"I'm not deserting her," he insisted. "I'm entrusting her to you, to your family." He swallowed, then searched the dark horizon beyond. "To the God your family believes in so strongly."

"You believe in Him, too." An acknowledgement she'd never given him credit for until now. "I saw you after rehab. You were different, peaceful."

A slow nod. "Aye."

His declaration plunged through her like a boulder crashing into the depths of the ocean, and for a moment, she feared she wouldn't be able to surface for her next breath.

"She'll hate you if you leave."

"I'd hate myself more if I stayed."

The earnest conviction in his voice scraped against her most fragile hope of a father returning for his daughter. Perhaps in a strange way, this moment was Hal's return to his daughter, too. Maybe not in a physical sense, but in a paternal one. A sacrificial one.

Hal offered her the ax, and Cece accepted it, blinking back tears before she followed through with his request to hand over the pills she'd taken. Then, she reached into her pocket and pulled out the folded piece of paper. "Your coordinates."

Hal stared down at the coordinates and blinked several times before he took them from her. No longer was he the larger-than-life Viking Cece had met in her youth. Nor was he the unrepentant villain she'd labeled him as an adult. This Hal, this weathered and broken man before her, was just that. A man. "Be good to my Elskede."

"I will," she choked out. "I promise."

With a final dip of his chin, he held her gaze. "Tell her I'm sorry and that I will love her until my last breath."

And then he was gone.

To the naked eye, the exchange between them looked like nothing more than a simple trade of goods. One highly valued possession for another. But as she watched Captain Hal motor her uncle's cruiser into the black waters beyond the Sound, Cece knew her view of the world would never again be the same.

The divide between love and hate and good and evil wasn't nearly as extreme as what she'd penned in her stories. Nor were her hands nearly as blameless as the heroes she crafted.

In her fictional world, she held all the control. It was her decision to allow justice to prevail and victory to reign. She was the one who could restore order and redeem the wreckage lost in life, love, and war. It was she who authored the happy endings for those most deserving and she who put to death those who lacked any true sense of virtue.

But here, in this world, she had no control over such things. God was the ultimate authority over justice, and His endings superseded what her limited mind could understand. She often disregarded the trivial role she seemed to play here, as if she were only a secondary character going through the motions in this life. But she'd never again see her role as inconsequential.

She felt for the bar napkin inside her pocket one last time before crumpling it into her fist and tossing this last piece of evidence into a lonely barrel at the edge of the dock. She would never speak of this night again.

Joel had been right. It was best for everyone if she was never here.

She couldn't have known then what was to come. She couldn't have predicted Hal's shipwreck any more than she could have predicted the shift in the winds, but if given the chance to do it all over again, if given the chance to trade her silence for the protection of the people she loved most in the world . . . she would make the same trade again. Her silence had come at a cost much higher than she could have ever anticipated, but even still, her conviction was stronger.

Because even when the words seemed lost and the world seemed bleak, Cece believed love would find its way back home. Just like the best stories always find their way back to where they first began.

29

When Joel and I finally come up for air, our gazes are anchored on each other, still braced against the undertow that's sucked us into its depth and spit us out onto this unrecognizable shore.

"That's not—that can't be all there is," I sputter. "She wouldn't just end it that way."

Joel's expression is a dazed kind of anguish as he lifts the final pages for me to examine on my own. Seized by a compulsion I can't control, I skim the last few paragraphs again and again. There's not even a *The End* underneath her last line—there's nothing.

I flip the page over in my hands and find it unacceptably blank.

On unstable legs, I move from the living room couch to collect the rest of the chapters sticking out from Joel's backpack. I riffle through the crinkled pages the way I did back in Marshall's office when I was certain he'd handed us the wrong words, the wrong story. Only now I'd give anything for this story to be the one that continues. But as I find no missing chapters within this weathered stack, I realize what I'm searching for doesn't exist on any page.

Because it's not more story I need but the storyteller herself.

I need Cece.

The sound that escapes me is guttural, scraped from the hollow husks of an ever-changing grief. Of a longing to have protected her the same way she protected me.

When Joel captures me in his arms, our embrace is that of two fractured people who can't possibly stand without the strength of the other. But even our combined strength isn't enough to sustain us forever. I realize only now, it was never meant to.

His voice is rough against my ear. "I didn't know, Indy. I swear to you, I . . ."

But when his words give way, I can do nothing but cling to the fabric stretched across his heaving back.

"All these years," he continues, "and I never once suspected she was keeping something like this from us." He pulls back, his eyes red and raw. "I should have listened to her, asked your dad about those men. I should have stayed with him until—"

"No, Joel. This isn't on you any more than it's on Cece." I fight to reverse the direction of the mental spiral we're both on. "My father—" My voice cracks. "My father made his own choice that night, the same way he's always made all his own choices. Even if Cece hadn't been there and even if you had stayed with him all night long, he would have found a way to take that last run." It's a revelation that sears itself into my soul. "Nobody could have talked him out of it."

Not even me.

Joel frames my face with his hands. "He made the only choice he thought he could to keep you safe. He loved you." He pulls me in close again, and I burrow into his shoulder, mourning a truth that hurts almost as badly as the lie I've believed, mourning a death almost as confusing as the life my father lived on this earth.

And yet rising up from the sorrow, confusion, and doubt, a spark of light breaks through the darkness. And as it grows, so does the clarity it illuminates. "I was so wrong to blame you, Joel. I was wrong about so much."

He presses a soft kiss to the top of my head. "You were hurting."

"We were both hurting." I pull back and stare into his mossy green eyes. "We still are." I hold Cece's face in my mind, wishing she were here with us, too. "It's so much to process—I'm not even sure where to start."

The muscles in his neck contract. "She shouldn't have kept this from us, it wasn't her burden to carry."

"It was an impossible situation." Much like the odds Cece faced only a year ago. "You know how smart she was, Joel. You know she didn't keep this from us out of ignorance or neglect or spite. For her to keep this kind of a secret for those four years she lived after my father died . . ." I shake my head.

"All the more reason to tell us everything in person, *before* her surgery."

A swift revelation sucks the breath from my lungs as I think back to what Madison told me in the cottage—not only about the dictation app, but about her recovery plans. "She needed to be certain we'd willingly be in the same place long enough to read it together. This is what she was planning for us during her recovery. It had to be."

Tension stirs inside me as my focus shifts to my father's good faith trade resting on the table near us, and then to the manuscript I discarded to the sofa.

"You know we can't turn it in, Indy," he says with quiet resolve. "Even if you could edit out every identifying detail and implicating sentence"—he points to the battle-ax on the coffee table—"we can't hand this off to anyone without talking to the authorities first. This is more than a memory, it's also a confession to a crime."

I close my eyes against the sting of that revelation.

"Your father's sins are not yours to atone."

I slip from his hold and sit beside my father's ax on the coffee table, working to make room for a story revision so far outside the conclusions I'd drawn on my own. "I always believed if I could just understand what he was doing on that boat, I'd find the closure I need to move on. But I feel like I do after I read a cliffhanger—like the new unknowns outweigh the old ones."

Before I even finish the sentence, a vivid recall of Cece's last published novel plays out in my mind—the notorious last scene her fans went savage over. A brutal image of a beaten and bloodied Merrick left shackled to a deserted harbor while the love of his life is captured by his own sister, the Pirate Queen. A plot twist absolutely no reader—or editor—could have seen coming. And yet it was never meant to be the end of their story.

Maybe this isn't meant to be the end of ours, either.

"There's always a final clue," I mutter to myself.

"What?"

"That's what she said during the scavenger hunt she wrote about at the tattoo parlor." I reach for where I'd abandoned the manuscript earlier and begin to flip back through the chapters, through each of the memories Cece chose to record for us, and land once again on the last page.

I read the final paragraph over carefully once more.

"'Because even when the words seemed lost and the world seemed bleak, Cece believed love would find its way back home. Just like the best stories always find their way back to where they first began.'"

I fill my lungs with fresh air. "I think this could be it. The final clue."

"Ingrid." Joel says my name like it's something fragile, something needing to be handled with care. "This isn't a scavenger hunt."

"Maybe not Cece's traditional kind, no." I tap the last paragraph. "But I think there's something more to this ending she wants us to find." I swallow hard and flip back to the first chapter. "And to find it, I think we have to go back to the beginning, to where this story first began." I splay my hand across the page. "Our story."

Our eyes lock, and in less time than a heartbeat, we say, "The library."

Once inside the sleepy lobby of the Campbell Hotel, Joel slips his hand in mine. He greets each member of the night shift crew by name as we pass the front desk, and I don't have to wonder at the kind of boss he's grown into—it's apparent in every warm inquiry and smile he receives in reply. A blaring contrast to the work environment I've been fighting to return to.

Joel swipes us inside the dimly lit library and taps the security panel on the wall to bring up the lights. But even under the full power of illumination, I feel just as uncertain about our next steps as I did in the dark. And by the way Joel scrutinizes me and the space around us, I'm not even sure he believes there is a next step to be taken.

"What now?" he asks.

"Now we search for a clue."

"I've been in this library dozens of times since she died. There are no yellow notecards hanging out in plain sight."

I twist to look at him. "When has Cece ever placed a clue for us in plain sight? We have to think the way she did."

With a compliant dip of his chin, Joel turns for the shelves while I, like a ship coming into the harbor, follow the pull of the beacon's light in the center of the room to the gorgeous display case Barry gifted the Campbells after Cece's death. Perhaps being in such close proximity to her creative genius will enlighten me to something unseen. To a hope I trust is banked on more than a hunch. On the tail end of a deep inhale, I close my eyes and visualize the warm summer day when she found me reading on her family's dock not too far from here. I think back to those first moments of Cece crashing into my private thoughts with her big personality and asking me a dozen questions about—

"Ingrid."

My eyes snap open at the rumble of Joel's voice from deep within the shelves. I weave through the quiet aisles. It doesn't take long to find him, but I'm surprised at the section he stands in front of. And then again, I'm not surprised at all.

He lifts his finger to the top of the children's reading section, to a shelf that is too high for most grade-schoolers and too uninteresting for most adults looking for a lighthearted vacation read. The novel rests peacefully on the far left side of the shelf, beckoning us closer. I tug at the unbroken spine, pulling down a special edition of *Island of the Blue Dolphins* from the shadowed stack of untouched classics. The shift creates a domino effect among the shelf's inhabitants, but neither of us pays it any mind. We're too enraptured with the yellow envelope taped to the front of the hardback cover in my hands.

Property of Joel Campbell and Indy Erickson.

"Unbelievable," Joel says with reverence. "You were right."

The hope between my palms feels like more than a clue or even a gift. It's the final piece of a legacy that ended much too soon. The idea that something could be waiting for us inside this cover, something Cece took the time and thought to prepare for us to find in this way, for this moment, is a miracle that shouldn't be rushed.

For the first time in nearly a year, Cece doesn't feel so far away.

"You do it." My request is little more than a whisper, but Joel responds by releasing the yellow envelope taped just below the embossed title and breaking the red wax *X* sealing the flap. There are two cards slipped inside: one to Joel and one to me.

I hold my breath as he unfolds his, only to realize my intrusion on his privacy a moment later. This isn't the shared memoir he's opening now, it's a personal exchange between him and his cousin. I take a step back and offer him the space he deserves.

His fingers still on the paper. "I have no desire to hide anything from you. There's been too many secrets for one lifetime as it is."

He moves in close for me to peer over his shoulder.

Joel,

If I were to tally up every eye roll and sharp-tongued word shared between us, I'm sure I'd owe you a thousand apologies (and of course, by my calculation, you'd owe me a thousand and one), but while those childish offenses are easy to forgive, I know the truth I've held back from you all these years will be much more difficult.

The day Ingrid packed her bags and left Port Townsend, I was certain

I wouldn't last an hour without confessing all the events that took place that night. I hated that you were hurting. I hated that your guilt and heartbreak were as palpable as the threats I'd felt so powerless to fight on my own.

I made two promises that night—one to you and one to Hal—and both were to love and protect Ingrid at all costs.

Despite my many doubts and shortcomings over the years, I hope I've honored them both. I hope even more that I've been the kind of friend to Ingrid that you have always been to me: loyal, patient, merciful, just, and faithful.

If God doesn't grant me the opportunity to sit with you and Ingrid in person after my surgery, then please know, I wrote this memoir as much for you as I did for her. What I didn't realize at the time was how much I needed to write it for myself, too.

Please forgive me.

I love you.

Cece

P.S. Merrick never had anything on you.

He exhales slowly as he lowers the letter in his hands, and I wonder if his silence has less to do with a loss for words and more to do with a loss of time—the time none of us will ever get back.

When I open my letter, there's something tucked between the folds. A newspaper clipping from the *Seattle Times*, dated nearly two years ago now.

We both stare at the article for several seconds until Joel's voice confirms that I haven't imagined the headline: "Coast Guard Busts Drug Trafficking in Puget Sound."

"'Three years after an anonymous tip from a man on the inside, the U.S. Coast Guard concluded an investigation that resulted in the arrests and confiscation of more than six million dollars' worth of illegal prescription drugs trafficked between Victoria, B.C., and the many ports along the West Coast. . . .'" Joel skims until he comes to: "'An officer recounts the night the call came in on the evening of . . .'" He stops, looks up at me. "Ingrid."

"I know," I say shakily. The date was the same night my father took out the Campbell's boat. "Do you think . . . do you think it could have been my dad who called the authorities?"

"Cece must have believed so."

A warring sensation rushes through me. Not only had these traffickers been stopped and prosecuted for the crimes, but perhaps . . . perhaps it was my father who helped put them away.

He turns to me. "Are you okay?"

I nearly laugh because I'm not sure *okay* is even an option at this point. "I have no idea what I am anymore."

He steadies me with a hand to my back, and I offer him the same invitation he offered me. I open my letter from Cece.

Ingrid,

If you're reading this letter, then you're reading what is likely my hundredth attempt at telling you a truth that has weighed on me ever since the moment I watched your father motor into the Pacific. Since that night, I've made and broken so many vows to myself, becoming overly obsessed with the details of the where, when, and how I should tell you instead of the <u>what</u> that robbed you of a father. It was so much easier to escape into my fiction, especially when you seemed to be happiest in Cardithia, too.

Turns out, there's no perfect way to tell a painful truth to someone you love.

And then, just a few weeks before my prognosis, I found the article. I'd been checking up on every news medium I could for years. I'm choosing to believe your father was the anonymous tip giver, that he made the best choice he could after a series of choices I know he regretted.

When I booked our girls' weekend in Oregon, I promised myself I wouldn't leave there without telling you everything. I practiced the conversation a thousand times on the way down, practiced how I'd transition from telling you about the prognosis involving my head before

I told you of the one that had been plaguing my heart for more than three years at that time. But I hadn't anticipated your tears over my surgery, any more than I'd anticipated my own. And once again, fear held my tongue captive.

As the surgery date edged closer, I pushed Merrick and Ember's fate aside and focused on a new plan. How could I possibly give my fans the ending they begged for when I was carrying around a secret that harmed the ending of the people I loved most in the world? I finished dictating the memoir only days before my prognosis changed, and outside of my mother, all I could think about was the "what if" of not getting to be there when you and Joel read those final words.

I wrestled for years over a secret I was scared to tell . . . until I finally got it all out on the page. If only I knew sooner the kind of freedom truth can bring, I never would have kept it so long from the people I love most. I pray you can know this freedom, too. I pray you both can.

I love you, sister.

Always and forever,
Cece

Much like Joel, I stand motionless at the conclusion of my letter for nearly a minute. There's so much to digest and sort, and yet one thing stands out amongst it all.

"She was scared to tell me."

"She had reason to be," Joel says in a tone that confirms his statement is only loosely related to whoever threatened and blackmailed my father. But Cece had witnessed more than my father's decision to board the Campbells' boat that night; she'd also witnessed my complete and total rejection of Joel and of the entire town I'd once called home. Was he right? If Cece had told me the truth sooner, would I have cut her out the way I'd cut Joel out?

To try to imagine my life without her friendship after my father's death feels wrong on every possible level. She was my closest friend, my confidant, my travel companion, my plus-one to every publishing event we were asked to attend. We'd plotted together, brainstormed together, built a fictional kingdom together. To erase her from any one part of my life would have felt like erasing a part of myself.

And yet, hadn't I done that with Joel?

I'd tried to erase him from all the best parts of my life.

And maybe that's what this had all been about—Cece's quest for us to read the memoir together wasn't only for me to discover the truth about my father's death, but for me to discover something else, as well.

Something I'd lost and wasn't sure I would ever find again.

"Joel, I—"

"There's something written on the back." His gaze freezes on the folded stationery in my hand. I turn it over to find two postscripts:

P.S. You asked me to wait to submit The Fate of Kings *to you until I could hand it to you over a bowl of caramel-cheddar popcorn, but due to logistics, I had to go with Plan B. So I left it where your favorite literary dog could stand guard over it until you were ready to find it.*

P.P.S. I have full confidence your masterful revision skills will bring this first draft of The Fate of Kings *to life. There's not a soul on earth who has loved this story more than you.*

Joel and I look to each other first and then to the bookshelf we're still facing.

"Does she mean . . ."

But he's already stretching for the top shelf I can barely see on my tiptoes. If there's something back there, then Cece would have needed the help of a stepstool. As would most staff and VIP guests who would have visited the library in the months following her death. Joel pushes the fallen books aside and reaches toward the back. Whatever he grasps is substantial, as it takes him some maneuvering to bring it down.

The stack of primary-colored notebooks he holds up is wrapped in twine, and at the sight of it all I can do is laugh. The raw sensation bubbling up my throat is so foreign, and yet the release of it feels almost therapeutic.

"Unreal," he murmurs. "Absolutely unreal."

Only it is real.

And all I want to do is verify that these four notebooks do, indeed, hold the ending of a story countless readers have been waiting on since *The Twist of Wills*, myself included. I drop to the carpet and use the shelf of beach reads at my back for support.

And then I open the blue notebook on top.

Dedication:
To the sister of my heart, Ingrid:
Sometimes the happiest endings begin after a cliffhanger.
May the same be true for you.

My vision blurs as I trace my fingers over the handwritten dedication in black ink before I turn the page to chapter one. Unlike when I opened Allie's digital manuscript on my laptop, I don't need my usual pre-reading coaching techniques. Within the first sentence, my mind relaxes into Cece's narrative, as if she were reading me the opening lines herself. Even though I've been away from this imaginary land for so long, the familiarity of it invites me in like a welcome guest and before I realize it's happened, I'm swept back into Cardithia.

There are errors and missing words throughout the pages, sentences crossed out and rewritten, notes in the side margins preceding arrows and asterisks, and yet I'd trade none of it for a polished product. Because these notebooks, with all their imperfections and flaws, are the kind of treasure a loved one cherishes forever. The kind of keepsake a loved one vows to protect at all costs.

It will take me several days, but I will type each and every word of this first draft into a digital format before I'll submit it to Fog Harbor Books. And even then, I have no intention of taking my eyes or hands off it for long. Cece entrusted me with her last written work, and I will do it justice. After she carried the burden of my father's secrets for so many years, it's the least I can do.

My lips curve slightly at the thought of everything this discovery will mean. Not only job security for me and story closure for Cece's readers, but also Wendy's protection and continued peace. Once I notify SaBrina of our findings, the search for the lost manuscript will be over and Fog Harbor Books will possess the long-awaited conclusion to the Nocturnal Hearts series.

Joel lowers himself to sit beside me, legs outstretched and back pressed against the same bookshelf as mine, but that's where our similarities end. Because on my lap lay four composition notebooks pointing to the future, while his holds a history summarized on a single piece of yellow stationery. There have been so many words shared over the course of this night. Some spoken, some read, some only hoped for, and many still unknown. But at least in this one moment, as Joel laces his fingers through mine and sets our joined hands on top of Cece's final book, there are no words lost between us.

30

It's nearly midnight when I finish inputting the final paragraphs of chapter three into a new document titled *The Fate of Kings* on my laptop. It's been at least an hour since my last sip of caffeinated tea and two since I sat with Joel in the library. The ride back to the cottage had been much too short and much too quiet.

"I should let you get to work," he'd said, idling in the driveway. *"I know you have a lot ahead of you."*

A fact I couldn't deny or argue with, and yet it didn't stop me from wanting to.

"Good night, Indy," he'd said before I could come up with something credible, some solution for how this could all fit together without us living nine hundred miles apart.

"Good night," I'd said, wishing for a thousand more minutes like the ones we'd shared in the library, where the pressures and realities of the outside world had all but disappeared. *"I'll let you know how the call with Fog Harbor goes in the morning."*

"I'm sure everybody you tell will be ecstatic."

And yet there was no question who wasn't.

I step away from my laptop and out onto the private balcony in Cece's bedroom. An ache has settled between my third and fourth rib. Even after I've left her fictional story world, I can still hear her voice like the steady heartbeat in my chest.

I love you, sister. Always and forever.

Reflectively, I twist my ring around my finger and take in the moon's glow on the dark, rolling waves just beyond where I stand. By my fifth rotation, I exit the balcony in exchange for a closer view.

Armed with the emergency flashlight I found in the kitchen and a quilt I snagged from the hall closet tucked around my shoulders, I take the steep steps down the bluff outside the cottage toward a shoreline narrowed by the tide. Yet even at this late hour, there's still plenty of beach to roam. I slip my sandals off near the bottom step, and the cold shock of wet sand sharpens my weary mind.

As I near the water's edge, I lift my gaze to search the heavens the way Cece used to search her mural of Cardithia whenever she needed direction in her story world. I click off the flashlight in my hand. Its power is nothing against the illumination of the full moon. And for just a moment, its stunning presence mutes the throb in my chest. But not even the mystery of creation can cancel out the loneliness of loss.

I love you, sister. Always and forever.

I close my eyes and open my ears to the sound of the breaking waves.

Sister.

The significance of that title hits me anew as I recall the day we met, which was supposed to end with her taking a one-way ferry out of town. How if I hadn't left the marina to read on her uncle's dock, or if she hadn't stepped onto that hotel patio to scribble a good-bye note to her cousin, the two of us never would have met. How after only a brief encounter about our shared love of books, she'd altered her plans, which had forever altered both our lives.

How even before I knew how to be a friend, Cece had chosen me to be hers. And she'd kept choosing me. Not only in life but even after her death.

I shift my stance in the sinking sand and work to find a new footing. For so long I'd accused God of being absent, of being silent . . . and yet now I can't deny the timing of how He'd used a spunky sixteen-year-old girl in my life at just the right time, in just the right place. Cece was a friend who held nothing back from me—not her mother, not her aunt or uncle, not her home or her faith, or even her only cousin. She'd given me a family, one who hadn't shied away from my father's struggles but had prayed for his victory and grieved over his losses.

The same way they'd grieved for mine.

The tears clinging to my lower lash line slip down my cheeks and fall to the sand at my feet. I adjust my stance again, and this time, when I step away from the deep footprints I've made to watch them fill with water, a glint catches my eye in the moonlight.

As soon as the shape and color of it comes into focus, emotion thickens in my throat. I squat down and scoop the triangle-shaped rock from the deep impression it made in the sand.

Only, it's not a rock at all.

Careful not to let it slip from my slick fingertips, I hold the small black triangle up to the moonlight to examine it further as the opaque surface morphs into a translucent center. Still not trusting my eyes, I pull the flashlight out and lay my treasure directly on top of the lens. When light slices through the rough, dark surface, my tears flow in earnest.

After so many years of beach combing with Cece, so many years of searching for a duplicate like the one my mother had worn and lost and like my father had found on a shore not too far from this one . . . this was the only black ocean tear I'd ever come across myself.

And according to Wendy, this is also a promise that *"no heartache has ever gone unseen and no darkness has ever been too dark for light to overcome."*

I cup the gift in my hand and breathe through a thousand new emotions. It's not grief I feel the strongest, but something else that seems to be reshaping my heart the way sand and surf and time have reshaped this tiny treasure in my palm. I hold it up to the moonlight again and marvel at a truth I simply couldn't see clearly until now.

There was no coincidence or accident when it came to the timing of a letter resurfacing in Marshall's office, and certainly not about the man who'd hand-delivered it to me. Suddenly the thought of leaving him all over again—without the chance to fight for something more, something different and new—causes me to pull the quilt tighter around my shoulders.

I look down at the promise in my grasp and wrestle with the resoluteness of the future that's ahead of me: Cece entrusted me with her final manuscript, and it's my responsibility alone to see that through.

In the same way I know Joel needs to stay where his family is, I know I need to go back.

The revelation causes me to squeeze the sea glass in my palm all the more tightly, to trust there is a plan even in this.

When the tide nips at my bare toes, I shiver and take a step back, hoping that if I stand out here just a little longer, a different revelation might appear before I head back to the cottage to catch a few hours of sleep.

After another spasm of shivers racks my body, I finally turn to face the bluff. But instead of an illuminated cottage, all I can see is the familiar figure lingering near the bottom of the stairs. When my own steps falter in the sand, his continue until we're standing only inches apart.

"I hoped you'd still be awake," Joel says.

My pulse ratchets higher, and I yearn to reach for him, to draw him closer. "How did you even find me down here in the dark?"

"When I pulled into the driveway, all the lights were still on in the cottage. I didn't feel right about going inside uninvited, but when you didn't answer your phone, I decided to take a walk . . . and there you were, bathed in moonlight like some sort of divine sea apparition."

I stare up into those beautiful green eyes as he steps in close to pinch the quilt tighter around me. Only now that he's here, I want to shuck the quilt to the sand and replace it with an embrace far better suited for the job.

"I don't want to say good-bye to you again," I say plainly, with exactly none of the moxie one of Cece's characters would have contained.

"Then don't." He reaches for my face and skims his fingers over my cheeks and down the line of my jaw. "Don't say it, Indy."

I'm so dizzy from his touch, from the way he says my name, that I can almost forget the reasons I have to do exactly that, and soon.

He cradles my face between his palms. "I know you have Cece's manuscript to manage in California, but 'see you later' isn't the same as good-bye. And I'm willing to say the former for however long it takes us to figure things out."

I nod in earnest, hoping this is a type of math problem that can actually be solved in real life, in real time. "I'll be managing all the ins and outs of the publication schedule as soon as the manuscript is officially submitted and accepted, which will be approximately nine months, ten at most, but there will be some breaks in between. I could fly up a couple of weekends a month, stay with Wendy if she'll have me, or in the cottage if it's available."

"It will always be available to you," Joel says a bit breathlessly. "And I can fly down to see you, too."

Only it's a bit more difficult for me to imagine Joel in San Francisco, and if I'm honest, it's becoming more and more difficult to imagine myself there, too. This is where he fits; where we both fit.

"And maybe once *The Fate of Kings* is set to release, I can look into what it might take to do some freelance editing work, transition my services to a new location. I've been told on good authority that one of my new friends here is actually quite brilliant when it comes to marketing endeavors."

Joel's expression is a mix of pain and hope. "Is that really what you want?"

Despite the chill of the night, my lips don't tremble when I say, "You're what I want, Joel Campbell."

And then his lips are on mine, and the quilt is at our feet. The warmth of his body, of his arms wrapped around me, is an intoxicating recharge that spans from my head to my toes. And all I can think is how much I don't ever want to let this man go again. The longer we embrace and kiss, the stronger the compass inked on my chest seems to pulse, as if to say *this is where you belong.*

Because this is exactly where I've always belonged.

When we finally break apart, Joel tips his forehead to mine, as if actively trying to talk himself out of closing the gap between our swollen lips once more. "I can't remember a time when I didn't love you, Ingrid."

Slowly, as our breaths intermingle, I press my palm to the left side of his chest, and say the only thing I can without having to use words. I barely make it to the third tap before Joel gives up his fight, takes me in his arms, and kisses me again.

By the time we've reached the top of Cece's beach stairs, where the path splits left to the driveway or right to the back patio door, we're already discussing plans for my return trip and how we'll tell Aunt Wendy and his parents about the many developments over these last ten days. We have much more than the early beginnings of a relationship to discuss with them. And while technically I still have three days left on my mandatory vacation, most of that time will be spent transcribing Cece's notebooks into a digital file so I can keep the originals locked away in a safe.

But as Joel and I walk hand in hand and veer left toward his car in the driveway, we notice a second vehicle parked beside it. The hotel's club car is empty, but Allie is sitting on the porch steps, her phone in hand.

"So . . . are late-night guests fairly routine for you, then?" Joel murmurs under his breath with a hint of humor.

The minute she hears us, Allie shoots up from the step, her energy palpable, as if it were one in the afternoon and not one in the morning. "I know it's late—I'm sorry, but I figured you'd be up, and I've been calling you for nearly an hour and this really can't wait till morning. There's something you need to see before you turn anything in to your boss."

I begin to shake my head, realizing there is so much I need to catch her up on since SaBrina's phone call to me at the storage units. "Oh, Allie, I should have texted you. We're not turning in the memoir." I smile as brightly as I can given the hour. "We found Cece's missing notebooks tonight—*The Fate of Kings*."

I expect Allie to scream or clap or do some kind of cheerleading maneuver with those super long legs of hers, but she barely seems to register my words at all. "That's super great, but you still need to see this."

She has her phone flipped out to us, a screenshot of a social media post with a profile name I don't recognize front and center. TaBitha Garwood. Once again, I start to shake my head, but Allie's too quick on the draw.

"Something you said to me earlier this afternoon in the club car has been bothering me all day, and I couldn't let it go till I figured it out. I've read all kinds of conspiracy theories about Cece after her death, across multiple platforms. There's a pretty significant range of stupidity to choose from out there, but I've only ever read one post about a publisher's offering a reward for bringing in the manuscript. It took me a while to find it, but it was posted on the memorial site about two months ago. We caught it and blocked it within twenty minutes, but still. It feels like more than just a coincidence that out of all the conspiracies, that's one of the ones your boss rattled off to you today."

Joel and I both take her phone and study the screenshot of the banned post.

TaBitha Garwood.

The profile is of an avatar with long brown hair, blue eyes, and huge ruby red lips.

The post reads:

Did you know Cecelia Campbell's publisher (Fog Harbor Books—San Francisco) is offering a hefty monetary reward for finding The Fate of Kings? Wanted to make sure all you #FindWendy trackers knew about this! DM me and I'll connect you with my source!

"What are you suggesting?" But by the drop in Joel's voice, he's already registered what Allie's suggesting.

"She thinks SaBrina could be behind this post."

Allie looks between the two of us. "I think considering what happened today, it looks pretty suspicious."

And then I study the profile name again, closer this time. "TaBitha," I say, with an emphasis on the second capital letter. "That's how SaBrina spells her name, too—with the B capitalized just like that." Was it coincidence or was it something more? "If she was behind this conspiracy . . ." I begin, my brain exploding with the implications of what such a discovery could mean and how far it might have gone if not for Allie's insightful investigating.

"Then it's likely not the only one of its kind," Joel finishes for me. "How would we substantiate something like this, Allie?"

She huffs a hard breath. "Tracking malignant behavior online isn't easy. Unless you could get access to her hard drive? But even then, it's a fairly big undertaking, and she would have to be dumb enough to have used her work computer or laptop."

"I don't have access to that," I say in a way that pulls both Allie and Joel's attention. "*But* I think I might know someone who could get us access."

I race into the cottage and grab my phone from the counter.

"Ingrid, it's after one in the morning," Joel reminds me, as if Chip is some kind of normal human being who operates on normal human hours.

"Believe me, it's not uncommon for Chip to be up this late, especially if the Nerd Herd is gaming online."

"The Nerd Herd?" Allie repeats.

"There's a reason our IT department isn't asked to help brainstorm book titles."

I tap Chip's contact and put him on speakerphone. He answers on the first ring, not a touch of sleep to his voice. "What happened today? You never called me back to—"

"Hold on, Chip. First, you're on speaker with my good friends here—Joel and Allie."

"Hey, good friends Joel and Allie."

"Second, we found the manuscript tonight." It's a better lead-in than, *Hey, I think our boss is the equivalent of an online hitman*. Although, he probably wouldn't blink twice if that had been my opener to this conversation.

"Wait—you found *The Fate of Kings*? Seriously? Ingrid! That's—"

"Yep," I cut him off. "It's incredible."

"You certainly don't sound like you were just handed job security for life at Fog Harbor. You realize SaBrina can't touch you now—"

"Actually, she's why I'm calling. We think there's a chance SaBrina might be involved in more than just blackmailing her employees for information. We think she might have been responsible for sending deranged fans here, too, to Cece's hometown, to harass Cece's mother for the missing manuscript. Given the nature of her threats to me and a post my social-media-savvy friend here just found, we could have a solid case against her."

The heaviness in his sigh is as telling as his next words. "I wish I could say I'm shocked, but this news is on par with Santa Claus not being real."

"Hey, some of us aren't ready to give that one up yet," Allie says.

Chips laughs. "Sorry. All right, so what's our plan? What do we need?"

The smile that touches my lips is a testament to Chip's outstanding loyalty. "I'm hoping you might have a contact in the IT department who can help us, someone I could send an urgent request to. Someone you trust." I swallow, knowing what I'm about to ask him goes beyond a pocket-sized favor fit for a coworker; it's potential career suicide. "But before you get involved, you need to be sure you've thought through the risks."

"Pretty sure I was *involved* the minute SaBrina eavesdropped on our private conversation, threatened me in her office, and black-mailed my boss about a memoir that was in no way hers to demand."

Joel smiles approvingly and mouths, *I like him.*

I point to the front door. "Then let's see if your IT contact feels the same way, and if he does, then I say we make a plan."

"Seeing as I'm on VR with Trevin right now, I'm pretty sure I can arrange a meeting. Keep your phone on."

31

THREE DAYS LATER

A lifetime of events has passed since the day I first saw Joel standing in my office at Fog Harbor Books, and yet I can't imagine being here today without him. He was at my side when I called to tell SaBrina we'd found the missing manuscript and when we formalized a plan with Chip on how our other discoveries would need to be revealed. Through all the unknowns to come, one thing is for certain: Whatever happens over the next few hours, the two of us are in this together.

Chip is the first to greet us in the lobby. Despite the constant, sleep-deprived communication we've kept with him throughout the last seventy-two hours, there is absolutely nothing about his appearance that suggests he isn't his usual bright-eyed self. In fact, he may even be a tad peppier than usual as he hands each of us a double-shot Americano from a drink carrier.

"I figured you could both use one of these before we head upstairs. I've already had two."

Joel arches an eyebrow appraisingly. "Let me say again, Chip, it's easy to see why Ingrid speaks so highly of you."

"He's one of a kind," I agree, taking the coffee and recalling the long hours we've spent divvying up tasks between Allie and Chip.

All of which were outside their typical job descriptions. "Do you have the—"

"Yep. The package is waiting for you on your desk, just like we talked about, and the conference room is booked for your one o'clock meeting. Figured it should happen there. Poetic justice and all."

Nerves take flight in my lower abdomen, and I attempt to drown them with espresso.

"Have you heard anything more from our White Horse?" Chip asks, using the code name he insisted upon as he escorts us toward the elevators.

"Nothing more yet," I say as Joel steadies me with a hand to my lower back. "But the White Horse has had a lot of red tape to wade through."

Chip stops to look between us, and I note the first hint of unease I've seen from him since this process began. I block the elevator panel with my hand before he can tap the up arrow, and lower my volume. "It's not too late for you to back out. Joel and I are prepared to—"

"*Too late* was cowering in a bathroom stall after being interrogated like I'd committed a war crime for talking to my editor after hours in the break room. Believe me, I want to see justice done as much as you do."

Joel claps him on the shoulder, smiles. "Have you ever considered a career in the hospitality industry?"

"No, but you'll be my first call after I'm fired for insubordination in roughly, uh . . ." Chip glances at his watch. "Thirty-two minutes."

"No poaching my assistant." I narrow my eyes at Joel before zeroing in on Chip. "And you. No more jokes about getting fired. I mean it. We are not the ones on trial here." But even as our elevator rises to the third floor, my stomach swoops low with anxiety, and I don't miss the silent exchange between the two guys behind me. It seems we're all a bit more tense then we're letting on.

Before the doors have a chance to open, Chip holds his thumb to the button at the bottom of the panel to ensure they don't. "Whatever happens in that meeting today, it's been a pleasure working for you, Ingrid. You've taught me so much about—"

"Chip." I squeeze my eyes closed and exhale through my nose.

"What? This is my pre-game pep talk."

Joel clears his throat. "Might be best if we wait for a post-game talk."

"Right." Chip gives a stiff nod. "Let me know if there's anything more you need. Until then, I'll keep my eye out for the arrival of the White Horse."

"Will do," Joel says, placing his hand on my back once again. "Thanks."

A dozen sets of eyes trail us down the hallway, and I do my best to appear calm and in control, but I have no doubt whatever rumors have been circulating about me—and what I may or may not have in my possession—are multiplying with the sighting of Joel Campbell. He's not exactly low-profile material.

We're behind the closed door of my office for all of two seconds before Joel reminds me to breathe. I assure him I am, in fact, still breathing, but he stops me before I can collect the package on my desk.

"Look at me." He touches my chin gently. "You're on the right side here. No matter who does or doesn't show up today, you showed up. That's what matters."

I will the tremor in my hands to still. "I just hope it's enough evidence to seal her fate without putting the target on anyone else I love." The faces of both Wendy and Chip surface in my periphery. Neither of them deserves to be the collateral damage in SaBrina's schemes.

"And that is exactly why we're here." He cradles the back of my neck with his hand and pulls me in to press a kiss to my forehead.

Like in so many meetings in this conference room over the last year, my gaze travels to the clock above the door. And like so many times before, SaBrina steps in one minute ahead of schedule. Unfortunately, our White Horse is still MIA.

"Ingrid," SaBrina coos as if she's greeting a long-lost friend and not a subordinate she was willing to stab in the back to rise to the top. "It's good to have you back in the office. And of course it's lovely to see you again, Mr. Campbell." She shakes his hand. "So glad you could join us for this very exciting day. Let me be the first to say on behalf of Fog Harbor Books that we're delighted to finally be making this happen. I'm sure the entire Campbell family is just as eager for the completion of Cecelia's series as we are." When SaBrina eyes Joel demurely, it's clear she assumes I've told him nothing of her intimidation tactics.

"I, for one, am definitely looking forward to some closure," Joel replies smoothly.

Joel is the picture of professionalism when he addresses her, though I see the tension that flares in his jaw as he settles in beside me at the table once again. There's no doubt he can see through her façade, but I tap his knee under the table in a silent reminder of our delegated roles inside this space. He's promised to let me take the lead, and I've promised not to back down. Two promises we talked through at length prior to this moment. Two promises that will require a healthy dose of patience and restraint for us both.

SaBrina eyes the package in front of me hungrily, but when I place a protective hand over the contents, she blinks and returns her attention to me.

"I've had our legal team reissue copies of Cecelia's original contract for the Nocturnal Heart series to include the updated information since her passing. My goal is for everyone to walk away from here today confident of the future." She opens a manila folder on the glossy tabletop and slides the contract in our direction. Joel flips through the first several pages regarding future royalty payments being issued to the trust. "As you can see, Mr. Campbell, the trust will receive the final installment of Cecelia's advance thirty days after today's submission." She glances again at the goods I've promised her. "Which would mean thirty days from today." She folds her hands on top of the table like a helpful grade-school teacher at a parent conference, only her blood-red fingernails don't quite fit the part. She stretches them out for the package. "If there are no questions, then I'll simply validate the full manuscript you've brought with you so we can get going on—"

"I do have some questions," I say, keeping my hand firmly in place as my gaze ticks to the clock above her head once again, hoping to buy us a bit more time. "On one of our recent phone calls, you mentioned the backlash Cecelia's last novel received from fans, along with the many conspiracies adopted by groups online. How do you plan on protecting Cecelia's reputation and addressing those concerns through the marketing of this new release?"

SaBrina doesn't so much as flinch at the mention of that phone call. "Rest assured, *The Fate of Kings* will have the full power of both marketing teams behind it—the San Francisco and the New York divisions." Her smile is as smug as her tone. "If we all play our cards right, I believe with the completion of this series, and the anticipation surrounding this last book, we could potentially break records held since Harry Potter fans camped out in bookstore parking lots in the late '90s. The unrest we've seen in Cecelia's fanbase as of late stems from a lack of closure to the characters they fell in love with over the course of four novels. Just imagine how they'll react when we hand them the very thing they want most: *redemption*." Her fevered gaze turns my stomach. "Not only will this final installment of the Nocturnal Heart series fulfill the film option agreement Cecelia signed, but each of us will play a part in this unforgettable milestone in publishing history. Can you imagine receiving the ending to a story you believed buried with its author?"

Yes, actually, I can imagine that. Just like I can imagine the kind of notoriety and advanced career track SaBrina will be on when she becomes the editorial director overseeing such an exceptional moment in publishing history. It was exactly as Chip had alluded weeks ago: People are willing to do crazy things in the name of power.

"Is there anything else I can answer for either of you?" she prompts, shifting her focus to Joel, whose gaze drills into the undisclosed package resting beneath my hand. I receive his message loud and clear. He's done being patient, and so am I.

"No," I say. "Thanks for clearing that up for us."

"Of course." Her smile suggests we're all on the same team, all after the same goal. But at the moment, I can't think of anything more repulsive. I slide the package forward and relinquish it to SaBrina.

White Horse or not, this is what we came here to do. And this is the hill my career in editorial will die on if it's not done exactly right.

Since the origin of our plan, I've imagined this moment multiple times. Imagined SaBrina's pointed fingernail flicking the gold brad at the back of the envelope and pulling out the stack of printed pages inside. But I couldn't get a read on her facial expressions. I've seen SaBrina annoyed. I've seen her indifferent. But I've yet to see her incredulous, until now.

When her gaze falls to the first printed page, it's like watching someone read their own eulogy.

She slips it to the back of the stack as if it's a mistake she can hide. However, she'll only find a hundred more just like it. Black-and-white evidence of the multiple fake online accounts she's hidden behind to manipulate, coerce, and fuel rumors and misinformation to Cece's fans for purposes I've yet to understand. The most predominant fake account being one Ms. TaBitha Garwood, a.k.a SaBrina Hartley.

"What is . . . ?" She riffles through it, as if the faster she can scan the pages, the faster she can make the evidence disappear. But that's the thing about a digital footprint, it *never* disappears. Her efforts to rise to the top have left behind a trail of scars.

Allie had been right about the difficulty in tracing destructive online behavior back to its originator, but thankfully, that part wasn't left up to us. Given that Trevin—Chip's favorite gamer pal and the head of Fog Harbor's IT department—was still reeling from the recent firing of his girlfriend by SaBrina's hand, he was extra willing to pull the web logs from her computer and send them to us. The task of sifting through her browser history and online activity had been tedious, but our findings had been disturbingly lucrative.

Allie had not only confirmed SaBrina's fake accounts inside multiple fan fiction groups, but she'd also confirmed that one of those fake alias accounts had started the #FindWendy hashtag that had become so popular last spring. Allie copied each and every post into an ever-expanding evidence file Chip had formatted and sent to the board of directors yesterday. In only a few days, the four of us had become savvy online detectives.

"*That*"—I dip my head to the pages in her hand—"is the reason we won't be submitting Cecelia's manuscript directly to you today. It's evidence of your handiwork pulled directly from your hard drive over the past nine months. Turns out, your threats to me regarding the conspiracies surrounding Cece's death and her family's well-being were not the first of their kind. Seems you've made a practice out of it. But it's like you told me once, *secrets like this only keep for so long*."

Her expression blanches and then resumes. "You can't prove intent with any of this."

"No, we can't, but we made sure to send the file in your hands to the board of directors, as well. We think it makes for a very compelling read."

"It certainly does." Barry, who is leaning against the doorway as if he's been there undetected for some time, pushes into the conference room. "Which is why I cut my vacation short to be here today."

Our fashionably late White Horse has finally arrived.

Barry winks at me. "Heya, kiddo." He dips his head to Joel. "Mr. Campbell. Please excuse my tardiness. Baja might be a quick flight, but traffic from the airport is always a beast." His loud, tropical-print button-up is a welcome sight, as is the familiar seat he takes at the end of the conference table. He steadies his gaze on SaBrina. "As the editorial director of this division for the last twenty-five years, I've seen my fair share of reprehensible behavior, but I've yet to stumble across something as blatant and damaging as this." His gaze sharpens along with his voice. "Our zero-tolerance policy for bullying and intimidation in the workplace extends to the use of work equipment and property."

"This was never about intimidation." SaBrina shakes her head as if this is all a misunderstanding she can backpedal her way out of, even though there are a hundred social media posts of evidence pointing to the contrary. "This is about strategic marketing."

"You're wrong, SaBrina," Barry says coolly. "There's no excuse that can justify your actions—"

"These fan groups hold more power than we give them credit for," she cuts in. "Their online chatter equals book sales, even the negative chatter. But once the discussions die, they move on. Nobody wants to start a series without the final book, and sales were declining because we had no final book to push. The only reason our sales didn't completely plummet was because I kept the dialogue about Cecelia Campbell alive." She stops herself from saying more, but in her silence, something starts to click.

"So you kept them talking by making up stories—conspiracies?" Outrage builds in my core at her audacity. "By sending them on wild goose chases through the Olympic Peninsula, searching for clues that they'd never find? Harassing the Campbell family and their community? You can't actually believe any of those things are responsible for an increase of sales."

"They're still talking about the Nocturnal Heart series, aren't they?" Her smug stare bores through me. "Because of me, they haven't forgotten about Cardithia or that horrible cliffhanger Cecelia left for her fans in book four. As soon as there's a publishing date for *The Fate of Kings*, you'll be thanking me for my interference."

"I will never thank you for the hurt you've caused innocent, *grieving* people."

"Don't be so naïve, Ingrid. Our industry is only one generation away from extinction. Everything I've done is to help protect our future readership, and every person in this room has reaped the benefits."

Heat sears through me at her words, but before I can fire back, Barry steps in. "Unfortunately, SaBrina, the board members I spoke with yesterday afternoon in an emergency meeting don't share your sentiments. And as such, we've decided to terminate your services at Fog Harbor, effective immediately. Our legal team will be following up with you shortly."

"You're making a huge mistake. This one publication has the power to bring everything back into the black. With the marketing efforts I have planned, this will be the biggest launch in the history of Fog Harbor Books—"

"You're right, it will. And your name will be nowhere near it," he concludes.

Her eyes flash. "You will be hearing from my lawyer."

"I count on it. Now, please go gather your things. Chip is waiting outside the door with security to escort you to HR," Barry calmly concludes, as if he's just placed a routine coffee order and not just fired his editorial director. "They're expecting you and will give you further instructions from there."

"I will fight this," she grits out.

"I would expect nothing less from you."

"This is about favoritism," SaBrina lashes out at Barry. "It's always been about favoritism. You've had a thing for the underdog ever since that little intern of yours stumbled onto the scene."

"No," Barry interrupts sharply. "*This* is about ethics. Ethics you have abandoned a dozen times over."

SaBrina steadies a hand to her chest. "I graduated with my MFA from Cornell and still had to work my way up the ladder—and what did she have? Nothing but a basic degree and a stroke of good luck. Ingrid is a one-hit series editor who knows nothing more than—"

"That's enough—" Barry tries to interject, but SaBrina talks over him as she rises to stand. Joel angles his rigid body protectively, as if ready to jump to my defense at any moment.

"Are you really going to sit there and act like *she's* done things the ethical way? We all know the story of how Ingrid lied about finding a manuscript on the slush pile when really she brought one in from her little Golden Goose." She glowers at me but speaks with a sickly sweet voice. "But then your luck ran out, which is exactly why I applied for this promotion when I did. I had a gut feeling that if I kept you around long enough, that missing novel would eventually surface, and I was right."

"Cece's storytelling won her that contract," I fire back. "Not luck, not me! You don't deserve to touch her work!" I struggle against Joel's tether on my arm, which keeps me in my seat.

SaBrina tilts her head and smirks ever so slightly. "At least I'm not the one riding the coattails of my rich, dead friend's memory."

"That's enough," Joel calls out at the same time Barry shouts for security with a final, "*You are dismissed, SaBrina!*"

Her chest heaves as she looks between us all one last time, her mouth twisted into the kind of grimace that's better read on the page than seen in person. The security guards are waiting for her in the doorway, along with Chip, and as she storms past him, he flashes us a thumbs-up before quickening his steps to follow after them.

Barry stares at us as if completely befuddled by the events of the last ten minutes. Not that I can blame him; I'm still spinning. And by the way Joel's jaw is jumping, he hasn't quite calmed down yet, either.

"I'd like to apologize to you both for every count of SaBrina's inexcusable behavior." Barry heaves a long sigh. "I'm not at liberty to go into detail about much, but she's been under scrutiny with the board for a while now."

"What did she mean by getting sales back into the black?" Joel asks in an all-business tone.

Barry purses his lips and then nods, as if deciding to share more than he planned to with us. "SaBrina grossly overpaid for a cookbook from one of our bestselling mystery writers, Harry Green. The launch flopped, one of the worst flops in our long history, to be frank. It put our whole division in the red."

"So she needed a huge payday, something that would buoy the financials and her career path," Joel fills in.

Barry's nod is grave. "That's the best I can come up with, but it fits her strategy of stirring drama with Cece's fans. I'm sure she would have kept feeding them all sorts of things throughout the publication process, too." He shakes his head. "I'm sorry, Ingrid. I wish I would have known what was really going on here—"

"None of this is your fault. I should have called you sooner." I smile at him, this man I've respected for years.

"We appreciate how swiftly you acted on the information we sent you," Joel says, taking my hand in his.

Barry props his elbows on the table, and I can sense what the coming weeks and months ahead will look like. As hard as this was for me, this nightmare will be ongoing for him.

"We can make things right here again, Barry," I say with an assurance I feel in my gut. "You've shown us what good leadership looks like; SaBrina hasn't undone everything you've taught us."

He tips his head to me. "I hope that's true. I also hope you'll allow me to recommend you to the board as my first choice for the editorial director of this branch. The position should be opening up in the very near future." He flashes me a knowing grin. "It will take some time to right this ship and bring back the sense of community and morale we've always been known for, but I'm certain that with some time and training, you'll be an excellent addition to our management team here at Fog Harbor Books."

It takes a moment for me to grasp what he's actually proposing. Only moments ago, I was waiting on the final verdict of the evidence we'd submitted to the board, and now here I am being offered the most coveted position in our division.

"I—I—" I clamp my mouth shut and then retry. "Wow, that's not at all what I was expecting." Dazed, I look from Barry to Joel, whose expression is unreadable. "I think I'm a bit shell-shocked."

"Understandable." Barry gives me a knowing smile. "Tell you what, I need to make an appearance down in HR. I have a feeling it's going to be a long night. Why don't you two keep the room. I'm sure there's plenty you need to discuss before we tackle the next steps regarding Cece's manuscript."

I nod absently as he stands to exit. But before he opens the door, he reaches out to pat my shoulder. "I'm proud of you, kid. Couldn't be more so, in fact."

And with that, he's gone, pulling a ripcord I hadn't anticipated.

"Is that what you want?" Joel's question is piercingly soft. "To be the editorial director for Fog Harbor Books?"

I rotate in my chair until our faces are mere inches apart. My heart beats wildly in my chest as I think through the ramifications of saying yes to a position that would ultimately keep me away from the man sitting directly in front of me for the foreseeable future. Long-distance relationships can't possibly last that long. "I don't want to go backward."

He strokes a thumb to my cheek. "Seems like this would be a pretty big jump forward to me."

"Not without you, it wouldn't."

He studies me in a way that feels like my rib cage might burst wide open. "It's not an either-or question I'm asking, Indy. It's an *and* question. I told you, I'm not willing to tell you good-bye again. So if this is the life you want, then I'll move here, to San Francisco."

My breath thins as I try to imagine Joel in any other place, in any other career than the one he's been destined for since boyhood. I could never in a million years ask him to part with a future connected to his family legacy. "You belong at that hotel, Joel. Your father—"

"I belong *with you*." His gaze travels a path from my eyes to my lips. "And if that's here or up north or on the other side of the planet, then that's where I want to be, too. I'm not letting go of you a second time. That's not how our story is meant to end."

And I know with a certainty I've rarely experienced that he's right. It's what Cece was trying to show us, the journey she was committed to taking us on even if she couldn't be here for it. Her words had led us through the formative years of our friendship and then into the foundational years of what became a love story we'd all but given up on. But Joel and I are no longer an interrupted happily ever after. Cece gave us the choice to pick up the pen and continue writing, one day at a time.

I press my forehead to his. "Please don't move here."

He pulls back to meet my gaze, and I don't even try to mask my joy. "Because I'm moving back to Port Townsend as soon as I finish the edits on *The Fate of Kings*. And it would be all kinds of tragic if you weren't there when I arrived."

He almost smiles at this, but refrains. "You need to think about what you'd be giving up to live in a small, slow town again."

"I happen to love that small, slow town."

"There's never going to be a huge publishing industry anywhere in the Olympic Peninsula. The closest would be Seattle, and that's still a hefty commute for—"

"We could change that, you know," I say with a shrug.

He quirks an eyebrow. "Change, as in . . . as in start a publishing house?"

I shake my head, laugh. "No, I have no interest in competing with Fog Harbor. I would like them as a reputable partner, though." I purse my lips for a moment and try to catch hold of my runaway thoughts. "What if I added on to my editorial freelance plan? What if it was more encompassing than that, and I could help equip an aspiring author during their pre-publishing journey? Identify their strengths while working to grow them in their areas of challenge. That's always been my favorite part of working in this industry— Cece's inspired that in me." I bite my bottom lip as the beginnings of a new dream start to take root. "There's still lots to think through, obviously, but at some point, I might need to call an official trustee meeting to discuss a few details pertaining to a future business matter. Do you think he'd be willing to schedule a meeting with me?"

"I think his schedule will always be open for you."

I lean in close and softly brush my lips against his. "Then for now, pencil me in for the day after the official launch of *The Fate of Kings*."

As he takes me in his arms, I can't help but hold on tight to this gift I've been given a second time around, one that came through devastation and loss, but also through sacrifice and love. I once believed the best way to honor Cece's memory was through her fictional works. But just as a life doesn't end after a final breath, neither does a story end with the turning of a final page.

Epilogue

People say the first year after loss is the hardest. They say that once you're through all those awful *big firsts*—first birthday, first Christmas, first death anniversary—that subsequent years will hit easier. But in my experience, *easier* is far too simplistic a word for describing the seasons that come with loss. Grief is ever-changing, just like the people who are left to navigate their way through it, one moment, one step, and one day at a time.

After living six years without my father, and nearly two years without my best friend, sometimes the hard days are just . . . hard. Which is why I know Wendy shouldn't be alone on this double whammy of a day: Cece's second birthday in heaven and the launch day of *The Fate of Kings*. A special scheduling request I asked the powers that be when I submitted the final, edited manuscript to Fog Harbor Books. *Happy Birthday, Cece.*

Wendy wasn't up for another elaborate affair at the Campbells' this year, and to be honest, I'm the last person who can fault her for that, as there's been no limit on activity and event planning at the hotel as of late. Thankfully, Joel and I were able to persuade her—along with our small army of family and friends—that a peaceful adventure on the open water was the best way to celebrate our beloved Cece.

366

I smile at the sight of Wendy's floppy yellow sun hat, bending and arcing in the breeze coming off the ocean. The stern, where she reclines on a white leather sofa, is perfectly situated underneath the shade cover of the upper deck, but still allows for fresh air and views. I've offered to store her hat inside the cabin multiple times, but Wendy, much like her daughter, is far too content soaking up the sights to be worried about losing something so frivolous.

It's been hotter than usual for this part of the coastline—highs in the low nineties instead of the mid-seventies—and after a day spent picnicking on the water, we're all a bit zapped from the heat. Honestly, before this week I've never paid such close attention to my weather app. Then again, I've also never been seven days out from becoming a bride, either.

Armed with a glass of lemonade and the small gift box in my pocket, I slip away from the happy chatter inside the living quarters of the main cabin and join Wendy for what I hope will be a couple minutes of alone time.

"Care for some company?" I ask after sliding the deck door closed behind me.

"Always," she replies, scooting over to make room for me on the sofa.

Her smile comes quicker these days, the spark in her eyes brighter than it was a year ago, but the mark of sorrow isn't always visible to an onlooker. And even though Wendy's beauty is striking, with her wavy gray hair and her golden bronze skin from mornings spent combing beaches for sea glass, there's a note in her voice that wasn't there before. A minor key that used to be major. I hear it when she talks and when she sings and even when she laughs. A reminder that even though there are still things to talk and sing and laugh about in this life, there are also things to miss and lament and grieve, too. Both are welcome and both are necessary.

In the same way that Wendy taught me so much about love in my formative years, she's teaching me now about the journey of grief, just by living her life one day at a time.

I snuggle into her side, and she puts her arms around me as if I've always been hers to hold. Apart from spending every day of these last three months with Joel since I said good-bye to my life in San Francisco and became a permanent resident of Port Townsend, living close to Wendy is a blessing I will never take for granted.

"I have a little something for you," I say, tugging at the box in my pocket and placing it in her palm. "I've been waiting to give it to you until today."

She sits up, her mouth shaped into a perfect O that makes me laugh. "You should have told me we were exchanging gifts on the boat. Yours is still back at the house." Her eyes grow tender. "Cece always loved giving gifts on her birthday—I was hoping this would be a tradition we'd keep every year."

"That was my hope, too. And seeing as today is both her actual birthday *and* her book birthday, I knew my gift had to be extra special to fit both occasions."

She hikes an eyebrow. "I'm quite intrigued now."

She slips the bow off the tiny yellow package and turns inward as if to shield it from any sudden gust of wind—unlike her hat, which is still flapping freely. When she pries the lid open, she lets out a happy sob, which I match almost immediately. "Oh, Ingrid—how—where—it's so beautiful."

"I found it a year ago, directly out from Cece's cottage. It was just waiting in the surf for me to find like a little gift from heaven. I measured one of the rings in your jewelry box so I could have it set for you."

With care, she pulls the ring from the box it's been in for weeks and slips the triangular black ocean tear onto her right index finger—the same finger I wear mine on. It's a perfect fit and the perfect size for her delicate hand.

She touches a finger to the surface of the glass, and I can't help but hold my right hand next to hers.

"No heartache unseen," I whisper her words back to her.

"And no darkness light cannot overcome," Wendy finishes. "What a sweet kiss from God you are to me, Ingrid. Thank you. I couldn't love anything more." She presses her lips to my cheek just as the door opens to the deck.

"Is there room out here for one more?" Joel asks, eyeing us both with a smile. "I'm not sure how much more wedding talk I can take. Between my mother and Madison . . ." He rubs at his temples good-naturedly, and I stand to slip my arms around his waist. Even though I only saw my fiancé ten minutes ago sitting at the helm with his father—who is now only five hours away from his own captain's license—I've turned into quite a fan of public displays of affection. Perhaps the nine months we spent sharing only every other weekend together are to blame. Or perhaps it's the five years we lost between falling in love as teenagers and being in love now as adults. Either way, I'm not complaining.

He takes my hand and then promptly steals my seat next to his aunt, pulling me onto his lap as soon as he's settled. He presses a brief kiss to the back of my neck and my entire body lights up in response. Again, no complaints to be found here.

"You should kindly remind them that nobody is supposed to be talking about the wedding today," I chastise playfully. "That was the only rule I gave when we planned this special excursion." Although, technically speaking, we are on our way back to the marina now. It's not hard to guess who the rule twisters are in that bunch.

"Ah, let them have their fun," Wendy says, admiring her new ring in the sunlight. "Weddings are supposed to be talked about—and Patti and Madison have such wonderful ideas for your big day."

"That may be true, Aunt Wendy. But if I have to hear, 'Well, what Carter and I did for our wedding was'"—he mimics in a high-pitched voice that sounds nothing like Madison—"one more time, I'm going to be the first man overboard *The Cardithia.*"

I smile at the new name of the Campbell's boat. They renamed it in Cece's honor shortly after we'd discovered *The Fate of Kings* in the library, and I happen to love it. Just like I know Cece would have.

Wendy laughs openly at her nephew as I point a finger at him.

"You will not be launching yourself over any railings on my watch, Joel Campbell. I happen to need you in seven days for a very important date."

"True." He plants another kiss on my tanned shoulder. My sundress came from Madison's Wardrobe—where I always receive the friends and family discount now—and the scalloped neckline dips just low enough in the front to show off the inked compass under my left collarbone. Joel very much approved of this purchase.

"Madison's been such a huge help to us," I reiterate for his benefit. "She was basically designing our wedding while walking down the aisle herself." As well as running her own local business and attending the early planning meetings for the Cecelia Jane Academy: a foundation for writers of all ages, talent levels, and publishing goals. My hope is to have it up and running by winter.

In addition to Madison's business and marketing prowess, Allie's input on the creative side of things has been pivotal in these early stages. I plan to hire her next summer after she graduates with her English degree; she knows she'll have a job with me if she wants it, as long as she promises to keep up with her own writing aspirations. So far we've worked through three drafts of *The Faerie Huntress* together, and she's currently working on her second book. She fights the discouragement every writer battles when it comes to revisions, and the restraints of school and her part-time jobs weigh heavily on her at times, but there is something special about these books. I can feel it, the same way I could feel it with Cece's early work.

And I'm not the only one to think so.

With Allie's permission, I sent off the finished draft of book one to Chip for his professional critique, giving Allie a pen name to keep her anonymous since I wanted Chip to be totally objective. His attention to story detail has grown exponentially this last year, and I trust his voice as an editor as much as I trust Barry's. His promotion to acquisitions editor last fall has been seamless, just like I knew it would be. He's made for this work, and I couldn't be prouder of him, even though I still haven't quite forgiven him for rejecting my offer to work alongside me in Port Townsend at the Academy.

At least he'll finally get to meet the rest of our wedding party in person next weekend.

Though he'd been my friend first—a reminder I brought up often—Joel claimed him as an official groomsman shortly after he'd asked me to marry him this spring on a dock decorated with flowers and candles and trails of glittering sea glass, thanks to Wendy.

By this time next week, we'll become husband and wife on that very dock.

Joel rubs my upper back and presses his lips to the tender spot beneath my right ear. "I should probably go check in with my dad before we get any closer to the harbor."

"Okay." I nod. "I'll go get the lines ready."

He locks his arms around my middle and traps me from escape. "Apparently, nobody is listening to the rules today. *You* are not playing the first mate on this glorious pleasure ride today. That's my dad's duty, at least for the next couple trips out. Don't rob me of the joy of getting to be *his* boss for once."

Wendy leans in conspiratorially. "And don't rob his only sister of laughing at the sight of him leaping on and off this dock like he's twenty and not sixty."

"Fine, fine." I raise my hands in surrender. "I'll stay put."

Joel lifts me from his lap and grips my hips to pull me in close. I've labeled this specific kiss of ours: Firm but Friendly. We've been practicing our wedding kisses. So far I'm more of a Soft but Lingering fan. Sadly, all of Joel's votes have been vetoed so far.

Once he's back inside the cabin, Wendy says, "Next weekend is going to be so beautiful. You sure you still want an old lady to be your matron of honor?"

I make a show of looking all around the stern. "I see zero old ladies present. But if you're double-checking my choice of wedding party, then I couldn't be happier with my selection."

As if on cue, the Spencer sisters—well, technically Madison is now a Worthington—wave at us from the other side of the glass door, beckoning us to come inside the cabin. Allie is miming what I think is supposed to be a person eating cake. I smile at them both and indicate we'll be inside in just a minute. Allie flashes a thumbs-up and Madison loops an arm around her baby sister's shoulders.

Who could have known these two curveballs would become some of my closest friends over the last year? We're all so different from each other—age, style, hobbies, career paths—and yet we share a common denominator that's turned into what I pray is an unbreakable bond: We all loved and were loved by Cece Campbell.

"I think they're wanting to do the birthday-slash-launch-day cake inside. You feeling up for that?" I ask Wendy.

"Is it in the shape of a giant treasure chest?" she asks, eyebrows raised.

Barb Spencer had made Cece's birthday cake today. She'd also be baking our wedding cake next weekend.

I shake my head. "Try again."

"Hmmm . . . a pirate ship?"

"One more try." I pull her up from the couch.

Wendy scrunches up her nose. "A treasure map."

"Ding, ding, ding! Complete with all the Kingdom of Cardithia landmarks. It's pretty amazing the detail Barb can add to a cake."

"It's pretty amazing the details my daughter put in her books. I loved the ending, by the way. You were right about the cliffhanger at the end of book four. It made everything so much more intense in *The Fate of Kings*, and so much more satisfying."

I'd given Wendy an early hardback copy of *The Fate of Kings* a few weeks ago, but she'd wanted to read through the entire Nocturnal Heart series again before she started it. Smart choice as I recently did the same, with only a fraction of the fog I felt last year when reading fiction.

I open the door for her, and together we enter the cabin for our final thirty minutes at sea. We sing happy birthday, give a toast to Cece for her book launch, and then pretend not to talk about the upcoming wedding—which, it turns out, is actually impossible for this group.

By the time *The Cardithia* has been docked and cleaned and all our guests are back on land looking windswept and happy, Joel and I are the last to leave the marina. Hand in hand, I relish our slow stroll back to the Campbells' property. I take in the soundtrack of my new, old life: the seagulls' cry overhead, the ding-ding of a ship's bell marking time at sea, and the dull lap of a rising tide.

Joel leads us to a private dock that holds so many memories for us both—some wistful and enchanting, others devastating and tragic, but all of them equally as crucial to the story of us. We stop at the end of the dock, where once a young, lonely girl sat reading, doing everything she could to escape into another world without realizing that her own world would soon be tipped completely upside down.

Joel pulls me into a close embrace and smooths my hair with his hand. His chest rumbles against my ear as he speaks. "Sometimes I wonder if she can see us, if she knows what her words gave back to us."

It's something I've wondered, too . . . and yet have no answer for. "I sure hope so."

"Me too." Joel plants a soft kiss on the top of my head and sways me gently in the light of a setting sun. "Because I'm convinced this right here might be the closest thing to heaven I'll experience until I'm there. I love you, Ingrid Erikson, soon to be Ingrid Erikson-Campbell."

My smile is watery as I recall the day he asked if I wanted to keep my father's surname. A year ago I would have declined the gesture. But a lot of healing has happened in a year, and while I can't condone many of my father's life choices, I loved him. And in his own way, Captain Hal Erikson had loved me, too.

I lift up on my toes, until our lips are only a whisper apart. "And I love you, my soon-to-be husband."

This kiss lands somewhere between Firm but Friendly and Soft but Lingering. It's a tender variation all its own, one meant only for today, on the birthday of a friend who gave us back a love we believed was lost forever. As Joel's mouth moves serenely over mine, I think again of that lonely girl whose only goal in life was to lose herself inside a book. Little did she know then that a dozen years of friendship later, it would take a different kind of book to find herself again.

THE END

Author's Note

Dear Friend,

For nearly a year, as I plotted, drafted, and revised this story, my thoughts never strayed far from this sacred space at the end of my manuscript. To be honest, this blank invitation was more difficult for me to fill out than any of the chapters I wrote before it. I've wrestled over what to say to you, and at times, even debated on saying nothing at all. But in the words of Cece Campbell, *"There is no perfect way to tell a painful truth."*

If I could sit down with you on a seaside bench overlooking the Pacific Ocean with a blackberry lemonade slush in hand, I'd tell you how prior to the fall of 2013, I wasn't sure I'd even spoken the word *grief*, much less understood the impact it could have on a life or on a family. But after my twenty-six-year-old baby sister was killed in a car accident on a foggy November morning, everything in my seemingly normal life as a young wife and mother of two flipped upside down. In the span of a single phone call, everything had changed. Suddenly, I had no earthly idea how to walk in a world where gravity no longer kept me grounded.

Much like what my character Ingrid experienced at the beginning of this story, even my voracious hobby of reading plummeted from three to four books a week to barely being able to focus on a single chapter. And much like Ingrid, I thought I could make the hurt less real, less true, if only I could figure out how to avoid the pain. But grief isn't like a well-mannered houseguest you can send home when you're not feeling up to hosting. Grief is far more like a permanent squatter who doesn't take no for an answer and who leaves your most cherished possessions ransacked and in tatters.

I was eight years into learning how to coexist with my grief when the idea for *The Words We Lost* first flooded my mind one winter evening. I questioned if I was ready to tackle a theme that would require so much of my personal experience, but ultimately, I felt the Lord guiding me to take this next step, the same way He'd been guiding me since my sister passed—one devotional time, one grief study, one counseling session, one coffee date, and one restorative prayer walk at a time.

But friend, I had little understanding before I sat down to write this story just how much these characters would challenge me or how much I would identify with their wounds and struggles. And somewhere in the middle of my first draft, I found myself wondering, often, about you. If you, like Ingrid, have ever felt isolated in your sorrow. Or if you, like Joel, have ever felt abandoned by God in the midst of chaos. Or if you, like Hal, have ever struggled to break free of addiction when reality feels too hard to face. Or if you, like Cece, have ever hidden a secret that's not yours alone to carry. Or if you, like Wendy, have ever suffered from anxiety when loss is too overwhelming to find your way forward. But just like in this work of fiction, these characters' stories didn't end there, and neither do ours.

You and I are not alone in our struggles.

We are known and loved by a God who collects our tears in a bottle (Psalm 56:8) and promises He is near to the brokenhearted (Psalm 34:18). There is no darkness His love cannot break through (Romans 8:38-39) and no suffering that will ever go to waste when we trust in Him (Romans 8:28). He is always working for our good and He is always on our side (Romans 8:32). There is no sin His blood cannot cover and no story of redemption better than what He has offered to us all (1 John 1:9).

As you close this book for a final time, I pray you will keep walking this journey of healing and hope with me. And I pray that no matter how big the heartache or its origins, you'll keep trusting in one step, one day, one promise from above at a time.

All my love,

Nicole

"May the God of hope fill you with all joy and peace as you trust in him, so that you may overflow with hope by the power of the Holy Spirit."

Romans 15:13

Acknowledgments

To my God of Hope, Jesus Christ: Thank you for taking my hand and leading me through the darkest seasons and into Your glorious light.

To my husband, Tim: Thank you for encouraging me to stay the course on this book even when things got tough, and for your many brainstorm hours and diagrams of allll things boat life and marinas. I'm so thankful you're my person.

To my parents, Stan and Lori Thomas: As I write this, we're just about to hit year nine without Aimee, and it's overwhelmingly beautiful to see what God has done in and through you both. Your example in compassion, empathy, care, and generosity to other grieving parents in your community is simply awe-inspiring. I'm so blessed to be your daughter and to follow in your footsteps. May God continue to abundantly bless your ministry.

To my writing sisters—Connilyn Cossette and Tammy Gray: This book is a byproduct of your friendship, love, time, support and at least a hundred hours of video chatting/laughing on Zoom. I will always choose to be an author by committee, and I am so thankful to have you as my people.

To my Coast to Coast Plotting Society sisters—Christy Barritt, Connilyn Cossette, Tammy Gray, Amy Matayo: Isn't it time for our big Hawaii retreat yet? I'm so very grateful for these last eight years together. Our plotting retreat is the highlight of my year and each of you are a highlight in my life.

To my early readers/reviewers—Lara Arkin, Renee Deese, Kacy Koffa, Ashley Espinoza, Rel Mollet, Rachel Fordham, Tonya Lowe, Toni Shiloh, Sarah Monzon, Joanie Schultz, Bethany Turner, Amanda Dykes: Thank you for making time to read my early drafts and for supporting my efforts to bring this story to final publication. What a treasure I've found in you all!

To my family at Bethany House Publishers and especially to my editors—Jessica Sharpe, Sarah Long, and Bethany Lenderink. Thank you for your expert feedback, brainstorm sessions, patience and flexibility with my schedule, and your sharp attention to detail on each and every draft. Thank you also for taking such good care of me as a writer as I work to balance my fiction life with my actual life.

To my church family at Real Life Post Falls and my life group: Thank you for discipling me and my family and for showing us how to be an active part of the body of Christ.

Special thanks to Rachel Fordham, author of *Where the Road Bends*: Thank you, Rachel, for combing through an early draft of *The Words We Lost* and for bringing Port Townsend to life. Though I've visited the area several times and LOVE the Puget Sound, my limited knowledge was no match for your local insight and expertise. You were so generous and kind to offer me feedback (even while on a deadline yourself) and dialogue with me back and forth whenever I had a question or concern. I appreciate the wealth of knowledge you offered, and I take full responsibility for anything I got wrong—especially when it comes to my directionally challenged mind. Thank you for being a part of my writing community.

More from Nicole Deese

After moving cross-country with her son and accepting a filmmaker's mentorship, Val Locklier is caught between her insecurities and new possibilities. Miles McKenzie returns home to find a new tenant is living upstairs and he's been banished to a ministry on life support. As sparks fly, they discover that authentic love and sacrifice must go hand in hand.

All That It Takes

Molly McKenzie has made social media influencing a lucrative career, but nailing a TV show means proving she's as good in real life as she is online. So, she volunteers with a youth program. Challenged at every turn by the program director, Silas, and the kids' struggles, she's surprised by her growing attachment. Has her perfect life been imperfectly built?

All That Really Matters

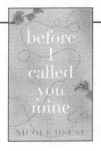

After many matchmaking schemes gone wrong, there's only one goal Lauren is committed to now—the one that will make her a mother. But to satisfy the adoption agency's requirements, she must remain single, which proves to be a problem when Joshua appears. With an impossible decision looming, she will have to choose between the two deepest desires of her heart.

Before I Called You Mine

 BETHANYHOUSE

Bethany House Fiction   @bethanyhousefiction   @bethany_house   @bethanyhousefiction

 Free exclusive resources for your book group at bethanyhouseopenbook.com

Stay up to date on your favorite books and authors with our free e-newsletters.
Sign up today at bethanyhouse.com.

You May Also Like . . .

Popular podcaster and ex-reporter Faith Byrne has made a name for herself telling stories of greatness after tragedy—but her real life does not mirror the stories she tells. When she's asked to spotlight her childhood best friend's missing-person case on her podcast, she uncovers desperate secrets and must face the truth before she can move forward.

What Happens Next
by Christina Suzann Nelson
christinasuzannnelson.com

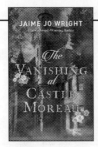

In 1865, orphaned Daisy Francois takes a housemaid position and finds that the eccentric Gothic authoress inside hides a story more harrowing than those in her novels. Centuries later, Cleo Clemmons uncovers an age-old mystery, and the dust of the old castle's curse threatens to rise again, this time leaving no one alive to tell its sordid tale.

The Vanishing at Castle Moreau
by Jaime Jo Wright
jaimewrightbooks.com

When Ivy Zimmerman's Mennonite parents are killed in a tragic accident, her way of life is upended. As she grows suspicious that her parents' deaths weren't an accident, she gains courage from her Amish great-grandmother's time in pre-war Germany in 1937. With the inspiration of her great-grandmother, Ivy seeks justice for her parents, her sisters, and herself.

A Brighter Dawn by Leslie Gould
AMISH MEMORIES #1
lesliegould.com

BETHANYHOUSE

Sign Up for
Nicole's Newsletter

Keep up to date with
Nicole's latest news on book releases
and events by signing up for her email
list at nicoledeese.com.

FOLLOW NICOLE ON SOCIAL MEDIA!

Nicole Deese, Author   @nicoledeeseauthor   @nicoledeese

Nicole Deese's fifteen heartfelt and hope-filled contemporary romance novels include her bestselling LOVE IN LENOX series as well as her award-winning novels with Bethany House Publishers, *Before I Called You Mine* and *All That Really Matters*. When she's not sorting out characters and plots of her own, she can usually be found reading near a window overlooking the inspiring beauty of the Pacific Northwest (most often while sipping a sparkling water). She lives in small-town Idaho with her happily-ever-after hubby, two towering-over-her teenage sons, and her princess daughter with the heart of a warrior. For more, visit www.nicoledeese.com.

Printed in the United States
by Baker & Taylor Publisher Services